I0831374

LETHE PRESS
MAPLE SHADE, NEW JERSEY

Published by LETHE PRESS
118 Heritage Ave, Maple Shade, NJ 08052
lethepressbooks.com

ISBN 978-1-59021-360-5 / 1-59021-360-2

Cover and interior design
by MATT CRESSWELL (INKSPIRAL DESIGN)

Cover Art
by BEN BALDWIN

LIBRARY OF CONGRESS CATALOGING-IN-PUBLICATION DATA

Daughters of Frankenstein:
lesbian mad scientists / edited by Steve Berman.
ISBN 978-1-59021-360-5 (hardcover : alk. paper)
1. Lesbians--Fiction. 2. Women
scientists--Fiction. 3. Short stories, American. I. Berman, Steve, 1968-

PS648.L47D38 2015
813'.01083538086643--dc23

2015012881

“I want to give fragrance to Breath of Life

(faces the room beyond the wall of glass)

—the flower I have created that is outside what flowers have been. What has gone out should bring fragrance from what it has left. But no definite fragrance, no limiting enclosing thing. I call the fragrance I am trying to create Reminiscence.

(her hand on the pot of the wistful little flower she has just given pollen)

Reminiscent of the rose, the violet, arbutus—but a new thing—itself. Breath of Life may be lonely out in what hasn’t been. Perhaps some day I can give it reminiscence.”

— Claire Archer, *The Verge*

Contents

INTRODUCTION

CONNIE WILKINS

I like to think that Mary Wollstonecraft Shelley, Frankenstein's "mother," would have been proud of these "Daughters of Frankenstein," her granddaughters. Their great-grandmother too, pioneering feminist Mary Wollstonecraft, would have approved of women portrayed with such limitless inventiveness and descriptive skill. Surely she would have appreciated the lesbian theme as well, with its flouting of convention and focus on strong female characters.

No scientists, mad or otherwise, have yet invented a time machine that would allow our literary foremothers to see how far our imaginations have flown over the centuries. We're lucky enough to appreciate all that has gone before, and to enjoy these new stories of invention, obsession, and wild adventure as well. I've enjoyed them so much that I'm tempted to say too much about each one, but I'll try to restrain myself. Discovery, after all, is a vital part of invention, and readers deserve their chance to discover each story as its author intended, with no "spoilers" to interfere with the experience.

The prospective reader does, however, deserve some general idea of what to expect. The book begins with Jess Nevins's scholarly overview of both real woman scientists and fictional portrayals of female mad scientists, from Alexander Pope's 1728 faux-goddess of mathematics, Mathésis, to the 2010 film *Caprica*. (I might have been tempted to include the Egyptian goddess Isis, who reassembled dead Osiris's body parts, with the addition of a golden phallus, and brought him back to life long enough to sire her son Horus, but calling that science would be too much of a stretch.) Nevins's list is a fascinating one, with more than its share of villains and/or cinematic fantasies aimed at males, making us all the happier to see this array of stories about wildly inventive lesbian women.

These stories take the theme in a wide variety of directions, set in many different time periods, sometimes in imagined or parallel worlds, but often in the one we think we know.

There's humor to be enjoyed when those four mystery-busting kids with their wacky Great Dane get the genuine adventure you always wished they would, and, in a different vein, when two clever women get their way in a society Bertie Wooster would have recognized.

In veins of a biological sort, there are tales of reanimators and experimental anatomists and zombifying drugs that skirt the edge of horror and once or twice ooze over that edge. In contrast, there are thrilling schemes and chases proving that Bonnie should have dumped Clyde and joined a gang of dykes; a future world of robots, weaponized cancer, and love transcending humanity; and steampunk scenarios with Victorian robots common as servants, but put to uncommon uses by uncommon women.

Viewpoints are as varied as the Russian revolution seen from inside a Fabergè egg, experimental psychologists running amuk with role-playing Minotaurs and Thebans, and Eva Braun (yes, *her*) with an infatuation for Rosie the Riveter.

The writing styles range just as widely, from slyly witty to technically precise to prose so beautifully evocative that it makes you shiver with delight or trepidation, whichever fits the story. For all their diversity, many of these stories have one factor in common: the presence of cats. The feline may be a cyborg, or a transdimensional dream cat, or a genetically enhanced creation, or a deceptively everyday tabby—or maybe just a subtle movement in the shadows. Some stories have no apparent cats at all, but really, who can be sure? I think this is a feminist author's answer to **Schrödinger's** thought experiment.

Enjoy the imaginations of these nineteen writers assembled by editor Steve Berman. They are truly the heirs, the daughters of that most infamous of mad scientists: Frankenstein. And their work is alive!

Connie Wilkins
Spring 2015

From Alexander Pope to Splice: a Short History of the Female Mad Scientist

JESS NEVINS

The mad scientist is an icon of modern popular culture, but critics have traced its origin back centuries. Yet there seem to be few female mad scientists. Which is odd, because the first significant fictional mad scientist was a woman.

Brian Aldiss, in *Billion Year Spree* (1973), puts the mad scientist's origin in Mary Shelley's *Frankenstein* (1818). Darko Suvin, in *The Metamorphosis of Science Fiction* (1979), nominates the Laputans [of Swift's *Gulliver's Travels* (1726)] as "the first 'mad scientists' in SF." Brian Stableford, in his essay "Scientists" (1973), goes farther back, stating that the mad scientist "inherited the mantle and the public image of the medieval alchemists, astrologers, and sorcerers." Robert Plank, in *The Emotional Significance of Imaginary Beings* (1968), claims Shakespeare's Prospero for the original mad scientist. And Peter Goodrich, in his "The Lineage of Mad Scientists" (1986), goes farther still, naming historical mad scientists, including the Persian scientist Alhazen (965-1040) and the English philosopher Roger Bacon (1214-1294), before tracing the origin of the mad scientist back to Merlin and to Prometheus, the Titan of Greek myth.

But the first mad scientist is undoubtedly Mathésis. She is the foremother of a long, but often neglected, tradition of female mad scientists in literature. Here we explore the history of lunatic ladies of in the laboratory.

Mad Mathésis, Her Feet All Bare

"Mathésis" is the ancient Greek term for learning/mathematics/knowledge/science, and in Alexander Pope's satire "The Dunciad" (1728) Mathésis appears as a captive of the goddess Dulness:

Mad Mathesis alone was unconfined
Too mad for mere material chains to bind
Now to pure Space lifts her ecstatic stare
Now running round the Circle finds it square.

But in Christopher Smart's "The Temple of Dulness" (1745), Mathésis takes on a more sinister tinge:

Next to her, mad Mathesis; her feet all bare,
Ungirt, untrimm'd, with loose neglected hair;
No foreign object can her thoughts disjoint;
Reclin'd she sits, and ponders o'er a point
Before her, lo! Inscrib'd upon the ground
Strange diagrams th'astonish'd sight confound,
Right lines and curves, with figures square and round.
With these the monster, arrogant and vain,
Boasts that she can all mysteries explain,
And treats the sacred sisters with disdain,
She, when great Newton sought his kindred skies,
Sprung high in air, and strove with him to rise
In vain—the mathematic mob restrains
Her flight, indignant, and on earth detains;
E'er since the captive wretch her brain employs
On trifling trinkets, and on gewgaw toys.

Smart altered Mathésis' madness. Rather than someone whose insanity is harmless, Mathésis becomes a "monster, arrogant and vain" who creates "trifling trinkets" and "gewgaw toys." There is not a lot of distance between Smart's Mathésis, with her "loose neglected hair" and "trifling trinkets," and the modern mad scientist, with his unkempt, wild hair and dangerous technology. But Mathésis is female, not male.

No rush of fictional mad scientists, male or female, followed "The Temple of Dulness." The Romantics in general saw scientists as either impractical theorists or wicked materialists, and an occasional mad scientist showed up in Gothic stories and novels, but it wasn't until Frankenstein that the mad scientist was fully transformed from the medieval alchemist to a modern character. Although male mad scientists began appearing with some regularity in the 1860s, in penny dreadfuls and dime novels, it wasn't until the 1890s, 150 years after "The Temple of Dulness," that female mad scientists began appearing.

Pre-20th Century Female Scientists

It might be objected that the delay in the appearance of fictional female mad scientists came from a lack of real-life models. But this objection, however reasonable, is based on false premises. Though small compared to their male counterparts, there were female scientists active in the 19th century, both amateurs and professionals, and some some of those women were notable even in their lifetimes. As far back as the 1650s Margaret Cavendish (1623-1673) was well-known for her work on "natural philosophy," the pre-19th century phrase for the study of the physical sciences, and one of the most important mathematicians of the second half of the 19th century was Sofia Kovalevskaya (1850-1891).

As Richard Holmes points out, women played an important role in the Royal Society of London, historically the most important scientific establishment of Great Britain. American women were active as scientists from the nation's beginnings, as shown by Joan Hoff ("Dancing Dogs of the Colonial Period," *Early American Literature* n7, Winter 1973), Sally Kohlstedt ("In From the Periphery," *Signs* v4n1, Autumn 1978), and Margaret Rossiter ("Women Scientists in America Before 1920," *American Scientist* n62, May/June 1974).

So there was no lack of real-life female scientists. Nor was there a lack of real-life female mad scientists on which to model fictional female mad scientists. During her lifetime Cavendish was thought to be insane, and Kovalevskaya was not only an active nihilist and revolutionary at times in her life—her partial autobiography is titled *Nihilist Girl*—but was also an inventor of "unusual" electrical machinery.

The explanation is likely sexism, but a particularly Victorian kind of sexism. Although the sexism of the 19th century prevented women from appearing in as wide a variety of heroic roles in popular fiction as men could, there were female amateur detectives as early as 1837 (William Burton's "The Secret Cell"), female warriors as early as 1842 (Timothy Savage's *The Amazonian Republic, Recently Discovered in the Interior of Peru*), female cowboys as early as 1847 (Charles Averill's *The Mexican Ranchero; or, the Maid of the Chapparal*), female professional private detectives as early as 1864 (Andrew Forrester, Jr.,'s *The Female Detective*), female Zorros as early as 1882 (William Manning's "Lady Jaguar, the Robber Queen"), female pirates in 1896 (Guy Boothby's *The Beautiful White Devil*), and even female astronauts in 1900 (George Griffith's "A Visit to the Moon").

However, none of these roles allowed women to be intellectually dangerous. No women scientists showed up in popular literature, and only rarely in mainstream literature, with the exception of historical personalities like Hypatia (circa 360-415 C.E.), who appeared in Charles Kingsley's *Hypatia* (1852-1853). The premiere model of dangerous femininity in British fiction in the 19th century was the Fatal Woman, the Victorian version of the femme fatale. But the Fatal Woman is dangerous sexually and morally, not intellectually.

The Effect of the New Woman

It wasn't until the 1890s, with the advent of the "New Woman," that fictional women were allowed to be mentally as well as physically and sexually dangerous. The New Woman was a woman who took many of the theoretical ideas of feminism and put them into practice as a lifestyle. She was usually a college graduate–women had begun being admitted to the better British colleges in 1847. She advocated self-fulfillment rather than self-sacrifice, and chose education and a career over marriage. The New Woman was direct in speech and forthright about her political views. She smoked and drank openly, decried restrictive fashions, exercised and played sports. And she was sexually active, or at least advocated sexual freedom, and avoided marriage, seeing it as a trap designed to rob women of their independence.

The fictional female mad scientist was one of the many negative fictional reactions to the New Woman. For many middle and upper-class Victorian men, women were the guardians of civilization and English culture's higher values. For the New Woman to strive for more than a role as wife and mother was deeply threatening to conservative moralists. For the New Woman to become an intellectual rival to men was even more alarming. Most novels of the 1890s portrayed the New Woman as coming to bad ends, and the novels with fictional female scientists are one version of this reaction.

The First Three, And What Made Them Different

The first significant female mad scientist–possibly the first at all–is the titular character in George Griffith's *Olga Romanoff* (1893-1894). The novel, a sequel to Griffith's *The Angel of the Revolution* (1893), is set in the future and is about the efforts of Olga, the last of the Romanoffs, to overthrow the Aerians, the master race which rules the world. Toward this end Olga Romanoff builds a supersubmarine and a fleet of airships, drugs two high-ranking Aerians and Khalid (a powerful Muslim ruler) and makes all them her mind-controlled lovers, and fights a number of bloody, losing battles against the Aerians.

Following quickly on the heels of *Olga Romanoff*, and overtly referencing *The Angel of the Revolution*, was T. Mullett Ellis' *Zalma* (1895), in which Zalma von der Pahlen, daughter of the leader of the international nihilist and anarchist movements and, after his death, the leader herself of those movements, plots to spark a socialist revolution by launching a fleet of anthrax-infested balloons into the capitals of Europe. And after Zalma came L.T. Meade and Robert Eustace's *The Brotherhood of the Seven Kings* (1898-1899), about Madame Koluchy, the leader of an Italian secret society who tries to seize power in England. Her chosen weapons include setting loose tsetse flies infected with encephalitis, composing a waltz with deadly vibrations, and killing through overdoses of x-rays.

These three characters provided the rough model for most of the fictional female mad scientists which would appear over the next sixty years. Like their male counterparts, fictional female mad scienitsts were usually portrayed as Faustian (overweening ambition) and Promethean (striving for utopia). But male mad scientists were usually based in their laboratories, and were static, forcing the heroes to come to them; female mad scientists were dynamic and were primarily active outside their laboratories. Male mad scientists were asexual, either past their sexual prime or, as creatures of intellect, above sexual desires; female mad scientists were portrayed as sexual beings, either using their sexual attractiveness to manipulate men or being sexually profligate as a sign of their moral perversity.

Male mad scientists were usually passionless (though not emotionless), where female mad scientists were passionate. Male mad scientists were usually obsessed with their research, and the results of that research—a million pounds sterling or conquest of the world—were of secondary concern; female mad scientists had some ultimate goal in mind which their research was meant to achieve. Male mad scientists were rarely portrayed in more than two dimensions; female mad scientists were usually three dimensional characters, or as much so as the authors could make them. Male mad scientists were rarely portrayed in a sympathetic fashion, while female mad scientists almost always were.

A Real Life Female Mad Scientist

The next significant female mad scientist, however, came from reality and was largely an exception to the proceeding. (Life is rarely as neat or programmatic as art). Dr. Louise G. Robinovitch (née Luisa Rabinowitch; 1881-1942) became internationally known in the first decade of the twentieth century for her experiments with electricity and anesthesia, but by 1921 she had withdrawn completely from public notice, and for good reason. In addition to her involvement in her brother's larceny (he was convicted in 1911, though her case was dropped by the police for lack of proof), newspaper articles about her brought to the public's attention that she had brought a dead rabbit back to life through electricity. Newspapers trumpeted that she was a proponent of "electrical anesthesia," though she refused to discuss her findings with the press, and in Paris she had revived an apparently dead woman through the application of electrical "rhythmic excitations." Allegedly she planned to prove, in laboratory experiments on animals (and, it was hinted, humans) that resuscitation of the dead via electricity would be universally possible in the near future. Taken singly or even two at a time, the public could accept these facts, but together they presented the image of a cold, deliberately reclusive genius of frightening capabilities and ambitions.

In this Robinovitch was seen as a photonegative of Thomas Edison, at this time the archetype, in both fiction and reality, for the heroic supergenius of popular fiction. Where Edison was a promoter, Robinovitch was a recluse who shunned the press. Where Edison projected a genial image, Robinovitch's was cool, verging on disdainful. And where Edison's experiments promised to advance human civilization, Robinovitch's ultimate goal was an archetypal Going Where Humanity Shouldn't Go experiment. Robinovitch was not widely imitated in fiction, but she provided a new archetypal version of the female mad scientist, the passionless, clinical researcher distant from human concerns and fixated on her research.

Experimental Theater and Comic Books

The next major (fictional) female mad scientist was Claire Archer, in Susan Glaspell's play *The Verge* (1921). Archer is a botanist who attempts to create new plants which exhibit "otherness" and "outness." She nearly achieves "otherness" with the the "Edge Vine" and the "Breath of Life," which is "the flower I've created that is outside of what flowers have been." Archer is emotionally frustrated and driven to distraction by the intellectual inferiority of those around her and the impossibility of communicating her ideas to them, and at the end of the play she shoots her husband. Archer's significance comes from Glaspell's status: at the time Glaspell was a major experimental playwright, and her use of a female mad scientist in experimental theater elevated the concept of the female mad scientist from the pulp ridiculous to something which could be taken seriously, just as Wells had done with Doctor Moreau in 1896.

The female mad scientist was a rarity in the pulps, but it only took eighteen months for a female mad scientist to appear in superhero comic books. Action Comics #20 (January, 1940) showed Superman's first nemesis, the Ultra-Humanite, putting his (male) brain into the body of actress Dolores Winters. As Dolores Winters, the Ultra-Humanite fought Superman in Action Comics #20 and #21 before disappearing for forty years. The Ultra-Humanite was not influential, but is interesting as a rare example of pulp/comics gender ambiguity, although this aspect is not touched upon in either issue of Action Comics.

Respectability At Last

The first female mad scientist to appear in respectable, mainstream science fiction was Barbara Haggerwells, in Ward Moore's *Bring the Jubilee* (1953). Haggerwells develops theories of time and space which allow her to create a time machine. But because she lives in a timeline in which the Confederacy won the Civil War, she manipulates the main character into going back in time and altering the past so that the Union wins. Haggerwells is abrasive and psychologically damaged and is a good example of a female mad scientist who is both mad and on the side of the good guys.

Haggerwells is also the first female mad scientist to strongly resemble her male counterpart. Haggerwells is as much in the mode of the traditional male mad scientist as the female mad scientist. Though three-dimensional, Haggerwells is an unsympathetic character. She is static and lab-bound. She is briefly involved in a relationship with the narrator of Bring the Jubilee, but sex is not central to Haggerwells' character as it was to earlier female mad scientists. She wants to change the past, but her emotions are mainly negative, unlike her passionate predecessors. Following Haggerwells, the female mad scientist would usually become indistinguishable, with the exception of physical characteristics, from her male analog.

The thirty years following *Bring the Jubilee* were a dire period for female mad scientist. The figure of the male mad scientist was increasingly used in a serious fashion in film and literature, from *Dr. Strangelove* (1963) to James Blish's *Black Easter* (1968), but the female mad scientist was relegated to low budget movies and cheap cartoons. Where the male mad scientist became a meaningful metaphor, the female mad scientist was used in the service of hack horror films. It wasn't until the early 1980s, first with Whitley Streiber's novel *The Hunger* (1981), that the female mad scientist was used in a serious manner, and since then the female mad scientist has been allowed the variation in character and seriousness that the male mad scientists have always had.

An Incomplete List of Female Mad Scientists

1893: Olga Romanoff. George Griffith's *Olga Romanoff.* British novel.

1895: Zalma von der Pahlen. T. Mullett Ellis' *Zalma.* British novel.

1898: Madame Koluchy. L.T. Meade and Robert Eustace's *The Brotherhood of the Seven Kings.* British novel.

1921: Claire Archer. Susan Glaspell's *The Verge.* U.S. play.

1926: Hilda Thorsby. Petterson Marzoni's "Red Ether." U.S. short story.

1936: Malita. *The Devil Doll.* U.S. film.

1938: Dr. Hamilton. Daniel Lopez's "Tommy Grey." Spanish comic strip.

1940: Ultra-Humanite. Jerry Siegel and Joe Shuster's Action Comics #20. U.S. comic book.

1940: Dr. Jackson. *Son of Ingagi.* U.S. film.

1947: Madame Voss. Steve Dowling and Gordon Boshell's "Garth." British comic strip.

1948: Dr. Sandra Mornay. *Abbott and Costello Meet Frankenstein.* U.S. film.

1953: Barbara Haggerwells. Ward Moore's *Bring the Jubilee.* U.S. novel.

1957: Miss Branding. *Blood of Dracula.* U.S. film.

1959: Dr. Myra. *Teenage Zombies.* U.S. film.

1964: Madame Atomos. André Carpouzis' *La Sinistre Mme Atomos* and its 17 sequels.

1965: "The Master." "If I Fell." The Beatles. U.S. cartoon.

1966: Dr. Faustina. "The Night of the Big Blast." *Wild Wild West.* U.S. tv series.

1966: Maria Frankenstein. *Jesse James Meets Frankenstein's Daughter.* U.S. film.

1966: Poison Ivy. Robert Kanigher and Sheldon Moldoff's Batman #181. U.S. comic book. Poison Ivy's mad scientist aspects were emphasized in later appearances.

1970: Dr. Elaine Frederick. *Flesh Feast.* U.S. film.

1971: Tania Frankenstein. *La Figlia di Frankenstein.* Italian film.

1972: Dr. Eva Wolfstein. *La Furia del Hombre Loco.* Spanish film.

1972: Freda Frankenstein. *Santo vs. La Hija de Frankenstein.* Mexican film.

1973: Dr. Caligula. *Alabama's Ghost.* U.S. film.

1973: Susan Harris. *Invasion of the Bee Girls.* U.S. film.

1973: Unnamed female mad scientist. *Supergirl.* Filipino film.

1977: Dr. Ellen Kratsch. *La Bestia in Calore.* Italian film.

1977: Dianne Ashley. *Kingdom of the Spiders.* U.S. film.

1981: Dr. Sarah Roberts. Whitley Streiber's *The Hunger.* U.S. novel.

1981: Dr. Gwen Parkinson. *Strange Behavior.* U.S. film.

1985. The Rani. "The Mark of the Rani." Doctor Who. U.K. tv series. The Rani later appeared in the serial "Time and the Rani" (1987) and the charity special "Dimensions in Time" (1993).

1987. Beth Halpern. Michael Crichton's *Sphere.* U.S. novel.

1990: Dr. Babs Blight. *Captain Planet and the Planeteers.* U.S. cartoon.

1992: Washu Hakubi. *Tenchi Muyo!* Japanese anime.

1993: Jane Tiptree. *Carnosaur.* U.S. film.

1995: Professor Helena Slogar. Keith Baker's *Gloom.* U.S. card game.

1999: Dr. Susan McCallister. *Deep Blue Sea.* U.S. film.

2000: Helen Narbon. Shaenon Garrity's Narbonic. U.S. webcomic.

2003: Doc. *Texhnolyze.* Japanese anime.

2005: Angelika Einstürzen. *Dogs: Bullets and Carnage.*

2009: Dr. Elsa Kast. *Splice*. U.S. film.

2010: Zoe Graystone. *Caprica*. U.S. tv series.

My thanks to Mike Ashley, Paul Di Filippo, John Eggeling, Denny Lien, and David Ringle for help with research.

AYNJEL KAYE

"I don't really sleep." Dawn walked through the front door, backlit by the afternoon sun, her burgundy curls glowing and her face in shadow. She paused in the entryway.

Alyssa closed the door behind Dawn, flipped the lock. "You don't sleep?"

Dawn nodded; the incandescent glow from the light overhead showed near-white roots. "I figured I should let you know." She looked around, then hung her coat on the coatrack and finger-combed her hair.

"At all?" Alyssa crossed her arms over her chest; a self-hug that might, in other circumstances, be mistaken for an expression of aggression.

"Insomnia." Dawn smiled with half her mouth; the expression never made it to her brown eyes.

"There are things you can take for that aren't there?" Alyssa held a hand out for Dawn's bag.

Dawn pressed her lips together, wrinkled her nose.

"Or other things you can do, if you're not one for chemical solutions? Hypnosis, maybe? I think I remember reading that." Alyssa frowned as she tried to pick out relevant memories from the information about chemical preservation techniques that cluttered the forefront of her mind.

"I know, but it's better if I don't sleep." She let go of the shoulder strap, surrendering her bag to Alyssa.

"You pack pretty light." Alyssa hefted the bag.

Dawn nodded.

Alyssa waited a moment longer looking at Dawn. She shifted the strap on her shoulder, then walked down the hall, opened the door to the library slash guest room and waved Dawn in.

"I just figured I should tell you." Dawn tilted her head and trailed her fingers over Alyssa's shoulder, down her arm as she walked past. "About the sleeping thing. So you don't wonder who is walking through the house at all hours of the night. Though maybe I should have mentioned it sooner?"

A shiver followed in the wake of Dawn's touch. Somehow, away from the club and the restaurants on the wharf, those touches were more electric. *What am I getting myself into?* Alyssa smiled. "Thanks. I'm sure it'll be fine." She set Dawn's bag down next to the daybed, then scurried to the desk, stuck her notes into the book there and shut it.

Dawn nodded toward the desk. "Did I interrupt you studying?"

"Checking my research, actually." Alyssa shifted the book, held it in front of her and looked at the floor. Heat and color rose in her cheeks. "And you didn't interrupt."

Dawn held a hand out. "Can I see?"

Alyssa pressed her lips together, looked up slowly, and handed the book to Dawn with a nervous nod. "It's..."

Dawn's eyebrows rose. "Heavy." She laughed, trailed her bubblegum fingernails along the spine, then over the alchemical symbols embossed onto the leather cover. A frown shadowed her eyes. "What is it?" She opened the cover, flipped a couple of pages in.

"Biology," Alyssa said. *Among other things.* She held her hand out for the book, the fingers of her other hand fidgeting in the air at her side.

Dawn continued her gentle turning of pages, paused where Alyssa's notes were. "Brain biology?" Dawn held the book up slightly to show a diagram.

"Among other things." She splayed her fingers. "Please?"

"Wha? Oh." Dawn closed the book, handed it to Alyssa. "The illustrations are lovely. Gruesome, but lovely. So much detail."

"It was my father's." Alyssa hugged the book back to her chest to conceal her trembling hands. "Originally. He..." She shook her head, took a deep breath and glanced around the room, then nodded to the door. "Bathroom is across the hall. Kitchen is the other direction from the front door."

Dawn nodded, fingers plucking at one of her belt loops. "And your room?" She lifted her gaze from the book to Alyssa, coy and confident both in the way that she tilted her head, in the slow spread of her smile over her pink-painted lips. Her smile went all the way up this time, lit her eyes like candle flame.

Alyssa swallowed. "To the right, end of the hall." *Breathe.* "I'm just..." She took another breath. "I'm going to put this away." Dawn looked across the room at the shelf where there were no empty places the right size to hold the book. Alyssa shook her head. "I mean, downstairs."

Dawn blinked. "Oh."

Dawn sat at the kitchen table, fingernails worrying at the frayed seam of the napkin lying beside her near-empty plate. While Dawn had managed to not drip dinner onto her turtleneck Alyssa had not managed a similar feat. She dabbed at the smudge on her own blouse.

"Tell me about your father?"

Alyssa set her napkin down and looked at her plate.

"If you want." Dawn added.

"He was a doctor. And he liked botany." Alyssa poked with the tip of her knife at the small lump of meat remaining on her plate. "He died when I was a girl." She didn't look up, brought her fork into play and focused on dissecting the remainder of her dinner trying to pull apart the fiber bundles neatly with tools not meant for so delicate a task. "It really is quite fascinating, even at a macro level. And the way that cooking changes the texture is..." Alyssa looked up from her plate. Dawn was staring. Heat flooded Alyssa's cheeks and she put the knife and fork down. "I'm sorry." She stood, gathered Dawn's plate along with hers and took them to the sink.

Dawn closed her mouth, shook her head. "Don't be."

Alyssa ran water over the plates. "No, I am. It's rude to play with my food." Even her father had said as much. *Dissection is not to be done at the dinner table, child.*

Laughing softly, Dawn stood. She walked over, put a hand on Alyssa's shoulder. "I like the way it draws you in."

Alyssa looked over her shoulder, studied Dawn's expression.

Dawn nodded. "So what do you do when you're not playing with your food or hanging out with me on the boardwalk and seducing me at Pier 38?"

"I didn't—" *Breathe.*

Dawn laughed. "I know." She brushed the backs of her fingers over Alyssa's cheek, tucked wild wisps of hair behind her ear, stroked her thumb along Alyssa's jaw.

Alyssa shivered. "I make things."

"Make things. Like art?"

Alyssa tilted her cheek against Dawn's hand. "Not really."

"Can I see?"

Alyssa looked into Dawn's eyes, squinted, then laughed. "You're worse than I am."

Dawn blinked, lowered her hand.

"No, no." Alyssa took Dawn's hand, squeezed it and dared a quick touch of her lips to Dawn's knuckles. "I meant the curiosity." She smiled. "I'll show you."

They walked hand-in-hand down the hall, and Alyssa unlocked the door that led to the basement stairs. She took hold of the doorknob, turned it partway, then paused, looked into Dawn's eyes again. "Just...don't touch anything when we go down there."

"Okay." Curiosity quivered in that word, and in Dawn's grip on Alyssa's hand.

"Oh." Alyssa wiggled her hand from Dawn's, took down the lab coat hanging on the hook beside the door. "And put this on. Just in case. And the gloves; they should be in the pocket."

Dawn looked the coat over, then put it on. It bunched her turtleneck's sleeves as she pulled it on, and it was tight across her back. She could button it, but only barely, and only at her waist. The gloves, as promised, were in the pocket. They squeaked as she put them on and she studied her hands. Her fingers and hands ended up too-short looking and the gloves left her wrists bare as well. "I look like a clown."

Alyssa shook her head. "Your makeup is all wrong for that; I'm sure that clowns wear more red." A quick look. "And usually their clothes are too big for them." She looked down the stairs. "Also, they are meant to look silly doing it." She touched the light switch, then walked down into the basement.

Dawn followed, two steps behind her. "And I'm not meant to look silly?"

"Of course not." Alyssa nudged her father's journal a bit farther onto the shelf across from the door as she snatched up the goggles lying beside it. "Oh!" One pair should have been in the other pocket of the lab coat.

"What?" Dawn looked around the tiny alcove.

"Goggles." Alyssa handed a pair to Dawn, then put the other pair on.

"Just in case?" Dawn pulled the goggles down around her neck, brushed her hair out from the band, then pulled them back up. Her hair ended up looking like a failed ponytail.

"Now? Now you look like a clown. Just leave the strap over the top of your hair. It'll be less uncomfortable and you won't end up with a gap." She helped Dawn fix her goggles. "And yes, just in case."

"In case of what?" Dawn tried again with the goggles.

"Just in case." Alyssa cocked her head raised her eyebrows. "Trust me, 'kay?"

Dawn nodded, hesitant. She tucked her hair behind her ear, fiddled with the band on the goggles.

Alyssa looked Dawn over. "As a temporary measure, I think that works." She made a mental note to acquire another lab coat and pair of gloves, both sized up from what she wore. She nodded forward. "Bathroom." Then she touched the light panel. Sickly yellow light stretched out beneath the gap between door and tile, then it groped along the wall as Alyssa opened the door to the right.

A dozen different scents assailed Alyssa and Dawn made a choking sound. Alyssa winced, rushed over to the control panel and flipped the switch for the exhaust fan, twisted the dial twice. The second click took more effort, but the when blades whirred faster, they pulled the muddied scent--ammonia, almond, sulfur, sage, amber, camphor, alcohol...*lord, what happened when I was last down here? And why didn't I clean up?*—out of the lab.

"Sorry." Alyssa looked from the control panel to Dawn whose eyes were wide, the whites of them stark behind the dusty tint of the lenses.

Dawn stood in the center of the room and crossed her arms over her chest and balled her hands into awkward fists. She turned slowly and her gaze washed over everything. Her lips moved slightly and her eyebrows raised and lowered comically, as though controlled by a puppeteer.

How much did she see? How much of what she saw did she understand? The spectrometer? The electrostatic generator? The fluoroscope? Did she notice the empty cages? Alyssa forced her hands to lay flat at her sides to keep from fretting in any obvious fashion. She'd never had someone who mattered down there, and Dawn was definitely someone whose good opinion Alyssa wanted to keep.

Impulsive little girl. Alyssa gritted her teeth.

Finally, Dawn completed her inspection. She walked to the control panel, reached her hand out, fingers moving over dials without actually touching them. "What do you make down here?"

Alyssa struggled with the childlike desire to swat Dawn's hand away. "Concoctions."

"Concoctions?" Dawn tilted her head, obviously awaiting something further.

Alyssa nodded. "Tinctures, elixirs, decoctions, infusions."

"Certainly you make more than potions?" Dawn walked from the main control panel to the workbench, tilted her head toward the wires and electrodes attached to an instrument panel with its own small control board and an amber display screen.

Nose wrinkled, Alyssa said, "I suppose you can call them potions, though the distinctions do matter, and that is for testing."

"Testing what?" Dawn's fingers hovered over an electrode.

"Chemical components in my," she sniffed, continued, "potions. Mostly."

Dawn didn't look convinced. "So the brain-book?"

Alyssa stalked over and nudged Dawn's hand away from the set-up. "My father's journal."

"But how does it relate?" Dawn squinted, as if tallying figures. She turned her head slowly looking from the electrodes to Alyssa. Dawn's eyebrows went up, goggles raising slightly as well. "Hallucinogens?"

"Accidentally, once or twice." Alyssa clicked the exhaust fan's dial down a notch, then shooed Dawn to the door.

"Is that how you afford this?" Dawn asked as she took the gloves off to reveal pruney fingertips.

"What?" Alyssa took her goggles off, hung them on a peg.

"Drugs." Dawn handed Alyssa her goggles, then finger-combed her hair. "You make drugs."

"Wash your hands." Alyssa nodded toward the bathroom.

Dawn did as she was told, and as Alyssa washed up as well. Dawn chattered over the running water as Alyssa took care to make sure she didn't have anything under her fingernails after being without gloves. "You make drugs, sell them, and that's how you afford this place."

Alyssa pressed her lips together, motioned Dawn up the stairs, then locked the lab door. "The house belonged to my parents."

Dawn stopped at the top of the steps, looked down at Alyssa. "Huh."

Alyssa stood two steps below Dawn, felt shorter than she always did. "You thought I was a drug dealer?"

"Not in a judgmental way." Dawn stepped back.

Alyssa walked up onto the landing. "When it comes down to it, I'm interested in how things work. Once you understand how something works, you can make it work differently."

"So you're a doctor like your father? A chemist?"

Alyssa shrugged. "I'm a dabbler."

They walked to the living room and Dawn sprawled onto the couch, one hand at the back, fingers playing over the throw blanket there. She rested her opposite foot on the floor, her knee bent. Dawn's lashes covered her eyes, though they were only half-closed.

Alyssa looked at Dawn for a long time: her hair—Alyssa never realized it was dyed—the dusky olive tone of her skin, the curl of her lashes, the shape of her lips, the dark arches of her eyebrows. "Take you, for example." Alyssa sat at the other end of the couch, wriggled her feet out of her boots and then curled her toes between the couch cushions.

"Me?" Dawn shifted, propped the throw-pillows behind her head.

"Mmhmm." Alyssa leaned forward, rested her arms on her knees and her chin on her wrist. "Insomnia."

Dawn tensed, drew her arm down from the back of the couch and hugged it across her chest. Her jaw twitched.

"There are a number of different drugs you can take to help you sleep, but they all work differently, do different things, and what works for someone else might not work for you." Alyssa tilted her head, hair falling in front of her shoulder.

"Look, I just don't..." Dawn sighed, reached up again and pulled the blanket down over her face.

"You don't want to fix it."

The short pause became an aching one as it stretched and Alyssa worried she'd pissed Dawn off. "Dee?"

Shadow twisted along the windowsill and a crow cawed outside.

The blanket jerked. "I don't want to sleep. I don't need to. It's not a problem."

Alyssa frowned. "Sleep deprivation isn't a good thi—"

Dawn sat up tugged the blanket away from her face, glared.

Alyssa caught her bottom lip between her teeth and sucked on it, then yawned. "Well. I need to sleep." She patted Dawn's foot, got up. "Stay out of trouble while I do, mm?"

Dawn nodded, chuckled in a way that made Alyssa wonder if she was forgiven for pushing the matter, then said, "I'll stay out of the basement."

Alyssa relaxed. "Thanks." She paused, tucked her hair behind her ear. "If you want to rest a bit, you're welcome in my bed." She swallowed, then hastily added, "And it's perfectly fine if you prefer the daybed in the library. Or, y'know, the couch. It's a comfortable couch."

"Thank you." Dawn leaned on one propped up knee.

Alyssa nodded. "Feel free to read whatever might catch your fancy in the library."

Dawn smiled. "Thank you."

Alyssa stood an awkward moment longer, then spun and scurried to her bedroom where she left the door cracked slightly as she got ready for bed.

Alyssa drifted off, her thoughts prodding at hazy memories of the effects of sleep deprivation on cognitive function, on the problems related to a lack of REM sleep cycles and the brain's need to go into REM more quickly when deprived of it.

Alongside that train another ran, and she mentally catalogued her collection of herbs, chemicals, and compounds, building an order that she'd have to give to the eaglet in the morning.

When she dreamed, it was of her father. He walked with her through the strange place he said wasn't real and identified the unusual plants they encountered—the glowing-edged roses, the aromatic whip-like ferns, the bush with serrated leaves so sharp they'd draw blood if you weren't careful—and he talked about their properties, encouraging her with each new plant to collect a leaf, a bud, a stem, some seeds. They did the same thing when they walked together in the parks and gardens at home.

You never know what you might need one day.

Alyssa woke to the scent of butter, brown sugar and cinnamon, gas from the stove. She shifted, reached out to the other side of her bed. Empty. Perhaps it had been all night.

A disappointed sigh passed her lips and she sat up, rubbed her face, tried to decide if she had really slept or not. She pulled on her silk robe as she walked out of her room and down to the kitchen.

Dawn stood in front of the stove cooking pancakes. "Breakfast?" She smiled, held one up on the spatula then flipped it onto a plate. "I would have made eggs in a basket, but you don't appear to have any bread."

Alyssa blinked.

"Surprised? Or are you always confused first thing when you wake up?"

"Yeah, a little." Alyssa took the plate Dawn offered. "Thank you."

Dawn laughed, summer-warm and at ease. She carried the other plate to the table and sat across from Alyssa. "Some weeks I've got a lot of spare time. Once in a while I do something useful with it, like learn to cook." She poured syrup on her pancakes, then nudged the speckled ceramic cream-pitcher across the table.

"You made syrup?"

"After a fashion." Dawn cut a bite of pancake. "I work with what I have."

Alyssa tilted her head, sniffed the syrup and smiled. Less like syrup, more like caramel, it went on thick and spread slowly over the buttered top of her pancake. She cut a piece and took a bite. Cinnamon, brown sugar, cayenne, all mingled with butter, the flavors smooth on her tongue. "This is lovely."

Dawn smiled, sipped coffee, then said over the rim of the mug, "It reminds me of the first time I kissed you. Sweet, with a little bit of heat that no one would expect."

Alyssa flushed and glanced at her plate.

"I've got an errand I need to run for someone." Dawn's expression was a mask, not blank, exactly, but completely unreadable. "Not sure how long it will take."

"Secret mission?" Alyssa winked and tried to shake the altogether unwelcome feeling that she'd done something wrong, or hadn't done something right.

Dawn shifted, put her fork down on the plate. "Something like that."

Alyssa picked up her plate, nodded. "I'll probably be downstairs. There's a spare key behind the address plaque." Alyssa scooped up Dawn's plate and took them to the sink. "Take it with you, or use it from there when you get back if the door's locked."

"I shouldn't be out too late. And I'll bring bread." Dawn squeezed Alyssa's hand, leaned in and kissed her cheek. "Thank you again for letting me crash here, Allie. I promise it won't be for long."

"No problem." Alyssa's heart sank and she forced a smile. "If I'm not upstairs and you need me, the doorbell rings down there, too."

Dawn nodded. She paused at the door, opened her mouth, then closed it and left.

Alyssa finished up in the kitchen, washed her hands, then wrote up an order, passed it off to the eaglet. The mechanical bird whirred, wheezed, then took off from the balcony.

While the warmth and sun in the living room appealed, Alyssa went downstairs, instead. She pulled her father's journal from the shelf and went into the lab, settled onto the least comfortable chair in the world and set the leather-bound book on the table beside the electrostatic device. She opened her father's journal and flipped toward the back where the notes and drawings were in her own hand.

She read through everything she had done using the whipweed, then read through her notes on common herbs and plants, the chemicals in them and their effects, scanning for anything that affected brain function in a way that might relate to dreaming.

She jotted notes on another notepad while she flipped back and forth between her notes and her father's, looking for connections.

A sharp raptor cry pierced the house all the way to the lab and Alyssa jumped, heart racing. She rubbed her face and got up, left her pencil in her father's journal and walked upstairs.

The eaglet sat on the balcony perch looking pleased with itself. It hadn't dropped its package, which wiggled and squirmed. Alyssa took the bag and fed the eaglet a bit of steak-fat left over from dinner.

The creature whirred, chirped and then spun down, bowing its head and lowering clockwork lids over, camera eyes.

"Thank you," Alyssa said as she carried the bundle into the living room.

She pulled out the lab coat and gloves, left them on the couch, then carried the rats downstairs.

Alyssa set the sack down next to the journal and pulled out one of the cages, sectioned it off, and set it up.

The rats in the sack made grumpy squeaking sounds until Alyssa took them out and put them into the cage. Four of them, an albino female, and the other three males with mottled white and brown coloring.

"Okay, kids, this might get a little weird." She pets the head of the albino with a gentle fingertip. "It'll be okay, though; I promise."

I hope.

Alyssa worked on the problem she'd assigned herself while Dawn was out running whatever errands it was that she did during the day, her earlier project less forgotten and more assigned temporarily to her hind-brain.

While she scribbled notes and decided ratios, Alyssa imagined that Dawn had a normal job. And then, as she prepared her third bioassay, she changed her mind; Dawn never talked about work and she seemed to come and go erratically. Between those excursions, and the insomnia, Alyssa couldn't be certain that Dawn was there at night at all.

Alyssa tested the various results of her research, first on rats, and then on herself. When she found something that seemed to work, she worked up the nerve to talk to Dawn about it. Dawn who, as far as she knew, hadn't slept since moving in.

Though the sudden crow infestation and their oddly timed outbursts were occasionally affecting Alyssa's sleep, too.

"So, I think I have something that might help."

Dawn looked up from her coffee. "Help with what?"

Alyssa nudged her egg around the plate with her fork. "You've been a bit, uh, flutter headed." Alyssa glanced warily at Dawn. "I mean, lately. From not sleeping, I assume."

Dawn set her coffee down, sighed. "Can we not talk about this?"

Alyssa sighed. "I just, I want to help. I hate seeing you not on top of things."

Dawn opened her mouth to say something, then closed it again.

"I know it frustrates you," Alyssa said. "I can tell." Alyssa caught her bottom lip between her teeth, worried at it lightly.

Dawn bowed her head, sighed. "What do you want to do?"

Alyssa smiled, leaned forward and reached for Dawn's hand across the table. "I made something that I think will help you. It won't put you to sleep, but it might trick your brain into thinking you have had sleep so it can do what it needs to do."

"It won't make me sleep, though." Not a question, a demand.

"No, it won't."

Dawn took a deep breath, squeezed Alyssa's hand lightly then nodded. "Okay. I'll try it." The words came out with reluctance, a sigh, giving in rather than being won over.

Alyssa smiled, rubbed her thumb over Dawn's knuckles. "Finish your coffee, mm?"

Dawn glanced into the mug, then did as she was told.

This, this was where Alyssa was most confident. There in the lab with a solution in-hand, her head throbbing with the thrill of understanding. Confidence prickled between her shoulder blades. She did this. She made this. She had a way to solve the problem she had been presented with.

Dawn followed her into the lab, her hair loose, a robe over her night dress, something Alyssa had never actually seen her wear.

"You know it isn't bedtime," Alyssa said with a nervous smile.

"Yeah, I know." Dawn's smile was equal parts tentative and hopeful. Does she even realize that she wants to fix this, no matter how many times she said that she didn't, that it wasn't a problem?

Dawn paused just inside the lab, head tilted, hair falling forward. She nodded toward the chair set up next to the main control panel. "That's..."

"Not meant for long-term sitting. It'll make sure you don't get too comfortable. Which...should help keep you awake in case you think that dozing off sounds like a good plan." Alyssa brushed the seat and dropped a threadbare cushion on it.

Dawn plopped down onto it. "Ow."

"Not a lot of cush to it." Alyssa patted the arms of the chair and Dawn scooted until her back was straight against the wood, then put her forearms on the shortened rests, let her hands dangle off the ends.

Alyssa stroked Dawn's wrist then gathered the EEG leads. "Welcome to planet gross," was the only warning Dawn got before Alyssa applied a dab of goop to her scalp then attached the first electrode.

The face Dawn made caused Alyssa to look away lest she be caught laughing. Her shoulders shook and she tried to keep her hands steady as she continued to work.

Dawn wrinkled her nose again when Alyssa finished. "It's getting sticky."

Alyssa squeezed Dawn's shoulder. "I know, it's awful. I won't get in the way of a shower after."

Dawn looked up through her lashes at Alyssa. "You sure?"

Heat spread through Alyssa's cheeks and her heartbeat quickened. "Mostly?"

Dawn laughed and took Alyssa's hand. "You are so adorable."

Alyssa smiled. "Thanks." She drew away, walked to the console, then turned back frowning. "You...meant that as a compliment, right?"

Dawn laughed again nodded ever-so-slightly, the wires skittering as she did. "Definitely."

Alyssa relaxed, flipped the readout on and watched the machine turn the work that Dawn's brain was doing into moving lines.

The difference between Dawn's readout and what Alyssa remembered of her own was almost as dramatic as the difference between hers and the rats. "Because different people are all the same," she said, scolding herself.

"Hmm?"

"Nothing." Alyssa glanced at Dawn then back to the console. "I talk to myself when I work."

"Do you answer?"

"If I ask a question? Of course. It would be rude not to."

Dawn's expression reflected in the console's glass display was priceless.

"Okay." Alyssa swirled the decanter then poured a small amount into a beaker and put a glass straw into it. She carried it over and handed it to Dawn.

Dawn sniffed it and her forehead wrinkled. "What's in it?"

"Other than alcohol?"

"Yeah."

Alyssa frowned and rattled off the list of plants that had gone into the decoction. She paused, thought about the poppy and whipweed. Before she could admit to them, Dawn said, "So that is why it smells like an unplanned garden."

Alyssa nodded. "Yeah."

"A drunk unplanned garden."

Alyssa nodded again. Really, the most overpowering scent--and flavor--came from the whipweed. Not licorice and not grass and not clove but a lot like all of them muddied together. Only sweet. Really, it made a lovely aperitif, and seemed to make Alyssa's dreams more vivid. If she hasn't had that initial vodka infusion to start from, it might have taken her longer to think through this problem.

Dawn's eyelashes fluttered and she gave her head a quick little shake as she drank the decoction. "Oh ew what." She looked like she was scraping her tongue against the roof of her mouth and she kept swallowing.

"Yeah, it is kind of unexpected."

"One way to describe it." Dawn hissed the words out and handed the beaker back. "You've tried it?"

Alyssa nodded; Dawn relaxed.

"So what should I expect?"

Alyssa shook her head, glanced at the readout. "Just relax. Tell me what you're feeling and what you think is happening."

Dawn sounds disappointed. "Nothing? I'm warm. Probably from the alcohol in it."

Alyssa chuckled. "Probably."

The lines on the readout danced as Dawn spoke, then went back to the strange resting pattern.

In the reflection, Dawn's eyes started to dart this way and that. The EEG reading showed a large spike and Alyssa turned to look. "Dawn?"

A whimper.

"Dawn, talk to me."

"Allie." The pleading in Dawn's voice broke Alyssa's heart.

"You're still awake, sweetie. It's okay." The spikes on the readout were alarming. Something more than REM was going on. "Talk to me. Tell me what you're feeling."

Dawn shook her head, tiny frantic movements totally out of sync with the movement of her eyes.

A glimmer, a shimmer, a swirling of light caught at the edge of Alyssa's peripheral vision, over near the generator. Perhaps the electrostatic machine? When she turned from Dawn to look, shivers went through her again and again and she hugged her arms across her stomach. Something was quite wrong. Something prickled over the head of the electrostatic machine, but it wasn't electricity. Through the warped and melted air, she saw that other place, the reality that no one else had believed in.

"Just a bad dream, little bookworm." Her mother, gentle and concerned when they found her after the first time.

"She'll forget about it eventually. Children are impressionable. Give her time." Doctor number one.

She forced herself to the control panel, but the electrostatic machine's switch wasn't engaged. The generator was producing power, though, was ramping up slowly but steadily.

"When are you going to grow up?" Her father, stern and disappointed that she wasn't being rational, logical, or sci-en-tif-ic.

"Stop telling stories, little girl." Mistress Esche, her grade school teacher.

The generator's temperature continued to rise and Alyssa re-routed the cooling from the refrigeration units to compensate.

"It's all in your head." Her mother, exasperated after she returned from her second disappearance.

"You must stop letting your imagination run away with you." Matron Everly, the principal.

The shimmering grew brighter, the image clearer. Panic and desire fought with each other inside of Alyssa's heart, her head.

"Stop lying to me!" Her mother, finally at her wits end after she disappeared the third time, hand swinging to connect with Alyssa's cheek.

She never doubted it was a real place, but she never expected to go back, either, not after the last time.

"Dawn?" *Breathe, bookworm. Just breathe.*

Alyssa looked back to Dawn. Her gaze darted this way and that, like she was caught in a nightmare with her eyes wide open, looking at things that weren't in the lab. Did she even hear Alyssa? The EEG display was... Alyssa had never seen anything like the readouts it showed.

"Wake up." Alyssa's fingers trembled as she removed the leads from Dawn's scalp, quick and careful as she could be.

"I-I..." Tears rolled down Dawn's right cheek.

The air prickled over Alyssa's skin and a familiar tugging sensation came from the other side of the lab. The rats squeaked and chittered, claws ticking at the metal mesh of their cage.

Alyssa removed the last lead, and took Dawn's hands, urged her up and out of the lab. She paused, looked back one last time at the half-warped image of that other place over the electrostatic generator, then slammed the door, pulled open the electric panel and flipped the circuit breakers.

The house went dark and the whine and hum from the lab faded into terror-quiet. She counted to ten, flipped on the breaker for upstairs.

Are you a doctor? Alyssa choked back a laugh at the memory of Dawn's question. If she was a doctor, she might be less concerned. Or perhaps she would be more. She settled Dawn into the lounge chair, brought water and a wet towel from the kitchen.

"Here. Water."

Dawn's hand closed on the glass, a reflex movement. Alyssa helped her bring it to her mouth. Little sips. Dawn's eyes still moved frantically this way and that but she didn't actually seem to see Alyssa.

Alyssa dabbed the cool wet towel over Dawn's face, wiped her tears away. "Dee?" Alyssa cupped Dawn's cheek. "C'mon, snap out of it."

Dawn's eyes kept moving; her gaze flicked, erratic and unfocused.

Alyssa ran to the bathroom, came back with smelling salts. She unstoppered the vial and waved it under Dawn's nose.

Dawn's head jerked back as she gasped. For a moment, her gaze focused, then she closed her eyes.

Alyssa made another pass with the smelling salts.

Dawn opened her eyes, turned her head, met Alyssa's gaze.

Alyssa capped the salts and tucked it in her pocket. "Are you okay?"

Dawn licked her lips, slowly shook her head.

Alyssa winced, tilted her head, looked into Dawn's eyes. Her pupils were closing and her gaze looked steady now.

"Leave me alone." The words came out of Dawn's mouth flat as tap water and she looked away, back out the window where the sunset was torn by a murder of crows flying off in the distance.

"Yeah." Alyssa went into the kitchen, came back with a pitcher of water, set it on the coffee table. "I'll..." She looked away from Dawn, sat down on the couch. "I'm right here...if you need anything." She picked up the notepad on the table, curled up and half-sat on her feet, scratched notes with a trembling hand and hoped that she would be able to read them later.

~

Pitiful meowing woke Alyssa. She shifted, groaned as the muscles in her back and neck scolded her for her choice of bed and sleeping position. She sat up, pulled the throw blanket around her and looked across the living room. Dawn stared in the direction of the window from her spot in the fluffy lounge chair. Pale, her unmoving eyes rimmed red and bruised looking.

"Dawn?"

"I hear it." She looked away from the window, blinked several times, rapidly as if afraid to let her eyes remain closed. Her jaw tensed, relaxed, tensed again. "I think it's coming from downstairs."

Alyssa nodded. "Are you..."

"Better." Dawn reached up and rubbed her eyes. "A little."

The meowing got louder and Alyssa glanced to the hallway, then back at Dawn.

"For the love of everything, do something about it." Was that exasperation or exhaustion talking?

"You're?"

"Just go." Dawn bowed her head, covered her face with her hands, pressed her fingers along her forehead.

Alyssa uncurled from the couch and walked down to the basement. The air smelled of ozone and singed wood. She flipped the other circuit breakers and then touched the light switch, unlocked the door.

As the door opened, something white and fluffy bolted from inside the basement, ran halfway up the stairs, then stopped, looked down at her and hissed.

Alyssa opened and closed her mouth, trying to make words. She closed the door, stared at the cat. "Treacle?"

The cat sat down, fur settling. Alyssa pulled the door closed again and walked up the stairs, held a hand out to her. Treacle sniffed Alyssa's fingertips, rubbed her face against Alyssa's hand, then bit her knuckle.

"Damnit." Alyssa pulled her hand back against her chest. "What was that for?"

Treacle licked her paw, then stood, padded up the stairs. Alyssa followed her.

⚗

"You have a cat? How did I miss a cat?"

Alyssa sat on the floor next to Dawn's chair and Treacle flopped down in front of her. She stroked Treacle's stomach and the cat seemed--for the moment—content to allow her to do so. Both of them watched Dawn. "Not exactly."

"It looks like a cat." Curiosity seemed to be drawing Dawn out.

"Her name is Treacle and she..." *You're going to sound crazy.* Alyssa took a deep breath. "And she's not my cat." Another breath to steady herself. "She's not from around here."

"I don't understand." Uncertainty hung in those words.

Alyssa thought about the image warped around the electrostatic machine. "I..." A dozen overheard conversations between doctors and her parents played back through her head. "I don't either." She swallowed. "Not really." She took a deep breath. "Do you know what happened down there?"

Dawn curled her fingers against the arms of the chair. Her nails dug into the leather. The rest of her muscles tensed and she pushed herself to her feet. The blanket slid down her legs to the floor and she stepped over it, paced. Short, angry steps back and forth in front of the window; fingers splayed and curled over and over.

Dawn shook her head. She still looked shaken, and a shadow of betrayal showed in her eyes when she turned to Alyssa. "I've never actually seen it happen before, seen what goes on around me, so I don't know how, or why, or what. I've always been *asleep* at the time." Her jaw clenched, relaxed.

"Because you don't dream when you're awake." Alyssa thumped the heel of her hand against her forehead. "Of course. It's the dreaming part, not the sleeping part that's the problem. Dee, I'm sorry. I'm so so sorry. It was stupid of me to do that and it doesn't matter that I just wanted to help because I should have listened to you and respected your decision and I'm so sorry." She looked up, her throat aching. "I will never do something like that again."

Dawn nodded. "And before you ask, I don't know what went on down there this time, either, because I couldn't see the lab, only..."

"Describe it?" Alyssa leaned forward. Silence answered and Alyssa leaned back. "I'm sorry." Treacle bit Alyssa's knuckle again, and rolled over, stretched, then walked over to Dawn, rubbed against her leg.

Dawn glared at the cat and stopped pacing rather than risk tripping. She spread her hands. "What?"

Treacle purred and rubbed her face on the buckle of Dawn's boot, then put her front paws on the top of Dawn's foot and sat down. The cat looked up, whiskers twitched forward. Treacle let out a single questioning meow.

Dawn squinted, then her eyes widened. She stepped back from Treacle. "No."

"Dawn?" Alyssa tilted her head.

Another single meow from Treacle and Dawn took another step back.

"Don't be stupid," Alyssa said, then slapped her hands over her mouth, her eyes wide.

"Stupid?" Dawn balled her hands into fists at her sides.

Alyssa shook her head. "Not you," she said, one hand still over her mouth. "I wasn't...that wasn't..."

Treacle head-bumped Dawn's leg and Dawn startled, took another step back. Treacle meowed again, more insistently.

"You know her." Alyssa stared at Treacle.

"How do you know that?" Dawn looked as startled by the question as Alyssa was.

Alyssa looked between the two of them. "I wasn't talking to..."

Treacle sneezed, then prowled out of the living room, her twitchy-swishy tail brushing back and forth through the air. Alyssa closed her eyes, bowed her head.

"How is she here?"

Alyssa shrugged as she shook her head. "Tell me what you dreamed?"

Dawn stepped up behind Alyssa, touched her elbow with trembling fingertips, then trailed them down her forearm, took her hand and drew her to the sofa. They sat down and Dawn held Alyssa's hands in her lap.

Hesitant, at first, voice soft, Dawn spoke. "I was there almost instantly. I've been there before, but I've never been so aware of being in a dream, and being here before. The chair, the cool air, the mothball smell, your perfume."

Heat rushed into Alyssa's face. She squeezed Dawn's hands.

Dawn continued, her words coming now with the rush of relief. "There are bioluminescent flowers and trees lining the walkways of the city. It's the rose quarter, named for the carvings on the doors, the shape of the metalwork, the scent in the air, but the roses don't look like roses. If I walk to the center of the city, I'm pretty certain that the spire will be there, crystal-studded, colored by the mood of the Martyr Queen, but the last time I was here she was angry. So very angry. The cats and dogs and mice and birds are out tonight, but none of the people. There's music in the air and it makes the stars dance, glimmering shimmering, raining from the sky like glitter and fractured dreams." Dawn drew her hand from Alyssa's and rubbed her head, ran her fingers through her hair. "Something else is there, though. In the shadows. It's always like that. Even though you're there, talking to me, calling my name. Something else is there, watching, waiting. Hungry darkness." Dawn shook herself and pulled the throw blanket to her chest, hugged it.

"I'm sorry." Alyssa rested her hand on Dawn's knee.

Dawn nodded. "I know."

Alyssa ran her front teeth over her bottom lip. "You've dreamed there before."

Dawn nodded, fingers rubbing at the blanket's edging.

"And you saw Treacle there."

"Yeah." Dawn took a deep breath, looked at the entryway. "She was different."

"A person."

Dawn jerked her head to look at Alyssa again. "How did you know?"

Alyssa swallowed. "She wore striped socks and a pinafore over a frock dress."

Dawn let go of the blanket, grabbed for Alyssa's hand, squeezed. "How did you know?"

Do you really want to say it out loud? Alyssa nodded. "I've been there." She took another breath; Dawn stared at her. Alyssa said, "The luminescent plant with the whip-leaves? I used a decoction from them. They're the only ones that grow here so they're the only ones I've been able to do much work with. I didn't bring enough back to work wi—ack!"

Treacle jumped onto Alyssa's lap, padded in a circle, then sprawled, her rear paws wedged against Dawn's knee. She kneaded Alyssa's thigh with her front paws and Alyssa flinched. "Claws. Claws!"

Treacle purred.

"She seems happy to see you."

Alyssa smiled, scratched Treacle's ears. "I'm happy to see her, too." She sighed. "I didn't think..." She shook her head, looked at Dawn. "You don't think I'm crazy."

"Not for this." Dawn nodded at Treacle.

Alyssa frowned.

Dawn laughed, squeezed Alyssa's knee. They sat in silence for a moment, then Dawn drew her hand back from Alyssa. "But I'm never drinking anything like that again." Her voice was cool.

Alyssa flinched and Treacle leaped from the couch, disappeared into the other room. "What if I could make something that does the opposite?"

"The opposite." Dawn's expression changed and warmth slipped back into her voice.

"Makes it so you don't dream when you sleep." Alyssa tilted her head to the side.

Dawn pressed her lips together and her forehead scrunches.

"You don't have to decide now. And I won't do anything unless you say yes." Alyssa held her hand out to Dawn, palm up.

Dawn rested her hand in Alyssa's.

"I promise."

"What about the...the other thing?"

Treacle padded back into the living room, sprawled on the floor and batted a dead mouse toward the couch.

Alyssa sighed. "Thanks, but we've eaten." She turned her attention back to Dawn. "I don't want to go back. You don't want to dream."

"You're not curious how it happened?" Dawn squeezed Alyssa's hand.

Alyssa bowed her head. "Of course I'm curious." She took a deep breath. "But I won't put you through that again."

Dawn shifted, lay down and rested her head in Alyssa's lap.

Alyssa's fingers trembled as she stroked Dawn's hair. "Tired?"

Dawn nodded. "That was..." She trailed off. A crow cawed in the distance.

"Coffee?"

Another nod. A soft, "Please."

Alyssa glanced at Treacle. "I don't suppose you could..."

Treacle sniffed, batted the dead mouse closer to the couch. At least it wasn't one of the rats downstairs.

Alyssa sighed. She curled down, kissed the top of Dawn's head. Dawn shifted again so Alyssa could get up. Alyssa looked at the cat still playing with the mouse. "Keep an eye on her, mm?"

Treacle meowed once and got up, hopped onto the couch and curled up on Dawn's feet.

Alyssa put a kettle of on the stove. The water boiled and as Alyssa poured hot water through the grounds, Dawn's voice carried from the living room. "Ow! Hey! Claws!"

That certainly was one way to keep her awake for the moment.

The scent of coffee filled Alyssa's head and she considered for a moment if the beans would be a terrible starting point, or if that was the wrong path to go down.

"Allie?"

Alyssa dropped two sugar cubes into her coffee, stirred it. "Coming."

DOUBT THE SUN

FAITH MUDGE

If a storm cell had not taken up residence over the Channel and grounded half a fleet of solar steamers in Port Geddes that winter, I would undoubtedly not be telling this story, or be doing anything else for that matter.

But it did, and I am. And it's too late to stop me.

⚡

I am spying on my father and it's not working out very well.

It's his own fault; if he lies all the time, what does he expect me to do? Am I meant to just not *notice* the sudden influx of spare credit? It's no use asking him, though, he'll only lie some more. Hence, spying.

His supervisor has taken the duties of overseer to a zealous extreme and if I hang around in Dad's sector much longer I'll get caught. When I look around for the hiding place the supervisor is most unlikely to disturb, I spot the depot. That part of the docks is a restricted access point, with the yellow hazard signs to prove it, but this is Port Geddes we're talking about, not Glasgow or Southampton. I grew up sneaking around the docks; I know the blind corners of the system as well as any long-term employee. It also helps that I'm wearing a pair of my father's old overalls and spent all night rewiring his security logo for universal access. The doors think they should let me inside, so they do.

I stop dead and stare.

The depot is roughly the size of an aircraft hangar and might have been one, once—there are so many in disuse these days; most planes were taken apart for scrap long ago, when the fuel shortages were at their worst. The current contents are probably on their way to meet a similar fate, but that doesn't make the depot any less of a wonderland.

Robots. Robots *everywhere*. I've seen ones like this in public parades, but the closest I've ever come was a cleaning drone broken down on the street, and it was a huge clunky thing. These are government service 'bots, deactivated for one reason or another and thrown carelessly onto vast heaps until they can be taken to the mainland for dismemberment and recycling. Some are minimalist outlines, others boxy and durable. A few could pass for sleeping humans in the right light. I crouch down to run my hand reverently along an exposed silvery arm, but jerk back when I see the insignia branded into its shoulder. Only an idiot would mess with Her Majesty's artificial legions, deactivated or not.

Most are marked as either military or medical, which makes sense given the proximity of Woolf Island, the local navy base. There's one symbol I don't recognise: a pair of concentric blue circles with a silver starburst at the centre. When I get closer, I see the points of the star are actually snakes. It's imprinted onto what would probably have been the unit's wrist, although it's scorched so badly I can't be sure. A pair of rigor-mortis stiff legs are the only parts of the body to survive intact. This one has been to Hell and back.

There are so many robots here. And they're all slated for recycling anyway. No one will notice.

That's what I'm telling myself, anyway.

Port Geddes is a harbour town, the population centre of Gaskell, which in its turn is one of the larger outlying islands of the British Archipelago. It is a grey place, permanently under the shadow of deep sea cranes, desalinator towers and bad weather; or at least that's my memory of it.

The docks were then, as they are now, the nexus of local employment. Among the thousands who kept the port running was Maranda Salvadore's father, a technician with ambitions he couldn't afford. He was a reckless man, and the black market became a profitable form of rebellion. He didn't tell his daughter what he was doing, and thought that meant she didn't know.

One day, when she was fourteen, she went to the docks to spy on him and came across a graveyard of robotic carcasses instead.

Perhaps 'came across' implies a greater element of chance in the encounter than was strictly the case. The locks happened to be in her way, so she went around them. The robot happened to be there, so she took it. Who knows what else she might have done if she'd had time to think it all through?

What she did, however, was slip into the staff room, purloin a pair of spare overalls and force them over the robot's immobile limbs. She staggered home with its half-melted arm propped awkwardly around her neck, her boots crunching through the frosty puddles of a winter afternoon, the tall grey warehouses turning blank faces to her crime like co-conspirators, and she concealed the evidence in a corner of the hurricane vault underneath the apartment building where she lived.

Ever since his demotion, her father had stopped bringing home spare parts and templates. The ensuing boredom had been intolerable, revealing a set of self-destructive impulses Maranda had not known she had. Robbing the government of valuable tech was probably symptomatic of a deep-seated suicide instinct, but that didn't mean she was giving the robot back.

Demonstrating her fundamental inability to not *anthropomorphosise everything in sight, Maranda gave the unit a name.*

⟷

I'm kneeling on the floor with Athene pulled awkwardly across my lap, neck bent so that my headlamp hits just the right spot inside the cranial cavity, and sweet Jesus is it a mess in there. This is the only part left that I haven't stripped because I am a born procrastinator and also, I am scared. What if I wreck her beyond repair? None of my templates have a pattern remotely like this. Doesn't help that about a quarter of what's in there is melted beyond all recognition. Groping on the floor for pliers, I start prising up one of the panels, then stop damn fast because my finger is suddenly tipped in blue. I twitch it experimentally. The spot of blue is transferred to my knuckle. Behind the panel, a light is blinking.

Did I do that? *How* did I do that?

A split-second of doubt is the only warning I get before a steel bar slams into the side of my skull.

I almost black out. If the punch had been any harder or at a better angle, I might be comatose. Instead I get the beginnings of an epic black eye and instinct screaming in my face to *get out, get out right now*. I'm scrabbling backwards as fast as I can through the debris of tools, metal filings scraping against my palms, but what I'm watching is my robot trying to stand up. She can't, of course. It can't? It's making a horrible grinding noise and I stop moving to listen.

I'm pretty sure Athene just said, "Don't."

"Wha—" I temporarily lose my grip. The hysterical explosion of laughter that bursts out of my mouth ricochets off the walls, which only makes me laugh harder.

"Oh *God*," I splutter, "oh God, you're *alive*."

With a working robot built from these parts, she could write her own admission scholarship to the tech academy of her choice. From there, who knew? The Reynolds Memorial College in London. The Venus project in Beijing. Japan, even, motherland of robotic science - every graduate dreamed of a scholarship in Tokyo.

She had never dealt with a machine this size before, though, or in such bad condition. Not knowing for sure how far the damage went, she stripped it down to a skeleton and began the slow process of piecing it all back together. She downloaded templates off the black market sites she wasn't supposed to know about, the ones she found on her father's data portal before the inspectors came to their flat and he trashed it. Where the templates failed, she poked buttons and jumped back fast.

Patching together an operating system that even looked like it would work took the better part of a year. She snatched time whenever she could, bounding down the fire stairs and calling out cheery greetings. "Bloody freezing this morning, eh, Athene?" "We're making an early start today. I'm taking apart your chassis to attach the new mobility node!" The robot went from an anonymous, inanimate drone in charred grey casing to an ever-changing patchwork, stripped down repeatedly as better pieces became available or as new ideas burst into Maranda's head, clamouring to be tried out. It was while she was fiddling with the central cortex that she woke me up.

It was an accident. Even Maranda's skill only went so far. I had no eyes to see her then, but some of my auditory functions had survived the fire and had been recording ever since, and now they downloaded into my consciousness.

People sometimes ask me if I understand the concept or sensation of pain. Doubtful, any more than they could understand what it is like to wake up with half their brain missing and someone's hands teasing the rest apart. I reacted the way any thinking organism would; I lashed out. The exposed steel framework of my left arm smacked into Maranda's face, knocking her to the floor, and as I had been pulled across her lap that meant I clattered down beside her. I heard her skid away from me as fast as she could, swearing in a breathless rush that was part amazement and part panic. I needed to explain before she ran away, but it was so hard to reach the words.

"Don't," I said, at last.

She listened.

Her primary memory cortex is shot and I don't have the skill to retrieve anything much from it, but a couple of secondary centres have survived somehow more or less intact and this is the great bit, *she knows where they are.* There's minor damage to the language core, which makes communicating a bit complicated, but point and nod works too and her vocabulary is improving every day. She hates the feeling of me fussing around inside her skull, so I put on music to distract her while I work.

"Wherein cacophony?" she says.

"Mmm?"

She flaps her arms, a gesture of frustration. "Divination of composition?"

"Oh! This is Bertha Oliver, Queen of Shakepop." I grab my mug off the floor for a quick swig. It's icy down here but I can't wear gloves - too clumsy - so the heat of the tea feels burning hot on my fingers. I wince and swallow. "She takes famous plays and speeches and put them together with a beat."

"Identification?"

I've been tuning the music out. When I stop to listen, I recognise the track. *Doubt thou the stars are fire,* Bertha croons. *Doubt that the sun doth move. Doubt truth to be a liar...*

"It's 'Hamlet'. Shakespeare. Do you like it?"

"Doubt," Athene murmurs. If that's an answer, I don't know what she means.

She sits still the rest of the night, only speaking up to warn me when what I'm doing feels wrong. By four a.m. I've closed up the back of her head with a triumphant click.

"Say something."

She considers. I sit back, squeezing my hands together with impatient excitement. I want to know if I got it right.

"Doubt thou the stars are fire," she says quietly. "Doubt that the sun doth move. Doubt truth to be a liar, but never doubt I love. Thank you, Maranda. That feels better."

This will take a lot of getting used to.

She asked me what I remembered, and I told her "nothing". Proof of two things: I could think, and I could lie.

My recordings from before the fire had been lost when my primary memory blew—but then the secondary system kicked in. Soon there were fragmented voices in my head, talking about a lost shuttle. "That's what things that can think do, doctor, they surprise you. Can you get this under control or not?" Later, incoherent shouting. The rapport of gunfire. "Load it in with the rest, we don't want them asking questions." After that, just clanking and groaning, the movement of the steamer. I didn't know where it had come from or where it had been going. I didn't want to know.

Who wants to remember being burned alive?

In the old days, when my insomnia got the better of me, I'd take apart old gadgets that my dad brought home and sit at the kitchen table with a mug of warm milk, teaching myself how to put them back together. When he started bringing people home, people who yelled about money and smelled of cigarettes, I started going to the local projection theatre instead. The night shift operator was a neighbour of ours and he'd let me in for free in the early hours of the morning to watch ancient horror flicks. I'd curl up in one of the thick nubbled seats up the back and watch the black-and-white ghosts of mad scientists rampage all over the stage, wreaking havoc for the hell of it.

I understood the urge to do that.

When I first started work on Athene, she was going to be the Igor to my Frankenstein—my stalwart assistant, who would say things like, "You rang, Mistress?" and follow me around holding the tool-box.

That didn't happen. Now when I can't sleep, I go down to the hurricane shelter to tinker and chat. Athene loves Shakepop and rock opera and memorising complicated recipes. She has definitive opinions about what casing she wants, the changes to her shape and colour scheme. We spend the night of my sixteenth birthday trialling hair styles with paper wigs.

"How do you know what you want? What's it like in your head?"

"You should know." Athene studies her reflection while she holds a mass of crepe paper ringlets against her scalp. She is not much more than a framework, still, most of her wires exposed, but I have scrounged up an old dressing gown that she always wears.

"How do you *think*?" I want to know. "Do you feel things? Do you get bored, or embarrassed, or lonely?"

"I don't know, Maranda. I do like it better when you're here." Athene tilts her head, copying one of my gestures. "I want curls."

"I wish I knew where you came from. What you used to be."

"I don't," Athene says flatly. Of course, her voice is always flat. She is not good at inflection yet. But there is an edge in her tone I have not heard before. "I was burned and cast out. If they ever find me, they will burn me again." She is silent for a moment. "Is this a feeling? Am I afraid?"

I don't know what to tell her. We sit on the floor in silence for a long time, then I reach out and hold onto her hand as tightly as I can. I won't let anyone take her away.

Frankenstein became Pygmalion.

My body elongated to more human proportions as Maranda sculpted the casings to a precise fit. The design was roughly Maranda's height but wider at the hip and bust, taking on a physical fusion of African and Greek lineage and the curvaceous dimensions of a Renaissance goddess. Maranda trawled junk yards and lurked in the alleys outside robot depots, cannibalised the most unlikely parts from any and every piece of technology that came her way and when all other measures failed, invented the necessary bridges. In the grotty apartment upstairs she might be a public education dropout incarcerated in minimum wage employment, making barely enough credit to cover the rent now her father was in Geddes Corrective, but in the hurricane vault she was an artist chasing perfection.

She exploited her position as Anonymous Lackey No.278 at the island's major hospital to salvage a pair of eyes—one the blue of the sea just before a storm, the other a dark coffee brown—and fitted them into a face casing she'd made herself from a freestyle template. It was round-cheeked and mulish-chinned, with full lips and a quizzical tilt to the left eyebrow. With the eyes in situ and flesh-coloured casing fitting snugly to my framework, I could pass for human, though getting the knack of facial expressions was hard.

One night Maranda smuggled me upstairs on the fire escape, sat me on the sagging sofa and produced a bottle of acidically cheap wine. I had never been in the apartment before. It was like walking inside her mind—the bits of miscellaneous circuitry scattered across the kitchen table with crumbs and forgotten cutlery, a mural of famous female scientists projected across one wall in fading colours, a scale model of the Colosseum made out of repurposed cogs gathering dust on a shelf—a scene of chaotic creativity. I would have liked to go around and look at everything carefully, but Maranda was excited and trying not to show it, which meant she had a surprise for me. I sat and waited expectantly.

"Athene, how do you fancy a trip outside?"

"Outside?" I stiffened. Outside meant other people. Other people meant an incalculable number of variables. I didn't like the sound of this at all.

Maranda produced a card from her pocket and flourished it at me. It was thick and creamy, printed with her full name and details, and headed with the name I had heard her sigh after so many times as an unreachable paradise. Port Geddes Institute of Technology.

"I did it!" Maranda bounced off the sofa, unable to keep still in the frenzy of her excitement. "I did it! That's one bonafide admission slip you're holding right there, Thena. Tomorrow I'm going in to prove what I can do." Her elation abruptly deflating, she dropped onto the sofa and took the card back. "I hope I'm good enough. I won't get another chance."

I tilted up my nose, a gesture mimicked from her. "Nor will they. If they don't accept you, we will go to every other academy in the United Kingdom, until we find somewhere with sufficient vision."

Maranda threw her arms around me. One of the advantages of my memory is perfect recall: that moment will survive, crystal sharp, for as long as I do. My sensors picked up the texture of her skin, the fine down of hair on her arms, the scratchy wool of her sleeves. The uneven tips of her hair tickled my cheek. I remember how it felt to kiss her for the first time, testing a tentative hypothesis, and how her first reaction was to pull back, clapping a hand to her mouth in surprise.

"You do feel things."

She kissed me back, inexpertly, awkward and half-laughing. We opened the wine, pouring it into two coffee mugs, and clinked them together in toasts. To discovery! To feelings! To every academy in the United Kingdom! She drank hers in between toasts, while I simply held mine, olfactory sensors recording every inhalation.

Later, she tucked her feet up underneath herself and fell asleep with her head on my shoulder. I don't know if this is what love feels like; how could I? Whatever it is, it's been enough for us.

ϟ

The superintendent of admissions introduces himself as Professor Keane. He is a lean, ascetic-looking man with an educated London accent and from the first second he looks at me I can tell he thinks I'm dock trash, possibly island trash, to be evicted from his presence with the minimum amount of fuss. He barely glances at Athene—it's my name on the ticket, after all—probably assuming she's my friend or girlfriend here to provide moral support.

Is she my girlfriend? Do we need to talk about that? As if I need more reasons to feel on edge.

Keane puts me through a standard test first in a projector field. I have to put together the translucent replicas of various examples of machinery, explaining what I'm doing as I go along. It's so simple I'm smiling as I work and Athene, waiting on a bench at one edge of the room, winks at me. *Of* course *you can do it.* The superintendent is less impressed. I don't think he likes the smile; obviously, all this is supposed to be hard. He purses his lips, considering me.

"Where did you learn your technique?" he asks.

"Ah..." This is all on my ticket, which is in his hand. The question feels like a trap. "I took regular VCs on—"

"Please refrain from using acronyms."

"I took virtual classes on an official tech share site for two years, and I've been experimenting by myself for much longer. My father is a technician too and he's given me a lot of guidance."

"Hardly glowing recommendations," Keane murmurs. "Your results are acceptable, but your style is irregular and undisciplined, as might be expected after that type of rag tag education. We have high standards here, Miss Salvadore, and scholarships are in high demand. I'm in some doubt about your dedication to this career. Applicants seek out higher training elsewhere before coming here, so that they are prepared for the rigours of the course."

Blood burns in my face. "I couldn't afford that kind of tuition, sir."

"Hmm," is his only reply. He's thinking of ways to get rid of me. I will, in his estimation, be a dead weight, a scrappy talent looking for a free ride. To cover my humiliation, I produce a winning smile.

"My results are acceptable, then?"

Keane inclines his head a bit. "Yes, but—"

Athene taps him on the shoulder. He turns around, surprised.

"If you don't let her in," she tells him, "you are an unmitigated idiot," and she strips the skin off her wrist with a flourish.

I will treasure the look on his face forever.

It was everything you'd expect from an institution that initialises as GIT.

There was a good reason that students were supposed to have prior qualifications before entering; the workload was gruelling, the awarding of scholarships a gladiatorial contest. Maranda would never have got her foot in the door without me as a bargaining chip. As it was, she walked a tightrope of negotiation—I hated being ogled, but there were too many people she couldn't afford to offend. When she took me on-campus for a session with her most persistent professor, he stripped the skin off my arm without asking first, and every time I spoke he either directed the answer at Maranda or ignored me altogether, like we were ventriloquist and dummy. When he reached for my head, I swung off the examination table.

"We didn't agree to that," Maranda told him.

"There's no point if I don't see inside the cranial cavity," the professor said, reaching again. I walked out the door without another word, leaving him to shout useless orders in my wake.

"I'm so sorry," Maranda said, on the way home. "I didn't know how to put him off any more—"

"You have to learn.*" I turned on her, hands stuffed deep into the pockets of my coat. It was an affectation I'd stolen from her. I could gauge the temperature with pinpoint accuracy, but I never got cold. "People will always treat me as an object. I expect better from you."*

She cried all night, even when I climbed into bed beside her and whispered my own apologies in her ear. It was like that, the first year. She was always overtired, often to the edge of hysteria. So I did what any highly advanced robot of dubiously legal status would do; I filled the gaps.

I could learn at treble her speed and could study twenty four hours in a day if necessary. Spending as much time as I did jacked into the administrative cloud, hunting clues to the latest exam, I was in a uniquely advantageous position for spying. By the start of the second year, I had amassed enough compromising data that I never had to go back to campus. It was a good thing Maranda wasn't out to make friends, because the only one she had was me.

I should have realised that someday I wouldn't be there to catch the bullet. Even I can be naïve.

•-WW-•

Halfway through my second year at the institute, I transfer into the Armaments course. There are two tracks - government service, which requires a background check, or private security. I take option B and end up studying internal defence. Essentially, that means learning how to turn a modern family home into an intruder's death trap without ruining the decor. Maybe I have paranoia issues to work through, because I ace every class and the professor starts giving me a cautious berth.

Athene spends a month immersing herself in architectural design while I fake a moneyed accent and call around checking defence packages with the big contractors. Each has its own jargon, but really all you get for a hefty consultation fee is the same standard set of features. For my end of semester project, Athene sketches the layout of a Tudor manor with the precision of a graphics printer and I go to town with a tailored defence system that includes stun darts shot from portrait frames and labyrinthine earthworks to swallow the unwary. We haven't had so much fun in way too long. I wish it was always like this, lying on the floor with shoulders bumping, surrounded by coffee cups and crumpled notes.

"It would be nice," Athene says eventually, "to have a house like that." She offers me a smile, close-lipped, because she's still getting the hang of teeth. "Protected by you."

The only places she's known have been a string of shabby apartments as I chase the lowest possible rent. The idea of one day owning a house on the mainland—a house centuries older than Gaskell itself—is about as achievable as planning to live on the moon, but in that moment I want desperately to make it happen.

One day, maybe it will. How can it hurt to dream?

I sit quietly and watch them take my wife apart.

Doctor Cross has tried to keep me out of the surgery, switching arguments three times as each one fails her, but the fact of the matter is that no one has the authority or brute strength to physically remove me. I sit with my hands folded primly on one knee, watching intently as Cross opens Maranda's skull. Initiating my higher functions, I compare the work against a mental log of similar operations. I have no reason to suppose Cross or any of her team are incompetent, but mistakes happen. They're human. I would have preferred to do the surgery myself, but management of the situation is difficult enough without alienating the medical team appointed by my wife's lawyers.

The truth is, no one knows what to do with me. On the one hand, I've been married to Maranda for the last twenty years and am her official next of kin. On the other hand - the one I wish I could cut off—I am a robot and therefore by definition a possession. A possession cannot manage other possessions. That, the lawyers of Copperfield and Co. told me, straight-faced, would set the wrong precedent.

Hoping to clarify the situation, I went into the firm's main office, prepared to undergo whatever evaluation they considered necessary to prove my personhood. The psychologist asked very personal questions, but it all seemed to go well enough. That is, right up until I went outside to sign some more forms and the woman—unaware of my auditory acuity—described me as having "an astoundingly well-constructed identity", but "about as much right to make decisions for a real human being as a toaster."

I know it won't be good news long before Cross says anything. If the operation was going to be successful, it would have been over hours ago. The survival rate for ECS victims is less than one in a thousand; from the moment the first shot hit, unloading a syringe's worth of serum into Maranda's blood stream, it's been a battle just to keep her alive.

Humans. They only live about ninety years anyway, but they go ahead and weaponise cancer.

At last, Cross murmurs to her assistants, "Close her up," and glances at me, gesturing to the door. I follow her out.

"The damage is more extensive than we thought," Cross begins. "Growing the cells for partial reconstruction will take time and she's got a limited window of that, but the real problem is how far the tumours have already spread. This is a particularly virulent mutation and it's proven highly resistant to all the conventional treatments."

"So what do you intend to do?"

My unshakeable composure often unsettles people who don't know me, but it brings out something close to open hostility in Cross. I'm not really surprised. Although medical researchers are not supposed to accept grants from the Humanity Line, the anti-robot activists are experts at professional recruitment. Scientists have spent centuries talking about the possibilities of artificial intelligence, but now AIs are actually out there, walking and talking and thinking for themselves, no one seems all that pleased with the discovery any more. I understand a fear of the unknown—that's how I feel about humanity all the time, messy, chaotic creatures that they are - but that doesn't mean I feel like putting up with a stranger's crappy attitude. It was someone like Cross, someone who thought of Maranda's work as an abomination against her own race, who shot her on her way home from work.

It wasn't Cross. I have to remember that.

"It's time to move her," Cross says, her undertone of belligerence grating on my already strained patience. "The facilities are too limited here. She needs to get to a real hospital."

"She stays. Any equipment you need can be brought here."

"I don't think you understand," Cross snaps. "The decision is in the hands of her lawyers and as her medical representative my strong recommendation will be that she is moved as soon as possible. This charade has gone on long enough—"

"What charade would that be, doctor?"

Cross shivers. Just by speaking it aloud, I have turned her title into a curse. Me and my terrible powers—I wish I felt like laughing. I have a wonderful maniacal laugh, even better than Maranda's, and that's saying something.

Instead of answering, Cross turns on her heel and goes back inside the makeshift surgery. I stand facing the door, thinking about the passive-aggressive resistance waiting on the other side and the series of inevitabilities lined up like dominoes, the momentum that will build from the instant the first one falls. That is how bureaucracy operates.

It's enlightening, being the avatar of demonic science. Everyone should try it.

I get everything I need from the academy on Gaskell in three years. By the time I'm twenty, we're travelling around the southern hemisphere, studying in Melbourne and Sydney, contracting in Hong Kong and Beijing. Everyone wants to meet us, particularly Athene. She's basically unrecognisable from the charred husk I rescued in Port Geddes, but she worries anyway and we're careful how much we say. I gain a reputation for being enigmatical.

One day we meet with a friend of a friend for yum cha and spend the whole time talking about the future of AI technology. No one understands this like Athene. The friend starts off aiming all his remarks at me, then goes quiet as he watches us bounce ideas like tennis balls, me scoffing dumplings and waving my chopsticks around to illustrate various points, Athene making deadpan jokes and breathing in the scent of her favourite jasmine tea. We look like any other expat couple in our mid twenties. Well, perhaps a bit more eccentric than some; I am scruffy and punkish in an oversized woollen jumper and steel-capped boots, while Athene is all thick black ringlets and Regency-style dresses. She is a centre of calm. I can't keep still. We are the perfect team.

Our new friend asks abruptly, "How would you like to work in Tokyo?"

"Doctor Cross wants to see you. She's waiting in her office."

I spent the night sitting beside Maranda's bed, lost in circular arguments with myself. I vaguely recognise the assistant in the doorway, but haven't bothered to register a name; most of Cross's team reflect her prejudice to varying degrees and some, like this one, add to that an air of badly controlled fear. I sometimes like to experiment with their tolerance levels, but today I'm too worn out to care. It feels as if I've been co-opted into a farcical drama in which everyone expects me to play Fool.

I kiss Maranda on the forehead and go down the hall to the spare bedroom that has been requisitioned by Cross as an office. My heels click a familiar rhythm against the glass floor. This house is a Heritage site with architecture dating back to the Tudors and traces from every era since, all maintained behind preservation glass and lit by decorative baubles suspended from the ceiling. This hallway, for instance, is lined in layers of Regency wallpaper, stripped into rows of floral memory. The bedroom is more Victorian, with an ornate fireplace emerging from the glass surface of the wall. Its present occupants are criminally unimpressed.

Dr Cross is indeed waiting. The assistant omitted to mention that she is backed up by six new minions, none of whom I have seen before. "My team are moving Ms Salvadore today," she says. "I have permission."

"No." My tone is polite, so polite, push-me-one-inch-further-and-you-die-a-painful-death polite. "The only permission that counts is mine, Dr Cross, it says so in her will, and I quite definitely have not consented to any transfer."

"The will is not valid."

I pause to consider the statement. "Who told you that, doctor?"

Instead of answering my question, Cross activates a wrist projector. The image of a document appears in the air between us, a close-written paper with the Copperfield and Co. letterhead; never a good sign, in my experience. It takes me only a few seconds to absorb the contents of the letter. Maranda's father—with whom she severed all contact nineteen years ago—has been exhumed from his latest incarceration to replace me as her legal guardian. Apparently even a petty criminal with a lengthy history of fraud is preferable to the robot.

It's over. I did everything I could. Maranda will understand.

"You have ten minutes to get out of my house," I announce. "In fact, I'd advise you get as far away from here as you can. I would have worked with you, doctor, but if I'm honest, I'll like this way better."

"I received the notification this morning," Cross retorts. "You have no legal right to make decisions on my patient's behalf. A state warden has been appointed in your stead."

"Is the situation that difficult to compute?" one of the assistants demands, sounding indignant. How dare the robot talk back! You'd almost think it was alive. "The warden will be here in an hour. If you have any sense of duty to Ms Salvadore, you'll recognise this is the most logical course of action."

Cross shakes her head impatiently. "Oh, don't bother, Gao. How can you expect a robot to understand death?"

On the tenth anniversary of our wedding, Maranda gave me an adorable little antique pistol and showed me how to use it. It would be completely pointless against all modern weaponry, of course, but I placed a lot of sentimental value on the thing and now I'm glad I kept it operational. Is there any surer way to get a human's attention?

"Well," I say, "it's funny you should ask."

•~~•

In Tokyo the revolution happened a long time ago. Robots are everywhere—driving trams and collecting rubbish in the big cities, operating the bulwarks and power plants on the coast, doing anything really that requires undivided concentration and a complete lack of ego. There is even an all-robot children's pop group, who have the commercial advantage of never getting sick of each other. This is a part of Japanese culture now, something so natural people look at me funny when I get excited about it.

To me, this is seventh heaven. Athene is not so sure.

"Are there any real AIs at all?" she asks one night as we're walking through the bright city centre, striding along at a relentless pace that parts the crowds with ease. It's lucky my legs are longer than hers or I would never keep up. "I don't like it, Maranda. There are robots everywhere and I can't talk to any of them."

"Maybe we're looking in the wrong places."

Athene thrusts her hands into her coat pockets. "Maybe I'm the only one."

We get a flat close to Hachi Academy, a soaring university complex on the outskirts of Tokyo that is so new it has disciplines you can't find anywhere else. I join a research program into multisensory simulations and pursue my own projects on the kitchen table at home (we have not used that table for anything food-related since our first meal there). Whatever surface is not coated in my microchips and partially completed models is occupied by Athene's stacked reference texts. She has always been a voracious learner, accumulating more than a dozen degrees that count for less than nothing just because she's the one holding them.

In Japan, it's different. The dean at Hachi offers her a junior lecturing post and within a month it seems like every university in the country is trying to poach her. Together we publish a series of papers on the future of AI technology. Athene agrees to let a select few of our scientist friends study her internal systems, the ones I have built and rebuilt out of all recognition over the years, but no one is allowed inside her head except me. One day I take footage of myself working so she can see what it's like in there and she watches it later that night while we're in bed. I know that because she wakes me up at three a.m. by shoving a screen under my nose.

"Do you know what this is?"

"Uh?"

"This is the design you found when you first opened me up, yes? Most of what you've done in my head is just repairs and research, isn't that right?" Her tone is urgent. Suddenly alert, I sit up, take a look at the screen and nod. "Maranda, I think I know how they did it. This is a brain. Someone recreated an actual human brain. It operates on electronic pulses anyway, that's not so great a step—some of your friends have been experimenting with the same thing - but whoever made me didn't do it from scratch. You know how surgeons use neural overlays when they're doing brain surgery?" I don't, I'm not the one with three medical degrees, but she's still talking, holding the screen so tightly that the casing cracks. "I think that's what they did here. Maranda, there is only one way to get a scan this detailed. The brain could have been living when they started, but it wouldn't have stayed that way for long."

Most of Dr Cross's team are only too happy to get out the door when asked politely by the deranged robot with a gun in her hand. Cross is made of stronger stuff. She says a lot of things like 'you'll never get away with it' and 'it would be better to just let go', as though she thinks she can actually reason me out of this. She gives up when I fire a warning shot at the ceiling (thank you, Maranda, for insisting on blast-proof glass) and runs to join the rest of the medical team. As I watch them disappear across the long sloping lawn, I finally get a message from Copperfield and Co.

While they are grateful for my cooperation, the psychological test has come up with a negative. In short, I'm not really a person. Have a nice day!

"Oh, fuck off," I sigh, and bring up the drawbridge.

Over the next few days, the authorities make concerted efforts to breach the household's defences, but are left baffled by the boundless creativity of one Maranda

Salvadore. She's always thought that locks are something that happen to everybody else, and took precautions to make sure it stayed that way. The defence systems embedded in and around the house could probably hold off a full-scale military invasion, at least for a short time, and that's good, because time is what I need.

No, that's not quite true. What I really need is Maranda.

⚡

I'm kneeling on the carpet in our flat in Tokyo, adjusting the work lights to the exact angle I need. Athene sits cross-legged, her back to me, the mass of her hair carefully removed and perched on a stand in our bedroom until the procedure is over. The back of her head is open. We're looking for clues.

As usual, there's music on as a distraction. The rich, mournful tones of Bertha Oliver float in the still air, punctuated by the odd clink or buzz as I work.

Doubt thou the stars are fire
Doubt that the sun doth move
Doubt truth to be a liar
But never doubt I love.

"Do you trust me, Maranda?" Athene asks.

I frown at the blinking lights inside her head. "Of course. What kind of a question is that? I mean, I'm poking around inside your skull, isn't this the point when you wonder if you can trust me?"

"No. I always trust you." Athene shifts a little, which isn't like her. She's upset and I'm not sure why. "I don't know what I'd do without you."

I think I know what's wrong. It's what keeps me up at night, sometimes, thinking about what will happen when I'm old and she isn't. It's probably easier for me. She's the one who will have to manage on her own, when I'm gone.

There's something else, though. Something not quite right.

I go deeper inside her head than I ever have before, making scans at every stage so that I can layer them later using my simulation equipment at Hachi. We go in just before four a.m., when the lab should be empty for a while. Athene sits on the edge of a worktable, watching me set up the sim. Together, we stare at the results, and I feel the full weight of everything I don't know settle on my shoulders.

She says aloud what we're both thinking. "We need help."

There are a lot of brilliant minds at Hachi, but the only one I trust not to share this around is Professor Hisaishi. He is the friend who met us in Beijing, the one who invited us to Hachi in the first place. At seventy, he's the oldest professor at the academy, a pioneer of modern robotics with enough discoveries under his belt to resist the siren call of ambition, or at least I really hope he can. Anyway, if Athene has to trust someone who isn't me, he's our best choice.

The professor studies the scans for a long time in silence. Even after he snaps off the projector, he doesn't say anything, just sits quite still with one finger absently stroking the bridge of his glasses. It's strange—usually Hisaishi is bubbling over with enthusiasm for everything from his latest project to his grandchildren's expertise at drawing dinosaurs. He should be asking questions. And he's not.

My stomach plummets. We have made a mistake.

"So you found a Gorgon," he says, at last. "I thought they were all gone."

"What is a Gorgon?" Athene asks, composedly, as if it doesn't matter in the least. Her fingers flex slightly on the arms of her chair, betraying her tension. I'm not that subtle; I jump to my feet and start prowling around the room, arms folded, waiting for Hisaishi to stop thinking and *answer the fucking question already*.

"I was sent scans almost identical to these eleven years ago," Hisaishi says, tapping the projector lightly. "My task was to turn them into a workable design. I wondered about that when I first met you, Ms Athene. There was a certain flair to the Gorgons."

"Who else was involved? Who were you working for?"

"I really don't know," Hisaishi says mildly. "I would receive updates to incorporate into my own work, so I know there were others. I never met them, though, and the company financing us was almost certainly a front."

"Why did you agree to be involved if you weren't *told* anything? Didn't you even know where the scans came from?"

Hisaishi smiles wryly. "Scientists of my generation, Ms Salvadore, are used to secrecy, even if we do not like it. I always assumed it was a government project. That is how they do things. How could I refuse such an opportunity? It was the greatest challenge of my career."

"You thought the Gorgons were gone," Athene says quietly. "Why is that?"

Hisaishi hesitates. "For some time, I was kept up to date with their progress. I was a senior member of the team. Then suddenly, the communications stopped. For months I heard nothing. One day I was sent a message: the project is a failure, the Gorgons are discontinued. I never found out why."

I stop, standing behind Athene. I don't know whether to believe him or not. There is a pressure inside my head, a sense of dissonance that is beginning to take the shape of a migraine. As I close my eyes, the room wavers around me.

"I am not sure you can be called a Gorgon, any longer," Hisaishi is saying, thoughtfully. "The changes run so deep. You are something new, though what that might be, I can't say—"

"Athene," I say, "come outside."

She looks up, startled, but follows me into the hallway. I push open the doors at the far end and step out onto a long balcony, taking deep breaths. It's early still, the sky an eggshell of pale blue arching above our heads, the spring air cool against my face. In the university grounds below, the first buds of blossom turn avenues of cherry trees into grids of pink and white. It all feels so real, but it's not.

"What happened?" I ask, turning to look at Athene.

"What happened? You interrupted the professor for no apparent reason, before I could ask even half of the questions I want—"

"We didn't come here," I interrupt. "What happened in our apartment, when you first told me about the scans? We researched for years before we went to Hisaishi. He didn't tell us about the Gorgons at the first meeting, either. You've compressed nearly eight years into a few days, and I'd like to know why. What happened to me, Athene?"

"You were shot." She comes to the balcony railing and looks away from me, towards the slowly rising sun. *Doubt that the sun doth move.* Oh, Athene. What have you been trying to tell me? "A needle full of ECS was fired into your bloodstream. You were in a medically induced coma for two weeks while the doctors tried to clear the infection, but it wouldn't respond."

I take a few minutes to absorb that. "I'm dying?"

Athene closes her eyes. "Maranda, you're dead. I'm so, so sorry. I did all I could."

We stand in silence for a long time. Birds trill in the trees, and in the distance I can hear the rumble of Tokyo traffic. I don't feel dead.

"So..." I smile numbly. "Is the afterlife a simulation, or is that just for me? If we're going to be revisiting the highlights of my life, I should get to pick where we go."

"The investigators said it was a lone extremist who attacked you. I don't think that's true. I think you were murdered." Athene turns to face me. "I didn't know what else to do. The only person I could ask for advice was you, and I wanted you to have just a little longer before you had to know."

The simulation flickers. The sky fades, the sun goes out, and I'm sitting upright in my workroom at home, in England. Athene is standing by my side, her expression calm as ever, her hands twisting as she watches my face.

There's a red light blinking under the skin of my wrist. I flex my fingers carefully, stretch out my arms. It's so easy to stand up, no aches and pains at all.

"So this is how it feels," I remark dreamily, studying the skin that isn't mine, that isn't skin at all. These eyes can tell the difference, but they aren't mine either. Well - I suppose they are now. It feels like I've arrived suddenly, a mystery destination finally announced. How else was it going to end, for us?

I'm alive. Close enough, anyway.

I look up at Athene. "You made me all by yourself?"

"Not really." She smiles. "I've been watching the best."

I crouch to test my knee joints and bounce upright again, enjoying the newfound speed. I could outrun anyone.

Which is good, really, because something tells me we'll soon be doing an awful lot of that.

TRACY CANFIELD

Outside the lab's gleaming windows, the wind from Bobcat Mountain whisked away the last of the Pennsylvania summer. Dead birch leaves swirled across Professor Isotope's view of the Sunset Drive-In screen far below. The Professor couldn't run a cable down the cliffside and wire her lab to the Sunset's sound system; Ken Hewitt, who owned the theater, wasn't taking her calls. So she watched the midnight show from her goop-splattered lab bench and tweaked her Tesla coil until its plasma filaments picked up the audio. A cat rubbed one head against her ankle.

"When the kittens come out to play, Ken, you'll be sorry." The Professor smirked down at a vast Malcolm McDowell slinking across the screen. "Maybe tomorrow."

The cat rubbed its second head against her other ankle.

"Maybe tonight," said the Professor.

⚡

Minna Biddle thought the guy in the striped shirt was on the wrong side of forty to be working a concessions counter. *Hi!* proclaimed his nametag. *I'm Ken Hewitt.*

"That's two Cokes," he said, "two Diet Cokes, and a bucket of popcorn for the dog."

Minna's teammates squeezed past her to grab their snacks. Shabba, true to form, shoved his head in the popcorn bucket and whuffed contentedly. Minna brushed a spray of kernels off her Linux tee. "It isn't every theater that'll serve a Great Dane," she said by way of apology."

Ken shrugged. "The Board of Health might object, but so what? Bulldozers are on the horizon. By summertime next year, this place'll be an office park."

Minna was the acknowledged brains of Mystery Five, founded when she and her friends fled their high school's Gay-Straight Alliance after the other kids had yet to decide in two hours what pictures went on the GSA's Tumblr page. Four kids and a dog in Hunter's SUV, scouring the country for the spoor of the inexplicable, fortified with gas, pizza, and dog treats financed via a loan from DJ's big sister. But after months of exposing scams, all Minna had discovered was that "amateur paranormal debunker" made a great hook for a college application essay.

Zee toyed with a blond dreadlock. "Man," he said, "I haven't had a fountain soda since Brady Lake."

"Brady Lake." Hunter popped the collar of his pink polo shirt. "Was that the abandoned sawmill and the art forgers with the rubber masks?"

"That was Catawba, silly," said Minna. Lightning flashed outside, but raindrops hadn't hit the windows yet. Maybe the weather would stay clear until the movie was over. "Brady Lake was the old pier and the smugglers with the rubber masks."

DJ inspected her auburn waves in her compact mirror. "Thought the smugglers haunted the abandoned factory in Shipshewana," she said.

Minna's beauty routine consisted of SPF-30 and concealing the occasional zit. DJ always carried an entire tote bag filled with name-brand make-up. One more reason DJ wasn't her type–Minna liked her girls less femme.

"Shipshewana was the decrepit funhouse," said Minna. "And the disputed inheritance."

"Ooh, I remember that one," said Zee. "They had rubber masks." Shabba barked his agreement, tail wagging like a windshield wiper.

Lightning flashed again and Minna caught her breath at what it revealed out among the orderly rows of economy cars.

"Ken," said Minna, "does the Sunset get a lot of freaky guys peeping at couples making out in back seats?" But that didn't sound right. She was pretty sure that dark, looming shape was female.

No one else spoke a word. They weren't even paying attention to her but stared at the large screen.

Minna turned. Overlaid on the retro carnage of Ed Begley, Jr. sticking his hand in the panther cage and getting bit, blazed an unauthorized message: COWER IN TERROR BEFORE MY MUTANT ARMIES.

"Gang, looks like we've got a mystery on our hands," said Hunter.

Minna polished her glasses. "Let's go pull off some rubber masks."

Outside the lobby, a line of cars snaked towards the exit. The blatting horns couldn't drown out the customers demanding refunds from the ticket booth girl. Lightning crackled above the mountain, but the summer night sky was still cloudless.

DJ fished in her Rebecca Minkoff clutch for a hairbrush. "And here I thought we might not have one last adventure before college started."

"Or, in Shabba's case, obedience school," said Zee. He chuckled awkwardly as his friends stared at their feet. Zee had proved to be no more college material than his dog.

One last adventure, Minna thought. *Then on to school, four years to study criminal justice, study accounting, study business administration; to become a prosecutor like Mom,a middle manager like Dad—or worse,, the dreary adult who tidies up the loose ends once the next crop of teenagers has had their fun and moved on.*

Ah, well. Dispirited as she felt, she had a mystery to solve. She pulled herself up to her full five foot two. "Let's split up."

"Man, I hate splitting up," said Zee. "Splitting up leads to falling through trapdoors."

"It's the only way anything gets done." Minna whipped out her trusty LED flashlight. "Team Chicks will collect that rubber mask by intermission."

"Is that so?" said Hunter. "Well, Team Dudes has a cross-country letterman, and a dog with a pedigreed nose, and, uh..."

"I'm a heteroromantic demisexual," said Zee.

"That means you're straight," said Minna.

Zee chewed a knuckle. "No, right, the dog's a heteroromantic demisexual. I'm—wait, I got this..."

Shabba dashed off, baying, into the night.

"See?" said Zee. "Found a clue already!" The boys sprinted after the receding howls.

"That dog has never followed a trail in its life," said Minna. "He'll lead the guys in a circle, and they'll find him back in the lobby, stuffing himself on Jujubes."

"On my sister's dime." DJ pursed her perfectly-lined lips. "I cannot begin to tell you how much I'm looking forward to getting a job and paying her back for all the junk food that's gone into his and Zee's mouths"

Minna chuckled. "You're not as shallow as you look, DJ."

"But I do look shallow, right? I want to pledge Phi Epsilon Mu in the fall. I'm worried they might discover my G.P.A.. Anyway, shall Team Chicks take the opposite direction?"

"I saw someone out here, earlier," said Minna, "sneaking between the cars." She played her pocket flashlight's beam across the gravel parking lot.

"Twenty bucks says it's counterfeiters,"said DJ.

"No bet." Minna pushed her glasses up her forehead and rubbed her eyes wearily. "Aren't you tired of crimesolving? I know that we've done a lot of good. There are criminals behind bars because of us. But when we created Mystery Five, I hoped to find things that were strange, things that were...*special.* Every time we expose yet another fake, every time the supernatural turns out to be spirit gum, fog machines and plastic masks...I feel like I'm the one who's been defeated."

"You won't be defeated tonight," said DJ. "Team Chicks never loses. Once more unto the breach?"

The gravel parking lot didn't show any tracks, but the the soft ground near the fence was trampled. Minna knelt for a closer look.

Footprints from massive work boots led through a gap in the fence–and there was something else, scattered along the trail, rustling in the warm summer breeze: something green.

"We haven't solved a drug case before, have we?" said DJ.

Minna giggled. "That's not pot."

"You sure? You don't think we should call in our subject-matter expert?"

Minna rubbed a crumbling leaf between her fingers and sniffed. "I may not be an authority on pot, but this? Speaking as the secretary-treasurer of the Animal Rescue Club in sixth, seventh, *and* eighth grade, this is definitely catnip—"

"Poor Zee. He'll be so disappointed."

"Why would someone spread...a trail of catnip into a drive-in theater?"

"Maybe Hewitt's allergic to cats," said DJ. "Let's see if I can get through this fence without snagging my tights."

The double trail of footprints and catnip traversed a vacant lot and stopped abruptly at the sheer stone mass of the mountain. "Trapdoor?" said DJ.

"Revolving wall," said Minna. "On the count of three." They leaned on the stone, laughing, anticipating the giddy spin. It was better than a carnival ride. *And unlike our adventures,* Minna thought, *carnival rides are actually dangerous sometimes.*

Inside the mountain, cobwebs thick as wedding veils festooned a winding staircase. The walls of the narrow passage trembled and boomed. Far away, something yowled.

"Sounds creepy," whispered DJ.

"Movie theater," Minna whispered back. "Echoing against the stone."

DJ wrinkled her nose. "It reeks in here. It's worse than Hunter's Hard Party body spray."

Minna nodded. "Worse than Zee's vegan cheese."

Workboot prints led through a carpet of dust–one set coming down, and another going back. "This corridor hasn't been used for a long time," Minna said.

"So what's special about tonight?"

"Stay alert," said DJ. "Stay quiet."

Something brushed Minna's ankle and she shrieked.

"Quieter than that," said DJ. "It's just a cat." She nodded at a shadowy form dashing up the stairs.

Minna kicked the floor. "It's always just a cat," she said. A plume of dust settled across her Oxfords. "Just a cat, just the wind, just a guy with Ben Nye greasepaint." She peered up into the darkness. "Although there was something weird about *that* cat. Did you get a good look?"

"It was black," said DJ. "And it crossed your path, if you want to pretend you're in unnatural peril."

"I just had a thought," said Minna. "We haven't seen any speakers, or a radio. So where's the movie soundtrack coming from?"

⁂

The stairs finally ended at a shadowy chamber flickering with red light. "Count of three sound good?" Minna panted.

A humming tube shed a red glow across Erlenmeyer flasks gurgling with chemical gunk. The smell was even stronger– rancid and sharp–and the rumbling louder. Another, weaker light wavered beyond the plate-glass window. The movie was still playing to the empty theater far below. Minna swept her flashlight beam across a door labeled *To Upper Lab*, and another labeled *Leave Open*. Both were shut.

"The mad science stuff'll be fake, same as always," said Minna. "Props, to scare Hewitt into or out of doing something. So where is the real clue?" She stole over to the red tube. "Helium-neon laser. Maybe this is how they wrote the warning on the movie screen." She pushed on the burnished casing but it was bolted to the stone wall. "Or not. Let's check in with the guys."

She dialed Hunter's cell–no sense trying Zee's, which was never charged. She wished he would change the ringback from Sam Smith's cover of "How Will I Know," which he insisted was the theme song for Mystery Five. "It's ringing," said Minna, "but..."

"They've probably already fallen down a trapdoor," said DJ.

"Shh. Listen."

Beneath the ever-growing rumble, they could just make out the muffled notes of his cell phone.

DJ inched over to the LEAVE OPEN door. "It's behind here," she mouthed.

The door creaked inward at Minna's touch. Even through the crack, the stench overwhelmed them. The entire floor of the room beyond was taken up by a wooden box piled with shredded paper, leaflets advertising the drive-ins, pages from the *Philadelphia Inquirer*. Somewhere in the mess, Hunter's cell rang forlornly.

"Well, that's where the smell's coming from," said Minna. "Someone sure has a lot of cats."

"I just know there's a clue in here somewhere," said DJ miserably.

Minna swallowed hard and plucked up a comparatively intact sheet of paper by one corner. "It's addressed to a Professor Stephanie Isotope, from some company called Sunnyview Commercial Property Developers." She shook it gingerly. "I can't make it all out, but it looks like Ken Hewitt's right–someone wants to build on his property." She swept her flashlight around. Deeper in the box, something glinted. With trembling hands Minna reached back in. "There's Hunter's phone."

But she was wrong. The glint was a familiar tag on a shredded dog collar.

"With a lot of cats," said Minna slowly, "you need a lot of litterboxes. Not one big one."

"So if there's one big litterbox," said DJ, "there's one big—"

Behind them, a low note trilled out, like a playful French horn. Minna and DJ pivoted, cringing, to stare into a gargantuan pair of slit green eyes.

Not a panther, not a tiger–a monstrously oversized housecat, a swirly-coated tabby as big as the Mystery SUV, swinging an immense paw like a sledgehammer full of steak knives. DJ's clutch took the blow. Purple pleather tore like tissue, scattering hairbrushes and keys across the lab floor.

"I-It's some kind of projection," said DJ, wide-eyed.

Minna shook her head. "Run now! Analyze later!" The cat took a soft step toward Minna, ears laid back, enormous pupils dilating in anticipation.

"Oh my God," Minna gasped, "it smells the catnip on my hands."

Animal Rescue Club flashed before Minna's eyes as the cat licked its chops. *They play with their prey because they haven't figured out how to kill it fast enough.*

She dove beneath a workbench, skidding up against something hard and humming on the other side. The laser. *Careful, a beam that strong's just as deadly as the cat.*

Minna dug frantically in her skirt pockets, but all she came up with was a Chapstick. Mystery Five never carried weapons. They had never needed them. The cat swiped its paws under the bench, extended claws clicking the floor tiles scarcely inches from her feet, batting some plastic trinket from DJ's purse this way and that.

Pepper spray? Minna snatched up the little container. Her hand brushed an ivory-smooth claw and she shuddered. *No, just her face powder. If I wore makeup more often, I'd have known not to bother. Then again...*

Shaking, Minna rose to her feet. The cat leapt fluidly onto the workbench, five hundred pounds of impossible muscle ready to spring.

Not daring to take her eyes off that glittering green gaze, Minna snapped the compact open and pushed it into the beam of laser light. The plastic edge hissed and sizzled–then the beam struck the mirror and danced, reflected on the lab walls.

"Good kitty," said Minna. "Good kitty."

The distracted cat dabbed its paw at the moving dot of red light. Minna rocked her wrist, skittering the reflection along the wall, careful to keep it where the cat could see. The cat's backside wiggled–it was ready to pounce. *Not yet, not yet...almost there ...*

With a warble, the cat leapt for the shining red pinpoint–and smashed through the glass window. A brief yowl Dopplered down the mountainside, ending in a thud.

Minna braced her head in her hands. "Oh my God," she gasped.

"Oh. Em," said DJ. "Gee. Could I have my compact back? It's Sephora Matte Cream."

Minna forced herself to take a deep breath of the foul air. "You saw that, right? You saw it too? There's no such thing. I mean there is, but there shouldn't be. DJ, that wasn't a closed-camera projection or an elaborate marionette. We have a real mad scientist on our hands. With an army of mutant cats. There's a real problem, and if we don't solve it, who will?" She bit her thumb. "Shabba's collar...for once I do hope the guys are stuck down a trap door somewhere. It could be so much worse."

When DJ didn't respond, Minna turned just in time to see her friend, a ragged hand clapped over her mouth, yanked into the shadows by a hulking woman in work boots.

One last adventure, Minna repeated grimly. She climbed the stairs to Professor Isotope's mountaintop lab like a soldier marching to battle.

The nimbus of purple plasma around the Tesla coil blasted '80s synth as the movie credits crawled down at the Sunset. Nutrient fluid bubbled through tanks of winged and scaled and eight-eyed kittens. A framed diploma hung on the wall next to a rabies vaccination schedule; tucked under one corner was a business card for a rubber mask manufacturer. A green cat groomed itself atop a filing cabinet, half-hidden behind a precarious stack of papers. Stuffed into the stack, Minna saw, was a manila envelope clearly addressed to Ken Hewitt.

The Tesla coil fell silent. The movie had ended.

Minna reached for the envelope. "You're not dangerous," she whispered, "are you, little mint kitty?"

The cat lifted a paw and swatted the whole pile down. Minna lunged and snagged the envelope before it could thump on the ground. "Return to sender" had been scrawled across it, even though the theater was right next door. There was nothing inside but a promotional DVD for a digital projection system.

The green cat licked itself, satisfied.

"Photosynthetic." A thirtyish woman in a stained lab coat stepped from the shadows. "You don't have to feed it–it recharges by sleeping in a sunbeam. Wait until I get those genes into the big ones. I'll save a fortune on Science Diet." She patted the layers of her brunette bob with a rubber-gloved hand.

"You must be Professor Isotope," said Minna.

"And you must be Wilhelmina Biddle," said the woman, with her odd accent adding emphasis on the *vil*. The green cat leapt to a lab bench sniffed her glove. "I saw Mystery Five on the news when you broke up that counterfeiting ring in Duquesne. Let me tell you, you are wasting your talents on this debunking business. The stoned kid and the dog find half the clues."

The Professor jabbed a blinking button. Three tremendous cats padded in and dropped Hunter, Zee, and Shabba in a quivering heap. Shabba cringed as if he could hide two hundred pounds of whimpering dogflesh in Zee's scrawny shadow.

Minna rushed over to the boys. "You're all right!"

"Under the circumstances," said Hunter with a groan. "This shirt's ruined."

"We fell through a trapdoor and landed, like, in the world's largest litterbox," said Zee. "Stay downwind of us. That would be west, no, hang on—"

He licked his finger and held it up. Then grimaced. "Oh man," he said thoughtfully, "I should not have done that."

"That's three of my friends," said Minna. "What did your Igor do with DJ?"

A towering woman in workboots stomped upstairs, DJ slung over her shoulder. "It's Ygraine, actually," she said. She settled the bound and gagged teenager in an ergonomic chair.

"Sunnyview Commercial Property Developers wants to build a mall here," said Hunter. He tried to stand, but a cat pushed him down with an impassive velvet paw. "You want to scare Hewitt off so he'll sell the drive-in to you for cheap, and you can turn around and sell it to the developers for a profit. You're busted, Isotope."

Shabba's ears pricked up at the word *busted*, but when the three gargantuan tabbies turned their cool gaze his way he tucked his tail between his leg sand cowered.

Professor Isotope waved a dismissive hand. "Owning giant cats means I don't have to listen to you."

The clomp of footsteps heralded Ken Hewitt, who stopped at the top of the stairwell, panting. "The cops...are on...their way."

Minna noticed what he clutched in one hand. "Is that a *gun*? Put that down!"

Hewitt's grip wavered. "You won't–wait, she really *does* have a mutant army?" A green blur whisked past. Then Hewitt was empty-handed, and the little mint cat was sitting on the floor, rubbing its cheek on his gun barrel.

"You're close, Hunter, but you're not quite right," said Minna. "You missed the key clue–the quote for the projection system." She held up the DVD. "All the movie companies are switching to digital projection, but it'd cost the Sunset sixty thousand dollars to convert. Hewitt *wants* to sell. It's *Isotope* who's holding out."

She turned to the Professor. "See, the drive-in lot by itself isn't big enough for a mall. The developers wouldn't buy Hewitt's property unless both of you sold. So he tried to discredit you and get you arrested. *He's* the one that projected that threat on the movie screen."

DJ wiggled free of her gag; people really ought to know better than try and bind her after all these months. "He also said 'she really *does* have a mutant army'," she said, "which suggests that he came up with the idea himself, and was surprised when it turned out to be true."

Hewitt peered into an incubation tank. The camo-print kitten inside pressed its nose to the glass. "I thought it fit with the mountaintop lab and the truckload of chemicals you get every week," Hewitt said.

"Ken, you tried to set me up?" said the Professor."

"Tried? I damn near succeeded," he snarled. "And I would've gotten away with it, too, if it hadn't been for these interfering, these snooping.... Damn, what's the word I'm looking for?"

Professor Isotope scratched a giant cat behind one umbrella-sized ear. The beast stretched languidly, flashing claws like Kukri knives. "You've got more pluck than I gave you credit for, Hewitt. So, now that you kids have heard his confession, I guess you'll all be on your way."

"Absolutely," said Zee. "Just call off the cats, lady, and we'll be out of here before you can say *zoiks*."

"You're not the good guy here, Isotope," Minna said. "Who left the trail of catnip over to the theater? You really were going to sic your giant cats on him."

"Technically I spread that catnip," said Ygraine.

"You don't have to take the blame. That was on my orders," said Isotope. She sighed and slouched. "But yes, I offered Ken a one-time payment to connect my stereo to the theater sound system, but he wouldn't hear of it." A glance at Hewitt seemed to revive her ire. "Tonight I was going to teach him a lesson he'd remember for the rest of his rather short life. And I still am. But I have one obstacle to take care of first...and that's you."

Minna spread her hands in exasperation. "All my life I've hoped to see something extraordinary," she said. "You see the extraordinary every day. You've created wonders the world has never seen. And what do you do with your discovery? You hide out alone on this mountain–"

Ygraine cleared her throat. "Ugh, she's not alone. Henchwoman, here. Tops at the academy, too. Just because you don't go for the tall, tough ones–"

Minna gave her an appreciative shrug and wink. "My point, Professor, is that you've reshaped the laws of nature to your will, and all you can think to do is wreak petty revenge. Who's next? The grad school advisor who kept postponing your dissertation defense? The health inspector who shut down your favorite pancake place?

"Enough," said Isotope sternly. "Ygraine, tell the cats to eat them."

Hunter fainted. Zee hugged his dog. DJ glared at Isotope.

Ygraine dragged the steel toe of her boot across the floor. "Uh, boss, do you think you should give that order? Because...that's a pretty serious decision."

"No," said Isotope. "I'm delegating that one."

"I kinda have some concerns about this," said Ygraine. "They're just kids."

"You two have never killed *anyone*, have you?" said Minna. "You're just a biochem PhD who likes cats."

A flushed Hewitt cleared his throat of phlegm. "They're breeding animals without a license."

"A misdemeanor," said Minna firmly. "You guys haven't done anything irrevocable yet. Have you even thought about the commercial possibilities of your work?" She pointed at the little green cat, which was touching its nose to Shabba's while the dog quivered in dread. "You've invented a photosynthetic cat that doesn't need a litterbox! You'll be richer than Meg Whitman and Bill Gates. Why not take over the world by becoming disgustingly rich, which is not only legal, but positively encouraged."

The notion silenced them all. Except Shabba, who whined at the thought of all those cats. And Zee who had started CPR on Hunter, who flailed for a moment at the mouth-to-mouth. And Ygraine, who had begun explaining tying knots to DJ. And Hewitt, who had begun sneezing.

Isotope laughed. "If I could think of things like that, I'd already be rich."

Minna closed her eyes and basked in a vision of a world where commuters rode giant cats to work and houses had carpet for siding; a world where lions as tame as lambs provided day care. Where the guy who discovered Claritin Non-Drowsy Allergy Relief got a congressional medal. A world remade by mad science. A world where no one had to go out searching for the marvelous; where no one had to be mundane. Not teenagers, and not grown-ups. She opened her eyes. "What you need is a manager." A manager of extraordinary things. Minna smiled. "I want a job."

ELDRITCH BROWN HOUSES

CLAIRE HUMPHREY

This is Salem at its oldest and spookiest: cold fog off the ocean, daylight dimming early, gables and gambrels looming at odd angles. I'm gazing out from the upstairs window of the Corwin place, from beside a case of age-yellowed cloth dolls. The streets are empty except for the tail-lights of a single car, receding.

The season ends today. I've already cartoned up the books and brochures and souvenir prints and stacked them under the admission desk, and returned the consignment soaps and candles to their suppliers. Mrs Gilman will come tomorrow to remove the textiles to cold storage for the winter.

I haven't seen another human being all day, except at a distance. I made coffee and toast in the kitchenette of my dorm, which the other students had already left for Thanksgiving. I didn't have anyone else on duty with me since visitor count was expected to be low—and it has been, not a single tourist so far.

I ate my bagged lunch at the admission desk, spilling bagel crumbs on one of the papers I was reading for class. I'm going to have the same thing for lunch tomorrow, unless my family suddenly decides to mend fences.

The house sways and creaks around me, wind-buffeted. Water trickles down the distorted glass. I check my phone: half an hour until closing.

Someone's struggling up the walk: a small person encumbered with a couple of gigantic bags. God, I hope we haven't forgotten to cancel a brochure delivery or something.

I scramble down the narrow stairs to hold the door open. It's a small door built for seventeenth century people, but this girl doesn't have to duck at all. Tiny, Asian, wearing orange Chucks dark with wet.

"I can take pictures in here, right?" she says, heaving one of her bags off her shoulder, and then the other.

"Sure, hon. School project?"

She cuts her eyes at me. "How old do you think I am?"

Voice crisp and grown-up, and oh. Shit. "I've seen you around," I say. "You're in my year, right? Sorry about that. I didn't recognize you at first."

"Was," she says. "Was in your year. Dropped out." She's looking down now, unzipping her duffels, pulling out a battered tripod and a heavy-looking camera.

"You were in my lit class." I remember. "You gave that seminar on Lovecraft."

"That was my last day," she snaps.

Awkward, Paige, awkward. I grope for a different subject. "Will you have enough light to work?"

"Don't need it."

"You sure? It's pretty dark in here. We keep it low so we don't damage the textiles and documents."

"Light meter," she says, waving a smallish box with a window on one side. She doesn't look at me, tight lines around her eyes as she pops open a canister of film, hinges the back off the camera and tucks the film inside. She snaps the camera shut and thumbs a lever on the top of it.

"What kind is that?" I ask. "It looks like it's made of metal."

"Yep."

"I can't even see the screen. It's like a stealth camera. How do you see what you're shooting?"

"It's analog."

"So if it's not for school, then—"

And a couple of last-minute tourists come through the door, two middle-aged women and a boy. The woman with the camera doesn't even look, just kicks her bags out of the way a little and keeps prepping.

I don't see her again until I'm nearly done showing the family around. I've got them clustered around the doll case upstairs, when I hear her clunking around in the next room. I'm partway through my tour spiel: "Several of these dolls were among the effects of the Corwin family when they sold this house to the state in 1940. They probably aren't old enough to have belonged to the daughters of Judge Corwin himself, but—"

"Creepy," the boy says. "Why doesn't this one have eyes?"

"It would have, when it was new. They would have been embroidered on by hand—"

"It looks evil," the boy says with delight. "Like it's going to come to life and murder you!"

"It's not," says Camera Girl, from the doorway of the Corwins' master bedroom. "There's nothing creepy about it. Nothing special at all."

The boy looks disappointed. One of the women ruffles his hair and says, "Why don't we take a look in here, Jayden? There are some interesting herbs and things that I'm sure this guide can explain to us."

So I have to follow them into the apothecary room and talk about blood and bile and phlegm and the way people had thought to manage them with dried rats and toads, which the boy seems to find thrilling.

By the time the family's had enough, I figure Camera Girl must be long gone, but once I've let them out, I return to the master bedroom and find her still there, pointing her box at things and shaking her head.

"Worthless," she says.

"The Corwin House is an important historical—"

"Yeah, whatever. Where's the magic?"

"All around you," I say in my best spooky voice.

"Hang on," she says, clutching at the light meter. It's pointed toward me, and I can see the little red needle swinging. "Wait—ah, fuck."

"What?"

"You were right," she says, voice going flat again. "It's too dark in here."

And without another word, she picks up her tripod and her camera and her light meter, and lugs it all back downstairs.

I follow. It's time to close. I staple the day's receipts—all two of them—while she packs her duffels.

"You didn't get the shots you needed, did you?" I attempt. "If you want to try on a brighter day, I can arrange to let you in. Some of the artefacts will be stored for the season but the furniture will stay here."

"What do you care?" she says, turning on me. Her eyes look brilliant and dark and really pissed off. "Why are you hassling me? Don't you have a family gathering to get to?"

"No," I say. I take a breath to explain, or something, but it just kind of gets stuck in my lungs.

"Oh. Ah. Sorry."

"It's fine—"

"Look at you. It's not fine. Come on, sorry, I'm being a jerk. I should know better—"

And her arms wrap around my shoulders, gentle and firm, while I sob into my hands.

⚡

Her name is Maya Wu. She tells me not to feel bad, she didn't remember mine, either.

All I do remember—other than the intensity on her face when she led that seminar—is the camera kit, which I saw her carrying around the green a few times. I always wondered what she saw in the campus architecture.

She gives me the lighter duffel to carry and leads me toward the sidewalk.

I follow, watching the night come all the way down over Salem, damp chill moving off the water and hazing the streetlights. The keys of the Corwin place jingle coldly from my free hand; I've left it locked and lonely, windows dark, and I won't see it again until spring.

Unless I let Maya in secretly for more photos. What am I thinking, offering to risk my job for a woman I barely know?

I'm about to fall back, tell her I'm going back to my dorm instead, but she stops in the doorway of a pub, holds it open for me, and inside there's heat and the smell of dinner and a low hum of music, and she's inviting me to go inside.

And she's smiling.

Maya orders a salad and a Coke. "Can't drink with my meds," she says, when she sees my questioning look. "You go ahead."

So I ask for a pint of Sam Adams and a burger.

While we wait for our food, Maya tears little bits off her napkin. I check my phone; nothing, as usual. Maya draws on the table with her fingertip. I clasp and unclasp my bracelet.

"That story," Maya finally blurts. "Do you remember it?"

"The Witch House story? Well, yeah, I should—you know what my workplace is called, right? I remember the guy in it has a nervous breakdown, studying too much, and he starts seeing weird meaning in architecture, and then, like, something eats his heart?"

"Yeah, pretty much. That's why I dropped out."

"Lovecraft wasn't your thing? Mine either—"

"I started seeing meaning in architecture," Maya says, eyes dark and serious.

I don't actually remember the story that well, except that it used the word "indescribable" to describe way too many things. So I'm not quite sure what Maya means. I take a careful breath to ask.

"I'm bipolar," she says. "Manic episode. Had to take some time off to get my shit together."

"Oh. So you weren't really..."

"You've spent plenty of time here—what do you think?" she says. "It's a bit too much like Disneyland, right?"

"Except Disneyland wasn't built on murder," I say. Probably a bit sharply, from the look on her face.

"I just meant..."

"That there's no magic here?" For some reason that kind of makes me feel like crying again.

Fortunately our food comes right then, and I have an excuse to look down at my plate while I spread mustard on my burger. When I look up again, though, Maya's watching me. She hasn't lifted her fork.

"You don't think I'm crazy," she says.

I shrug. "I mean, clinically, you are, right?"

She laughs at that, thank God, but she still waits for an answer.

I shake my head. "I don't think you're crazy."

"Good," she says. "Because you don't have plans this weekend, and I need some help with my research."

Maya's staying at the Ocean View Inn, which doesn't have an ocean view unless you stand somewhere on top of the roof, up by the rusty old lightning rod. I hold the duffels while she pulls out the key, an old-school metal one on one of those plastic diamond keychains with the room number stencilled on it.

"Atmospheric," is all I can come up with, surveying the room: red and beige striped bedspreads, chartreuse floral carpeting, and a clutter of esoteric equipment. Jugs of brown liquid on the counter by the sink, rectangular trays laid out on the dresser and desk. Television disconnected and tucked in the corner, replaced by some kind of adjustable lamp contraption. And are those blackout curtains over the windows?

"My brilliant plan," Maya says, with a self-consciously dramatic flourish. "I've been researching how to capture magic on film. I've figured out a new coating for my camera lens that will magnify the refraction of magical energy through the aetheric layer—"

"Whoa, Lovecraft."

She clears her throat. "Point is, I know I'm mentally ill, but some of what I saw was real. And I think I can prove it."

"Awesome," I say, because it is.

"Only there's a problem with my meter. I couldn't get much of anything in the house." She pops the back off the little box, probes a fingertip at whatever's inside.

"Maybe the house just doesn't have it. I mean, it wasn't really a witch house at all. It was the home of one of the judges in the trials."

"Huh," Maya says. "I knew I'd be happy I picked up a tour guide."

"Was that a pickup?" I can feel myself blushing. "You weren't just feeling sorry for me?"

"Bit of that too," she says. "You still haven't told me why you're spending Thanksgiving alone." She snaps the back on the meter and jiggles it.

"It's kind of a long story..." I start.

"Holy shit!" Maya jumps. She points the box at me. Points it away toward the wall. Points it back. "Maybe that's it..."

"What? What's what?"

"Paige," she says. "Paige. Want to be in some pictures?"

Maya sits me on a chair in front of the blank wall where the television would normally be. She sets up a light on a tripod near me, and gets me to turn my face half toward it. I can feel the heat of it on my cheek.

All I have to do is follow Maya's instructions, and if I don't get it right, she just gently moves me into place, hands warm through my cotton blouse. Between that and the two pints I had at the pub, I'm as relaxed as I've been all week.

I smile at her, easy.

"Just like that," she says, from behind the camera, and I hear the sliding click of an old-fashioned shutter, and then the whir of the film advancing.

A lock of hair tickles my cheek. I raise my hand to brush it back.

"Right there. Hold," Maya says, and I do, pinned in place by her voice, her eyes.

Maya processes the rolls of film in a canister of chemistry, each one wound onto a spindle so that none of the surfaces will touch. She does this in complete darkness, narrating it to me while I sit on her bed. It's hypnotic, her voice and the crackle of the film and then the sharp smells of developer, stop bath, fixer.

We each drink a bottled coffee from her bar fridge while we wait for the negatives to dry. Then she clips the negatives into a frame inserted in the enlarger, which casts an image onto the desktop a couple of feet below the lens.

The red rectangular box by the sink glows dim red, throwing weird upward shadows on the contours of Maya's face. The other lights are off, the blackout curtains pulled tight. I watch over Maya's shoulder as she looks at each of the images in turn. My features are weird in reverse: bright white eyebrows, bright white bangs, black teeth showing between my parted grey lips.

"How can you tell what it's going to look like?" I say.

"You get used to it after a while," she says. "Here, this one." She draws her finger through the beam from the enlarger, its shadow pointing to a crackle of darkness in the image.

"What's that, a flaw in the film?"

"Nope," she says. "That's what we're looking for."

She gets out her photo paper from a thick black plastic envelope, sets it in place and exposes it for a carefully chosen length of time. She does a few more at slightly different settings. Then she slides all the papers into a tray of chemistry.

"Whoa—won't they be wrecked by the wet?" I ask, and then I see, in the dull red light, the images begin to form.

Maya and I sprawl on our stomachs side by side on one of the beds, facing the array of still-damp photos spread out over the bedspread. They all show pretty much the same pose, me seated, half-turned, eyes looking right into the camera. I snicker a little at the look on my face; Maya doesn't.

In more than half of the images, I see something I've never seen before.

"Why do I have a halo?" I ask. "How did you do that?"

"I didn't," Maya says, rolling onto her side to look at me. "That's all you."

It isn't exactly a halo, because it's all around me, stronger in some pictures than others, nearly obscuring my features in a couple of cases. Kind of crackly pale light, like aurora borealis.

"Do I have a halo all the time?"

Maya shakes her head. "I'm not about to go off my meds to find out."

I roll half onto my back to look at her face. I want her to tell me what happens next.

She doesn't hold my gaze, turns away and goes to the window, pulling the curtain open, showing an inch of pale early light.

"Holy crap, have we been up all night?"

"Come on," Maya says. "Let's walk."

The sun must be rising somewhere behind the fog, because I can see colours now: Maya's purple jacket fuzzed over with tiny beads of mist, curling red leaves drifting at the edges of the street, a blue and white flag on one of the few yachts still in the harbour.

Hands in jean pockets, I follow Maya downhill toward the water. She walks quickly, head down. I can't quite see her face.

Then she reaches the seawall and turns to me, flinging her hair back in the rising breeze. "Paige," she says. "I really did it, right?"

"Nah, it was all me. You said so." I grin, and I watch the answering grin blossom on her face.

"Witch," she says. "Come here, come here." And she wraps her arms around my ribs, squeezing tight.

Behind Maya's head, the sun is starting to burn through the harbour fog. Her eyes are puffy and red from being up all night in the reek of chemistry, and probably mine are too.

"Hey," I say. "It's Thanksgiving."

"Which you're spending with me."

"Yeah."

"I'm going to buy you breakfast," Maya says, "and we're going to figure out where there's witchcraft in your family tree."

"I had no idea—"

"And then we're going to take a nap," Maya goes on. "And then we're going out for pie."

"Yes," I say, and as I say it I can feel the weight of my body settling heavier in her arms. It's delicious.

She looks up at me, squinting in the brightness. Seems like she's looking for something in particular. Whatever it is, she smiles, satisfied, and slips her cold hands into mine.

"I know a great little diner over by the Common, with a three-ninety-nine breakfast special," she says.

We walk away from the harbour, up past the House of Seven Gables, in the clearing mist. We pass wax museums and houses of horrors and purple-draped Magick Shoppes and palm-reading stands, but all of them are closed for now, and the streets of old Salem are ours alone.

I haven't told Maya the long story of my family's estrangement. I'm pretty sure I will, if she tells me to. I'm starting to think I need a safeword with her; and somehow I can see she'll know what I mean by that, and she'll be careful with me.

I can smell cinnamon and burning leaves on the morning air. The frost on the Common is melting into sparkling dew. I tug Maya to a stop for a moment, gesturing.

She gazes. Takes in a breath. Then she's on her tiptoes in her orange Chucks, hands wrapped around the back of my head, pulling me into a kiss.

And I can feel it, the halo, bright with promise, crackling around me.

THE MOOREHEAD MAZE EXPERIMENT

TIM LIEDER

Transcript

Narrator

In 1972, in the basement of the English Department of Moorehead State University, researchers set up a labyrinth for a social and biological psychology experiment that would rival all predecessors.

Dr. Elana Adler, Social Psychologist

Shortly after the Stanford Prison study, I knew that I would have to implement the maze study immediately. Universities were cracking down on what you could do with human subjects and if I had waited, Moorehead State would have cut the funding.

Sharon Barry, English Professor, Dr. Adler's Longtime Companion

Elana is not a cruel woman by nature. She has her moments, but you can't call her a sadist. And it was a different time. Milgrim and Zimbardo were doing their experiments on obedience and authority. Mind control cults were popular. Men and women who seemed normal and even boring were running into the desert to take peyote or dance with rattlesnakes.

Text (Narrated)

Abstract—The effects of phencyclidine, commonly known as PCP or angel dust, on the memory have been documented in several mice tests. However, the studies fail to incorporate the human element, particularly the human capacity to remember complex directions when under the influence of PCP. In this study, subjects who ingested PCP managed to perform complex tasks and with effort, remember the directions learned in a previous experience, despite reactions which included euphoria, anxiety, weightlessness and paranoia.

Adler

I did not believe in animal testing at the time. I still do not believe that mice running through mazes can produce compelling repeatable data. And I never liked vivisection.

Barry

I was the one that suggested that Elana do a mice maze experiment with humans. I thought it would be a fun summer study.

Tom Robinson, Former Unification Church Minister, Cult Educator

When people ask how Timothy McVeigh happens and how Osama Bin Laden and Charles Manson attract followers, they are often trying to distance themselves from the cult members. In truth, we all have the potential to follow these movements. As human beings, we are capable of rationalizing anything. Once we believe, we will use all of our intellect in order to maintain belief, no matter how irrational.

Michael Edelman, Minotaur—Moorehead Maze Experiment

When I heard the tapes for the Jonestown Suicide, I felt a sense of recognition. I knew that something was wrong but I was trying to argue my way out of it.

Dr. Jeremy Rosenberg, Social Psychologist

We did use Kool Aid. The pictures we took horrified us, but if you look at them now, you just see people in Mickey Mouse hats running away from people with papier-mâché heads.

Edelman

I still don't know why I was wearing a minotaur mask. I think I could have been just as effective with a bag over my head. By the end of it I was just happy that I was one of the minotaurs instead of one of the mice.

ADLER

Sharon convinced me to use the minotaur masks and the mice ears. I know she likes to make it sound like she was always against the experiment and that I was out of control, but she insisted we use the minotaur masks from her Spring production of Phaedra. She had some graduate design student make about a dozen minotaur masks because she thought that the chorus should symbolic. Something. I didn't get it.

BARRY

Theseus killed the minotaur! And in Phaedra, he is old and nostalgic. So of course he's seeing minotaurs everywhere. His greatest triumph is commenting on his worst tragedy. How is that complicated?

ADLER

She thought it would be funny.

BARRY

It wasn't funny. It was tragic.

[SCENE: The curtain call for Phaedra with the chorus in minotaur masks surrounding the four principle actors. Besides the minotaur masks everyone is dressed in street clothing]

ADLER

It was the goofiest thing I ever saw. I had been planning the maze experiment and once I saw Sharon's piece, I agreed with her. I had to use masks.

ROSENBERG

Generally, social psychology experiments are conducted in order to study the way we perceive stimuli and how we conduct ourselves in certain situations.

ADLER

When images of abuse, torture, murder and mass suicide are broadcast, there is an instinct to go on the defensive. In the Mai Lai massacre, the military outright stated that it was just a few bad apples. When the Manson murders happened, we wanted to assume that everyone associated with the cult was already evil, but a set of socio-psychological variables can make ordinary people into monsters and victims.

NARRATOR

In Cambodia, Rwanda and Uganda, ordinary people perpetrated extraordinary abuses. Examining the lessons of the Moorehead Maze Experiment can help us understand.

Dr. Judith Gross

I think that the experiment stopped being an experiment for most of the subjects and they just saw it as their life.

Minotaur

Fuck this maze! Fuck you! Would you like a piece of candy?

Theban

I am not a mouse!

Minotaur

Squeak! Squeak! Would you like a piece of candy?

Rosenberg

We had no idea that it would go so far. We all talked about how we did not want to reproduce the results of the Stanford Prison Experiment. We were just trying to test the power of the environment, but with a puzzle experiment.

Adler

The experiment was for memory only. Dr. Rosenberg is lying when he claims that it was anything else.

Newspaper Ad on Screen

Male College Students needed for a psychological study involving memory and puzzles. $10 per day for 2-3 weeks, beginning August 3. For further information & applications, come to Room 137, Jasper Hall, Moorehead State.

Narrator

Over fifty subjects volunteered for Dr. Adler's experiment.

Adler

We screened the candidates and then picked twenty-four healthiest ones. Then we chose eight to be minotaurs and the rest to be Thebans. We just flipped a coin so initially half were minotaurs and half were Thebans and then we winnowed down the minotaurs by flipping the coin until we moved enough into the Theban category.

Edelman

On the first day we were fitted into the masks but we were told to wear black pants and white button down shirts with black ties. Then they gave us whistles, hand cuffs, billy clubs and fake blood to spray on the walls.

ADLER

I wanted the minotaurs to be as bland as possible without the masks, because the first few days they would be without masks and I wanted everyone to feel like they were safe.

HERBERT MITSUME, FORMER THEBAN

They told us to be at the Psychology Building at noon. I arrived about ten minutes late and I saw several people sitting on benches with blindfolds. A student checked us in and I thought that he was administering the test. I later found out that he was another subject. Everyone was very friendly. They started telling us that they were honored to have us as sacrifices which seemed strange but I was on a college campus with a Greek System. I saw pledges running through campus in their underwear. I just took my blindfold and sat on a bench.

EDELMAN

I was in my Mormon uniform before the check-in, but they didn't give me the tools. All eight of us participated in the check-in with two in the van, two at the table and the rest of us in charge of greeting the other subjects. I had two lines that I was supposed to say: "Welcome" and "We are honored to receive you". I know that Carl was saying "Thank you for your sacrifice" but he only said it a few times. He kept looking at me as if I knew what was going on.

CARL RINDELAUB, MINOTAUR

My lines were "Thank you for your sacrifice" and "This is going to be fun." I was supposed to say them with a smile.

ADLER

Dr. Rosenberg wrote the greetings. I wanted the experience to feel like an initiation because the Moonies were just starting at the time and we knew about the Jesus freaks and the Hari Krishnas. Of course, Charles Manson was still in the news. So we were all very interested in the ways that cults worked and Dr. Rosenberg was the one that reminded everyone that cults always started out friendly, maybe a little weird, but always welcoming. Judith Gross wanted insisted on the minotaurs only saying two lines at first and one of them being about sacrifice.

MITSUME

I just put on the blindfold and waited. Someone tied my hands in front of me and said "welcome." It wasn't until we were loaded into the van and brought to the site that I started to worry.

ADLER

The minotaurs or alphas blindfolded them and tied their hands at the extraction site. When they got to the experiment site, the Thebans or betas were told to strip naked and then put on dresses with belts that were supposed to seem like the ancient Greek outfits. They were all called Blessed One in order to both dehumanize them and give them the human sacrifice experience. I didn't think that the minotaurs would be able to intimidate them—especially without the masks—but then Michael Edelman started repeating his lines while staring them in the face.

MITSUME

They locked us into the room and we started talking about what was going to happen next but every time we tried to speak someone yelled at us and we heard the nightstick hitting the door. We tried whispering but the...guards, I guess... they weren't in their masks yet...would come in and tell us to stop.

EDELMAN

I decided that I was going to have fun.

[Security camera in the waiting room with most subjects dressed in gowns]

EDELMAN

Welcome.

THEBAN

Thank you.

EDELMAN

Welcome.

THEBAN

Thank you.

EDELMAN

Welcome.

THEBAN

Okay.

EDELMAN

We are honored to receive you.

THEBAN

Okay.

EDELMAN

We are honored to receive you.

THEBAN

Thank you.

EDELMAN

Welcome.

EDELMAN

I was fascinated with my behavior. I wanted to see where I could go with it. If they tried to ignore me, I would get in their face and shout. Someone should hit me. I would have hit me.

ADLER

The minotaurs then left to go to their room and the Thebans were released from the Theban room one at a time.

ROSENBERG

We told them that they were going to be tested on their ability to find food and water in a maze. I was at the front with the lab coat. At that point, they were very happy that they were given something to do.

ADLER

We didn't spike the Kool Aid the first day.

ROSENBERG

I didn't know about the phencyclidine. Actually no one knew about the phencyclidine except for Dr. Adler.

GROSS

I thought that we should have used legal narcotics, but Dr. Adler insisted on hallucinogens and since LCD is vulnerable to heat, PCP was the drug of choice. I don't know how Dr. Adler got it.

ADLER

When you are a young lesbian in the Midwest, it pays to become friends with cops. I'm not going to say anything more about it, because most of the people who helped me are still alive. They have pensions.

ROSENBERG

I did not agree to the drug part of the experiment. When Dr. Adler published the paper, I did not want to be named.

GROSS

Jeremy had a fit when he found out that he was going to be called as a witness.

EDELMAN

We were told that we would stay in our room until the second day. They gave us beer. I didn't like sharing a room with seven guys for the experiment, but the money was good. Ten dollars a day went farther in those days. And unlike the Thebans, we all had cots.

ADLER

I just want to make one thing clear. The rooms that we used for minotaurs and Thebans both had bathrooms with showers attached. This was not the Stanford Prison Experiment. We did not want to see the subjects standing in their own feces and crying. Some of the test subjects stopped bathing but they always had the option.

BARRY

She was using the dressing rooms for the Theater department. I approved of the usage of the basement and rooms, but I explained everything to the department head.

MITSUME

The walls were green. There were mirrors on the door so you could see yourself. Supposedly that was not part of the psychological torture but how could it be anything else?

EDELMAN

It was a green room. Even my high school had a green room.

MITSUME

The first day, we were just sent through the maze and everything was pretty basic. I found the room by noon and they had food for us.

EDELMAN

The first day was boring.

MITSUME

I heard the noises.

ROSENBERG

We played tapes for the Theban subjects.

ADLER

Sharon made the tapes. She paid some actors to make them. Got some of the actors from her play to make them. First they were scratching sounds and then as the study progressed she added singing, crying and there was even one girl going "please don't hurt me". No wait. It was more like "please...don't...hurt me" but she had this weird accent that could have been Japanese or from Vermont. It was unsettling.

BARRY

I didn't know why she wanted the tapes.

ADLER

The next day we started the harassment.

EDELMAN

I didn't put on the mask until the fourth day, but on the second day, I had the character in place. I would come through the maze and order the subjects to go one way.

ROSENBERG

The minotaurs didn't hesitate. They really wanted to play with the Thebans.

EDELMAN

Every time I saw someone I would push them. But I would still say my lines. Hello. We are honored to receive you. Now get on the floor and lie there! I made them do pushups. I told one to sing. I followed one through the maze saying "Hello?" until he was crying.

ROSENBERG

That night we introduced PCP into the Kool Aid.

INTERVIEWER

Didn't you say that you didn't know about the drug?

ROSENBERG

I didn't know about it before the experiment. Once the experiment started I felt helpless to stop it. I was a graduate student. Dr. Adler had tenure and her recommendation had the power to determine my future.

GROSS

I wonder if Jeremy believes anything he says.

Adler

We immediately saw results. The low dosage of phencyclidine made everyone more susceptible. The noise tapes were causing a host or reactions from wall slapping to laughter. Their motor reflexes were slowed but jerky.

Mitsume

I didn't know that I was high that first night. I just knew that everything was much sharper. I felt very light, as if I could fly to the sun and back.

Rosenberg

They were normal the next day but sleep deprived.

Edelman

Some of them tried to avoid me and I could shove them much more easily. One actually tried to punch me, but he fell on his face.

Rosenberg

On the fourth day, we were increasing doses but not getting the desired results. The minotaurs were becoming accustomed to the Thebans but they weren't dragging them by the hair or making them strip. I could tell that Dr. Adler was frustrated.

Adler

The experiment was going slowly. Incrementally the minotaurs were stepping up the harassment and seeing what they could get away with. I did not want to torture the Thebans so much as bring them to a place where they doubted their memories.

Edelman

I hated the mask. I couldn't see anything and at any moment one of the prisoners could have punched through it and I'd have papier-mâché in my eyes.

Mitsume

I knew on some level that they were students in stupid masks. Hell, I even knew where those masks came from, but I also started to think "what if they are real?" I don't mean that I didn't know that they were wearing masks, but what if the masks were hiding real minotaur faces? What if I took off the bull head and the head underneath the bull head was a real bull telling me that I was honored or welcomes or whatever they kept saying.

Edelman

I want to point out that we were not told to use our opening lines throughout the experiment. But when we were relaxing after the day, Carl said that it would be hilarious if we kept talking like we talked the first day but with the masks on. Since most of us were still using our two lines on the prisoners, we all agreed that it would be hilarious.

MITSUME

Thebans started disappearing. I wanted to assume that they had just begged to be removed from the experiment, but I saw blood on the walls.

ROSENBERG

I want to stress that the minotaurs did not receive the drugged food.

MITSUME

Welcome. Thank you for coming. Have a nice day. Your sacrifice is worthy. I...this fucks me up. Sorry. People died in that maze. They claim that everyone was fine, but I heard it.

EDELMAN

We didn't know what we were supposed to do except harass the Thebans, so we improvised. Carl would throw water on them and I would just walk up to groups and push them into each other. By the end of the week, I was putting Thebans in handcuffs and tying them to the radiators; then laugh as the other Thebans saw their comrade tied up and crying.

MITSUME

A week into the experiment, it was no longer an experiment. The minotaurs would pee on us. They released bears into the maze to hunt us down and everything smelled like blood. I touched a wall and it grabbed me and it wouldn't let me go. Aliens were clinging to the walls just staring at us with their big eyes—and all the aliens were wearing SS uniforms.

EDELMAN

(singing) Wilkommen Bien Venue Welcome...I love that musical

MITSUME

The bear took advantage of me.

ROSENBERG

By the second week, the drug mixture was increased. We gave the prisoners stale crackers with their Kool-Aid. Some of them were falling and screaming. Some of them were vomiting in the maze.

ADLER

We made certain that the vomit was cleaned up by the next day.

ROSENBERG

I had to clean up the vomit.

GROSS

Jeremy started cleaning up the vomit but then he came up with the idea of making the minotaurs do it.

EDELMAN

You know how hard it is to force a Theban prisoner to clean up vomit when he's tripping? I would stand with a bucket of water and sponge, just waiting for one of them, so I could grab him and make him clean it. I started making them clean imaginary spots.

MITSUME

The minotaurs were threatening to eat us if we didn't behave ourselves. By the second week, they were real.

[SECURITY CAMERA FOOTAGE: Theban on his hands and knees]

THEBAN

Please Jesus please get me out of here. I am sorry. I am so sorry. Please just kill me.

MINOTAUR

Thank you for your sacrifice. Clean that up. Get it. Over there. Harder. Thank you for your sacrifice.

EDELMAN

I suppose you could say that I was dehumanizing the subjects. At the time, I would have said that they were the ones that were dehumanizing me because I was the one in the silly mask.

ROSENBERG

The minotaurs started to take advantage of their power and escalated the games. They would tell prisoners to stay in one place. Tear their clothes. One minotaur poked all the prisoners on their foreheads. Some of them were severely paranoid by the second week.

MITSUME

When the minotaur touched my head, light entered my skull.

ADLER

I think that you have to take a lot of this in context. The minotaur myth itself makes Theseus out to be the hero because he was the one actually managed to kill the minotaur, but if you are recreating the myth, you need to let the subjects feel like what it must have been like to be prisoners in a place where they are being sacrificed to a half-bull creature.

GROSS

I didn't think that Dr. Adler knew much about Greek mythology when the study started. Or when it ended. She started talking about it at an ethics board a year later but...we never heard about it when we were doing it.

ROSENBERG

It took longer than the Stanford experiment, but the minotaurs started to get sexual.

TAPE RECORDING

You are my little Esmeralda. Oh yes, you are. The world needs more like you. Walk over here and say you love the hunchback. The world needs more like you.

EDELMAN

Humiliation was not the prime goal, but it became the part of the experiment that we all wanted to do. Fear and intimidation are great, but we were feeling like those guys who worked the haunted houses in carnivals. You can only get so much work satisfaction out of standing around in a mask, threatening to touch people.

RINDELAUB

People have sexual hang-ups, even in the seventies when we were all supposed to be going to coke orgies. Or key parties.

THEBAN

I want to fuck the wall! I want to get fucked by the broom! Thank you! I can fuck the floor.

MITSUME

The bear was very gentle.

MINOTAUR

Now give me ten! You are a beautiful flower!

THEBAN

Yes!

MINOTAUR

With your ass out! You are a beautiful flower!

THEBAN

Yes, master!

MINOTAUR

Fuck the floor! You are a beautiful flower!

THEBAN

(inaudible)

ROSENBERG

Everyone knew that they were college students playing at being Thebans and minotaurs and yet, they were so committed to the roles that they stopped seeing the Other as human.

ADLER

That is the point of the Greek myths. If you are born blind or born a slave, you have to make the best of it. Hubris only makes us think that we can overcome our fate, but in reality we are just a road trip away from killing our father and sexing up Mom.

BARRY

Elana is really a sweet woman. We have been together for over forty years and we got married as soon as it was legal. I would not have stayed with her if she was as bad as her reputation. She's Jewish. She would not turn a basement into a concentration camp.

MITSUME

No. I don't think that she wanted revenge against me for being Japanese. It was an experiment. I don't feel comfortable talking about her.

GROSS

No. I don't think that Dr. Adler was racist.

ROSENBERG

There were only two races in the world by the second week. Thebans and Minotaurs. The Thebans were drugged and the Minotaurs were vicious, so it was like *The Time Machine,* but less British.

THEBAN

I did a bad thing. I did a bad thing.

THEBANS

Fuck you. Fuck you.

MITSUME

They would make us chant things and I would go along with it. I think one guy had breakdown. He was crying for the rest of the experiment. He even broke one of the ears on his hat.

EDELMAN

The crying prisoner made me laugh. Is that wrong? It was really funny. Sorry.

ROSENBERG

The Theban breakdown was genuine. He really upset us.

MITSUME

I used to see that guy around campus and sometimes he would see me and there would be this look on his eyes like we shared a secret, but I better not tell anyone.

GROSS

A year ago, I was speaking at a symposium on Ethics of Human Experiments and after my lecture, a former subject came up to me and told me that he was in the experiment. It took three cocktails to remember that he was the one that cried.

ADLER

Gross and Rosenberg would make bets on how long it would take the crying prisoner to break down after he was pushed from the Theban room. It was always five minutes and thirteen seconds. Yet, every day they would bet as if they had not seen it the previous day. Rosenberg even tried to count the crying from the lip quivers at the four minute mark in order to claim victory one morning.

ROSENBERG

At some level we understood that we were no longer in control of the experiment and that we were damaging these people. I think that we should have had more stops on the experiment to examine the kind of torture that we were imposing on our subjects.

EDELMAN

We didn't start making the Thebans fight each other until the experiment was almost over.

MITSUME

By the end of the experiment, I hated everyone—especially the Thebans.

MINOTAUR

You want this? You want this? Fight for it! Thank you for your sacrifice!

NARRATOR

At the end of the second week of the experiment, Dr. Adler invited her girlfriend, Professor Sharon Barry, to visit the maze.

BARRY

I had heard about the experiment from Elana and I helped her plan it, but I did not know what was going on until I was right there in the middle of it. I wanted to run down and stop everything. The part that got me was the alpha subjects grabbing the betas by their genitals and leading them through the halls.

ADLER

She really hated the part where the Thebans were covered in bags and being forced to hold onto each other by the shoulders and kick up their legs.

BARRY

They were just leading them through the site and slapping them. I could tell that Elana was excited. It was turning her on. I just started crying. It was torture. I couldn't watch it.

ADLER

Sharon was not happy. We discussed it but she was always very emotional. I told her that psychologists needed to learn these things. If we were going to deprogram cult members, we needed to know how they were programmed in the first place.

BARRY

The next day I came back and it was still terrifying, but I could see Elana's point.

MITSUME

I forgot that I had a name.

GROSS

Because Dr. Adler was in charge of the experiment, she could bring her girlfriend into the booth. I couldn't bring my boyfriend. Jeremy couldn't bring...I don't think Jeremy was dating anyone at the time.

ROSENBERG

Professor Barry brought an outsider perspective and that was interesting for our notes. I do think that Professor Barry allowed us to step back and question the morality of the experiment.

GROSS

Jeremy was the one that suggested we start changing the maze set up to confuse the Thebans and Minotaurs. So we would go into the maze and move the walls around. He also wanted us to put whoopie cushions at various locations to increase the disorientation, but Dr. Adler stopped that idea in its tracks.

ADLER

I never liked fart jokes and I did not want to present the videos if there was any possibility that the most dramatic scenes would involve a Theban reacting to a fake fart.

MITSUME

A few days before the end of the experiment, it began to change. I was still afraid, but I had stopped hallucinating.

EDELMAN

The prisoners became less easy to push into walls. I could still order them around, but they didn't fall so easily. I stopped seeing blood on my hands.

ROSENBERG

We decided that we should see how the prisoners reacted without the phencyclidine.

GROSS

We ran out of drugs.

ADLER

The phencyclidine was supposed to last for the entire three weeks, but we were using more of it than we had planned for. And my suppliers were becoming reluctant to aid our research.

ROSENBERG

The prisoners reacted just as subservient in their sober states as they did in their drugged states. The drugs might have gotten them in that place of servitude faster, but they were going to be there regardless.

NARRATOR

At the end of three weeks, the experiment ended and everyone was paid.

MITSUME

One day, the door opened and three researchers came in and told us that we could go after we answered some questions. I was told to remove my Mickey Mouse hat, but I kept it on.

ADLER

We combined qualitative with quantitative questions. The Thebans—or the beta group—was generally unhappy with the experiment and they were very much in agreement that they were going to lose sleep in the next week. Several reported hallucinations including large killer bunnies, bulls and singing walls.

MITSUME

I think that the questions were the last torture before they sent us out with severe PTSD.

ROSENBERG

Only one subject reported symptoms of PTSD and we sent him to campus psychological services. We even set him up with a therapist who had nothing to do with the experiment.

ADLER

There was one student that I referred to my ex-friend Robert. Robert was the one who reported on the experiment for the ethics committee and testified against me. He also convinced the student to testify against me.

GROSS

We were all in trouble for a few months, but then Dr. Adler had tenure and the experiment report was published by *Abnormal Psychology* so the University decided that we may have been improper, but not worthy of official censure.

EDELMAN

I kept the minotaur mask.

THE EGGSHELL CURTAIN

ROMIE STOTT

At first, Koshka went to the train station for the trains; later, for the two ladies; and still later for Nyusha.

The two ladies were Peterburzhec of the nobility, true cosmopolitans. Older women, they wore scandalous amounts of makeup—one as heavily rouged as a theater performer, and the other barefaced but so spectacularly clothed the lack screamed of nakedness. They met every day at 4 o'clock and drank coffee at the station café. The barefaced woman paid.

Although they chose to meet in a busy station, they ignored everyone. Occasionally, a man passing through (for it had to be a man waiting for a connecting train; who of the station regulars wouldn't know better?) would try to join the table with one excuse or another—loneliness, friendliness, a shortage of chairs—and the two ladies would carry on with their conversation as if no one had said a word, as if no one occupied the third seat. Once, a man settled the bill before the barefaced woman got to it, and as the ladies finished their coffee, the barefaced woman set her own stack of rubles on top of the man's, paying all over again, as if his money didn't count.

Koshka thought they were wonderful. She bought a little fur cap like the rouged woman wore, just a little beaten up along the folds, with just a few gaps in the fur, found secondhand at a street market. The hat's implied history was insouciant, dishabille, redolent of old money and the boudoir. Koshka's father forbade her from wearing it out of the house. Koshka's father was not concerned with its daring; he did not understand that it was meant to be daring.

"Papa," tutted Koshka, "this is how the aristocrats wear them about town." She tilted the cap forward over her eyebrow, set at what she supposed was a rakish angle.

"People with a great deal of money often enjoy looking poor," said her father. "Money is central to the effect."

"I love this hat," Koshka insisted. Her father looked up from the technical drawings he'd spread over the kitchen table, up past her eyes, up to the crown of her hat. He stared through two blinks, giving the matter his full consideration. Koshka held her breath. Although her father was a man of strong opinions, he formed them from observation, and his weighting of variables, though obvious to him, was difficult to predict. He lowered his eyes and resumed work on the drawings.

"If your hat keeps your ears warm, it's a good hat," he said. "But only in the house."

The hat did not keep Koshka's ears warm, and she did not wear it in the house.

Koshka's father was the physicist Zinon Faddein Kunetzov. If she spoke to an engineer—not an engineer who drove a train, but an engineer who designed a train—the name was repeated with an exclamation point, "Zinon Faddein Kunetzov!" If she spoke to anyone else, the name brought at best a "who?" and more often "so?" But he worked for Fabergé, and that was a name everyone knew. Fabergé made a jeweled egg that glowed in moonlight, a silver cigarette box that never seemed to empty. Sometimes, very wealthy men would ask about Fabergé's secrets.

Koshka also asked.

"We feed rubies to ducks," said her father, or sometimes, "I paint myself with radium and sit on them like a hen."

He joked often, but Koshka was never sure whether he enjoyed it, or whether it was a protective strategy.

When spring was just beginning—when every third day seemed it might be spring and the rest held on to winter—Koshka began to notice another spectator at the train station, watching the ladies. She might have attended already for months; she might have kept vigil for longer than Koshka. Koshka, who was fond of writing diary entries chastising herself for her faults, imagining they might one day be read and admired, often took as her subject how oblivious to others she was, how self-involved, how egocentric was wicked Koshka. These entries were perhaps not as exaggerated as she believed. In fact, she only noticed the girl because the girl was staring at her, as though Koshka was as absorbing as the ladies. It was thrilling.

The girl, Nyusha—for this was Nyusha, promised and pivotal—dressed in padded clothes with clumsy but effective quilting, and her hair was short and spongy, like the center of a pumpernickel loaf. When she smiled, her mouth twisted at the edges as if it held in a secret. Her puffy clothes made her seem tiny and giant at the same time; Koshka could never make up her mind.

The weeks after Koshka noticed Nyusha staring, she looked for her in the crowd, but Nyusha, maddeningly, wasn't looking at Koshka anymore. Not when Koshka wore a bright purple scarf or curled her hair into ringlets or dangled tiny bells across her wrist. She could stand in the same place or another place or even against the railing of the café. Nyusha did not look. She smiled her twisting smile, but gave Koshka no clue what she smiled at. Koshka didn't even know her name.

Then one day Nyusha strolled over easy as you like and handed Koshka half an egg and onion pirozhki and a jar of mint kvass, and said:

"You should know that I'm not a man or a woman; I'm a worker, and that's all that matters. I enjoy beautiful things, but I can also see that they are decadence, so long as wealth is not evenly held." She took a swig of the kvass, and then put it back in Koshka's hand.

"Oh, I quite agree," said Koshka, who had no idea what she was talking about. She immediately took a large bite of pirozhki in a strategic maneuver to ensure she would not be expected to say anything further.

"Look at us," said Nyusha, and she paused to run her eyes up and down Koshka's body, which felt like being buzzed with a low voltage galvanic current. "I work all day in a factory and make just enough money to eat and sleep, and if I'm sick and can't work that day, I starve, as though I am worth nothing. You spend all your days not working, not striving, not using your hands or mind, as though you are worth nothing. We look different, but we are both caught in a system that values machinery over human people. I seem to act freely, because I don't let the system inside my head, but we will not be truly free until the system is abolished."

"You seem to have given this a lot of thought," said Koshka. "I like the way you make kvass."

"Thank you," said Nyusha. "I use a bit of birch bark for extra flavor."

It occurred to Koshka that Nyusha was perhaps one of the Bolsheviks, but Koshka hesitated to commit to this view, because in all honesty she wasn't sure what the difference was between Bolsheviks and Mensheviks, if there was a difference, nor was it clear to her what she herself was. Koshka's father had mostly kept her at home during the bread riots, and they'd used the occasional factory strikes to vacation in the country. Koshka had seen enough to suspect "Tzarist" meant her, although she had never met the Tzar and anyway didn't see what her support had to do with it: he'd been born the Tzar, and seemed like a fairly nice one, all things considered. Several months ago, she'd worked up the courage to ask her father about it, and they'd had a long and serious conversation late into the night, in which he seemed to suggest they weren't Bolshevik or Menshevik or Tzarist; instead, he'd talked a lot about science and the political neutrality of pure discovery, about how the scientist looked beyond emotional attachments to state or even family, considering only what might serve to improve the future of the human race. At the time, Koshka had thought she'd understood it all, but when she woke up the next day, she couldn't remember most of it—just the thrill of briefly being able to make sense of her father. She wanted to ask again, but was afraid he'd be disappointed. He was ever so efficient.

Nyusha, in contrast, seemed like someone who might be very happy to explain things over and over again.

"Perhaps you would like to walk with me," said Koshka, "along the river, if you have time?" She smiled a smile she'd practiced in the looking glass, lips slightly parted the way she'd seen in a hair tonic advertisement. Nyusha smiled back, and it was crooked and thinned out her lips, but there was something nice about the way it drew attention to her jawline.

Several weeks of afternoon walks passed pleasantly, and soon they were spending Sundays in the park together. Nyusha favored entertainment of a physical sort—rowing, and as the weather warmed, swimming. Koshka preferred to wave a flag, or more accurately a brightly-colored handkerchief, from the sidelines, but she did it with a whole heart. She embraced unreservedly her new friend's notion that a body striving for perfect action was the highest expression of freedom-in-community, but found her own body, when pressed to exertion, felt decidedly not free—felt decidedly non-communal and smelly, and a bit prone to sunburn. Bicycles seemed perhaps debonair enough to be worth it, but Koshka suspected they were, for the moment at least, bourgeois. Nyusha didn't seem to mind Koshka's not being a Communist, but Koshka didn't see any reason to rub it in. She sat happily under a parasol and watched the powerful rotations of Nyusha's shoulders, the smooth rhythmic dips as her hips shifted. Nyusha's form, she thought, was very fine, and it did inspire in Koshka desire to commune freely.

In June, Nyusha gave a speech at a workers' rally that preceded another strike, and Koshka didn't go, but she did look in all the papers afterward to see if Nyusha was mentioned, and clipped out the single sentence in the single handbill that spoke of one comrade whose voice "inspired in the listener irrepressible longing for collective action," which sounded enough like Nyusha to Koshka, at least, to be kept secretly underneath her powder box. Koshka and her father spent the duration of the strike in Petrozadovsk, where Koshka was encouraged to visit various monuments and make watercolors of Lake Onega, and Zinon spent his time at the mines, performing experiments on rare ores, some of which proved satisfactory enough to be sent back to the factory in an otherwise unoccupied railcar.

Koshka worried that Nyusha would lose interest in her absence, but couldn't figure out how to address a letter to a person who lived in a co-operative dormitory. She considered asking Zinon, but this would make her subject to inquiries both probative and tiresome. Instead, Koshka spent the vacation alternately testy, elegantly tragic, and deliberately carefree, until they returned home. Her relationship with Nyusha picked up exactly where it had left off, and she could go back to being herself. A delivery man commented that she looked refreshed, and indeed she felt positively ebullient.

By now, they were spending most afternoons in a disused warehouse Nyusha had somehow gotten a key to, which she made comfortable with bits of discarded furniture. She talked about adding a printing press, or maybe holding free classes, or setting up a labor exchange where one comrade could fix another's shirt and later be given a free haircut. These plans changed by the day, but Koshka understood why someone might want to linger in the pleasurable moments of rising possibility.

Koshka wished she could tell Nyusha, without telling Nyusha, that she recognized a certain level of commitment in the friendship—something special and slightly foreign to her, an intimacy based on potential and shared space rather than biography and shared history. She wanted to say, "I accept you into my life in a way I can't define, a way that is important to me." She wanted to say this without smothering the strange and comfortable trembles she wished to celebrate. It seemed like the kind of thing that might be expressed by the right nickname, but Nyusha was already the most intimate, infantile form of "Anna" available, and Nyusha insisted on it from everyone—one of her notions about removing barriers to the truth of communal interdependence. Instead, Koshka said:

"I like that slogan about 'no end to war without an end to the class system.' I like the idea of people from different classes being able to love each other instead of fighting."

Nyusha reacted as though this was the funniest thing she'd ever heard.

"Oh Kisa, no," said Nyusha, using a finger to blot the last tear from her eye. "No, I think the end to social classes will not happen because everyone gets along. I think it will be violence beyond what you've ever imagined."

Koshka's cheeks got hot, and she couldn't tell whether she was embarrassed or angry, so she spoke softly and quickly.

"I thought Capitalism might naturally move to Communism as people got more aware of each other, and the factories would pass to the workers who knew them best, and since they'd be more invested and efficient, we'd make more of everything and there would be enough for everyone. I didn't know you wanted to go around killing people."

Koshka bit down on her lip and stared very hard at the floor of the warehouse, at the line where the wall met the floor.

"Hey," said Nyusha, carefully. "Hey." She nudged the side of her foot against the side of Koshka's. "Nobody wants to kill anyone. Nobody in this room, anyway. I think."

"No?" said Koshka, the kind of no that means "I hate you."

"What I hope will happen and what I think will happen are two different things."

"What? You're mumbling," said Koshka, although she had heard Nyusha perfectly. She was finding that she was, in fact, mad and not embarrassed. Another part of her filed away the sound and image of mumbling, to examine later; this was a new Nyusha.

"I said," said Nyusha, "that I don't have a rosy opinion of industrialists. I don't think their ideas of fairness have much to do with mine, and I don't see them handing over their assets to the collective peaceably. It's not—if a mob of factory workers told you to share all your house and your food and, yes, your bed, and your clothes, and your soap, and if it was all gone, you wouldn't get any, wouldn't you call that a robbery? Wouldn't you fight back?"

"Well," said Koshka, "I could be seduced."

"Seduced?"

"Yes. I believe I could be seduced. You could try to seduce me."

"One of us has misunderstood this conversation," said Nyusha, "and I'm beginning to think it was me."

By the time there was more talking, it was nearly an hour later, and their clothes were indeed jumbled together in a shared pile. Koshka languidly draped her silk scarf around Nyusha's bare shoulders.

"To wear into battle," she said happily. Nyusha snorted.

"If anybody saw me with this, I'd be denounced as a Capitalist. But—" she quickly added, "I will wear it always, wrapped around my waist, underneath my shirt, so I can feel you secretly embracing me."

"Oh yes, that's much better," said Koshka.

The next few weeks were the happiest of Koshka's life. Her father was so absorbed with his new ores that he set up a cot in his laboratory and was only home to fetch old paperwork or drop off grocery money. Consequently, Koshka was free to come and go as she liked, without questions, and was able to fit in assignations with Nyusha whenever Nyusha wasn't working or going to block meetings.

Nyusha, she discovered, was frequently working or at block meetings. Using a series of "no, not then"s, Koshka tried to piece Nyusha's schedule together, but she could never make it come out. There just weren't enough hours, not with the extravagant length of factory shifts, even assuming Nyusha ate all her meals while working, which she didn't. In fact, Koshka was finding factory work ought to preclude all other activity. It almost seemed structured that way.

In a pleasant doze on the pile of rags that functioned as the warehouse's improvised bed, Koshka heard more than felt Nyusha get up. Koshka opened her eyes just enough to peer through her eyelashes, half dreaming, and saw Nyusha pick up a folded envelope and tip a small pile of white powder into her hand. This was inhaled with the efficiency of long practice.

At that moment, Nyusha looked up at her and froze.

"It's not what you think," she said. Koshka frowned, puzzled.

"It's not cocaine, then?" Koshka sighed, not bothering to fill her lungs. The world had fit together for a second, like a too-small shoe finally stretching to free her foot. "I thought it was. It made so much sense."

"I don't usually use this much," said Nyusha, "just a little, just to give myself a little time of my own." She smiled, but it looked painful. "You don't know what it's like, owing every hour to people who don't even like you. Then I wanted more time with you..."

Koshka jumped into the pause, "Oh no, don't worry. My father does it all the time. It's very fashionable and efficient."

Oh, wasn't Nyusha special beyond her station, as if Koshka needed further evidence!

"I just thought it was expensive," Koshka explained.

"It is, yes," said Nyusha, subdued.

Later that evening, in comradely spirit, Koshka ransacked her deserted house. This, then, would be her contribution to the movement. She would beneficently redistribute some of Zinon's cocaine, which he would never notice as long as she left him enough, the same way he didn't worry over eggs or pencils or clean shirts until the supply was nearly exhausted. That was what bourgeois meant, Koshka was finding—wincing at the cost of a ball gown, but not bread, not the day-to-day. Which for Zinon and Nyusha included cocaine. So Koshka would skim from Zinon, Nyusha could continue her brave campaign, and incidentally there would be time for more warehouse trysts. Assuming Koshka could find the jar of powder in the first place.

The house was full of hidden cabinets and experimental latch designs, like a magician's trunk or a pharaoh's tomb. And Zinon tinkered with them constantly, either for research or relaxation. He'd shown them all to Koshka, every change, but she found it difficult to keep track. Or not difficult—boring. Dull to remember clever sequences to open a box of old letters in a language she didn't read. Dull to blow across the surface of a sugar bowl to make it play a little tune, and have to wait through repetitive music before she could sweeten her breakfast. And within the cabinets, Zinon's organizational methods could be esoteric, their tidiness a misleading veneer. Koshka preferred to set up parallel systems and manage them as she liked.

Perhaps two hours into her search, Koshka realized Zinon would have taken the cocaine jar with him to his laboratory.

Perhaps two hours after that, Koshka remembered he kept some in a snuff box in his best jacket, for getting through unpleasant parties.

The box was a marvel of enamelwork, smooth and cupola-shaped. Even when Koshka brought it close to the lamp wick, the seam between lid and case was invisible, hidden by tiny fish scales in varied metals. When Koshka tried to twist the top, the scales rotated fluidly, as though she was pushing balls of mercury. When she let go, they flowed back into their original stripes, as if they'd never been disturbed. She sat on the floor of the dressing room, trying one approach and then another, pausing only to adjust the lamp wick.

The downstairs clock tolled three. Koshka noticed her eyes were watering. She balanced the box on her palms and raised it up to her eye level, hoping for a new perspective.

Zinon's slim, large-knuckled hand reached past her shoulder to gently lift the snuffbox. His thumb slid back and forth across the enamel, rearranging the tiny plates in an almost effortless glide, until the box shuddered like a yielding pet animal. The lid went limp and loose, as though it were an uncurled orange peel. The box was empty.

"Needs a refill, I'm afraid," he said.

Koshka looked up at her father, not sure what to expect. He wore a half frown; whether for her or the box was difficult to fathom. Koshka realized he was swaying slightly. He looked very pale, slowed by exhaustion but full of anxious energy. She wondered how long he'd been watching her.

"How is work?" she said. Zinon considered. The silence stretched until Koshka thought he wouldn't answer. Then longer. And then, to her surprise, he said:

"Come to the lab with me."

And then—

"I haven't been a good father to you."

It occurred to Koshka he might not be feeling altogether well. As a loving daughter, she ought to implore him to sleep, or even call in a doctor.

At the same time, never had she been offered an opportunity to see the lab. Even when she had lunch for him, or a message, these had to be dropped at the gate, to be handed up by the doorman.

"Let me get my coat and boots," she said.

The Fabergé Building had every window lit, even at an hour when the city slept; electric lamps hung from the ceiling of every room, and there were boxes by which machines could be hooked into the current itself. As Koshka followed her father up stairwells and down hallways, she peeked into room after room, hoping in vain to catch a glimpse of extra electricity leaking out to pool on the floor. When they reached Zinon's office, it took her a while to understand they had arrived; the lab was large enough to comfortably fit six sitting rooms, far from the single table Koshka had imagined.

"Please, explore," Zinon said with a dismissive wave, turning to fuss with a contraption that looked like a box full of geared lightning rods. Despite his grant of free access, Koshka restrained her exploration to her eyes; touching experiments in progress did not seem prudent.

"That's a fluoroscope, there," said Zinon, "if you'd like to see your skeleton. The gaps in the things that hold us together." This last sounded like one of Zinon's jokes, and like most of his jokes seemed to be for his own amusement rather than his audience.

The back wall seemed to be taken up by a tunnel of black accordion fabric, stretched right across the room, tall enough to fit a man. Coils of copper wire protruded at regular intervals. Or not regular—mathematical, as though the troughs of a wave had been marked and then methodically compressed, starting at one end. Like a spring at the moment of tightening, before periodicity had been restored. As Koshka walked alongside it, she noticed progressively less dust on the fabric, as though it were being attracted by something at one end. Or repelled by the other.

"I never thought you'd become a Communist," said Zinon, raising his voice to be heard across the room. It was all Koshka could do not to jump; as it was, her back went very straight, and her hands felt cold.

"What makes you think I'm a Communist?" she said.

"Your diary. I thought some of your observations were quite intriguing, worthy of further exploration. It surprised me, though. I always thought you meant to go the other direction."

"I love the Tzar," said Koshka, trying to remember what exactly she'd written in her diary. She'd lately been trying out thoughts she wasn't sure of, but the last few weeks had been love poems addressed "the lover" or "the dear one," which she understood to be the fashion. She suspected they were very bad, but had not yet worked up the courage to show them to anyone who could confirm this. The idea that Zinon had read them made her feel hot and desperate. Although really he had no taste in poetry, so figs to his opinion. "And I am mortified that you would read my diary," huffed Koshka. "It isn't the least bit seemly."

Zinon harrumphed, seeming to take Koshka's objection as no more weighty than a preference for one after dinner cordial over another, maintaining the tone that had always seemed too casual in formal situations and oddly formal for his intimates.

"Come, now," said Zinon, "I read every book in the house. And it's clear that you write for public consumption." He adjusted a twist of wire.

"Well," said Koshka, "well, I'm not a Communist."

"No?"

"I'm not even sure I like Communists. I just like a specific Communist."

"Yes?"

"Yes."

"And I suppose it can't be helped?"

"No."

Zinon nodded, flicking a switch so that the lightning rod cabinet spun into action. Here, then, was Koshka's leaking electricity—arcs of purple-blue fire, leaping between twirling metal spears, first at random, but then, as the thing achieved full speed, coming together to form a twirling, many-petalled flower, like a firework caught in a birdcage. Koshka came to stand shoulder-to-shoulder with her father, wondering.

"I blame myself, of course," he said. "It's a failure of the genes." He put a reassuring hand on her back, the way he had when she'd been a little girl, looking out at the ocean. But only for a moment. He sighed.

"It ends tonight, though," he said.

"Oh, Papa," said Koshka, her eyes instantly full of tears—real tears, her own and not his, he who had never cared for tears. "I won't talk anymore about Communism and I won't take any of your cocaine, but please. Please just a little while. Please let me keep my friend. Nothing will be broken by it."

Zinon watched her, impassively, waiting until she'd said her piece. The bright electrical glow made the blood vessels under his eyes visible beneath the skin, as though his gaze was its own dynamo. Or perhaps he just looked very tired.

"The trouble," he said, "is that it would end, and you'd put it behind you and marry respectably. But your child would have the same unnatural genes." He breathed deeply, as if steeling himself.

"I love you, my Kiska," he said.

Then he lunged toward her like a mosquito darting across a raindrop, and pushed her, with iron strength, into the mouth of the black tunnel.

When Koshka came to, there was daylight, and everything was much larger. Her father was across the room, speaking to a man in a laboratory coat. She couldn't hear either of them. She snapped her fingers in front of her face; they made a noise.

"Hello?" said Koshka, not really expecting a response; it was hard to distract her father from a technical conversation. She started to walk toward him and tripped over a gigantic, scaly, knee-high...log, was it? A conic beam of ebony, carved with ridges like mushrooms.

There was something queer going on. Nothing sounded right. The lab looked like the lab, but Koshka seemed to be standing in a glassed-domed room within the lab that hadn't been there a few hours before. This inner room had strange proportions, as though it had been hacked from an enormous block of ivory, from the tusk of an elephant the size of a building, using rough tools that left every surface pockmarked. Rough ivory furniture fused seamlessly to the floor, in funhouse sizes not fit for a human—chairs with seats as high as Koshka's collarbone, a bed with hard carved pillows that took up half its length.

Koshka's father and the other man walked up to Koshka. As they leaned close, a single eyeball took up the entire fourth wall of Koshka's room within a room. The eye's slick jelly surface jiggled frenetically. Its blood vessels pulsed like muscular arms. Koshka realized the strange log was an eyelash, and she herself as small as a grain of rice.

The eyeball pulled back, and the men resumed their silent conversation. Koshka focused very hard on their lips, and not on how fast her heart was suddenly thumping against her chest.

The scientist said, roughly: "Quite a remarkable resemblance. Your daughter must be flattered."

Her father said, roughly: "I thought that since, as a little girl, she dreamed of living in the palace..."

They both laughed.

The scientist said: "So you send a clockwork daughter to the Empress. Ingenious. But how did" something something something something, words Koshka couldn't recognize.

Her father: something something "Rutherford's lab, which" something (and here Koshka concentrated with every atom, for this was sure to be her best chance to understand her situation and reverse it) something something something something something something something something "suggests that every piece of matter in the universe is projected from somewhere else, like the sunlight that reflects off the moon, and so, roughly speaking, I focused on the other end and *pushed*."

Scientist, awed: "So the simulacrum isn't truly small, so much as distant, allowing a full-sized level of detail. Ingenious."

The rest of the conversation was hopelessly trivial. Koshka tried to concentrate, but her mind was battering against the inside of her head like a bird shut in an attic. Eventually, the scientist left and Zinon sat down to his notes. Koshka shouted to him, but he didn't seem to hear her. She yelled every cruel thing she could think of, every joke he might laugh at. She sang irresistible songs and devilish riddles. She beat her shoe against the wall. Zinon never once looked her way.

The next several days were the same. Koshka investigated her ivory egg and its crystal cover, but there wasn't much to do. Zinon left a crumb of her favorite walnut honey candy where it was mostly hidden from view, but Koshka went on hunger strike. It was surprisingly easy; Koshka had never managed to keep a diet more than a day, but after three days passed without hunger pains, she began to suspect her lack of appetite came from more than grief. She realized she didn't need to eat anymore. Nor, it seemed, did she urinate, or bleed, or need to breathe. She could breathe if she liked; she needed breath to make words. It occurred to her that in all her screaming, she hadn't needed a sip of water, and throughout her rage and fear, she hadn't cried. She and the world were cleft, running the same route on parallel tracks.

Candy aside, Zinon appeared to make a deliberate effort to ignore his daughter, or perhaps the fact of his daughter, or perhaps the fact of her current state. She, in contrast, could focus on nothing but him. She stood and watched until she was tired of standing, then sat and watched until she was tired of sitting, then stood. He would interrupt his work to stare at nothing, something Koshka had never seen him do. At a guess, Koshka would say he was sad, or tormented, but she admitted this might simply illustrate what she wanted to see. If Zinon truly felt regret, there were things he could do about it, things he plainly did not do. At night, or when he left for meals, Koshka lay on the floor and let her mind drift, the closest she could come to sleep. Fantasies of reconciliation bled into fantasies of revenge or rescue; stray memories mixed with unrelated images—

waves, beetles, street performers.

Koshka's isolation was intense, but not, she found, that different from her life before Nyusha. Koshka in a room, watching people come and go; Zinon working on his own. The sounds were different, and novel; when the glass cover of her room was lifted, Koshka was beset on all sides by shrieks and unearthly wails. She thought at first that she was going mad. However, her madness proved predictable, stable. She ventured a guess that the noise came from rats in the walls, bats outside, and some of the machinery. She began to welcome it; it was better than silence, and she grew tired of her own voice, which had to stand in for everyone else's. When silent visiting giants admired her with magnifying glasses, Koshka felt she ought to do something bold—make an action of such great dignity as to instantly arouse sympathy for her plight, or such profanity it would register inarguably as a protest. But she could never think of anything, and in a sense, quietly waiting to be admired was the most comforting reassurance that nothing much had changed.

Koshka's hopeful denial was broken when her crystal and ivory egg prison home was placed on a velvet cushion in a teak box and carried to the palace—a journey Koshka spent in darkness, wedged under the narrow table, bracing with all her strength, as though passenger on a ship in a typhoon. As her teeth rattled and her indestructible head smacked the floor again and again, Koshka realized this new life was forever. "Forever" perhaps not hyperbolically, given that she couldn't bleed or break or feel hot or cold. Maybe she could be crushed like an ant. Or maybe she could be swallowed by a dog and come out the other end, unaffected. It was not clear to her which would be more horrible.

Thus, Koshka did not care when she was presented to the Empress. She did not care when she was presented, with greater ceremony, by the Empress to Princess Marie. After a lifetime of skimming newspapers for the slightest elegant detail, Koshka did not care about the palace or the hair or the jewelry, or that the princess ate aniseed to keep her breath sweet, or that the young prince looked brave despite his delicate health. She did not care when she was taken into the princess's private rooms, set on a table beside the princess's bed. She did not care that the princess fell asleep talking to her about her secret crushes and private hopes.

Instead, Koshka spent these moments, and every moment, nurturing her new hatred for her father. After a lifetime of excusing him, of accepting herself as inadequate, the emotion was almost invisible at first, but Koshka carefully winnowed it out from among her more tender feelings, mote by mote, as though panning at a sluice. Each night, uncomplicated words formed on the princess's enormous lips; as Koshka watched the lips move up and down, in and out, she imagined them as fleshy pink threshers—as a machine on which Koshka could lay her biography, one day at a time, until it was reduced to mush, leaving only what was sharp and hard. She built an internal funnel for this precious dust of hate. She spent her days carefully prodding it, finding new connections, new resonance, until it became stone solid enough to stand upon. When Koshka was finished, no observer could see the difference. Her body was just as miniscule; her voice was just as unheard. Yet Koshka stood as a general on an invisible cliff molded from her hate, able to survey the enemy's movements and set traps long before they reached the battle.

Nothing had changed. Everything had changed. Koshka began to pay very close attention to Princess Marie, or at least to seem to. Before, when Marie had spoken, Koshka had watched passively. Now, Koshka walked right up to the edge of her ivory egg and pressed her ear against the crystal case, hanging on every word. At first, it was a novelty, but as days passed and Koshka's friendliness didn't waver, Marie got used to leaving the case off. Their friendship firmly established, Koshka danced and curtseyed with abandon, yet retreated into becoming shyness when shown to others. She began to ape some of the princess's movements. When Marie spoke to her, she leaned forward, nodding sympathetically with every word, until Marie got used to holding the egg in her in her hand to whisper her most embarrassing fears. Koshka would walk right over to her thumb and pat it comfortingly.

When, after many weeks, Marie fell asleep with Koshka's egg on her pillow, Koshka calmly climbed out and crawled into Marie's ear until she reached the eardrum. She waited a moment for signs the princess might be waking; she looked out from the hot waxy darkness, through the ring of light and hair to the palace beyond. Koshka waited to feel doubt or certainty that this plan was better or worse than any other, but it didn't come. Certainty, she supposed, came when you showed your plan to other people. Absent an external check, she'd simply moved forward, awaiting an obstacle which never came. Koshka supposed that was sufficient evidence in favor of the plan.

Turning away from the warm pink light, she tugged off her boot, with its carefully sharpened heel. She braced her knees and began slashing through the princess's eardrum.

By the time they managed to remove her, using long tweezers after a saline flush had failed, Koshka was quite a bit further in. How far, she didn't know. She had felt fluids that weren't blood. Some slick walls had deflated; others had swelled. The tweezers removed a few gibbets of flesh before they caught Koshka's leg—intentionally? Accidentally? As she was dragged backward, Koshka left her boot lodged in the depths of the princess's head, like a climber's piton—a secret maker's mark, the kind Zinon hid in his eggs.

From what she could see before she was shut in a guard's cigarette box, there was quite a lot of blood and Marie was howling. Here, then, was Koshka's moment of certainty. Her jailer, accidental or otherwise, had been vanquished. Koshka was stonily satisfied, although later, when she was safely clear of the field of combat, she was able to feel something like regret. Not truly regret; Marie was a necessary casualty. Even an indifferent chess-player like Koshka knew you had to kill a pawn to reach the king. But Koshka felt the same sadness she'd felt when Nyusha insisted on bloody revolution. It seemed so stupid that violence had become the only means of communication between her small, proscribed life and the grander world.

That morning, before even sunrise, Zinon was arrested for attempted murder of a member of the royal family, by means of ornamental egg.

At the trial, it was hard for Koshka to make out what was going on, because she was placed under a microscope for observation. Zinon looked as though he had aged twenty years. There was white in his hair, and he couldn't seem to raise his eyes past his shoes. Gradually, Koshka realized he wasn't going to be executed, which she had been sure he would, although he was to be sent to a work camp. To her surprise, he threw himself on the mercy of the Tzar, and admitted Koshka was Koshka, which she'd been sure he wouldn't. He poured out his heart. He allowed himself to be messily emotional. He told a story that resembled the truth, although with several departures—Koshka's size shift had occurred in an accident when she tried to sabotage his lab, and it was his love for her that led him to give her what he thought would be a safe and harmless life. Koshka's Communism was made much of, her Communism, her Communism. Never lesbianism. There was no mention of Nyusha. And Zinon's explanation that he hadn't known Koshka was dangerous seemed to Koshka to contradict his claim that she'd sabotaged his lab, but this didn't seem to bother anyone.

By the end of the trial, which lasted several days, Koshka's hatred had burned out. Looking at her gray, defeated father, and his fight for survival, she found she missed him, and she pitied him. None of the aristocrats seemed like real people. She looked at her father, who had spent his whole life hiding who he was, who had shut himself firmly behind the scenes, building beautiful locks that looked like magic. She wondered who he'd loved, whether it had been silent, where the disappointment had come from. There was so much they could have talked about.

A date was set for Koshka's execution, but the Tzar was perplexed by how to do it. She didn't have enough bodyweight to hang. A firing squad seemed ludicrous overkill; beheading by scalpel grotesquely intimate.

Before he could make the decision, the Communists stormed the palace with a mob of Cossacks, a large group of military students, and a women's battalion left over from The Great War. Soldiers, it turned out, were Workers. And they were very impressed by the symbolism of what Koshka had done. As Vladimir Lenin lifted her from her tiny prison, he wept openly.

"You are the least among us, and through your courage you have brought about great change," he said. Then there was a lot of shouting and looting. Koshka scanned the crowd in vain, hoping Nyusha might be among the women's battalion, but she never saw her.

Koshka spent the rest of the revolution, and some time after it, mostly sitting for portraits. One of the artists was clever enough to set out an inkpad and a sheet of paper, so that if Koshka ran around she could write out short messages, but this was both time consuming and exhausting, so she kept things terse. "Nyusha?" she wrote, but there were too many Nyushas, and "a Communist" didn't clear things up. They did bring her a few Nyushas who claimed to be her Nyusha, but none of them were. After a few years, she gave up.

Similarly, when the Communists liberated the Fabergé facilities, they found a machine that seemed to make books very tiny, something called microfilm, which they brought to Koshka, but nobody knew how to use it and it quickly fell into disrepair. Koshka sometimes received reports that her father had been executed, or that he'd been spotted in another country; either way, she never saw him again, which was a shame. He was the only true comrade she might have had, not to mention her only hope of returning to full size.

As the years went by, the reign of the Communists came to resemble a shabbier version of the reign of the Tzar. Koshka hoped the rouged woman and the barefaced woman from the train station had made it out; it seemed to her they might have. She did wonder why Nyusha didn't come. She couldn't or wouldn't imagine she was dead. She supposed it had to do with the size difference, or the difficulty of conducting a relationship in public. Nyusha was awfully practical. And Nyusha did like being "of the people." Koshka hoped at least that Nyusha had heard she was wanted. That was the main thing.

One of the many "Nyusha" letters she got—a few every year, for decades, none of which ever mentioned the scarf or the warehouse or cocaine or anything which might suggest they had ever met—read simply, "Although I am unable to reach you, I am consumed with thoughts of The Beloved," no return address. It didn't sound like Nyusha at all, but Koshka decided it was. Nyusha might try to write in a style like Koshka's. Zinon might have given her Koshka's bad poems in apology. That sort of thing wasn't impossible.

When Lenin died and Stalin took over, he wasn't sure what to do with Koshka, so she was displayed in Lenin's tomb for a while, and then in the national museum. A worker was designated to hold books and newspapers far away from her, so she could read them.

The years passed, and Koshka didn't age, but this was so much less a curiosity than her size that it went unremarked upon. Since she was a national treasure, her lack of change seemed appropriate.

Several decades after Koshka had mostly been forgotten, some clever university students worked out a way to use a radio to slow some sounds down and speed some sounds up, so that Koshka was able to talk to them through a kind of telephone. Stalin immediately destroyed the telephone and all evidence of the telephone, out of fear of what Koshka might say. But after he died, it was rediscovered or reinvented, and schoolchildren across the USSR were invited to submit questions for Koshka to answer.

"What is your favorite kind of animal? Mine's rabbits," was one question.

"Did you have to eat turnips when you were a kid? My mom always says to eat turnips so I can grow up to be strong but I bet you didn't eat turnips and you're a hero, so did you?" was another question.

It was a pleasant way to spend time, Koshka found. She'd never thought enough about children before to like or dislike them, so she decided to like them.

Still later, when Communism itself was dead and buried, and researchers from around the world fought for the opportunity to interview her, and paid enough to fund both the museum and an attached university, Koshka realized with a shock she was now extraordinary not for her size or Communism or bravery or historical significance—none of which were really, as far as she was concerned, her doing—but simply for the length of time she could remember. She could reassure everyone that people had been people 100 years ago, and would still be people 100 years further on. She offered people the hope of remaining in living memory. What a strange closeness she had developed with the world after being pushed away from it.

In one of her many interviews—she restricted herself to one a day, and the slots were booked well into the next decade—she was finally asked the question she'd been waiting for. She didn't know until she heard it.

"What do you think about all the advances in technology?" asked a long-haired Hindu working on a doctoral thesis.

"I am a great fan of technology," said Koshka. "It saved my life."

POOR GIRL

TRACI CASTLEBERRY

From across the cobbled street, I watched the rag-clad girl who huddled on the leeward side of the Dolphin Inn. She held one trembling palm extended toward a passing gentleman. "Spare a copper, mister?" The man, like all the other passers-by gave the girl a wide berth, especially when she let out a barrage of coughs.

She was perfect for what I needed. The difficulty breathing was bad enough to be indicative of pneumonia or consumption, either of which would probably kill her soon. From the livid red scar and the fused fingers clutching at the collar of her worn dress, she'd been burned, and not all that long ago. No one would miss her, and she was near enough to death that if she passed on I wouldn't feel bad.

My missing hand itched as it always did when I was excited. I wound my way through the crowd and crouched in front of her, ignoring the stares of those walking past. "Spare a copper, mister?" she asked me.

I touched the knuckles of my good hand to my cap. "Morning, miss. I don't have a copper, but I do have a hot bowl of stew to fill your belly and a nice warm bed to rest in."

It was hard to make out her expression beneath her dirt-stained face, but her eyes widened as she gazed suspiciously at me. "I don't have nothing you want. I got the consumption. Ain't fit to lie with."

"I don't want to lie with you." I held out my hand. "I'm just trying to be gentlemanly and help the less fortunate."

"You ain't no gentleman."

I inhaled sharply, wondering if this pathetic urchin had guessed the truth I hid beneath my jacket and trousers. Then again, those near death were often delusional. "It's your choice. Come with me or stay out here in the cold." A night on the streets of Whitby was nothing to wish for with the constant threat from the sailors, traders and dockworkers as well as the bitter sea wind that almost never stopped.

Another round of coughing left her bent double. When the fit ended, I saw defeat in her eyes. She was so worn and tired that any risk would be better than enduring another moment begging on the street. She accepted my hand. I had to help her rise as she stood on unsteady legs. The poor girl was barefoot, her feet black and thick with calluses, and shivered when I put an arm around her waist for support. She was hot, feverish, and I wondered more than once if she'd make it to my dwelling, which was not in Whitby proper but hewn into the cliffs below.

There were still a couple of functioning alum mines up north in Boulby, but for the most part the ones in Whitby had been abandoned, leaving me the ideal place to hide. The only time I feared trouble was when overzealous scientists had discovered the fossilized skeleton of a gigantic crocodile and incited searches for more. There were also those searching for veins of jet, the black mineraloid locals carved into crosses and beads and other jewelry. Men and boys scoured the cliffs after each high tide and storm, looking for any veins that might have been exposed. Fortunately, few came near my mine, and when they did, I scared them away with strange noises, letting them think the place haunted.

The main entrance had been sealed up but I'd found another hidden beneath an overhang which made it all but invisible from above or below. It was here I guided the girl, who by then had nearly collapsed from exhaustion. I had to catch her when she stumbled, though having her half delirious was to my benefit. The less she was aware of, the less she could reveal later—if she lived to say anything at all.

Once inside, she gazed in childlike wonderment at my decorations, most of which must have seemed wondrous or foreign to her. She gaped at the ceiling where I'd hung Chinese paper lanterns from the wooden beams. "Pretty," she said. Then she stared at the rest of the furnishings, the mahogany dining set missing only one chair, the shelves lined with books, the bed frame shaped with elegant nautical themes which could only have come from a captain's cabin. "You have everything. How's you get all this stuff in here?"

"I carried it." All of my furnishings had been scavenged from the multitude of shipwrecks along Yorkshire coast. A few things, like the lanterns, I'd bought from traders. I even had a small, pot-bellied stove, properly ventilated, to cook, heat water and maintain the main room at a pleasant temperature.

"It's just like a proper home, even if it isn't." She coughed, hard enough that she bloodied the handkerchief she yanked out of her pocket. Poor girl. She wouldn't last much longer.

I guided her over to the bed and sat her down, where she stared at me as if I was something miraculous.

"Why you being so nice?"

"I have my reasons." None of which I was going to tell her. I lifted the kettle from where I'd left it simmering and poured hot water into a mug already prepared with one of my favorite blends. "Here. This will ease your cough."

"Been an awful long time since I had a proper cup of tea." She wrapped her hands around the mug and sipped. She paused with a thoughtful expression. For a moment, I feared she'd tasted the hemp and wouldn't finish, but, no, she was only taking her time and savoring the rare treat.

It wasn't long before the drug took effect. I caught the half-empty mug before it fell from her limp fingers. She slumped over, fast asleep.

I carried her over to the table and laid her out. With a knife I stripped her filthy dress and shawl and tossed them into the stove to burn. Her age was difficult to discern, sixteen, perhaps eighteen, as she was skinny, bony, and covered in flea bites. The burn which had ruined her hand extended all the way up to her shoulder. Despite my intentions to remain aloof, I pitied the girl having ended up so poorly.

Once I scrubbed the dirt and salt from her face, I discovered something. She was pretty. Illness had sucked much of the color from her complexion, but her lips were a soft rose-pink. Her shift did little to hide the curves of her breasts or the shapely legs.

I shook my useless fancies aside. If she were anything like my previous subjects, she wouldn't last the night. With a length of rope I bound her to the table, no easy task with one wooden hand, but I didn't want her to fall off when she thrashed. That done, I went to fetch my prize.

George screeched at me as soon as I opened the steel door to my workshop. He thrust a fuzzy hand through the bars of his cage and hopped madly until I cut an apple in half and gave it to him. I snatched my fingers back in time to avoid his sharp teeth. I'd bought him off a sailor who'd gone to India and brought back several monkeys. I don't think he forgave me for letting his mate die when I used her to test an elixir to heal wounds. He probably hated me for trying it on him, too, but at least he'd lived.

The table was covered in glass vials, copper tubing, mortars, pestles, and herbs, but my real prize rested inside a golden pot covered with hardened six-and-one mud. The present mixture, one meant to restore balance in the body, had been simmering for nine days and nights, and I couldn't leave it much longer.

Carefully, I poured it into a bowl of pure gold and carried it out to the main room. I lifted the girl's head and held it to her lips. She didn't wake but swallowed the concoction of silver, mercury and other minerals easily enough. In ordinary circumstances, the mixture would be deadly.

If I'd done everything right, it would cure.

I spent the night seated on a cushion and reciting the proper incantations in Chinese. My ghost hand itched and tingled. The pictograms I'd carved into the table seemed to shift and waver, although I dismissed that as fatigue on my part. After a half hour, the girl moaned and started to writhe. I didn't stop speaking, even when her moans increased to terrible screams that echoed throughout the mine.

The sound didn't worry me beyond possible damage to my hearing. It only increased the likelihood of someone thinking the place haunted. Besides, after a while, the screams dulled to a whimper then ceased altogether. I was certain I'd killed her. She'd gone even paler, her breaths almost imperceptibly shallow. I continued to chant fervently, keeping both hope and disappointment at bay. The pictograms twisted and writhed, and for an instant there was...something. An energy, a spirit, I didn't know which, but its presence left my skin warm and tingling.

When the prescribed nine hours had passed, I rose and felt for the pulse in her wrist. It was faint but regular. Her breathing was steady with no sign of consumption.

I dropped her wrist, not quite believing what I saw. The girl had surprised me.

She'd lived.

There were numerous ways of disposing of a body, which included burial or hauling it out to sea, but dealing with a live girl was something I hadn't prepared for.

Added to that was the risk that she would leave and expose my work to the wrong people. I could keep George in a cage, but callous though I was, something within me resisted keeping a young woman locked up until I had the next elixir ready. A chain would do well enough.

But first, I had only the one bed and I wasn't about to risk it to lice. She was weak and feverish and didn't wake as I untied her. My initial thought was to simply shave her head, as it would have been simpler, but I couldn't bring myself to deprive the girl of a piece of her beauty when she'd nearly died. So I washed it with a potion to kill vermin, dragged the comb through it, and it turned a pretty, pale blond.

I tucked her into bed, certain she wouldn't wake while her body continued to replenish itself. After growing up amongst the slaves in Batavia, I loathed the thought of chaining the girl to the bed, but I couldn't risk her running away and exposing me. I did wrap a length of cloth around her ankle so the manacle wouldn't damage her pretty skin. It wouldn't do to have her die of infection before the next elixir was ready.

I should have been exhausted, but after the excitement of the night I was wide awake. I hurried into town, passing through the marketplace to pick up a loaf of bread and other essentials, and then to a modest store on Church Street. It was rarely busy; the locals tended to distrust foreigners like Xiao Liu unless they were desperate.

But I was neither a local nor desperate and headed right in. The store was empty except for Xiao Liu, who stood behind the counter grinding some dried leaves in a mortar. As soon as he saw me, he poured two cups of tea, as was our tradition. "You're up early," he said in Chinese.

"I'm out of arsenolite." I replied in kind.

"Poisoning rats again?" Xiao Liu asked with a raised eyebrow that indicated he knew I was doing anything but.

"I need it for the six-and-one." Alum, soapstone, oyster and salt I had no need of buying since I could find them in the mine or nearby, but the arsenolite was not native to England and had to be imported. I needed a few herbs too and passed him a list.

Xiao Liu glanced at the items then rummaged through the hundreds of drawers lining his wall. "And what are you concocting this time? A cure for the lepers at the hospital?"

He was always trying to suggest something altruistic for me to do. I hadn't taken him up on the offer. "My hand is bothering me. I'm having trouble sleeping."

Xiao Liu frowned. He was my friend and I hated lying to him, but neither could I admit the truth. "Does it hurt?" he asked, genuinely concerned.

I nodded, not trusting myself to say anything. In truth, my missing hand did cause me pain on occasion, but not enough to keep me awake.

"Let me see."

I pushed up my left sleeve to the elbow and unbuckled the leather straps that secured the wooden hand to the stump at my wrist. Xiao Liu poked and prodded, muttered something to himself then brought out his dish of fine needles and inserted a few into points along my arm. After a few breaths, the phantom itching eased. I let my arm rest while he went about collecting the herbs I needed and organizing them into paper packets.

Finished, he removed the needles and massaged my arm and shoulder. He put a new supply of lamb's wool between the hand and my stump and buckled it on, checking the fit as he did so. "Feel better?"

"Yes, teacher. Thank you." I set a few coins down, but when I reached for my supplies with my good hand he grabbed my wrist and set his fingertips on my pulse.

"Tell me the truth, Jackie. What are you up to?"

"I..." arguing was useless. So was escape. Xiao Liu could break my wrist with little effort. "Testing an elixir. On monkeys." Human ones, but I didn't dare say that.

"Which elixir?"

"The one meant to restore balance to the body." That was the truth.

He let go, but his gaze was hard. "When you were my apprentice, you had all the makings of a good physician. Your mind is bright. These are gifted hands." He took both my palms and turned them upward. "But you lack compassion. You keep your heart locked away."

I yanked my hands back, stung by the reminder of why Xiao Liu had dismissed me. I didn't care. I'd learned enough to experiment on my own, and Xiao Liu wouldn't approve of what I meant to do. My skin tingled. He'd struck closer than I'd hoped. "Goodbye, teacher. Thank you for your assistance." I collected my packets and tucked them into various pockets.

"If you're working evil, the spirits will know. They will turn on you."

I left the shop without looking back. The tingling didn't stop until I reached the market.

When I returned laden with parcels, the girl was awake. She hadn't moved from the bed, but she watched me organize my packages. "I bought some fresh ox tail and vegetables at the market. I'll make a stew. I promised you that."

"Am I your prisoner?" The chain jangled as she kicked.

"For now." I had no reason to lie to her.

She lay passively as I sliced meat and carrots and set the pot over the stove to cook. "What's wrong with your hand?"

"It's missing." I held up my wooden appendage so she could see it better.

Her chin dropped. "How'd that happen?"

"None of your business." I wasn't in the mood for stories. To my relief, she asked nothing else while I finished preparing dinner. Done, I went over to her and asked, "How do you feel?"

"Ain't never felt better. Almost like I was cured."

"That's because you are." I checked her pulse just to be sure. Strong and regular, just like her breathing.

"How? You didn't use leeches or bleed me or nothing."

"Why would I rob you of something your body needs?" I examined her hand, the burned one, mentally going through the recipes in my book of elixirs and thinking of which ones I might try. "English doctors have a lot to learn about balance within a body."

"You ain't English, are you? Your eyes is different and you talk strange."

I should have cut out her tongue when I had the chance. "I was born in Batavia. My mother was Chinese. My father was Portuguese."

Her eyes grew big. "Do you speak Chinese? Will you say something?"

I was fluent in Chinese, Portuguese, Spanish, and English and knew a smattering of Dutch and French, although I didn't tell her that. It must have been her innocent fascination which moved me, but I recited a poem I'd learned in childhood. She had no idea what it meant, but clapped her hands in delight. "It's pretty. Say something else."

"Later. I have a few things to take care of while the stew cooks. Rest for a while and then we'll eat, all right?"

She pouted, but she was still too tired to leave the bed. I grabbed my packets of herbs and arsenolite and hurried off to the workshop where George greeted me with another screech of rage.

"Shut up, you." I tossed another apple to him. In the other cages, the doves and rats clamored for their dinner as well. I fed them all, and at last could turn my attention to my mixture. The mud would take a month to prepare. In the meantime, I had to figure out what to do with my unexpected guest.

The girl eagerly downed her dinner, the spoon awkward in her damaged hand. I wondered when she'd eaten last, but she hadn't complained during the long wait for the stew to cook. "I don't know what to call you." She sat on the edge of the bed, legs swinging, the chain going clink-clink-clink.

I had half a mind to yank her onto the floor to stop the din. "Jackie will do."

"I'm Violet. At least, that's what Milady called me. She liked all her maids to have flower names." She wrinkled he nose. "It's better than the name Mama gave me, though."

Since she obviously expected me to ask, I said, "Which was?"

"Harriet."

No, she was right. Violet suited her better.

"You get a lot of visitors?"

There was a note of worry in her voice. "No one comes down here. They think this mine is haunted."

Violet paled and went still. "Is it?"

I shrugged. "It's true there was a cave-in and twelve men died, but if there spirits are hanging about, I haven't seen them."

"Oh, Jackie, I don't like ghosts." She shivered. "I'm scared of the dark."

I bit back annoyance at her childish behavior. "I'll leave a lantern burning, all right?"

I did just that when it was time for bed. I could have evicted my patient but decided it wasn't worth the effort. I collected a few blankets and a pillow and made do on the ground. The chain rattled as Violet made herself comfortable. She patted the mattress. "There's room for two."

"I'm fine here." In truth, I could sleep anywhere and wake rested.

"You sleeping there 'cause I'm sick or 'cause you want me thinking you're a man?"

Her observation struck me dumb for a few moments. I had to fight to keep my composure.

"I knows who you are," she said sleepily. "You're Jacqueline Rivera. You killed your husband and stowed away on a ship where you pretended to be a man. You turned pirate, but it wasn't treasure you wanted, it was books. The English captured your ship but you escaped. The butler read us your story from the paper."

The girl was too keen by far. I should have altered my name more than I had, but since it worked as a male moniker I'd kept it. "Don't believe everything you hear. Jacqueline Rivera's husband was a lecherous lout more than twice her age. Now she's dead too. She jumped overboard and drowned."

"They never found her body."

"It's a big ocean."

"Do you miss being on a ship?"

My missing hand suddenly ached with a sharp, burning agony akin to that of the day I'd lost it. Crippled, I couldn't return to the sea I craved and I hated the girl for reminding me of what I couldn't have. "Go to sleep. If you don't, I'll give you a draught so deep you won't wake until next week."

She watched as I readied my blankets and pillows on the floor. "Do you dress like a man because you don't like being a girl? I mean, I knows you can't be a girl on a ship, but why do you dress like that on land?"

There were several females serving openly on other ships, but I didn't bother arguing. I wondered if she'd always been so observant or if her brush with death had heightened her senses. "Shut your mouth before I do it for you."

I glanced back at her, glaring, but she gazed resolutely at me. Sighing, I kept my back to her, stripped off my shirt and unwound the lengths of cloth I used to bind my breasts. The relief was worth feeling her stare.

"You're awful pretty, Jackie."

My ghost hand throbbed. I pulled up the covers without looking at her.

It must have been past midnight when Violet's trembling voice woke me. "Jackie? The ghosts ain't gonna come, are they?"

Damn the stupid girl. "There are no ghosts. I told you."

Silence stretched. The chain clinked, then, "Jackie? I'm too scared to sleep alone."

I sighed. I should never have told her about the cave-in, but I'd forgotten how frightened the young could be.

"Please, Jackie?"

Figuring I'd never get to sleep if she kept pestering me, I climbed in next to her. She was soft and snuggled against me like a puppy. When she curled an arm around my waist, I stiffened. I'd never had any desire to lie with a man, but I wasn't entirely comfortable this close to a woman, either.

"It's all right," she whispered. "I used to share a bed with Rose, before..."

Before the fire had put her out of a job. I didn't ask for details. I didn't want to know.

But then she began to cry, a choking, muffled sound that turned into a sob and dampened my shoulder. I lay there stiffly with no idea how to comfort a hysterical female.

It turned out I didn't need to do a thing. Between gasping breaths, she said, "It were my fault. Milady's brother—he went to sea and had just come back. He'd been out for a long time with no womenfolk."

It wasn't hard to guess where this was going.

"He came in my room carrying a lamp. He put his hands on me and I..." She took a long, shuddering breath. "I kicked him. He dropped the lamp. The bedclothes caught, and then the curtain, and he was burning and screaming. I would've burned, too, if Mr. Jenks hadn't fetched me out of there."

"The butler?"

"Aye. He was a good man, was Mr. Jenks. Always looking out for us. But even he were too late. Milady's brother died. Half the house burned before they could put the fire out. Milady let me go, she did. Called me such awful names when I tried to tell her what happened. It were terrible, watching him die."

Terrible for her, perhaps. I'd killed men, only I'd felt intense satisfaction rather than fear as their life drained away.

"Will you hold me, Jackie?"

I didn't care to. I wanted my nest on the floor where I could curl up alone and forget she was here, but the calculating part of me was curious as to what it would take to make the girl stop trembling. After so many years at sea and living alone, femininity was a mystery to me, and I was never one to let a puzzle go unsolved.

So I rolled over. She pressed against me, her slight figure warm against mine and not altogether uncomfortable. I swept her hair aside and rubbed her back through the thin cotton shift. I fingered each bone in her spine, taking in the curve of her body.

And later, when she kissed me, I didn't resist.

As was my habit, I woke early and went out to walk the shoreline. I needed the smell of the salt air, much as it hurt to watch the ships come and go with supplies. I wanted to be out there with them, but I couldn't, not until I was able to restore my hand.

The past few days had been calm, so I didn't expect to find any usable scraps washed ashore. I was right on that account, but I did find a pair of ammonites. The locals called them snakestones after a legend in which Saint Hilda had rid the area of snakes by turning them to stone. I tucked them in my pocket, wondering if Violet had ever seen one.

When I returned, the iron door to my workshop stood ajar with a length of chain leading inside. Fury pinched my temples as I followed the trail of links. Violet, dressed in a patched shirt over her shift, stood in front of George's cage. The door was open.

"Leave it alone!"

She swiveled around. The monkey was in her arms, his fingers curled in her hair. "He's very sweet. Wherever did you find him?"

"He's a vicious little creature that—"

George hissed and bared his teeth. Violet cooed to him, and to my shock he settled down. I took the hint and left him alone. After all, I didn't care whether he befriended Violet. The less I had to do with him, the better.

"What are you doing in here?"

She waved a dust rag at me. "This place ain't bad for a mine, but it could use some tidying up."

I couldn't disagree. Housekeeping was never a priority and it was impossible to be rid of the dust. "Did you touch this?" I pointed to my iron pot of six-and-one.

"No." She gazed at it. "What is it?"

"It doesn't matter. Go near it, and I'll cut off your good hand."

She didn't seem fazed by my threat. Instead, her eyes widened. "Is that a magic potion? Is that what you used to cure me?"

"It's not magic. It's science. A simple mixture involving complex preparation."

"I gets it." She gestured to the bowls, jars and vials upon the table. "I was a good lady's maid. Milady had me make all her creams and lotions. I know a good one for making hands smooth. Smells like peaches."

The last thing I needed was smelly concoctions for fancy women. "You're too young to be a lady's maid."

Violet hung her head. "I wasn't, but Milady's maid Rose taught me how to act proper and all that. I stood in for Rose sometimes." She scratched George's head, and he chittered in pleasure. "I'll help you. I'll do anything you want. Mix, grind, stir, cook, clean, you just ask."

George's adoration—and consequent good behavior—was enough for me to tolerate her presence. "Fine. But clean the main room first. I've got work to do."

She hurried out, George perched on her shoulder.

As she'd boasted, she was a deft hand at mixing draughts, lotions, and anything else I might require. Besides that, she was an excellent cook and housekeeper but never touched my equipment unless I asked her to.

"If you let me go out, I'll sell the potions for you. I swears I won't betray you," she told me one night while we were in bed together. "I likes it here with you."

Of course she did. She nowhere else to go. I provided her with plenty of food, shelter and the possibility of earning an income. That sort of independence was something I understood and didn't want to discourage.

"But if I goes out, I needs a dress. I can't wear this." She tugged at her shift.

A dress. Part of me recoiled at the thought of even touching such a garment, but she was right. She couldn't go out in a shift and old shirt, and she was far too feminine to wear boy's clothes. "I'll see what I can do."

"I want a blue one. Blue as the sky."

So I went into town and stopped at a shop which sold castoffs from rich families. Most were too fancy and would attract too much attention, but there was a day dress of blue muslin I hoped would work. Not knowing what possessed me, I bought a hair ribbon to match.

She was thrilled and tried it on right there in front of me. "Needs some taking in, but it's perfect, Jackie. I never had no better."

I had to admit it suited her. The bodice was moderately low and hugged her breasts. Her hair was pulled back in a braid and tied with the ribbon so her pale shoulders were exposed. The only thing out of place was the chain, and that I removed. "Run, and I will hunt you down. Betray my secrets, and you'll regret it."

"I won't." She stood on tiptoe and kissed my cheek. "Just you wait. I knows the market, I does."

And so she proved true to her word.

She turned out to be a shrewd bargainer, and once she convinced me to make herbal cures started selling or trading them along with her lotions in exchange for food or supplies. Often, she took George, who ended up being a great draw for children and their parents and earning a few additional coins.

I suppose I looked on her presence as an experiment in itself. I'd been around women so rarely that I was fascinated by the way she moved and the kindness with which she treated George.

Strange, how I could admire in another that which I hated in myself. I loved to watch her bathe, as she sat in the tub and let the water trickle through her hair and between her breasts. When I took my turn in the water, I arranged a folding screen around the tub as a hint I didn't want to be disturbed.

She ignored it.

She dashed around the screen, cloth in one hand, bottle of one of her smelly concoctions in the other. I just had time to grab a towel and wrap it around myself. "Get the hell out of here!"

Playfully, she tried to pluck the towel from me so she could play the lady's maid and wash me, but I caught her good wrist and dug my fingers deep. "Leave me alone."

She sucked in her lower lip, and for a moment I was afraid she was going to cry. I couldn't stand weepy females. Then her gaze dropped to where my left arm ended. "Tell me what happened."

Cursing, I let her go and stepped out of the tub, hiding the stump beneath the towel's folds. Her curves, visible through her thin cotton shift, made me uncomfortably aware of my bony, damaged body. "Cannonball." The loss of my hand wasn't the extent of it, just the worst.

She rubbed her wrist. I'd probably bruised it. "It must've hurt."

I'd just turned to gather my clothes when she took my arm. I was too stunned to thrust her away. In bed we'd both worn clothes so I'd had an extra layer of protection. Now I had no defenses, and I hated being helpless. I'd fought and killed men armed with pistols and sabers. I'd survived storms, battles and a long swim to shore, yet this wispy girl I'd found on the streets held me captive with touch alone.

"Come on, Jackie."

She took my good hand in her thin fingers and led me to the bed. I sat hunched over while her soft fingers worked at the towel.

"I'm not afraid to look."

Perhaps not, but I was afraid to let her. Eventually, her kindness wore me down. Eyes closed, I told her how a cannonball had struck the Santa Isabella. Wood had gone flying. Several large splinters had driven into my flesh. The biggest one had gone through my palm and shattered most of the bones. The Santa Isabella was captured by the English and the wounded transferred to their ship. The surgeon had cut off my hand at the wrist and cauterized the stump, but once he'd seen I was female, I knew my career was over.

I wouldn't let the captain hang me or turn me over to the authorities, so I'd jumped overboard and clung to a piece of flotsam until I reached English shores. The cold and the salt water kept my wound fever at bay, but once I climbed onto dry land, illness struck hard. If Xiao Liu hadn't found me, I would no doubt have died in the local hospital. Instead, he laid me on a cot in the back of his shop and tended my wounds with remedies thousands of years old. Once the fever passed, he gave me strengthening exercises and taught me the rudiments of Chinese medicine.

Violet listened with rapt fascination. She traced my scars with her fingers. "You're amazing, Jackie."

Her shift joined my towel on the floor. What followed was an experiment and all in the name of science. My reactions. Hers. How this touch made her moan and that one made her wriggle. I didn't mind the warmth of her body against mine, though I felt none of the enjoyment she seemed to as I ran my hands over her naked flesh and delved into her deepest parts. I let her touch me, kiss me, probe me, but my heart remained as cold as it had when I was Xiao Liu's apprentice.

I felt nothing beyond the physical. I couldn't.

The next elixir would soon be ready.

I didn't want to deal with any protests Violet might have, so I dosed her tea with a light sedative. While she was dazed, I urged her onto the table, removed her pretty blue dress and tied an elaborately-knotted rope around her. I made sure her damaged arm was exposed up to the shoulder where the burn ended.

George hopped and shrieked, alternately trying to bite me and pawing at Violet's motionless body. I finally had to grab the creature by the back of his neck and thrust him into his cage, which he hadn't used in weeks. The screeching increased, muted only when I slammed the iron door shut.

"Jackie?" Violet's voice trembled. She was afraid, but it couldn't be helped. "Jackie, what are you doing?"

"I'm going to fix your hand."

At this she awakened fully. "It don't need fixing! Please, Jackie. Please leave it alone."

I ignored her protest and brought over the bowl. The liquid, while still warm, was no longer hot. "It's meant to return a body to its true form." Carefully, I poured it down the length of her arm and pooled most of it on her damaged hand and fingers.

For several moments, nothing happened. Then she tensed, and a wail broke from her throat. "Take it off, Jackie! Take it off! It burns!"

She jerked and thrashed. Tears slid down her cheeks. I could have used acupuncture and herbs for the pain but I didn't. The dark part of my soul wanted to be certain I could watch her suffer and remain unaffected. "It's only for nine hours."

This brought a renewed barrage of pleas and screams. "Jackie! Jackie, please!"

I took my seat on the cushion and repeated the incantations to go with this new elixir. After a while, I couldn't take the screaming. I stuffed a gag into her mouth, ignoring the tears and look of betrayal.

If she hadn't been tied down I'm sure she would have torn at her own flesh, but my sailor's knots held true and she was helpless to free herself. It took over two hours for her strength to fail. By then, she was a sodden, sweaty mess, exhausted and trembling.

I continued my chanting. As before, the words wriggled and twisted on the table. I had the vague awareness of shadows flitting back and forth, darting in and out of the mixture drying on Violets hand.

Spirits. The creatures brushed against me, too, but instead of a tingle, they pinched and burned before they flew away.

I resisted the urge to rub my arm, wondering if the violence had been a threat...or a promise.

Come morning, I rose to check on my patient. The mixture had hardened around her hand and I had to use a knife to peel it away, but there, like a butterfly emerging from its chrysalis, I revealed healthy pink flesh and five separate fingers. I examined each of them, bending every joint to ensure functionality. Violet stared at me with such hatred that I shuddered.

"Look. Your hand is perfect. Just like new." I plucked the gag from her mouth then worked at untying the multitude of knots.

"You hurt me." Her voice was barely a whisper. She sat up and glared at me. "You hurt me and you didn't care."

I had her untied. "But your hand—"

"Bully my hand!" She used it to strike me across the face.

My cheek stung. I should have put the chain on her to keep her from leaving, but I couldn't seem to move. I watched as she dressed and packed her few belongings into a satchel. Then she went into my workshop and returned with George in her arms. He hissed and spat as they passed me on the way to the exit. Neither looked back.

I didn't care if she hated me. In childhood and at sea, I'd learned never to love, never to trust. Death was always with us, whether from illness, injury or drowning. And since I had more to hide than others, I kept to myself as much as possible.

It didn't matter that I'd grown used to her presence and would miss her idle chatter. Within a month, I would be back at sea.

I would be whole.

Unencumbered by my guest, I went about preparing my next, and last, elixir. I opened the cages for the rats and doves and set them free. They fled, just as Violet had.

I had enough ingredients from the last batch of six-and-one that I didn't need to visit Xiao Liu. I'd also collected the necessary minerals for the elixir itself. Gold. Mercury. Arsenic.

When the mud was ready, I coated the golden crucible and put in the elixir's ingredients. For nine days and nights it brewed. I scrawled Chinese characters into the ground around the fire and myself. I chanted and sang and fasted, drinking only water. I alternated various breathing exercises and meditations, focusing on the success of the experiment.

I refused to let it fail.

On the tenth morning, I lifted the crucible from the fire with shaking hands. I removed the wooden hand then stripped and lay naked on the table amidst the graven characters. I had a rope ready and secured my legs, waist and my shortened arm. With my free hand I poured half the bowl's contents over my stump. The rest of the elixir I drank. It was hot, slippery and filled my mouth with an acidic, metallic taste. My belly churned, protesting the poisonous brew.

I clamped a stick between my teeth then tucked my hand into a small noose and pulled it tight. I was trapped, unable to free myself until I regained sense enough to do so. For a few moments, I reveled in the fact that I'd done it. Whatever came of this elixir, I'd poured my heart and soul and will into it.

Then the pain came.

At first, it was a heat within my belly and a light burn on my skin as if I'd been in the sun too long. Then the brew sunk into my flesh and guts and turned excruciating.

I bit hard on the stick and let out a scream Every nerve had caught fire. I'd thought Violet weak for enduring her pain so poorly, but now that I experienced it for myself, I knew just how terrible it was. Like childbirth, I tried to tell myself. Hundreds of thousands of women had suffered when they used their bodies to create something new and had been just fine.

I didn't care to remember that thousands more had died in their attempt to bring a new life to completion.

I twisted and writhed atop the table, yanking hard at the rope as my muscles twitched and jerked by their own accord. The characters on the table twisted into deformed parodies of themselves, and I was certain it was my own fevered brain seeing things that weren't there.

Until I felt...them.

Spirits. Hundreds. Thousands of them. They flitted and poked and jeered. Their breath burned my skin. Other drove beneath my flesh, ripping and rending. Agony blinded me. I screamed, but the sound was distant.

Xiao Liu was right. The spirits had turned on me. The elixir proclaimed that by drinking it I could transcend to my true nature, but this was no angelic lifting of the spirit or transformation into the body I craved.

This was hell.

•—∿∿∿—•

I must have clawed myself free of my restraints. Anguish drove me out of my cave and into the open air. Bitter sea wind clawed my naked flesh, but I didn't care. I roamed the shore, barefoot, heedless of the sharp black rocks. I was red and ragged and burned, but the truest shock came when I gazed where my arm had once ended.

I had a hand, but I could not call it such. A paw was closer. It was a frightening, ugly thing, covered with the bristled fur of a boar and bearing claws as sharp as a hawk's. The skin was tough as old leather and just as impermeable. The rest of me was covered in burns and blisters which stung with the merest touch of cool air.

The elixir had transformed me into what I truly was: a monster.

I howled my fury. The sound echoed against the cliffs and mingled with the loud rushing of waves. Seagulls shrieked in response. I lashed at one too slow or stupid to get out of my way. It fell in a spray of blood and feathers.

The sea would never be mine again. No crew would take a deformed creature like me aboard. I was worse than female. I was...inhuman.

I dropped to my hands and knees and raked the sand. Hatred and disappointment burned as deeply as my skin. I'd failed. I deserved it. Years of preparation. Dozens of deaths, both human and animal.

All for nothing.

"Jackie?"

I struck before the voice registered. Hot blood spattered my face and arm. I licked the coppery fluid from my lips.

Then someone screamed.

I thrust the heels of my hands against my ears, but I couldn't shut out her anguish. The sound went on and on. I raised my paw, ready to silence the screamer for good.

Teeth sank into the back of my neck. I yelped and swiped at the little beast, but it was too fast. It darted away, and it was the pain coupled with the sheer incongruity of seeing a monkey scampering on a shell-strewn beach that reached past the feral madness which had taken over my soul.

And then I caught a glimpse of blond hair trailing over a sky-blue dress.

Violet dropped to her knees. The screams turned to moans of pain as she clasped her hands around her belly. Red leaked from between her arms and fingers, trickling down to join the wet sand in soaking her skirt.

"Violet?" The word emerged cracked and broken. My fury disappeared beneath a sudden terror. I didn't have to see the wound to know it was bad. With that much blood, it couldn't be anything else.

I don't know how she managed to smile, but she did. "I brought you back, Jackie. Took me a while but I figured out what you was up to. Came back to stop you, I did."

"It's too late."

"Ain't never too late." She keeled over.

"Violet!" I dove toward her. Blood kept coming, running from her belly in torrents. She was dying. I'd killed her after all.

George screeched and pranced, leaving little monkey-prints in the sand. I'd already murdered one female he'd cared for. I'd be damned if I let another die.

I scooped her up and held her against my body as I hurried up the switchback trail leading to the top of the cliff. "Keep your hands there. Press hard," I told her, and she whimpered.

I must have been a frightening sight, naked, blood-covered and carrying the girl I'd just maimed. I didn't care. For once, George didn't screech at me. He wrapped his furry arms around my neck and hung on as I raced toward Xiao Liu's shop.

I didn't have to knock. He was already at the door, probably alerted by the commotion rustling through the street. He waved me inside.

"Here, Jackie." He swept an arm across his counter, abruptly clearing it of bowls, herb packets and a pair of unlit candles.

I set her down, watching dumbly as Xiao Liu ripped her dress apart to expose the wound. Her intestines glistened. "How?" he asked.

I held up the inhuman thing at the end of my arm.

Xiao Liu didn't reprimand me, but his gaze was accusatorial enough. "Put on a robe. You're going to help me."

"I can't." It galled me to say it. I was a monster, now. Unfit for human company. I headed toward the door. Better that I leave now before I hurt someone else.

I glimpsed sympathy beneath his unhappiness. "Prove the sprits wrong. For that matter, prove yourself wrong."

Even George had gone silent. He sat on the counter, picking at Violet's hair. "I wanted to go back to sea. That's all I ever wanted." To be part of a crew. To have a place in the world where what I could do mattered more than what I was or where I'd come from.

"Hurt or heal, Jackie. What will your choice be?"

She was pale, golden hair sticky and red as her life ebbed away. Twice before I'd been willing to let her die. I'd had nothing to lose. This time, I did.

I took a robe from behind the counter and slid it on. The silk cooled my burns. "Tell me what to do."

There was no six-and-one mud this time, no mixtures of mercury and arsenic and gold. Just Xiao Liu's expert hands as he used his acupuncture needles to minimize pain around the wound.

My talons had an unexpected benefit; the tips were as fine as Xiao Liu's needles. I dug them gently into points used to induce sleep while Xiao Liu rinsed the gash. Violet's twitching slowed to something more manageable, allowing Xiao Liu to work unhindered. Remembering how much Violet had enjoyed hearing me recite Chinese poetry and children's tales, I called several to mind and spoke softly as Xiao Liu used silken thread to piece together what I had so callously torn apart.

I spent days and nights at her side, waiting, hoping, changing the poultices and dosing her with draughts to ease the pain. When wound fever turned her body heated and raw, I fretted and bathed her with cool water. I kept my vile arm hidden, unable to lay eyes upon the method of Violet's destruction.

Xiao Liu watched me with the same intensity as I did Violet. "You would make a good physician," he said.

I laughed bitterly. "I've killed men without regret. I didn't care what happened to Violet. I'm a cold, unfeeling creature. I always will be." George screeched softly. I knew he'd agree.

Gently, Xiao Liu drew back my sleeve to expose my disfigured hand. I longed to snatch it back, but I was afraid I'd hurt him, too. "You might have a man's soul, but not an animal's. This," he said with a slight shake of my hand, "is not who you are. Each of us has darkness inside. Don't let it swallow you whole."

I met his gaze. Something inside me cracked. "I'm sorry. For everything."

"I know." He patted my hand and left me alone.

Two days later, Violet's fever broke. The following morning, she opened her eyes and focused on me. She raised a shaky hand and brushed my cheek. "Jackie?"

For the first time since I was a child, I wept.

Two weeks later Xiao Liu suggest we go out for a walk. I still refused to wear feminine attire, so Xiao Liu lent me a cotton shirt, pants and cap which brought out my Chinese heritage. Between that and the ever-present George, Violet and I earned more than a few stares as we walked to the end of Church Street and up the nearly two hundred stairs to St. Mary's church and the ruins of Whitby Abbey. Violet clung to my arm from weakness, but she was determined to reach the top. Once there I led her through the church's graveyard to a bench overlooking the sea. For a long time, the only sounds were the wind and the distant roar of the waves.

When Violet broke the silence, her voice was bitter. "I suppose you'll go back to the sea, now that I'm well."

"No." I clenched my paw, careful of the sharp claws. "I can't."

"You got what you deserved, and I ain't sorry for being glad about it. Not after what you done."

I couldn't refute this, so I didn't.

"It ain't so much that you almost killed me, but you didn't care. I didn't matter no more than those rats or doves."

"I care now." I gazed at the ships docked and either loading or unloading supplies. The sea would never be mine again, but it had never been as important as I thought.

"Jackie?"

I gazed at her. Strands of blond hair fluttered in the wind. I'd had to buy her a new dress. This one was green with lace and ribbons around the bodice but not too tight around her still-healing belly. I knew what she wanted. An apology. Some sign that I loved her and would stay with her forever.

So I kissed her.

Gently, she put a hand on my chest and pushed me back. I was crushed, especially when I met her gaze and saw the sorrow there. She reached inside my sleeve and withdrew the clawed thing within. "How can I trust you?"

How, indeed? I had nothing to give her. There were no promises I could make that she would believe. My scars would never fade. I looked at the hairy, inhuman hand in hers. I didn't deserve her. Not after what I'd done. "Burn everything in the workshop and chain me to the bed." It hurt to say it. I'd spent years perfecting elixirs and herbal remedies. I didn't want to lose those recipes, but it was preferable to losing her.

"Chain you to the bed?" There was a hint of mischief in her voice. "Make you my prisoner and do devilish things to you?"

George chittered softly as she slipped a hand between my thighs and cupped me there. The hot tingling took me by surprise. I nuzzled her neck, taking in the scent of peaches. George hissed, but I ignored him. This was my girl, no matter what he thought.

"I want you to promise me one thing," she said.

"Anything."

"Don't fix my scars again."

I rested my paw on her belly. "Never." She was perfect as she was. We both were.

BANK JOB BLUES

MELISSA SCOTT

Miriam Smith sank lower in the stained bathtub, letting the tepid water lap up and over her breasts even as her knees stuck further out into the air. This was probably the only moment all day that she would be cool, and she wished she could make it last, but she could hear the others in the kitchen, and knew she'd already taken more than her share of the morning in the bathroom. She hauled herself up out of the tub, the water sloshing, pulled the plug and reached for the thin towel. The rented house had come furnished, but everything was worn, and had been cheap to start with; she was desperately tired of threadbare towels and shiny upholstery and holes in the linoleum. But it had come with a garage, and that was the main thing. With a garage, they could work: Doc could build her weird machines, and Miriam herself could keep the cars going. At the moment, there were only two, the Ford for everyday, the one they let the neighbors see, and the Frankenstein Special, sleek and black on its Packard chassis, the souped-up twelve cylinder engine—more of Doc's work—ready to carry them out of trouble. They'd need another car soon, if Doc was serious about the job, a replacement for the Ford once they'd gotten the Special hidden away again. She wanted a Terraplane this time, but with the money they had in hand, she'd probably have to settle for a Buick, or another cheap Ford. At least the Fords lasted forever.

She dressed reluctantly, well-washed underthings and a plain cotton shirtwaist dress, but couldn't bring herself to put on stockings in the rising heat. Instead, she left them on the foot of the bed she shared with Doc, and padded downstairs barefoot to the kitchen. Everyone else was there ahead of her—everyone except Doc, she amended, and she plastered a smile on her face in spite of the heat and the smell of bacon grease.

"Good morning."

Rue Isbell grunted something from the end of the table. She was tall and raw-boned and homely, a country girl with stringy mouse-brown hair and a missing tooth at the side of her mouth, but she was strong enough to fire a BAR—when they'd had one—and she was the best shot of all of them with the pistols and shotgun and Tommy gun that formed their current arsenal. Mattie Markham managed an actual word in answer, looking over the top of the local newspaper, and Clea Lusky turned away from the stove. She had put on lipstick and rouge and mascara even at this hour, and the frock beneath the patched apron had been expensive, but her scowl could have melted steel.

"Good morning to you, Miss Priss. It was your turn to cook, you know."

Mattie lifted the paper, barricading herself behind the sheets, and Rue heaved a sigh. "Baby, I said I'd cook—"

"That's not the point." Clea stabbed angrily at the bacon, spatula rattling against cast iron. "The deal was, share and share alike, and she ain't doing anything like her share of the cooking."

It was true, Miriam knew, and she gave a guilty shrug. "I'm sorry. Do you want me to take over, or I could do it tomorrow—"

"I want you to do what we agreed," Clea said. She looked at the others. "It ain't right. She's not any better than me."

Rue pushed back her chair without a word and started for the kitchen door. Mattie heaved a sigh.

"Baby's right," she said heavily, and Miriam gave her a look.

"Well, she is." Mattie folded the paper beside her empty plate. She was the butchest of the bunch, even by Chicago standards, stocky and broad shouldered in slacks and a man's shirt with the sleeves rolled up neatly to her elbow. She was taken for a man more often than not, which came in handy, and more often than not she acted like one, too.

"What do you want me to do?" Miriam asked again, and heard herself defensive. "I can take over—"

The kitchen door banged, and she glanced toward it, expecting to see Rue slipping away from the quarrel the way she always did, but instead Alta Holliday stopped just inside the door, looking around the room.

"What's the problem?" She was wearing men's wash pants, grease-stained at the thighs where she'd forgotten and wiped her hands: she'd been out in the garage again, trying to move things along.

"I forgot it was my morning to cook," Miriam said. "Sorry, Doc."

"Like she did last week," Clea said, "and the week before that."

"One reason Smitty doesn't cook is she's no good at it," Doc said easily. "But you're right, if it's her turn, she ought to do it." She gave the kitchen one swift, assessing glance, and moved toward the stove. "Tell you what, Baby, Smitty and I'll take over, you go sit, and we'll take tomorrow, too."

"That's fine for now," Mattie said, "but Baby's right, we need to settle this. It's not right that she should do all the housekeeping."

"Go sit," Doc said again, to Clea, and the other woman reluctantly unwound her apron. Doc took it, wrapping it around her own waist, and began forking the bacon out of the pan. "Smitty, pass this out, will you? Then cut me some more bacon."

Miriam did as she was told, carrying the plate of bacon to the other women. Rue slid back into her place, looking up without expression.

"Maybe another pot of coffee, too?"

And that was rich, coming from Rue, who worked just as hard to get out of the cooking. Miriam's mouth tightened, but she managed not to say anything and kept serving up the bacon.

"I can do that," Doc said cheerfully, as though she didn't feel anything wrong. "Smitty, you want to cut some toast as well?"

Miriam did as she was told, trying not to let her resentment show. She supposed it wasn't fair for Clea to do all the housework, but Clea was the one who fussed about being a lady, about always having silk stockings and a nice hat, the one who expected them to open doors and carry her suitcase. Under the circumstances, she damn well oughtn't complain about the cooking—

Doc was still talking, bright and happy like the gang wasn't starting to fall apart around her. Three times they'd picked out a bank to rob; twice someone else had got there first, and the third time there had been so many guards with shotguns and rifles that there hadn't been any point in even stopping to case the joint.

"I know it's been hard on you, Baby, and I just want to say that we—all of us—really appreciate the efforts you've put in. This place is a rat-hole, but it would be twice as nasty if you weren't taking care of us. And you're right, the rest of us have been slacking, and we need to step up. And we will."

Clea sniffed, but she put away her handkerchief and began to poke at the bacon.

"Who wants eggs fried?" Doc said. "Because that's pretty much what I can do." There was a murmur from the table that could pass for agreement, and Miriam slid the bowl of eggs across the counter. Doc took them, began cracking them one by one into the spitting grease. "Sunny side up, or over easy, and I don't promise perfect either way."

"Over easy," Rue said.

"You got it." Doc checked the eggs again. "Cut me about three more slices of bread, will you, Smitty?"

Miriam picked up the bread knife and began slicing, carving careful slices from the loaf. They had maybe ten dollars among the five of them, and that had to last them—had to pay for rent and food until they picked out another bank, and have money left over to gas up all the cars.

Mattie shook her head. "It ain't working, Doc."

"What do you mean?" Doc slid Rue's eggs out of the pan, and Miriam carried them to the table.

"What I said. We ain't seen a bank we could knock over since January, and we got no money left. Ain't no point sticking around here. Baby and I were doing just fine in Chicago."

"Except for pissing off Scarface Al," Doc said.

Miriam glanced sideways in time to see Mattie grimace. Clea's face was pale beneath her powder; she obviously hadn't intended to push things this far.

"But if you want to go," Doc said, "I'm not the one to try and stop you. We always said, we'd run this gang fair and square, and that's what we're going to do."

"So you'll give me my share?" Mattie fixed her with a stare, and Doc set down the pan.

"Sure. If that's what you want, you can have it. We all agreed to that, and I keep my word." She smiled then, so bright and happy that if Miriam hadn't been standing next to her she would never have noticed the strain that tightened Doc's hands. "But.... You might want to hear me out first."

Rue lifted her head from her plate, sharp as a hound and just about as ugly. "You found us a bank."

"I did." Doc lifted the pan again, slid the last of the eggs and bacon onto a plate for Miriam to dish out, then set the pan aside and reached into her hip pocket for a sheaf of folded paper. "Ladies, let me introduce you to the Third Farmers Bank of Clarendon."

"Never heard of it," Rue said.

"Not likely you would," Doc answered. "Clarendon's not much, but it is a railroad stop, and—more to the point—it's a clearinghouse. Twice a month, they transfer it, and the week before, there's serious money in that vault."

She unfolded the papers and laid them on the table. Miriam served a plate for Doc and finally for herself, and took a seat opposite Mattie, careful not to draw too much attention to herself. There were letters on bank stationary—answers to letters Doc had sent inquiring about safety deposit boxes and the like, one of her ways of finding out if a bank was worth the risk—and a map of the town and finally a brochure from the bank itself. Mattie picked that up, then turned it around so that everyone could see the drawing in its center.

"Wait a minute, Doc. This here's a Wiggins Time-Lock double vault. Two doors. Even during business hours, they'll keep that inner door locked, and there's never time to blow it in. All we'll get's the money in the tellers' cages, and that's not worth the risk."

"Unless we did it on a transfer day?" Clea began, then shook her head. "No, they'll have too many guards."

"Absolutely right on both counts," Doc answered. "But that's exactly why we're going to hit them. They think they're safe with a vault like that, and they're not going to pay extra for guards when the inner vault's locked up tight. But they're not reckoning on Hercules."

There was a little silence, and then Mattie whistled softly. Rue said, "So that's what that thing is you been working on."

"That thing," Doc said, "is Hercules. And he's going get us thirty thousand dollars."

After breakfast, they trooped out to the garage to examine Doc's latest creation. The garage itself was huge, having begun life as a four-stall barn back when the house had been in a nice part of town, but someone had converted it to a workshop and garage sometime in the early Twenties, and a lot of the equipment was still in place. Doc had brought her own, of course, and hooked them up to the town electricity, so that she could flip a switch and bathe the entire space in harsh, blue-toned light. Miriam's eyes slid at once to the Special, hidden under its canvas shroud. She loved that car at least as much as she loved Doc, even if she never got to drive it except on a job. It was too strange—too long, too sleek and lean, the supercharger too obvious—for them to allow it to be seen in daylight, and even in the safety of the locked barn it had to be hidden. Doc had painted it midnight blue, even the trim and the spokes of the wheels; only the hoses of the supercharger showed silver. It was four-doored, with had a boat tail like a speedster, and fenders that swept up and over the wheels as though they'd been sculpted by the wind. She loved it even more than the little roadster she'd had in college, the one she'd raced... The Special was faster than anything the police had, and it could carry all of them in a pinch, and that was all that really mattered. The Model A that was their workhorse was pulled in close behind it, mud still caught in the wheels and carefully obscuring the license plate.

Beyond the cars lay the workshop, the long reinforced bench running along the back of the barn, hoist and chains rigged to the strongest beam, a set of shelves full of half-finished components. In front of the bench squatted a metal object that looked like a cross between a box turtle and a turnip, with rhomboidal caterpillar tracks like a tank on either side. Three arms were folded tight to its round sides, looking like something out of the Irish manuscripts Miriam had studied at college, back before the Crash sent the whole world into a tailspin. The thing had been given a coat of glossy black automobile paint, but it still didn't look like something that could open a Wiggins double-doored bank vault.

"That's Hercules," Mattie said, sounding dubious, and Doc reached for a box lying on the workbench.

"Give me a minute here." She flipped a switch, and light began to glow on the top of the box. Twin wires unfurled, rising toward the ceiling; she flipped a second switch, and a thin blue filament of electricity began to rise along the wires, buzzing and snapping as it went. A light flashed on in the top of Hercules's dome, and metal clattered inside the carapace. A moment later, an engine spun to life, and the three arms lifted away from the metal. Doc fiddled with a pair of dials, and the caterpillar treads began to turn, jerkily at first, and then more smoothly. Hercules inched forward, its biggest arm beginning to unfold. Clea gave a little scream, and Mattie swore, pulling them both out of the way, one arm protectively around her girlfriend. Miriam edged back, too, nearly stepping on Rue, and Doc frowned over her controls. Hercules ground to a halt, and then began to rotate, its treads moving in opposite directions; a smaller arm reached down to sink three thick claws in the dirt floor, while the biggest arm extended itself, its claws opening and closing.

"You're going to use that," Rue said, "to open the vault."

"Got it in one." Doc worked the controls again, folding the arms back to their resting position, then turning the machine and driving it back to its place. "He's got a supplemental engine for extra power, and the arms are designed to give us all the leverage we could possibly want. He'll rip that door right off its hinges."

"Are you sure it can handle that?" Mattie asked. "Those safes ain't exactly made of tinfoil."

"I've done all the calculations," Doc answered. "It'll work."

Rue narrowed her eyes. "How are we going to get it there?"

"We're going to modify the Special," Doc said. "Not much, Smitty, don't look like that. I'll just extend the rear platform and add a roll-out ramp, and he'll trundle right off."

"What about steps?" Mattie demanded. "That picture you brought says there's stairs in front of that bank."

"We back the Special up to the door," Doc answered. "You can do that, right, Smitty?"

Miriam nodded, glancing from Hercules to the Special and back again. The Special could handle the extra weight, especially if she shifted the balance just a little bit forward; the Special could handle the kind of stairs she'd seen in the picture, too, five shallow granite stairs that were supposed to make a plain building look imposing. If Doc said Hercules could handle the vault door, it could handle it, and that meant that everything was already decided. They'd talk it out, work out the escape route and the rendezvous and the split, but that was just details. They had a job in hand.

It took a little longer than she'd expected for Doc to modify the Special, but by the second week, the plan was starting to take solid shape. She'd made a couple of trips to Clarendon and the surrounding towns, until she knew which roads were good enough to let her fly, and then she'd done the boring job of filling up the Ford and siphoning the gas over into the Special, until the big tank was full. Now it was just one more run to fill the Ford for their getaway, so that they could switch from the Special to it and then to the brand-new Terraplane that Doc had gotten them, and they'd be ready to go.

Dinner was over, a small pork chop apiece stretched with a big pot of greens and a round of cornbread, coarse and salty. Miriam chipped some more ice from the big block in the chest, then poured a careful two fingers of bourbon over it, swirling it so that when she sipped at least some of the liquor had begun to cool.

It was still light on the porch, the sun at the horizon, the summer twilight stretching late. She collected the magazine she'd bought in town and settled herself on the step, drink beside her, resting her shoulder against the newel post. For a minute, she could have been twelve again, curled up with a book in her grandfather's house, before she'd found out what she was.

That wasn't a pleasant memory, and she took another swallow of the bourbon, making herself concentrate on the thin pages. The cover promised another Race Williams story, and with any luck—yes, there it was, and it was indeed one of his adventures with The Flame. The Flame always helped him, in spite of her own nefarious plans, and she always got away in the end.

"What're you reading?" Rue asked, looking up at her from the bottom of the steps, and Miriam scooted aside to let her past.

"Black Mask. 'The Girl with the Criminal Mind.'"

"Say." Rue looked more interested than Miriam had ever seen before. "Is she one of us?"

Miriam shook her head. "No—well, I mean, she's a criminal mastermind, but not—" She stopped, afraid she was blushing. She knew there were words for what they were, but they were all ugly, insults or something to snigger about. Well, except "Sapphist," maybe, that was the word they'd whispered at college, but that just felt silly, here in a tumbledown rented house in the middle of Missouri.

"Oh." Rue sighed. "I read a book once that was about us. Stole it off my brother. They all died in a fire, but before that—I kind of liked it."

"You can have this," Miriam said, and held out the magazine without thinking. "I'm done."

"Thanks anyway." Rue shook her head. "I ain't much for reading."

She climbed past Miriam into the house, and Miriam was careful not to watch her go. She'd watched Rue with writing before this, had seen her print her name and a few straggling words, had heard her ask Clea to read things to her rather than puzzle them out herself. She should have known better than to offer her a magazine.

The thought nagged at her, though, as she climbed into bed next to Doc, the fan on the dresser stirring the cooling air. Rue had stolen a book—Rue, who could barely read a grocery list, could just about write her own name and nothing more, Rue had stolen a book and worked her way through it, just to read about women like them. Miriam had seen those books herself, cheap paperbacks with lurid covers that you had to get from behind the counters at the newsstands and the drugstores. She'd never dared buy one herself, for fear of what she might find out.

"Penny for your thoughts," Doc said, and wrapped an arm around her.

"Just thinking."

"Worrying about the job?"

Miriam shook her head. "Thinking about us—about women like us. How we are. How we're supposed to be."

Doc's arm tightened, pulling her close. "What do you mean, how we're supposed to be? We're bank robbers and dykes and we're trouble on four wheels. We're making this up as we go along."

"That might be our problem," Miriam said.

"What problem? We're going to knock over this bank, and that'll be at least six grand each—enough to make a real start—"

"At what?"

"At whatever we want." Doc's voice was suddenly very serious in the dark. "With six grand, you could be respectable. You could walk away and never look back."

"We both could," Miriam said. They were both college girls, they could move on, Los Angeles or New York or just about anywhere, scrape together a respectable job, secretaries or librarians or teachers, and no one would ever know what they'd done. What they'd been. She wouldn't even have to get married, not in the city; she could stay a spinster and no one would suspect a thing.

"But I don't want to," Doc said. "I figure, six grand buys me two years to work on the next generation of Hercules. There's lots of people who'd want a machine like him—he can do a lot more than rip doors off their hinges if I can just fix a few little problems. I can find people who'll pay good money for him. And by then there'll be another project—I've got some ideas already."

"So you'll stop robbing banks."

Doc shrugged. "Unless I have to take it up again." She paused. "You'd be welcome to stick around, you know."

"Thanks," Miriam said, and settled against her shoulder, knowing that wasn't the answer Doc wanted to hear.

They got underway a little before dawn, taking the long road out of town so that the noise of the engines wouldn't wake too many people. Miriam nursed the Special along at the tail of the line, the engine protesting the low speed, headlights off until they were out in open country. Doc put her foot down then, the Model A getting a surprising turn of speed, and a little after sunrise they pulled into the copse of trees just over the Clarendon town line. The surrounding fields were fallow, a broad-leafed cover crop Miriam didn't recognize rising knee-high from the parched earth, and the trees gave good protection from the road. They climbed out of the cars and huddled together in the shadows, passing around the thermos of coffee.

"Everybody clear on what to do?" Doc asked. It was really too late if they weren't, but everyone nodded anyway. "Let's synchronize watches."

They stood close together, Rue holding a flashlight, and Miriam adjusted her watch to match Doc's own. Her part was simple enough: wait until the town clock started striking ten, then bring the Special down Main Street and back it up the bank steps to loose Hercules into the bank.

"Time you were going, Baby," Mattie said, and Clea nodded. She stood on tiptoe to kiss her girlfriend's cheek, and then Mattie held open the Terraplane's door so that she could settle herself behind the wheel. She was heading south and east, toward the Arkansas border, where they'd hide the Special and find someplace to hole up until the worst of the heat was over. Then they'd reclaim the Special, and go on with their lives. Assuming, of course, that everything went right, and there was a decent amount of money in the bank.

Miriam killed that thought, and watched as Clea backed the Terraplane out of the shelter of the trees. She was wearing a neat hat and a respectable dress, looked more like a doctor's wife than a gun moll or the chorus girl she had been. But that was their stock in trade, and she made herself look away as the Terraplane turned south toward the border. Doc checked her watch again, and Miriam saw her shoulders rise and fall as she took a deep breath. They still had a couple hours to wait, time for Clea to get into position, time for the bank to open its doors, and not incidentally the vault, and for the first rush of the morning's business to pass.

It was a pretty morning, the dew rising from the fields in thin wisps of steam, gone by the time the whistle sounded at the Ardec plant on the far side of town. The sky was pale with haze, promising a hot afternoon, and birds hung high against the white, soaring over the fields. On the far side of the highway, beyond the fallow fields, a man was driving a mule cart along the fence line, his head and the mule's bobbing to a matching rhythm.

Doc checked her watch again, and finally nodded. "Right. Rue, we're up."

Rue nodded, and slithered behind the wheel of the Ford. It would be left behind in Clarenden, abandoned as a roadblock if they could manage it. She was wearing her best dress and a flat straw hat, her hair pulled back into a ruthless bun, and looked ten years older than her years. Doc was in a dress, too, a nice flowered frock that went badly with her enormous purse. But that was where she'd hidden Hercules's controller, and there wasn't any way to make that any smaller.

"When the clock stops striking," Doc began, and Miriam nodded.

"We'll be on the steps and Herc will be heading through the door."

Doc looked as thought she wanted to say something more, but instead, she gave a crooked smile, and settled herself in the passenger seat beside Rue. Rue mashed the starter, and then with a clash of gears they were gone. Miriam looked at Mattie, who rested her hip against the Special's sleek front fender. She and Miriam were the only ones in trousers, and the gray suit made her look like a man. She reached in through the Special's open window and drew out their prized Tommy gun, pointing it carefully away as she checked the magazine and the safeties. Miriam fumbled for a cigarette—she didn't smoke much, but right now she was desperate for something to do—and lit it with fingers that surprisingly didn't tremble. She shook out the match and glanced at her watch: not long now.

"You got plans for your share?" Mattie asked. "Or are you and Doc going to stick together?"

"Maybe?" Miriam shrugged. "I hadn't really got that far yet. How 'bout you?"

"Baby and me were thinking California. There's nightclubs there, she can always find work, and I can probably come up with something. All those film actresses—maybe they need a bodyguard or something."

"Could be." Miriam checked her watch again, annoyed that the hands had barely moved.

"Probably better not to make too many plans," Mattie said. "I don't want to jinx this."

"Yeah." Miriam stubbed out her cigarette, the smoke acrid on her tongue, and looked at her watch. "Time."

She settled herself behind the wheel of the Special, working her shoulders against a seat that had been made for her. Mattie climbed in beside her, Tommy-gun on her knees, shotgun and two pistols on the floor between her feet. Miriam worked the starter, feeling the twelve cylinders rumble to life, the power building under the long hood. She backed the car carefully out of the woods and onto the highway, pointing the nose toward Clarendon.

The Special ran heavy with Hercules in the back, but, as Doc had promised, the suspension could handle it. The highway here was decently paved—and paved all the way to the county line, though she wasn't counting on it as an escape route—and the Special hit forty-five before she brought it back to a more reasonable speed. Ten minutes to the town line, she thought, glancing at her watch again. Ten minutes to the town line and the town clock would chime and it would be time to go—

She downshifted as they passed the first outlying buildings, a gas station where the boy tending the pumps stared slack-jawed at the Special, then the feed store, and then a scattering of houses. Main Street was just ahead, a sharp right turn off the highway and a straight run to the downtown. She controlled the impulse to hurry, easing the Special decorously through a turn she would rather have taken on two wheels.

The clock struck, and she put her foot down on the throttle, the Special jerking forward as she ran through the gears. Mattie clutched at the door, swearing. There was a wagon in the way, and she slipped around it, leaving the mule backing and trembling in the traces. A battered Buick blocked her path for an instant, and she twisted the wheel left and right again, dodging the old man before he could think to put his brakes on. The other cars had seen her, all four of them, were pulling out of her way, right up onto the sidewalk, scattering pedestrians and pigeons. Someone was shouting, several people were shouting, but all her concentration was fixed on the road ahead, on the clock chiming, six, seven, eight.

It struck nine, and she grabbed the handbrake, flung the Special into a screeching turn that left its rear bumper at the foot of the shallow stone stairs that led up to the double doors of the Third Farmers Bank. She shifted into reverse, one hand on the back of Mattie's seat sat the clock struck ten, and gunned the car up the stairs. The reinforced rear smashed the doors open, holding them and blocking both escape and rescue. Mattie grabbed the Tommy gun and jack-knifed out of the window, swinging it to cover the locals still on the street.

"This is a stick-up! Stay back and nobody gets hurt!"

Miriam pulled the lever that released Hercules, looked over her shoulder to see the trunk lid lift and the ramp come down and Hercules trundled out of the compartment.

"Stay back," Mattie yelled again, and punctuated the words with a blast from the machine gun.

Miriam reached for the nearest pistol, cocked it, and laid it between the front seats. In the mirror, she could see Rue waving her sawed-off shotgun, herding tellers and customers into a corner, while Doc, her hat lost somewhere, bent over the sparking control box. Hercules kept coming, traveling the straightest line without regard for obstacles. A table crashed to the floor, and then the machine went through the nearest teller's cage, the wood splintering. Women were screaming, and Rue shouted for them to shut up; Mattie swung the Tommy gun to cover the street, whipping her head from side to side as she searched for the law.

"Come on," Miriam said, under her breath. They didn't have much time, just enough to open the vault and run, and that was only as long as Doc didn't have any problems—

There was a whistle and a ping as a bullet hit the Special's front fender, and Mattie cursed again, taking careful aim. She fired another burst, this time into the window of the store across the street where the shot had come from, and Miriam thought she saw people duck hastily into shelter.

"Damn fool," Mattie said. "Doc! Get a move on!"

In the mirror, Doc had got Hercules up to the vault's first door, had planted two arms and engaged the supplemental motor. The third arm stretched into the vault, and Miriam could hear the sudden whine as the supplemental motor revved up to full power. There was a sudden crash and more screaming, and abruptly Doc backed into view, her enormous satchel dangling by one handle. It was full of money, Miriam saw, so full that bills were spilling out, flicking away onto the floor.

"Smitty!" Mattie turned in the window and fired another long burst at a car that was poking its nose out of a side street. It screeched to a halt, but Miriam could see a man in uniform at the wheel.

She put the Special into gear, pulling forward enough that Rue could jump over the ramp and duck into the back seat on Mattie's side. Doc stumbled after her, the satchel under one arm as she tried to work the control box. Hercules was coming, slower in reverse, but he was still a good yard from the end of the ramp.

"Leave it, for God's sake," Mattie yelled, and ducked as more bullets struck near them, throwing up chips of stone. Miriam grabbed her pistol, stuck it left-handed out the window and pulled the trigger three or four times, aiming the general direction of the police car. She didn't think she hit anything, but the noise of the shots was enough to drive the men into cover.

"Doc!"

Then at last Hercules was on the ramp, up the ramp and into the compartment, and Doc came flying past, diving into the back seat beside Rue.

"Go!"

Miriam worked the levers that closed ramp and lid and pressed the throttle. The Special lurched down the stairs, and she swung right, back the way they'd come. Mattie fired one last burst in the general direction of the police car, and slid into the seat beside her.

"Got it?" Miriam called, shifting gears, and in the mirror saw Doc grin.

"Everything we came for."

Behind Doc, she saw the police car lurch awkwardly out of the side street where it had been sheltering, a blue-coated arm reaching out the window, revolver leveled.

"Look out!" She yanked the wheel from side to side, the tires squealing on the pavement. A bullet sang off the roof, but the rest missed.

"Gimme," Rue said, and Mattie passed the Tommy gun over the seat. Rue went up on her knees, rolling the window down, and fired two short bursts at the pursuers. The police car dropped back a little, swerving in turn, and Miriam put her food down.

The Special leaped forward, the big engine howling as she ran through the gears. They were in third before she'd reached the end of Main Street, shifted up to fourth as they crossed the town line, the highway stretching flat and open ahead of them. Five miles of paved road, she had memorized that from the maps, then gravel all the way to the county line. In theory, the town police couldn't chase them past the county line, but they were bound to call head, warn the next town and the next counties—

A mule-drawn wagon was pulling onto the road ahead. Miriam sounded her horn, but the driver froze, the mule laying its ears back as though it wanted to kick. Doc swore, and Miriam braked and downshifted, swerving around the wagon with her left-side tires on the yielding dirt. She pressed the throttle again, and felt the front tire grip, hauling them back onto the pavement. The wagon would tangle the police even further, she thought, seeing the dark-blue Ford falling behind again. Keep on to the end of the highway, then dodge west, and as soon as they were out of sight, cut back south and east. There were three different roads that would take them the way she wanted; none of them were paved, so she wouldn't make as good time, but it would surely be enough.

She focused on the road ahead, the line of pavement stretching now between trees, rising slightly over one of the little ridges. There was a house in the distance, a thread of smoke rising from its chimney; the junction was coming up not a mile beyond that.

"We're losing them," Doc called, looking over her shoulder. "That farmer's all across the road now. Keep going, Smitty, you're gaining."

Miriam braked gently, downshifting, then harder as they reached the end of the paved road. She made the right turn onto the gravel at speed, collecting the car as it started to skid, pressed the throttle again as she straightened. They couldn't make much more than forty on this road, but that would get them out of sight—yes, there were the trees the map had promised, and the road dipped down into a hollow at the same time. That would cut the cops' line of sight.

There was no sign of pursuit in her mirror as they came up on the next junction, and she turned south onto another gravel road. There was more traffic here, an old truck, another mule-drawn wagon, a Model T belching oily smoke, and she saw Doc grimace.

"They'll remember the car."

"It's hard to forget," Miriam answered, slowing to avoid a flock of chickens. A woman was staring from the porch, and there were men working in the fields: Doc was right, there were too many witnesses. "There's another road coming up, we'll go west again, and double back."

"You sure there aren't farms that way, too?" Mattie asked.

"I'm sure," Miriam said, and hoped she'd read the maps correctly.

She'd read the maps right, the country was wooded and empty, but the roads were narrow and more dirt than gravel no matter what the map said. She couldn't go more than twenty without skidding, the tires slick on the greasy clay, and there was an unexpected stream, not marked on any of the maps, that held them up for almost fifteen minutes as Doc and Mattie climbed out to check the depth and look for potholes before Miriam would risk the Special. Break an axle here, and there was no escaping, not matter how much money they had in the back seat. The Special lurched and groaned in first gear, the water splashing, but they made it across at last, and Miriam gunned the engine. They were almost at the state line, and from there it was only twenty miles of back roads to make the rendezvous.

Even pushing the Special as fast as she dared over the worsening roads, the sun was almost down by the time they pulled off onto the rutted road that led to the Mclaren farm. Doc had paid the old man to leave the Special in the tumbledown back barn, and Clea would be waiting with the Terraplane to take them blamelessly south and east to hole up somewhere—Memphis, for preference—until the heat was off and they could recover the Special and Hercules.

It was dark between the trees, but she didn't risk the headlights, squinting through the dusk until she saw the Terraplane drawn up at the edge of the woods. That was outside the plan. She frowned, and heard Rue snap the shotgun into readiness.

"Take it easy," Doc said, but her voice was nervous, too. "Go slow, Smitty."

Miriam nodded, letting up on the throttle as much as she dared, one hand hovering over the shift in case they had to run. The Terraplane's door opened, and Clea climbed out, a cigarette in one hand as she came toward them down the dirt road. That had to be a good sign, Miriam thought, but couldn't relax.

"Mattie," Doc said. "Check it out. Rue, cover her."

"Right." Mattie's voice was grim but she levered herself out of the car without hesitation. Miriam flicked on the headlights, the beams stabbing through the dark, but there was no sign of anyone else in the car or among the trees to either side. Mattie moved forward, her right hand holding her automatic along the side of her leg, but then Clea seemed to say something, and she relaxed. She put her arm across Clea's shoulders, and they turned back toward the car.

"Trouble," Doc said. It was not a question.

Clea nodded, leaning on the roof beside the open window. "Old Man Mclaren says we can't use the barn. The Clarendon police called their state troopers, and they've called the troopers in Arkansas and Tennessee."

"Maybe I should talk to him," Doc said.

"It won't do any good," Clea answered. "Don't you think I tried?"

"I know, but we've got money," Doc said.

"That's the last thing you want him to know," Clea said. "He thinks he knows we did it, he'll turn us in for the reward."

"How much?" Rue asked.

"Five hundred," Mattie said.

Miriam whistled. That was a lot of money, enough money to make sure every farmer from here to the Gulf would be looking for the Special.

"He would, too," Doc said. She took a deep breath. "All right. Change of plan. We still have to hide the car—maybe there's somebody over in Greene County that we could lean on—"

"Don't look at me," Mattie said, and Clea shook her head.

"Not with that reward out. There's nobody I'd trust."

"All right," Doc said, drumming her fingers on the top of the door. "All right, we need to stay away from people—" She looked up sharply. "Caves! Rue, didn't you tell me there were a ton of caves around here?"

"Some," Rue said, cautiously.

"Any we could drive to? Drive into?"

"I don't know," Miriam began, but it wasn't as though she could see any better option.

"I heard of one," Rue said, though she still sounded doubtful. "We could try."

"Anybody got a better idea?" Doc asked.

"We could just leave the Special," Mattie said.

"You know how much it cost me to build this?" Doc demanded. "I'm not giving her up without a fight."

"Doc's right," Clea said. "Come on, Matt, let's go. We'll follow you."

They switched around the seats, Rue riding shotgun to try to find the roads. Miriam put the headlights on their lowest setting, and they crawled along the back roads, skirting the settled farms and the occasional town, until at least Rue peered up at a rising hill, then looked back at the land they'd come from, and said, "Here."

There wasn't a road, and barely even a track. They left the Terraplane parked behind some bushes, and Doc and Mattie went ahead with flashlights to scout the path. Miriam followed, wincing every time the Special bottomed out, or a stone clanged against the undercarriage. It was all too easy to rip a hole in the oil pan on an unseen rock, or break an axle, and then where would they be? They'd have to leave the Special out in the open, and someone was bound to find it before it was safe enough for them to come back.

The ground was getting steeper, the wheels jolting over bigger and bigger rocks. The trees cut off the stars, and Miriam risked turning up the headlights. The brighter light showed a rising hill, dirt and moss and heavy pine trees, and then, beneath it, a deeper patch of shadow. Doc held up her hands, motioning her to stop, and Miriam pulled the handbrake and cut the engine.

Mattie disappeared into the cave, brushing aside a trailing vine that released a shower of dead leaves. Miriam watched her flashlight flickering in the depths, and then she poked her head out again.

"Looks ok to me, Doc. It's not deep, but I think deep enough?"

Doc stepped in after her, and Miriam folded her arms on top of the steering wheel, resting her forehead against them. She was suddenly exhausted, her hands aching, her shoulders burning from muscling the Special around curves and up and down hills. They gotten the money—there was supposed to be at least thirty thousand, Doc said, but they hadn't counted it yet, and every other time the take had been less than they'd expected. But it was money, cash in hand, and maybe, just maybe, there would be enough to let her quit this business. She couldn't help thinking about college, her cozy room with its clanking radiator and the boarding-house landlady who policed visiting boys with protective ferocity but never once checked to see what two girl friends might be up to behind their closed door. She had loved the libraries, too, at the college and in Boston, riding the train in to the city to settle in the reading room, where silent attendants brought her books, and she left the lamplit quiet in a swirl of snow, bound for a tearoom and a laughing fair-haired friend... Maybe enough money could make that world hers again.

"Smitty?"

Miriam lifted her head. "Yeah?"

"It'll just fit," Doc said. "Ease her on in, till the front bumper just about touches the wall."

"Okay." MIriam pressed the starter, feeling the big car rumble to life. The others held the vines apart like the halves of a curtain, revealing a dark opening.

She checked the gas gauge automatically—less than a quarter tank; when they came back, they'd need to bring a can or two of gas—and eased the Special into first. It crept forward, complaining, a vine trailing dirt across the windshield, the headlights turning the rocks the color of cream. She edged it into place, turning it to the right to fit the tail inside, looked in the mirror at last to see Doc giving her a thumbs-up. She cut the engine, and only then realized that she'd blocked her own door. She sighed, too tired to swear, and crawled across the front seat and out the passenger door. Doc caught her arm, steadying her, and for a moment she leaned gratefully on that support.

"Now what?" Rue asked. She stepped back, hands on hips, and Mattie let her light play over the cave's mouth. The Special seemed enormous in the narrow space, hardly hidden at all. Mattie tugged at the vines, draping them to provide better cover.

"When those vines fill out," Doc began, and faltered. Miriam swallowed hard, tasting her own tears. When the vines filled out, yes, it would be better, but that was a long time from now, months in which any passing hunter, any moonshiner or farmer and his girl looking for a place to make out could come past and see a car where no car should be.

"We could divvy up the money," Mattie said. For once, she didn't sound happy about the idea, and Clea moved up beside her, tucking her arm into the other woman's elbow. "You done good, Doc, we had a good run, but—maybe we ought to quit while we're ahead."

Doc shook her head as though she'd been slapped, but straightened her shoulders. "We could. I always said you could walk away—any of us could walk away."

Rue heaved a sigh, but was silent.

Clea said, "I don't—we never—" Her voice trailed off, and Doc looked at Miriam.

"How 'bout you?"

Miriam took a deep breath, as though she were stepping off a cliff. Surely there would be enough to give up robbing banks, to send her back to Boston and a rented room, and even the inevitable economies would be better than this. Surely. "What do you think we should do instead?"

"Give it time." Doc's head was up, her shoulders squared the way they'd been when she got kicked out of school right before graduation. "Let's not split up yet. Let's let it ride, let the heat die down. If the cops haven't found the Special by then, we're jake. We come back, we collect it, and we make some new plans."

"What if they find it?" Miriam asked, looking at the cave mouth. Even in the light of the flashlights, it was too easy to see the Special's fender, the sleek curve that protected the right rear wheel. "They're bound to find it."

"Then they find it," Doc said. "And then we split up the money, and all of you can do what you want. But I'll tell you this, Smitty. I'll build you another Special—I'll build you a better Special, after everything I learned on this one, and

I'll make another Hercules and by God we'll do it all over again. Because I am not going back to Boston. I'm not going to be that girl ever again."

"So who are you going to be?" Miriam whispered, as though there was no one else listening. "Who are we going to be?"

"We'll figure it out," Doc said. "We'll experiment. Come with me, Smitty?"

Back to Boston, the boarding house and the snow and pinching pennies and teaching kids whose mothers looked down on her as a spinster, never any time for her own research while she typed papers for lesser men. Never to drive the Special again, never to share Smitty's bed, feel the hands and lips that brought her to the peak as surely as she moved the Special through its gears... "Yes," she said. "Yes, I will."

Doc grasped her hand, their fingers knotting in the dark. She was holding so tight it hurt, but Miriam didn't care.

"Well," Rue said, after a moment. "Reckon it can't hurt to wait a little longer."

Clea and Mattie exchanged looks and then Mattie pursed her lips. "Okay. Let's see what happens."

"Right." Doc shook herself. "Okay, then. Let's get back to the car."

"I got a friend in Nolan County," Rue offered. "She'll put us up for a bit. Plenty of room, and no near neighbors."

"That sounds like just what we need," Doc said. She flicked on her flashlight, keeping it low to the ground. After a moment, she found the path they'd followed, and started down it, Miriam's hand still in her own. Miriam followed willingly, glad of the light and of the unexpected certainty. Outlaws and bank robbers and deviants and criminals—she didn't care, because that wasn't nearly enough to encompass this. So they'd keep trying, keep experimenting, and maybe she'd eventually find a word or two, and maybe not, but she felt the rightness of it in her bones.

A.J. FITZWATER

i.

The evening call to prayer rang out as Cinnamon Darling dashed up the wide steps of the Symposium. Her pilot's heart racing in time to the thap-fwump of the airship rotors at ease above the smooth, dark archways, she ignored the imperative. At any other time the ululation and comforting bass beat served as a counterpoint to life in the river city, but now cut with the tinkle of crystal, laughter and the hum of finely tuned strings, it composed a martial beat towards doom.

Darling hurried past the Major Domo, barely acknowledging as she eyed her oil stained apron and hair falling from pins. The Major Domo, with hands at first prayer position, preferred to usher Darling into the party rather than deliver a vocal introduction due an esteemed guest.

A lively tune belled skirts and pant hems as Darling's long legs ate the gold flecked marble dance floor with efficient strides, advancing on the three women whose presence dominated the airy chamber.

"Were you going to tell me about it, or were you planning your death to be a pleasant surprise?" Darling stamped her booted foot and pulled a fist full of papers from an apron pocked and shoved them at a woman with a face the colour of the sun islands.

Attendant cats scattered and one yowled in protest as Darling's boot caught a tail tip. A river city elder, her silver streaked braids coiled tight about her head, hid a smile behind a sun lined hand. Her Xin companion with ankle-length black hair unmarked by age took a keen interest in her goblet.

The sun islands woman stepped forward to intercept Darling and turned her away from the gawking crowd.

"Auē, Cinn. How could you forget what tonight is? Could you at least have—" She pursed her thick lips and fluttered her fingers up and down at Darling's apron. "—changed? Your lack of attention to social etiquette makes most parties brighter, but this is a bit too much, tonight considering."

Darling glanced down and heat worked its way from battered high lace collar to grey-edged auburn hairline.

"I am not sorry, Aroha. I came straight from the hanger, where I was preparing flight plans and maps like a good pilot should."

Juggling the papers from arm to arm, Darling slid apart the ties of the apron and rolled the spatters of lubricants, ink, and other unidentifiables out of sight into a pantaloon pocket. A tie flapped loose, and the previously put out feline took a bat at it.

"You should know better," Guild Engineer Aroha Raharuhi said in a tone that implied the woman would not. "It is not very hygienic. What would Chifwe say?"

Darling grimaced an apology over at the silver-haired woman in the guise of a plainly dressed aunt of a reclamation house. Chifwe tapped her feet to a lively air at play and fussed at her scrupulously clean nails.

"Your party goers need not fuss, my hands are clean." Cinn held them up as evidence. A few pages of the stack fluttered to the floor and she fumbled to pick them up. "I will apologize later, but for now there are more important things. Like when you were going to tell me about this little...addition to the airship?"

Aroha Raharuhi folded her hands primly across her stomach. "You have been reading personal files again. What have I told you about that before?"

"River wash, Aroha. Do not play your wife for a fool."

Aroha's features softened, falling back into lines that aged her beyond the seasons of any of the three women. "I will tell you everything soon enough, kairoro. It was not my intention to lead you astray. But tonight is an important moment in the city's history. I have guests to attend to."

Cinn shook a finger under Aroha's nose. "We are not finished tonight, not by a river fathom."

"Understood." Aroha kissed the tip of the finger, and smiled for the fierceness barely holding the lanky body upright. Cinn responded with a tense giggle. "Now, take yourself to the water closet, find yourself a boy to tidy your hair, and borrow an evening mantle worthy of an engineer's house from the Symposium's communal wardrobe."

The boy on duty from the tailor houses was more than willing to fine tune Cinn's unruly curls, and even added a dusting of gold powder across her eyes and cheeks to enhance skin the envy of many city folk of all genders. It always amused her when successive generations rediscovered the fashion for sleeping in river mud packs in an effort to emulate her famous rusty skin tone.

Upon her return to the dance floor, the great Xin engineer and her former employer Long Ba Luen, who now preferred the simple appellation of 'tinkerer', bowed her into their presence. The city's animagus Chifwe Aito-wel, Ba Luen's closest friend for a dozen dozen seasons and more, offered a firm handgrip to show her trust in cleanliness between city folk. A scuttle of Chifwe's famous domestic cats on security detail weaved their way about their feet, though most avoided Cinn.

Chifwe's most famous attendant, the copper-leaved and glass clockwork cat Tin, steamed and hissed gently. Originally one of Ba Luen's famous constructions from her family's circus, Tin had been at Chifwe's side as long as the two women had been friends. Many whispered its age derived from Chifwe's strange powers discovered during a plague of unnaturally fierce rodents. Then only an apprentice to her reclamation house, Chifwe's connection to felines had made the jump from warm body to metal. It made a good tale passed over ale tables, but there was still much about that part of river city history Chifwe and Ba Luen held behind sad, dark eyes.

"Do you know anything?" Cinn snagged a goblet of precious sweet wine from a passing waiter's tray, and stepped in beside her old friends.

Aroha stood apart, shuffling her speech notes, mouthing words. She had excellent retention for design and could reconfigure a circuit board in her sleep, but performing in public was Cinn's forte.

"The cats can smell something strange." Ba Luen leaned in and lowered her voice, breath heavily scented with mint juice, as liquor made her "itchy inside and out."

Cinn looked to the animagus, who sipped carefully at her favourite meaty ale and nodded her agreement. "Tin says so, Ma confirms it." She indicated the metal and albino cats in turn.

"Smell what?" Cinn pondered. Party guests advanced with requests for a performance.

"Lightning," Ba Luen shrugged.

"Death." The word came easily to Chifwe, the vital function celebrated by river city folk.

Enough guests offered donations to the orphanage where Cinn taught that a small performance was deemed appropriate. The Major Domo set to clearing a space on the dance floor while Cinn went through a too short stretch that her joints would punish her for in the morning. The conductor, having accompanied Cinn many times before, saluted with her baton and picked the orchestra into an ambient air, reminiscent of the water so precious and vital to the port city.

Cinn removed her boots, buttoned her mantle, and drew the strings closed on her pantaloons. She patted her auburn curls, firmly secured with decorative bone sticks. The tresses would only fall out if she bumped the fastenings, which she had not done since she was an apprentice of the circus mistress Long Ma Bai.

By the time she had completed the routine of walkovers, splits, curls, limb weaves, balances, and abdominal manipulations, she had the crowd spell bound with everything from fascination and lust to out-right revulsion. It had been a combination of all these things that had won a young ocean-shocked Aroha Raharuhi's heart far away and so long ago when hired to assist on an overhaul of Long's famous circus airship. The work had given her two life-long passions which Cinn often thought were as immortal and unchanging as Chifwe's sun-powered cat.

With the crowd still alight from Cinn's performance, Aroha took to the small dais, throat clearing lost under a small orchestra fanfare. She clutched her notes, but her smile for so many familiar friends and acquaintances, investors and enthusiasts was genuine. Her bones had lost some meat recently, but that was not unusual after long hours spent on the hanger floor during the hottest days of the rain season.

She greeted them in traditional Ao, then continued in Rah'bik: "My dream has always been to return to my birth place, the home of the white clouds, Ao, amongst the sun islands far across the oceans. Steam ships and paddlers, for all their usefulness upon these glorious coasts, do not provide the power required to mitigate months spent on a wild ocean. Our sailing fleets are vast and beautiful, but we lose too many good people, crew, and cargo to sickness, storms, pirates, war, and time."

Cooks and wait staff crept from the shadows to listen, and cats peered up at her attentively. Aroha forced a long, slow breath against the firm stays of her mantle, the kind of exhalation required when meditating over difficult circuitry or blueprints. A keen longing crept into her tone.

"With the help and extraordinary vision of our city's friend, the grand tinkerer Long Ba Luen, I believe we have discovered a way to safely and quickly traverse the oceans of our great world, linking us all for the greater good."

Applause buzzed. Ba Luen bowed a few angles towards the crowd, though the fingertips of her strong hand massaged against the other.

At a gesture from Aroha, youngsters from the biggest city houses began pulling on great ropes to open the crystal skylight that sealed the Symposium roof. Aroha's voice rose above the growing applause and creaking pulleys.

"With an eye for the finest materials, the great skill of this great city, and your unceasing belief, we have strived to create a vessel unlike any other seen upon this continent, nay in all the skies of the world!" She was really getting into it now. "This, distinguished guests, is a revolution in cross-ocean travel. This airship will bring our friends, family, and peoples closer together. For trade and travel. For commerce and the spreading of good will and peace. No more long months spent in perilous pursuit across the vitriolic ocean. We will join hands in mere days across the equator."

The skylight fell back with a definitive clang, and the crowd gasped.

"I present to you...the good airship *Tāwhiri-mātea*!"

The applause reached a crescendo as newly installed electric lights, harnessing the power of the river and sun, flickered to life. The slim-line black airship, named for the Ao ancestor of the wind, tugged at its moorings as if eager to be away, gleaming metal struts taught and ready.

Cinn closed her eyes for a moment. Against the after image left on her eyelids, she saw her beloved as she often saw her in dreams; her body as the inflated belly of the ship, her face the cut-glass nose cone, and her glorious hair the tendrils of cloud whipping about and away from the ship.

Her eyes snapped open as Ba Luen clapped once, like a circus ring mistress. A clap of thunder rattled the Symposium hall though the skies were clear, the waxing moon a wedge above the upper curve of the ship. Cats skittered, and the audience laughed, applauding towards the orchestra's timpani section for the good sport, but the drummers simply shrugged. Aroha and her incredible group of engineers, designers, and crafters were swallowed up by a sea of congratulations.

Third watch was well underway before the party disbanded and the four women finally collapsed into a rented carriage dressed with filmy veils. A strange silence settled across the group despite the excited partygoers echoing through the streets.

Aroha loosened the stays on her bodice, fanning the humid air upon her bosom without embarrassment. Neither Chifwe nor Ba Luen blinked; the animagus had chosen devotion to her city and animals, while the daughter of a circus mistress had seen much behind the curtains of her family circus.

Cinn broke the silence first. "Where do we begin?"

Aroha drew her hands together into a lazy second prayer position, for levity. "Auē. Not tonight, kairoro. I am very tired."

"If not tonight, then tomorrow morning. And tomorrow morning you will be wine-sick and crawling to Chifwe for one of her cures. And then it will be lunch and siesta time. Then it will be afternoon and work at the hanger and you will not get home until late and miss dinner and..."

Aroha cut her off with a laugh, flinging her fleshy arms around Cinn's neck, smothering her face with kisses. "Yes yes, I understand. And so, an all-nighter. Are you two up to the task?"

Tin, settled between the animagus and tinkerer, made a questioning 'mrrrh' and Chifwe bit her bottom lip to hold back any offending mirth.

"Yes little one, this is about you, in a way," Aroha cooed at the cat.

Chifwe and Ba Luen exchanged glances and Cinn puffed out a breath.

"Chifwe and Ba Luen say the cats saw two things. Lightning and death. The lightning I can understand at this time of the season. You are hale, and certainly not ill. At least, not that I know of?" Cinn aimed a hard look at her wife, and

Aroha shook her head in such a way that Cinn knew to be satisfied.

"Then these designs of yours do not entirely make sense." Cinn jumped to another thought as she pulled a crumpled paper from her pocket and smoothed it on her knee. "It outlines a death celebration, and corpse transportation aboard the air ship?"

"My first choice has always been to return my remains to the burial grounds of my ancestors," Aroha said matter-of-factly. "No offence to your family's excellent work, Chifwe."

"None taken." The animagus dipped her head. "It would be an honour to reclaim your bodily remains, but you should do as you see fit."

"I do not understand. You profess a love for life, for *me.* Why do you want to *die*?" Cinn burst out.

Any further conversation was frustrated as the carriage rattled to a stop in the back courtyard of the factory and hanger that doubled as Aroha and Cinn's home. Chifwe paid the driver and thanked the horses, then they climbed the spiral ramp to the top floor living quarters. Cinn grimaced at the ache in her knees and hips, muttering a curse to the humidity of the day, the long routine she had performed beyond her daily stretches, and her wife's recalcitrance.

Ba Luen saw to making root tea in the galley kitchen as Chifwe rearranged colourful cushions into a talking circle. After pushing open the river-side shutters, Aroha sank into a nest of cushions with a grateful sigh.

"Well?" Cinn pushed, standing above everyone with her arms folded.

"Patience, kairoro." Aroha held up a hand, deep lines around her lips and eyes cutting further with the strain of the day. "Let me gather my thoughts. You caught me off guard, before I was ready to explain myself to you. To you all."

Ba Luen served them all tea, and Cinn pouted around her cup as they saluted each other in the river city style, cup to forehead and heart. Aroha wet her mouth and began to speak.

"I want to assure you all that I am of sound mind and body. The cessation of my moon phases was difficult and protracted, but that is many seasons behind us now. I thank you all for your patience in that."

Chifwe acknowledged her with a dip of her head, and sipped silently at her tea. Usually she had a lot to say on the subject of death and the myriad uses of a body after the spirit had passed on, but this was not her time to talk. Cinn circled her free hand to hurry Aroha along, cup to mouth, then held the empty vessel out for a refill.

"Slow down, you will burn your mouth," Aroha admonished, the rote words laced with amusement. "So. My mortality is not impending due to the vagaries of the human body. I will attend a healer house in the morning, if that will avail your spirit of some quiescence."

Cinn gave a single sharp nod.

"You are correct, kairoro, that due to my dislike of ocean travel, the desire to return my earthly remains to the urupā of my whanau has been just that, a desire. Until now."

"The *Tāwhiri-mātea*." Ba Luen smiled, rolling her long hair absently between her hands to warm and distract her skin.

Enthusiasm washed seasons from Aroha's face. "But it is more than that. It is about journeying the *entire* globe. Traversing the continents available to us in your family's airship Ba Luen has been a privilege, and I thank you for those times we travelled together—"

"—And I piloted," Cinn broke in, a small grin creeping back as memories of her other occupational passion she had not indulged in many seasons flew through her head.

"Yes, kairoro. And you piloted." Aroha took Cinn's free hand and squeezed it gently. "That is to do with my plan as well. It means we can always be together, and you can assuage that fear of out-living me because of the difference in our ages."

Chifwe sat forward, tea cup cradled in laced fingers between bent knees. "What do you mean 'always be together'? I thought you were speaking of your death."

"This talk of death is...the incorrect way, though I do not fear it." Aroha glanced towards the grey river as dawn pastel-washed the horizon. "I am not sure there is any easy way to say this."

"I am ready for anything you have to tell me," Cinn said, eyes narrowing back to a speculative squint.

Aroha winced. Two of her knobbed knuckles clicked where she had broken fingers in gears over the years as Cinn squeezed her hand harder than intended.

"Auē, I do not believe you are, but here it is regardless."

She supped at the last of her tea, sighed, and licked her lips, capturing the three women's gazes in turn.

"I wish to fly. Not just pilot, but feel and manipulate the wind and sun and rain. If my calculations are correct in what I can do, the airship will be my flesh, and I will become its heart and brain. I will *be* the airship. I will fly as far and high and as long as the *Tāwhiri-mātea* will fly."

Even Cinn was silent for so long that the day's first call to prayer rippled out from temple, weaving through shutters and dreams. Tin trotted over and stared up at the engineer, while other cats watched from window sill, balcony, and interconnecting building ladders.

Finally, Ba Luen found her voice. "Lightning."

"Are you insane?" Cinn whispered, reclaiming her hand.

Aroha massaged her fingers and smiled gently. "Quite possibly."

ii.

Insects and shadow business stroked through the humid darkness beyond a dirty skylight.

Chifwe peered down into the interior gloom of the hanger, bending her ear to the scuff of feet of the reclamation teams as they removed waste from house cisterns, and the whisper of a robed traveller upon the shadow highway nearby. The *Tāwhiri-mātea* was a large smudge to the right, pulling against its tethers as if eager to embark on the promised maiden voyage.

Below, a lone figure worked in a pool of light that made the rest of the hanger clean by comparison. Chifwe reached to her cats to provide greater visual detail; hair tucked out of the way within her tinkerer's vest, Ba Luen fussed over a long metal pole of about two woman-length, affixing to the tip a metal bulb almost as big as her head.

Cats at other points of the city also relayed things shared and shared again; the taste of wind and the hot snap of dust. A storm was coming.

Ba Luen attempted to lift the large rod from its cradle, but her exhausted arms wobbled and the rod fell back. Chifwe flinched at the noise and slipped down the gantry and poles, a soft foot amongst the shadows.

The trill of a cat alerted Ba Luen to Chifwe's presence a moment before she stepped into the light.

"I will never get used to seeing you do that," Ba Luen breathed, a hand too pale against her chest.

Chifwe held her hands up in combined greeting and apology. A small bow sent unpinned braids tumbling around her face, silver and obsidian. "I am sorry."

"No you are not." Ba Luen back-handed a thin sheen of sweat on her brow leaving behind a thicker smear of grease. "I was expecting Aroha."

Chifwe folded herself into a cross-legged position atop an empty workbench, and Tin settled in beside her. "Aroha will attend shortly. I simply...adjusted the meeting time."

Ba Luen fussed with her tools, aligning them with the edge of the bench. Chifwe unclasped her cloak and passed over a clay bottle of water, from which Ba Luen drank from deeply.

"You must have questions." Ba Luen patted the metal rod.

"When do I not?" Sun-lined fingers working swiftly, Chifwe teased a knot out of a braid and began re-wrapping it with a bead and colourful fabric scrap found in one of her copious pockets.

A look passed between the two, of memories that were old but too sharp edged and chill to fade.

"Secrecy is most unbecoming of you," Chifwe continued, trying to keep her voice as light and steady as possible. "Surely this is something Cinn and I can bend our strength to."

A grey cat, one of Ba Luen's family of three, insinuated itself under the tinkerer's cleaner hand. "I am afraid to admit that I am...afraid. This is something you have always warned me not to tinker with. Shadows have not always bent to my will like they do yours."

Chifwe examined the experiment closer, with her eyes and those of the cats who had witnessed the culling of the metals. "It looks very much like the lightning rods you built for the council chambers and library."

Ba Luen nodded, and her mouth worked silently for a moment, trying to find the right words, until she said simply: "I have been building a weather machine."

"You know how I feel about the manipulation of the elements," Chifwe scowled, her fingers working faster at the braid.

"You are one to talk," came another voice, echoing out of the darkness.

Cinn stepped down from the office entrance, and offered a wry smile in apology. "It seems no one can sleep in this humidity," she said, fanning herself with a hand.

"The older I get, the less sleep I need," Chifwe admitted. She gave her milling cats a glare tinged with exasperation and love.

"Oh, do not fuss over them." Cinn flipped a hand then grabbed a clean rag and began polishing the metal bulb so hard it rattled in its cradle. "The older *I* get, the less they can smell me. This is not a bad thing. We keep our distance and that suits us all fine."

The other two women laughed for the vagaries of Chifwe's brood, and the tension broke before the coming storm.

"*My* apologies," Chifwe said, putting her hands into fourth prayer position, crossed over heart. "We shall have a...discussion, my cats and I, once this is over."

Some of the cats made disgruntled whuffing noises and wandered off into the shadows, and Tin just clicked a blink.

Chifwe looked to the office entrance a moment before the fourth voice spoke.

"The party has begun without me. Late to my own death celebration, how rude."

The three women laughed and threw greetings as Aroha emerged into the pool of light. She had not donned the white robe and gold-trimmed red scarf, instead still favouring factory stained pants, sleeveless jerkin, and apron in concession to the heat.

Aroha wrapped a tool belt around her hips. "It seems we have enough muscle power to manoeuvre the rod into place. Friends, if you please?"

She gestured at the rod and without question they all fell into place along its length, donned leather gloves for grip, and lifted it carefully from its cradle. With much grunting and cursing, they picked their way out the main doors and wove up the outer hanger ramp, emerging on the upper gantry just below the airship tugging against its creaking stays.

Catching their breath for a moment, they laid the rod against the scaffolding of the gantry. Chifwe gazed along the length of the ship, admiring the dark symmetry. The aesthetics of length, size, and balance which would be perfected by this new rod struck her anew; Aroha had planned this from the beginning.

Ba Luen wiped her brow free of stray hair strands, leaving another smear. "This machine is not one to help predict the weather, like the ones we have built for the meteorology houses. Weather is an exacting science, and a good barometer and varioscope can only go so far. They are in no way helpful when you need to move swiftly when the wind, or lack thereof, impedes."

Chifwe's dark eyes glittered in the low light oozing up from street and hanger, and Ba Luen shivered.

"I suspect it is not the wind which is impeding you," Chifwe said blithely.

Aroha picked up Ba Luen's lost words. "No. There is wind aplenty at the heights and distances we will achieve in the airship. But the big storms are moving away. Chasing after them would be time consuming and frustrating."

"You want to create a storm."

"We are not quite that skilled," Aroha laughed, as if the idea was quite mad. "But we do want to control its fury."

Chifwe frowned and stroked the metal rod like a cat, her eyes on her oldest friend. "I know your memory is not impaired, jir-ii." She had used the term of affection for a non-blood relative sparingly over the years.

"This will be different from the time The Piper used the weather against us." Ba Luen's voice came swift and quiet, like a small breeze that will become more. "We will be prepared, it will be short and swift, with as little precipitation as possible. There is no leeway for floods with the cisterns full, and the fields fertilized. We are more interested in harnessing the lightning's effects."

Cinn's eyebrows laced as she listened to all this. "You never speak of your encounter with this piper. Whispers and stories run free. Help an old contortionist who uses her body and not her mind understand."

Ba Luen pinched Cinn's chin gently, leaving behind a small smear like a handsome tuft of hair. "He was a difficult man whose powers overtook his sense, and sought to dominate the city through a plague."

"Yes, we all know that..." Cinn began, but Chifwe cut her off.

"It is not a story worthy of a glad day such as a death celebration." She looked towards the river mouth, hidden by the night, as if drawing strength from the turning of the tides. "Just know his weakness came from being unshakeable. He believed that the elements, people, animals, maybe even the earth itself, were at his bidding. This is why I teach failure as well as success, respect as well as a faith." Chifwe tapped Cinn in the centre of the forehead, and the contortionist chuckled, swiping the hand away like she would an insect. "You are not stupid, jir-ii. You can fly an airship, have a feel for the wind that many simply cannot be taught. And you chose your friends well."

As if by unspoken command, the four women lifted the metal rod again and shuffled into place on the scaffolding beneath the nose cone. The wind had dropped enough that only a minimum of cursing and fuss was required to slip the rod into a specially constructed cradle. Despite the height above factory and ground, Ba Luen swung through the railings without a harness, tightening the cradle, while Aroha worked the clamps around the flat end of the rod.

Next came the long struts that would prevent the rod from bending or snapping under its weight. Each woman brought one each up from the factory.

A hint of dawn greyed the edges of the city before Aroha was satisfied with their placement.

Collapsed against a balustrade, they all stared at their night's work, silent for a job well done. Chifwe's silence sat the heaviest, until Aroha felt compelled to speak.

"You have seen how lightening hits a diffuser atop a building, or how it affects a tree or airship in flight." She drew slow pictures in the air with her tired hands. "I heard tell of a scientist who was able to harness this great power. Facts were few, and his papers were forbidden amongst our community, as many said what he did was against the laws of nature but—" She sighed and rubbed her blood-shot eyes. "—though he sounds a lot like your piper fellow, I believe, I *know*, there is validity in such a theory."

"Harness? How?" Cinn asked, curious and horrified at the same time.

"By moving one type of life force to another vessel. The details are scant, but there was enough that Ba Luen and I could extrapolate to our needs."

Chifwe bore the weight of her dark gaze down on the tinkerer.

"What did you tell her?" The animagus said, voice full of shadow.

"By The River, I said nothing!" Ba Luen backed against the bricks and tiles of the roof almost bereft of the previous day's heat. A grey cat grumbled and jumped into her lap. "It is not my place to impart such knowledge."

"Tell what?" Cinn found a comfortable spot and looked between all the women, and her eyes narrowed as she gleaned triumph from her beloved's face.

"If I am correct, it is part of their history with the plague magus," Aroha said, wrapping her dirty fingers in Cinn's. "What I plan to do with the lightning, Chifwe has within her own blood."

Cinn stared at the animagus, who under the imperative stood and paced the flat roof, though she moved slow and careful after the night's endeavours.

"It is my position never to pry into a friend's history," Aroha continued. "The rumours of your...ability...make good ale-house telling Chifwe, though I do not ask you to explain how Tin came to be. I would never ask such a thing, which is why I choose this path to rebirth instead."

Cinn hugged her knees. "So it true. You *did* bring Tin to life."

Chifwe scowled, but not in castigation. She paused her pacing, staring at the tiles deep in thought. When she chuckled, the three other women let out their breath as one.

"Having someone other than Ba Luen know the truth would be a weight shared," she admitted. She took a moment longer to stare up at the bulk of the airship. "Yes, it is true that I gave life to the metal cat and life back to one other after The Piper had harmed my cats, but it is something that I have only done once, and it was a very long time ago. It is not something I would even consider attempting on a human, as my skills do not extend to those of a healer. The risk would be too great."

Cinn stared up at her friend in fascination. "It may be your worst kept secret," the contortionist said.

"You have no inkling of my secrets," Chifwe replied, though the corners of her eyes crinkled to counteract the shadows within.

"I thank you for your honesty Chifwe," Aroha said, hauling herself up by the balustrade and dodging through the scaffolding to give the lightning rod another pat and polish. "And I understand the limitations of use on such careful magicks. I would never ask such a thing of you."

"And yet you would ask this—" Chifwe gestured at the nose cone and quirked an eyebrow. "—of Ba Luen. Much and the same."

Now it was the turn of the tinkerer to scowl. She stood and drew her frame as straight as her old bones would allow, muttering in Xin for a moment before lapsing back into Rah'bik. "For once, I wanted to do something right. Offer my abilities to something greater than I."

With a sigh, Chifwe cupped her friend's face in her hands. "But your clockwork creations, your family's circus. You have always done right by them."

"I wanted to do right by the currents of *death*."

Chifwe nodded slowly, absorbing the idea. "Perhaps it is time I should too. Perhaps I can prepare Aroha's spirit for the journey, ease the passing across the veil."

Perching on the edge of the balustrade, Cinn flexed her knuckles and neck, keeping herself carefully between her beloved and the animagus. The sun was due and her limbs were stiffening from the extra work and cool tiles. "What do you mean? Aroha has said only her body is going to pass, and she is going to... move on."

The animagus gazed along the length of the airship, as if judging its heft and pull against its stays, not its size. "This has been a purely engineering feat that I could offer little to. Allow me to give what I can."

"But jir-ii-"

Before Ba Luen could finish the thought, Chifwe stepped in a single flowing movement towards Aroha at the far edge of the roof, holding her hands palm outwards in a gesture to initiate intimacy. Cinn swallowed her breath. The grey cat and Tin leapt a safe distance away, while the rest of the cats sat as still as the fortune statues that dotted house roofs.

"The Great River Swells and Flows, I will only do this with your consent," the animagus said, low and smooth. "I do not know if there will be pain."

Aroha tilted her head, looked up through her lashes, and took Chifwe's hands. "What do you require?"

"Only your body."

Ba Luen chafed her hair between her hands. A long sigh expelled from Chifwe's lips, as if she was beginning a meditation or prayer. The sound was filled with regret and longing none of the women had ever heard.

It happened fast. The animagus took Aroha's face between her hands and covered her lips with her own. Aroha's eyes widened then her eyelids drooped and her body relaxed. Despite the long drop behind them, the two women held each other up easily.

The kiss went long, but nowhere near reminiscent of desire. The perfunctory connection shared information along breath and tongue that could not be shared through deed or thought. They helped each other breath for a long time. Ba Luen and Cinn watched on, breathless. When they finally pulled apart, the air smelled faintly of burned metal and the freshness left behind after a storm. Aroha breathed long, slow and deep, smiling up into Chifwe's face. A calm overtook the two watchers, obliterating any jealousy that may have lingered.

Ba Luen watched her best friend limp away down the inner stairs. "What do we do now?"

"We wait." Chifwe's voice was as weary as she looked.

"And we celebrate." Aroha lifted her face towards the sun as it cracked the horizon. "A new day is here. Our guests will be arriving with it."

"Wait for what?" Cinn whispered, checking her wife's vitals at throat, wrist, and eye, sniffing her breath in hope of garnering just a smidgen of what had passed between the two. The sun-islander shooed her off, the skin around her eyes and mouth more taut than Cinn could remember in many a season, as if the kiss had sloughed away the vagaries of time and worry.

The three women and cats vacated the rooftop as the shouts of delivery boys from the courtyard mixed with the morning's prayer wafting over rooftops. While they were occupied with water rations, bunting, and pastries fresh from the city ovens, Chifwe slipped back up the stairs and into the shadows of the airship. She took the narrow footholds of the scaffolding much slower than the engineer and tinkerer.

Perching in the scaffolding beneath the nose cone, she listened to the pluck of a stay, and ran her hands along the glass and steel. Choosing a panel, she pressed her lips against metal. Once the contact was complete, she smiled, licked her lips, and retreated to rejoin the already vociferous party.

iii.

The rising wind wrung a sweet counterpoint from the airship's stays and struts, harmonizing with the voices still celebrating in the factory below. The push and sway of the music and wind reminded Aroha of the rise and fall of her people's waiata. Fists clenched around the pilot's wheel stripped of its protective leather upholstery, she squeezed her eyes shut and brought forth memories of hands fluttering in greeting. She had been taught of death as solemn, revered, but this celebration by peoples in so many ways different and alike—Cinn's dancing, Chifwe's storytelling, Ba Luen's colours and food—this too was a grand death. She leaned into the sway of the great machine, embracing it all.

With a gentle hiss of steam to attract her attention, Tin stared up at her as if appealing to her sensibilities one last time.

"Auē. Do not fret, little one," she said to the cat. "We were made for the sky. You can come with if it pleases."

Tin's eyelids made a languid click.

Storm clouds gathered up river of the city, and a few rumbles of thunder promised a good show. Soon the call would ring out from the meteorology houses to shutter up, protect the cisterns, and open the river gates.

Chifwe's albino, Ma, slipped through the cat flap in the outer bridge door and touched noses with the metal cat then settled her gaze on the engineer. Her absence from the party had been discovered.

The bridge door creaked open just enough to allow through a shadow and a gust of wind. A pleasant grass-salt fragrance followed as Chifwe scattered the funereal river reeds across the polished wood floor. The animagus kissed the last handful and spread them around of the pilot's chair and navigation board, then brought her hands to third prayer position with a little bow.

Aroha simply kissed Chifwe's tattooed cheeks left-right-left, to honour family, house, and family again. Everything that needed to be said had been said over the previous seven nights of death celebration.

With warm fingers smelling of the rich river mud, Chifwe took the engineer's chin and twisted her face this way and that. She nodded, satisfied.

"My mind is...quiet. Perhaps beaten a little thin. But the silence is not unwelcome. I do not remember a peace quite like it." Aroha answered the unspoken question in Chifwe's gaze, whose eyes were as soft as the wind outside the airship. "I have dreamed much these last three nights. Of darkness, thick and warm. The waiata of my people." She shook her head. The strange seed planted by Chifwe's kiss shifted again, squeezing around her heart and lungs, a good pain. "I apologize. Cinn is the better poet."

Chifwe took Aroha's hands and placed them back on the wheel. A boom of thunder had them searching beyond the nose cone windows in a silence formed from seasons of words long past.

The stomp of dancing feet mixed with the hum and twang of the airship turning to the approaching storm. Aroha imagined Cinn's limbs insinuating this way and that, unable to fight the lure of song even in her exhausted state. Even with everything laid bare in a death celebration, stubborn, loyal Cinn, who had fought and loved with the tenacity and vagaries of the wind, could still not speak of her time before joining Long's Circus or her real name. Wherever Aroha Raharuhi was, she had drunkenly told the raucous party, that was home.

A gaggle of airship cargo pilots just arrived from up river had joined the party on the third evening, slapping gloves against thigh, stinking of sweat and grease, and Aroha had watched as Cinn's hands flexed as if around an imaginary steering wheel. Circus bred, the contortionist-cum-pilot needed to pack little, and already the task was done in her head.

The bridge door creak once more, and Aroha flinched when Cinn's cool, long, lined fingers folded over her free hand. "There you are, kairoro. I take one moment for a nap, and this is what you do. The cats gave you away."

Chifwe raised a bushy eyebrow, still able to be surprised by the actions of her large feline family.

Cinn gave Aroha a sideways hug and smiled over at the animagus. "By the riptide and the storm, it is an odd sight indeed. They all appeared quite quickly along the line of the hanger roof and the gantry."

The airship dipped again, and Aroha set a stance like a captain heading down a storm. Fat droplets splattered against the glass, adding extra timpani to the bass hum engines.

"Should we call for Ba Luen?" Cinn asked.

The albino cat brushed against Chifwe's ankles and the animagus' eyes clouded over. "No need. She is already here."

The upper maintenance hatch popped open, and a damp shadow dropped into the bridge. The ululation of the call to storms was whipped away by the singing struts, the party now faint.

"Well met, friends," the Xin tinkerer said, breath coming easy despite the dangerous climb. She had no safety equipment about her person, not even a rope. She pulled a small red banner from her pocket marked with the characters of good fortune and death in gold Xin script. "It is indeed a most fortuitous and special occasion."

The four women tied the banner to the pilot's navigation panel to Aroha's exacting specifications. Tin jumped onto the panel and stared at Cinn as a definite boom shook the city.

"What were you doing out there?" Cinn asked, nibbling on an already ragged nail. Though an expert pilot and long time river city resident, storms made her nervous.

"A few final adjustments to the equipment." Ba Luen picked up a coil of thin wire that terminated in the floor near the front end of the nose cone. At a sharp nod from Aroha, she began wrapping it around the engineer's hands, tying them to the pilot's wheel. The sharp smell of metal mingled with that of the reeds and blood.

When her hands resembled electrical coils, Aroha held each of the women's eyes in turn, her wife's the longest. "The time has come. If you do not care to watch, I do not blame you."

The thunder boomed, much closer now.

"I am not leaving," Cinn said, folding her arms and planting her feet.

Chifwe rubbed her temples with her fingertips, but did not move away either. "You honestly think this will work?"

"You have given me the seed. You, your expertise. And you, my purpose." Aroha smiled to Chifwe, Ba Luen, and Cinn in turn. "I could not have done it without all your love".

Gauges flickered with the charged air. The engines thrummed up a notch, though Aroha had not touched any of the shining brass levers or switches. A flash of lightning etched diamond and silver across the sky, picking out the lines of the white and ochre city, eliminating shadow for one perfect instant. The animagus imitated the tilt of a feline's head, eyes glazed, appreciating the view from within and without.

Aroha licked her lips, smiled. "Auē. I cannot hold it for much longer. It tastes like darkness, and will eat me from the inside. It is now or not at all."

"I hope you were right with what you have done." Cinn laid her hands again on her beloved's shoulders, but looked askance at Chifwe. Ba Luen tugged on her arm, trying to manoeuvre the slippery limbed woman into place.

"I, too." Chifwe's eyes had lightened to the grey of the storm tossed river, seeing what her cats would show her. "I only gave her what she needed. It was a leap of faith, and By The Current of the Great River, she has held up longer than I imagined. Perhaps there is something long hidden in her blood."

"A gift from my ancestors," Aroha murmured. A line of blood disappeared into the cuff of her white and red robe. "But do not fear the dark, kairoro. Magic is only science we have not yet quantified. Perhaps this experiment will help. I give you permission to donate my blood to a healer house for examination."

Now Ba Luen was tugging on Chifwe's arm as the albino cat twisted frantically around their ankles. "As fascinating as this discussion is, the lightning is close."

Cinn leaned in and kissed her beloved's cheek and mouth, easy and sweet. The time for farewell was long complete. "May your journey be all you hope it to be."

"When this works, we will fly anywhere you care to. Anywhere you go will be wondrous seen from the air." Aroha's soft voice was almost lost beneath the now raging storm. The airship shook with the fury of the wind and the press of thunder. "It will be beautiful."

Chifwe had to look away. Ba Luen twisted her hair, biting her bottom lip.

"I wish you no pain," Cinn whispered.

Another crack echoed around the bridge; Ba Luen took on the power and appearance of circus mistress as she clapped her hands. Human and feline alike stiffened to attention.

With a voice that completed the transformation from stolid tinkerer into her strict and potent mother, Ba Luen ordered the two women to a cushioned pad set into the bridge floor holding the visitor's chaise lounge patterned in Aroha's favourite purple velvet, well away from any metal fittings. "In the event of an emergency, please do not step outside the square until I say it is safe."

The albino cat circled into a comfortable spot amidst feet and robes. Tin, however, could not be coaxed to leave the engineer, and settled into the cushioned pilot's seat. The glass ball of its inner workings steamed gently, as if only mildly curious of proceedings.

Lightning struck somewhere close, and they all flinched. Ba Luen muttered counts and wind direction in her Xin dialect. Aroha's eyes closed as if to ward off the cacophony.

The airship lurched and Aroha leaned against the captain's wheel at an alarming angle, her face slack as if her spirit had left her body a moment too early. Despite schooling herself for days not to undertake anything rash in the final moments, Cinn reached out for her beloved, but Ba Luen restrained her with a strength her small body belied.

The bridge bucked beneath a slap of noise and a burst of light which drowned the senses.

With a crash of scaffolding and a snap of ropes, the airship almost pulled free of its berth. Blue-white light cracked along the long thin metal rod attached to the nose cone. It spread through the window frames, following along the floor-anchored wire and into the tangle of cables attached to the navigation board. Some of the thick windows cracked but held. Gauges popped and smoked, and exposed metal surfaces blackened.

The blue-white light crackled from the wires, running up and down Aroha's body. Her back arched at an impossible angle, clothes and hair burning away. First the lace and ribbons in streamers of sparks, hair turning molten, then the buttons and seams popped with the echo of cracking bone. All three women cried out as a smell of burning meat hit their nostrils.

After many revolutions of the energy stream, a green-tinged wash of light the same colour as the Northern Lights shot out of Aroha's mouth, passed once over her body, and then into the machinery.

Through it all, the engineer said nothing; never cried, did not pray, or beg.

And then she was still.

Though Ba Luen moved first, Cinn reached the body slumped over the wheel quicker, unwrapping the wire that cut blackened hands and wrists to bloody shreds. She shook off a few painful residual zaps as she felt for pulse, breath, rhythm.

Smoking from the ears and joints, metal calico leaves black at the edges, Tin clicked a blink and tilted its head.

"She is gone," Cinn whispered. Mindless of the stench and gore, Cinn kissed Aroha's forehead and whispered something in an Ao dialect too low to be discerned into the hair frazzled and burned back to only a few inches of length.

Ba Luen dashed away tears with her sleeve, and bent over the navigation panel to hide her face. Chifwe picked up the closest cat to hand, and buried her nose in the albino's fur. It purred loud enough to overcome the swiftly retreating thunder and wind. The time for crying was done.

"Did it work?" Cinn's voice came thick and low, her lips stained with blood.

Ba Luen shrugged, still unable to find her voice, hands fluttering over the gauges broken and locked into position. Chifwe held her breath.

A strange whisper fluttered from the inter-communal link grill near the captain's phono-horn. A hum like wind through the electric wires, a voice smoother and younger than Cinn had heard in many a season, the way it had been so long ago when they had been sure of changing the world.

I am here.

Cinn shook her head as if trying to lodge an insect buzzing in her ear. The communication grills around the ship all picked up the whisper, smooth as the polished wood, gleaming with the pride of the copper and glass, an echo of the wind that had gone and was yet to come.

Here. And here. Here too. Over here.

With a smile tugging at the corners of her peeling mouth, Cinn pressed her bloody lips to the still hot navigation panel, leaving an imprint quite distinct from any tarnish. Ba Luen and Chifwe placed their own offerings of the same.

The animagus gently covered the body with finely woven shroud pulled from a robe pocket.

"Aroha?" Cinn placed Tin in her lap as she took her place in the battered pilot's seat, hands hovering over the gauges and levers and wheel. The clockwork cat did not pull away.

I am here.

"It worked." Surprise coloured Chifwe's tone as she dandled the happily limp albino like a baby. "I cannot fathom...it worked."

Your shadow seed. Grew true.

Ba Luen busied herself checking the panel for damage, grimacing as she delicately plucked at wires and brushed away broken glass. She gasped then chuckled as a green light flickered through and reset the gauges. "She sounds disorientated."

"Give her time," Chifwe said, as if speaking of someone recovering from a simple fever. "You would be too. Tin was stiff for some weeks after their change."

Cinn could not help but laugh at the unintentional joke.

The metal cat left off a little hiss of steam that smelled of burnt wires. Cinn patted its head absently, promising to look it over. Ba Luen, hands still busy in the guts of the machinery, arched an eyebrow up at Chifwe, but Chifwe just shook her head and smiled.

Cinn stroked Tin one more time then put it down. The clockwork cat strutted stiff legged around the panel, murring and sniffing, unable to find the source of their mistress's voice, completely ignoring the inert shrouded body.

Cinn leaned in to whisper to the phono-horn grill, which pulsed a languid green. "What do we do now, kairoro?"

Fly away. Be free. We are free. We are whanau.

"I already have a large enough family." Ba Luen dropped her eyes though the corners of her mouth twitched upwards.

Always room. For more.

Chifwe stretched, her spine popping. "I wonder if the cats get air sick? I have not travelled in many a season."

Remedy that. We can.

"I promise to be your pilot, and theirs. To take care of you as long as you wish to fly." Cinn whispered a renewal, a readjustment of vows spoken so long ago.

She kissed the grill and it pulsed green again."And as always, we will have *fun.*"

As the storm abated, washing the sky rich blue and gold, Aroha turned on her ropes, putting nose towards water, towards the promises of the ocean winds. The airship pulled at her anchor, ready to be off, impatient to find many new friends and adventures, impatient to be free.

IMAGINARY BEAUTIES: A LURID MELODRAMA

GEMMA FILES

...hitherto we have been permitted to seek beauty only in the morally good—a fact which sufficiently accounts for our having found so little of it and having had to seek about for imaginary beauties without backbone!—As surely as the wicked enjoy a hundred kinds of happiness of which the virtuous have no inkling, so too they possess a hundred kinds of beauty; and many of them have not yet been discovered.

—R.J. Hollingdale's translation of Friedrich Nietzsche's *Daybreak.*

Rice Petty was leant up against the University of Toronto Medical Sciences Building cafeteria wall with Rammstein blasting in one ear, admiring the slick purple vinyl sheen of her own boots and wondering idly if she could get away with charging (yet another) new strap-on to her Daddy's VISA, when Horatia Wint slouched in: All head to toe in black, a weird Renaissance-style sugar-loaf wool cap with a gold brocade top jammed haphazardly down over her ears, dripping melted snow from the January blizzard outside. She stood there a moment shaking her head, waiting for her glasses to unfog; as they did, Rice saw her eyes were both slightly squinted against even this dim light, and probably far larger than that heinous degree of prescription made them look—a pale, peculiarly penetrating shade of green, like mouthwash, or maybe absinthe. Her nose was snub, her jaw square, her mouth decisive. She didn't look like she had any friends, or wanted any.

And: ***Oh*** *yeah, uh huh, save some of that for* ***me****, please. Hey baby, hey baby, hey.*

For Rice, it was violent pull at first (close-up) sight—like, lust, whatever. Certainly worth a walk-by, anyhow.

After relentlessly and heteronormatively fucking her way through high school, Rice had called dick break on university (with occasional time-outs to peg some random male bitch, here and there), and was enjoying the result; nice to have a different sort of reputation, if nothing else. Besides which, she'd played various girls' sports competitively since age ten, so it wasn't like any of the basic mechanics were exactly unfamiliar ground.

Meanwhile, though she'd also thus far coasted through her courses by playing the hypercognate card—previously registering Horatia's existence mainly through smart-dar, as potential competition rather than possible prey—Rice knew her own complicity in accepting that particular categorization had always been little more than a scam, a quick hit of public recognition without academic expectations. Sure, she had enough eidetic memory to ace any test she'd ever taken, but her study habits were for shit—and it was there, in the personal projects part of the equation, where the cracks were already starting to show.

Where Rice'd always excelled were the soft-skill areas of social intelligence: Linking, cross-referencing, playing seat-of-the-pants mix-and-match games with names, faces, relationships, motivations. All the things that ubergeeks like Horatia, the real deal in terms of sheer cerebral cannon-power, found either too boring or contemptible to master; from what Rice had observed, Horatia seemed to be virtually people-blind, in much the same way Rice was—and always had been—rule-blind.

Notoriety clung to both of them in roughly equal amounts, an ill halo—automatic separation from the herd. It gave them something in common, a connection virtually begging to be built on. Add up the sum of *these* parts, and whatever alchemical combination you ended up with would probably blister paint, eat through walls, dissolve fools on contact: Major damage in a Klein bottle, times two by infinity. And fuck knew, Rice had never felt up to resisting *that* sort of open challenge.

As Horatia scouted 'round for a seat, eventually deciding on the caf's single least passersby-accessible table, Rice pondered her plan of attack. She knew she must be having a pretty good face day, judging by the cat-calls she'd gotten on her way down-campus, and that gave her an extra advantage: When the casual sex gods smiled, she'd been reliably informed, she looked eccentric but exotic—a skinnier Uma Thurman with good teeth, spiked-up hair and a lanky jock charm. On bad days, though, she just looked...goofy, would probably be the word. Like she'd been put together at top speed by a committee, all of whom were working under the influence of something truly second-grade.

Horatia popped her MacBook Air open, revealing a screen mostly occupied with some chemical equation roughly the size of Pi to 1,000. At the same time, Rice did a complex, basketball-inspired shimmy through the crowd and slid right in next to her, so close she was almost in Horatia's lap. "Hey," she said, grinning. "Antisocial much?"

Horatia scowled without looking around. "Do I know you?"

"Rice Petty, major Chem, minor Bio. And you—*you*'re Horatia Wint, Girl Genius. Got the full ride on home-school, did 100 across the boards on your extrance exams, won that big...*thing* last year..."

"The Lasky Award for Excellence in Chemical Recombination Studies?"

"...yeah, that's it, comes with $25,000 and a lab grant; think we've got, like... Prions for Perverts together, or whatever." Rice leant a little further forward, deliberately invading Horatia's space to see what she'd do in response, if anything (answer: wrinkle her nose and stare at Rice like she'd grown another head, apparently). Then cocked her skull to one side confidentially, while resting her chin on her steepled hands, and continued: "But anyhoo, enough shop talk... you like cunnilingus?"

"What?"

"Well, I'm just throwin' it out there, man. In my experience, though, most chicks do."

Horatia considered her again, a bit longer, and more closely. "Why are you even talking to me?" she asked at last.

Rice shrugged. "'Cause you're the only one here?"

"This place is full of people."

"Well, sure." Murmuring: "But, see...I've slept with most of *them* already."

Back at Gilmore Petty's West End screw-pad, to which Rice had had a copied key since she was around fifteen, Horatia watched with studied I'm-so-not-impressed 'tude as Rice cooked her up a quick batch of home-made MDMA. An hour later, she was explaining her thesis research to Rice at top speed and volume, gesticulating like she was on crack; a half-hour after *that*, Rice had her bent over the breakfast buffet, her tongue in Horatia's ear, three soaked fingers and an equally-wet thumb urging her girlie parts towards full, fist-ready dilation.

Why would she have even taken that first hit? On some level, Rice supposed, Horatia probably thought she was immune—that she could defeat simple chemistry through sheer Nietzschean will-to-power. The basic fact was, really smart people could sometimes do the dumbest shit imaginable; Rice herself was living proof of *that* truism.

For most of her sexually-mature life, Rice had taken deliberate pride in cultivating a policy of enthusiastic polymorphous perversity—*live life to its most lurid extremes* was her motto, paraphrasing Rimbaud (or maybe Verlaine).

In her time, she'd seduced teachers, friends' parents and parents' friends, the occasional pet; she'd inserted any object inside her which would fit, plus many which really didn't (though she'd certainly had fun trying to make them). Hell, she'd spent the better part of prom night sucking off her best-friend-who-was-a-boy's same-sex date in the faculty lounge girls' washroom, while simultaneously taping the whole encounter for later Youtube distribution on camera-phone. If it was doable at all, she'd pretty much already done it.

But even in a short life of complex thrills, sex with Horatia had to qualify as a serious career high. Cold and efficient to near-Spockian degrees under almost every other circumstance, Horatia only really came fully alive in pre-, post- or orgasmic mode; she had no moral hang-ups, a vivid carnal imagination (Rice suspected she'd attended the School of Porn for some time now, functional virgin or not), double-jointed thumbs, and seldom remembered to wear underpants. Considering her entire *modus vivendi* revolved around a constant diet of hypertension and overwork, it probably shouldn't have been any sort of surprise that with the proper encouragement, she could—and did—go off like a string of firecrackers, almost every single time.

They spent the next day in bed after a pleasantly exhausting night out of it, in various other locations (and positions). Rice lounged back and watched Horatia elaborate on the experiment that'd consumed her life up to this point, eventually breaking in to clarify—

"So you're working on, like...human flesh spackle."

Horatia, flushing: "I most certainly am *not*."

Rice really had to laugh, long and loud. "Aw, c'mon! You know you are, man—that's *exactly* what it is, and that's totally fine; very...chick-friendly. Very marketable."

"It's a damn *cellular matrix force-growth reagent* in a *collagen unguent base*, you whore."

"Comes in a jar? Goes on with a spreader?"

"...I hate you."

Ah, but *that* didn't last too long.

Just supposed to be a simple hook-up, a trick, like everything—or everyone—else Rice did. But she found herself taking Horatia's numbers anyhow, and actually <u>using</u> them; indisputably, there was *something* about finally having another high-three-digit I.Q. case on speed-dial. About not having to go through the day always censoring yourself, constantly talking down, up or sideways so you didn't frighten those really pretty dumb-asses away, long before you had a chance to slip them the high, hard one.

Besides which, Horatia had...qualities, and those qualities were already starting to grow on Rice, like sympathetic mold. She didn't sleep much, for example, snored when she did, and refused to admit it; in class, she took her notes with both hands, promiscuously ambidextrous. While deep into working she liked to listen to opera up *loud* on her iPod, and sang along in a horrible fake Italian mish-mash, all Chef Boyardee accent run through a string of random vowels. Rice soon got used to having her around in the background while she ran through her normal daily grind of low-level super-villainy—so much so, after a lamentably short while, it almost seemed like she couldn't function optimally *without* Horatia. Which was...

(creepy)

...evolution, maybe. Like calling to like. And likin' it.

By the end of February Rice had bought Horatia in on the bottom floor of an only half-built, all-but-discontinued condo out near the old abandoned sugar factory on Lakeshore, and put up for a bunch of shiny new lab equipment on top of it. A few weeks later, she let her dorm roommates kick her out at last, and moved in too. By April, when her Dad wanted to know just where the fuck her perfect GPA had gone and just what the fuck those $40,000 worth of unspecified expenses on his VISA bill were, she told him to go screw himself and he told her—fucking *finally*—that she was officially cut off: Annoying, but not unexpected.

After all, it wasn't like she didn't have a viable back-up plan.

-ww-

But: "Listen," said Horatia, with surprising patience, "I am *not* going to let you boil the greatest potential discovery of the 21st century down for parts and sell it as a recreational drug, just because we have bills to pay. I'm just *not*, Clarice."

"Rice, please. 'Clarice' is Doctor Lecter's long-distance crush."

Horatia rolled her eyes. "Why would you want everybody to think your parents named you after a staple foodstuff?"

"Why would your parents really-for-truly name *you* anything that reduces down to 'ho'? 'Cause that kinda had to suck, back in school, right?"

"Moving on..."

It was April 22, Earth Day—that ridiculous, fake-ass Hippie holiday, usually used as an excuse to smoke "organic" ganja, watch BBC nature documentaries while tripping and ignore the planet dying around you. Good time of the year for moral debates generally, but Horatia's position on this one would've rung a whole lot stronger had she not just been turned down for a follow-up grant to her now-exhausted Lasky Award funds—as Rice well knew, having overheard at least one half of the entire shrieking phonecall which preceded this particular plot-twist.

As far as Rice could make out, the Lasky Foundation's main objections had seemed to be a) but what are we supposed to *do* with something which keeps functionally-dead rats alive indefinitely, yet unable to breed? ("Sell it to rich people who think they're too important to die at a ridiculously inflated price, you morons!" Horatia had screamed. "Then use half the initial profit to mass-produce it, give it out gratis to everybody else, and freeze Earth's population explosion!") which then led directly into b) shut the fuck up, you freak.

"You do get how you just kinda shot your credibility wad there, right?" Rice had asked, helpfully, after Horatia threw the phone across the room. "I mean, fighting Death-the-archetype *mano a mano* for the salvation of the world is... pretty cool, but to the corporate mindset? Counter-productive, to say the least. They *want* mortality left in the equation, man. Makes it a whole lot easier to sell people shit they don't really need, when they're scared."

"I took the same Intro to MicroEconomics requirement you did, thank you very much."

"Okay, sure. But were you actually paying attention? Or were you maybe just working on Reagent Draft One under the table, while making fun of the prof's heinous nose-hair?"

To which Horatia had snarled something unintelligible under her breath, then banged out of the lab/loft space like her former benefactors had said they might reconsider if she only slammed the door hard enough...but not really, Rice was guessing, since that had been a few weeks ago now, and SugarBox Developments was already threatening to cut their utilities off.

"Look," she began again, taking it nice and reasonable. "You already stacked the deck at the design stage so this stuff would induce euphoria, right? With no side effects?"

"That we've *seen*, yet."

Rice nodded. "And you *could* make a real big fuckin' lot of it, pretty fast, if you needed to."

Horatia, shrugging: "Absolutely. But *I* don't need to."

And there it was again: Horatia's marvelous people-blindness—so endearingly hilarious when watching her trample over everybody else's feelings, so infuriating once you realized she really didn't even grasp that *you* had them too. Obviously, Rice would have to fight for at least a convincing semblance of Horatia's beloved, ruthless logic, even if that involved stepping hard on her own natural impulse to counter: *Well I need you to, bitch; what say we just work with* that?

"Don't you?" Rice leant back in her chair as if the whole topic was boring her. "'Case you hadn't noticed, 'Rashe, you're not the only one whose income just dried up–I mean, you do remember who paid for all this, right?" A dismissive wave at the lab. "Sure, you take what you've got to any major Big Pharma group, you could get a decent *salary*, but you know how that'd go. They'd keep you on rats for at least another ten years, you could lose intellectual property rights at almost any stage of that curve." Sly: "And it's not like you *made* it for animal testing, did you?"

Horatia looked at her, green eyes glinting beneath her glasses; gave a slow, single nod. Agreeing, softly—

"No. I didn't."

"It'd be just like skipping straight to human trials...if you can even call junkies human."

"Says the woman who thinks 'E' makes any first date better."

Rice smirked. "Hey, I do that shit for *fun*, dude; kicks, no chaser, Daddy-o. Not 'cause I'll go cold turkey if I don't, or anything."

"And you'd find a paying customer base—where, exactly?"

"Where wouldn't I? All over. Some of my best friends...oh, all right: More like all of 'em, actually. Everyone I've ever taken a class with, shared a club with, hooked up with..."

"...except for me, that is."

Now it was Rice's turn to nod, her grin stretching wider, as she locked Horatia's hot gaze with her own, even hotter stare. "All except for you, yes. 'Cause..."

(...you're *special*. Congenitally so.)

Now where's my money, honey?

And yeah, Horatia did hem, haw and fume a bit more after that, but by post-Afternoon Delight snack-time, it was a fully done deal. They attacked the sub-equation together that night, worked 'til 5:30 A.M., and spent the rest of the weekend on cooking/packaging. Friday evening after that, the hot new party favor known as "reA" was officially out on the street. Rice hit the circuit with fifty tiny baggies stashed in her purse's lining, wearing a winning combination of Victoria's Secret lingerie on top, red pleather fetish gear on bottom and a big, cheese-eating grin: Salesperson mode, plausible and charming. Her twin trade secrets were a head-full of previous contacts and a complete willingness to do that all-important first little bump while her targets watched, ostensibly to prove she wasn't "wearing a wire", or some shit.

(And: ***Where** would I be wearing it, exactly?* she often thought, at such moments. Because once you excluded all the parts of her <u>not</u> barely covered by translucent or skin-tight fabrics, the only options left for concealment seemed fairly unconducive to good audio pick-up).

Test passed, the marks would soon take a snort of their own, and sag back, eyelids fluttering—*oh **man**, shit, that's **good***! Followed at speed by the one-hit-you're-hooked routine of immediately double-dipping, rubbing it on their gums, all the while wondering out loud: *Uh, Rice...it wears off kinda fast...can you, like, shoot this stuff, or what?*

Well—

—let's find out, shall we?

⚱

Sometime later, Rice too would have occasion to wonder, the way she once had on Horatia's own behalf: *So why* did *I even take that first hit, anyway?* Fully knowing, in her heart—and elsewhere—the only possible correct answer:

...oh yeah. 'Cause I thought I was immune, too. Or indestructible, at the very least...

And the funny thing, in hindsight? *That* was the part which turned out to be true.

⚡

Start-up fees alone kept their penetration of the GTA's synthetic drug market fairly shallow at first, though Horatia's demented insistence on tracking—and analyzing—their clients' habit-based bell-curves in as much detail as possible (given they were, after all, dealing with people who spent more than half their waking lives getting high) rendered functional invisibility not really an option. Still, Rice made sure they stayed close to the radar, if not actually under it. She had no doubt their main competitors knew *of* them, but it seemed unlikely they could gauge exactly how much of their profits reA sales might be cutting into, let alone who its creators were or where they lived.

By summer, however, the inevitable finally became evitable...and Rice and Horatia woke, one way-too-early morning, to find their lab-loft suddenly full of thugs with guns. Their leader, Dieter Dorfmann, was a rooster-proud flyweight boxer of a guy with a shaved head, albino-blond eyebrows, inept jailhouse tats and a scary little lisp; Rice had bought crystal meth off and on from his various club dudes for about a year now, watching him from afar as she did, and always maintained there wasn't much wrong with him that a good swift dick up the ass wouldn't cure, plastic or otherwise. Still, it was funny how much less innately ridiculous he seemed when bolstered by five other well-armed guys of varying sobriety, all of them busily tossing the place for whatever they could find.

Rice and Horatia froze, stranded, halfway down the stairs from their sleeping platform—both barely dressed, with Horatia maintaining a white-knuckled clamp on Rice's wrist. The good part: Nobody'd knocked over anything likely to explode, as yet. The bad part...everything else, pretty much: Guys with guns, no guns of their own (not that Rice even knew how to shoot a gun, but she thought she could probably work it out fairly fast, given sufficient contextual pressure). No way to reach the door without being seen and/or stopped...

...so Rice went with her most basic instinct, instead—chill hard enough to cool down the whole room, thus keeping people calm enough for she and H. to stay alive. In her best amused drawl, therefore, the knot in her gut thankfully inaudible—

"Yo, D, man...I *can* call you D, right?"

A rippling wave of pistol-cock clicks brought six separate barrels their way, at this; Horatia had already ducked behind Rice before Rice could even react, which might've looked bad from the outside, but provoked a weird rush of affection: *That's my girl.*

Dorfmann turned, cutting her the only-slightly-curious wall-eye. "*DD*," he said.

Rice shrugged. "Yeah, well, whatever, D-squared—looks like you're looking for something, so maybe I can help. What's the issue?"

"Uhhh...*you* two rich bitches, shitting where *I* eat? Pushing your homebrew crap in my territory, without even kicking some back to me for the privilege?" Adding, as his chief button-men–equally large, brown and unimaginatively monickered brothaz Big Trey and Lil Trey–smirked, behind him: "That's just *rude*, dude."

"Granted. How 'bout we rectify that right now, then?"

"Okay. You turn over what you got, you don't make *any* more, and you pay up for what you screwed us out of. Then you get to live...maybe."

Rice clicked her teeth together, "thought" a moment, then smiled wide. "Nah," she said. "Not really workin' for me, as an offer. Care to try again?"

"Listen, little miss gay-'til-grad—"

And now Rice could feel Horatia's nails *really* start digging in—but fuck it, her blood was up, and if she *had* to die today, she just didn't feel like doing it while sucking anybody's dick (metaphorically or otherwise). "Oh, fuck *you*, little mister Aryan Brotherhood-'til-parole," she snapped back, a contemptuous sweep of her hand taking in both Big and Lil's multiracial faces at once. "Your White Power click-pals know exactly who you got carrying the weight for you, out here? Or do you just skip conveniently over that part, come contact visits day?"

"Hey, insults. That'll make me *want* to cut you a break."

"Dieter, who the fuck do you even think you are, aside from the guy who couldn't cook up a new drug if somebody made you deep-throat an Uzi? Get out of my damn place!"

DD flushed (creepily deep, even given his coloration); he cracked his neck from side to side, then said, with remarkable restraint—

"Make me."

—and shot Rice, right in the chest.

Horatia's shriek was louder than the bullet's impact itself, and weirdly more painful. Rice lost her balance and fell backwards, like she'd been punched hard in the ribcage. Her ears rang. The light felt heavy. As she lay there, she saw Big Trey and Lil Trey moving slow-mo past her to grab Horatia in a double arm-lock, hauling her down right on top of Rice's body to sprawl on the steps. DD was blabbing on, thick and dying-battery deep, about "teaching" somebody some fucking thing, while Lil Trey undid his pants; Big Trey had put his weight on Horatia's shoulders, holding her down on top of Rice's body. Horatia flailed, scratching at Lil Trey's eyes, and got a backhand in return that looked like it almost cracked her jawbone.

Oh, you don't *hit her. Ever.*

Without thinking, without even planning to, Rice simply reached up, grabbed Lil Trey by his ears and broke his neck with one sharp twist, yanking his head clean off like snapping a pencil in two. Carotid and jugular popped, spouting blood over everything like a busted hot-water tap. With a single wordless cry,

Big Trey fell off the stairs entirely, base of his skull connecting hard against the lab/loft floor; Horatia scrambled backwards up the steps, mouth gaping, glasses smeared with crimson. A second later, Rice had vaulted to her feet, Jedi-style, and kicked Lil Trey's twitching body off the steps too before heading straight for DD at full-out stalk, ignoring the shots he kept pumping into her body until the gun ran dry, until she was close enough to lift him off the floor by his throat. As he dangled, gurgling, she leaned and hissed, right in his face:

"*Now.* Like I already said...you wanna try *again*?"

(Or *what*?)

Perhaps because he also spent much of his own time constantly caffeinated, DD seemed to get broken in to the whole *Herbert West, ReAnimatED* idea a whole lot easier than most other people—people not Rice or Horatia, specifically—might've. But he did have to work his way through it at least once, maybe just to hear it out loud:

"So...you're all dead but not, 'cause you been gettin' high on your own supply?" Rice, leaning on the kitchen island counter as Horatia fussed around her, nodded. "Which means...you must'a been makin' that shit out of shit that, like—makes you all not dead, and shit."

A snort: "Oh, you're *smart*," Horatia observed, not even vaguely sounding like she meant it. Switching over to Rice: "You do know what you've obviously done to yourself, I take it..."

"'Obviously'? No, not really—and your bedside manner *sucks*, by the way." To which Horatia just scowled, taking yet another blood sample (though what she thought she was going to learn from this one she hadn't from the pint or so she'd already taken, Rice seriously didn't know); as she did, Rice turned back to DD, snapping—"And as for you...seems to me like *you* got crew problems that go waaay beyond the whole total-lack-of-discipline thing." She glanced significantly past him, first at Lil Trey's bisected body, then over at the still-open door, through which the rest of his gang (all but Big Trey, now lying semi-concussed on the couch) had already booted. "So if you still want to get in on this with us–"

DD blinked. "What?"

Horatia wheeled back up from the microscope, jaw dropping. "Excuse me, *what?* He *shot* you, Rice!"

"Yeah, thanks—might've missed that, you hadn't pointed it out to me." Rice ignored Horatia's near-purple flush and looked back to DD. "Like I was saying, the assholes who tore out of here, they're *your* guys. What are they gonna say happened, once they're back on the street?"

DD shrugged. "Nothing anyone'll buy; shit, I'm lookin' right at ya, and *I* don't even buy it." He scratched his head, oddly quizzical. "So, you like Wolverine now? Whatever happens, you just heal back?"

Horatia shook her head, impatience-quick. "Not how it works, not at this stage; the reagent builds a collagen-silicon neurocompatible tissue scaffold that sustains cells while they're living, redirects around them when they're dead or damaged...."

Rice yawned. "Tech, tech, techitty tech tech...."

"You're not even listening to me."

"Not as such, no. There a chase we can cut to?"

A slow, deep breath. "I'll need more tests to make sure, but I'm guessing your whole nervous system is probably more reagent than living tissue, now. You don't need blood or oxygen anymore, so the only way to put you down for good would be the classic Romero maneuver: Headshot, brain-death. But since inert cells means no reparative process—"

"—I can't die, but I can't heal. Meaning I'm stuck full of holes for...ever, basically."

"I'd tell you to be careful with yourself from now on, but..." Horatia shrugged, helplessly, as Rice shrugged back: *Given.*

Big Trey looked at them, then at Lil Trey's corpse, then back at DD; his face twisted, half-disgust, half-sorrow. "Listen, boss-man—what these bitches got, this, this is really ill, man..."

Rice: "Says the on-command *rapist enabler*: Just step the fuck off, Sasquatch."

"Hey." Dorfmann raised his hand, abruptly hard. "*My* call, not yours, even *if* we partner up on this, and that's a way fucking big if. 'Cause I'm still not sure how much I trust you, Zombie Hooker from Mars—"

"Oh, you have *got* to be kidding me!" Rice exploded. "You shot me in the fucking *chest*, you dork, and I'm the one offering *you* free fucking money—does the A.B. only take retards these days, or what? You unbelievable fucking pussy!"

"Okay, okay; Jesus!" DD took a second to get composed, then braced himself against the other side of the kitchen island, lowering his voice like he thought 4-0 might be outside right now, listening in. "So...how soon before we can start to ship this shit?"

And: Far too many fricatives to that sentence for comfort, which Rice almost felt like telling him—but didn't, 'cause she'd already been shot more than enough times today. Besides which, at least he'd finally remembered that the primary active ingredient in dealing was making fucking *deals.*

•ʌʌʌ•

Later, though—long after DD and Big Trey had gathered Lil Trey's remains up in a couple of sacrificed pillowcases, and departed—

"I'm beyond pissed, Clarice," Horatia began, almost conversationally. "Using the reagent recreationally is perhaps the single stupidest thing you've ever done, let alone using it *this* much—and now you're planning to play Scarface with some moronic meth-head meatbag?" Considering that her voice didn't even rise while cursing, Rice actually found herself paying attention. "Not to mention how we don't know nearly enough about prospective side effects to begin mass-producing *anything....*"

"Those seem pretty cool, to me." In an infomercial announcer's voice: "'Side effects may include: If it so happens you end up getting shot in the chest, don't even worry! Plus, as an extra-special bonus offer, free head-ripping ability; super-strength, virtual immortality...'"

Horatia shook her head. "You really don't get it, do you? For fuck's sake, Rice—you had the same course-load as me. Is it really too much to ask that we *occasionally* approach the science part of all this like, oh, I don't know...scientists?"

Rice straightened up, grabbing for the old familiar sweet, hot flush of rage—though now, even with effort, all she suddenly found she could conjure was an offputtingly uncomfortable tinfoil-bite sting which rippled her nerves, from dry mouth to equally dry crotch. "Define terms, bitch," she said. "Did *we*, or did *we* not, just already spend three months manufacturing this exact same shit in large quantities, then selling it to people to get high on?"

They stared at each other for a long moment. Then:

"Oh, *fuck*," they both said, at pretty much the same time.

It wasn't until two weeks after the first major incident that CITYPulse 24 co-opted the street-name, and started referring to people who unwittingly overdosed on reA, wandered into some public area and then spontaneously combusted in a spray of potentially contaminative material as "dusters". Rice and Horatia watched shaky black-and-white security camera footage of one poor bastard, as narrated by an equally-shaky newscaster: He came weaving up to the counter of an all-night Tim Horton's and started negotiations, before abruptly dissolving in a dusty explosion which covered the horrified, easily-infectable people around him in dried-out human matter.

Horatia stared. Muttered to herself: "Probably heart attack, aortic pop-shock, embolism, or...for him to go off like that, he must've died weeks ago, overdosed and just not noticed. So—one of the initial buyers, the first wave..."

"Yeah, I guess." Rice tried vaguely to summon some faces from that particular party run, but couldn't. "Eeeugh."

"We've released a damn plague of zombies, and all you have to say is 'eeeugh'?! Rice, this is *bad*."

"Look, that's not going to be me, if that's what you're worried about."

"What? *How? How* is that not going to be you?"

Rice grinned, and lowered her voice, conspiratorially. "Human flesh spackle. We got it; they don't."

"I *really* wish you'd stop calling it that." A pause. "Besides which...they aren't supposed to O.D.!"

Which Rice supposed was true—but to be fair, they probably weren't *supposed* to be taking drugs at all. Thirty years after Nancy Reagan, however, it seemed increasingly to her like that whole War Against Drugs thing had simply never really worked out quite the way it was supposed to.

So she started macking on Horatia instead, to change the subject—grabbed her in a clinch, set in for some serious tonsil excavation. Horatia relaxed into it initially, but soon began finding it difficult to put up with, and not for the usual breath-control issues; she drew back, nose wrinkling. Said: "Your tongue tastes... weird."

Rice drew back too, took a swallow, considered the result. "Huh. It sort of *feels* weird, too..."

She turned away, snagging an empty coffee cup, and spit. It came out black.

And: "Well," Rice said, at last. "Probably some new kinda side-effect, huh?"

Horatia, barely able to keep herself from spitting too: "Oh, you *think*?! You *see*? You *see*?"

"Man, stop being all *Plan 9*, and let's just fix this shit."

"Again, **how**? *You* don't know—I don't know! *Anything*! Because both of us were too Goddamn busy getting high or fucking with each other to ever run any motherfucking *tests*!"

"Okay. So here's what *I* don't get, H.—if you think I'm such an irredeemable idiot, why don't you just up and *leave* my dumbshit ass?"

Horatia breathed out through her nose, just once, a short, controlled huff. Saying, eventually—

"I'm certainly not going to do *that*. Because—"

(you took my virginity)

(you're the only friend I have)

(you're the only person, friend or not, I actually know...let alone *like*)

"—this is *my* apartment, too," she finished, finally. And went right on back to whatever she'd been doing, before Rice getting herself living dead-ified in the service of keeping Horatia's narrow ass strictly reserved for Ladies Only had so rudely interrupted her.

(Un)naturally enough, of course, black spit soon proved to be only the tiniest tip of the New Model Zombie iceberg; Rice careened blithely from symptom to symptom, dead heart not even skipping a beat between fresh new disasters—already starting to shrink a size or two overall, like the Grinch's leftovers. Her tapetum began to scrape away, eyes throwing light like a cat's, while her skin grew iridescent with dust, proteins calcifying and rising everywhere she looked, fine and sharp as mica. A pheromonal miasma, decay-in-the-mist, exuded through her pores. She wore her shades all the time now, even at night, like the old song went—but it didn't look so cool anymore, not even in a retro way. Just...

tired.

As things cooled off between Rice and Horatia, meanwhile, DD began hanging around a *lot*—far more so than their mutual three-way business "relationship" really warranted. One lazy summer afternoon, Rice walked out of yet another soothing, collagen-heavy Spackle bath—stark naked, natch—to discover him sprawled out on their bed, all shirtlessly inviting, like he'd picked up his entire idea of how a Cool Guy Who Wants To Impress A Cool Girl acts from watching home-made pornos.

"Oh, man," Rice said. "Necrophile much? Pervin' away on the Living Dead Girl; no, *that*'s not creepy at *all*."

"You don't look dead. You look...slammin'."

"Oh, do I? Hadn't noticed." Rice sat down to gel her hair, and grinned at him in the vanity mirror. "Dieter, you do get that some people are just *gay*, right? All DC, no AC? And thus unlikely to be quite as interested in your eight inches as—say—you are, or would like them to be?"

"Sure, I get that—like *her*, right? But you..." He grinned at the thought, offputtingly wide. "I think I might'a found, like, clips of you doin' it old-school, all penis in vagina and what-not, right there on the Internet. True or false, missy?"

Rice shrugged. "Busted."

"So you *can* get down with the bone, if you wanna."

"Well, proven—but see, that's just not what's gonna happen, with you and me. 'Cause I don't even like you *that* much."

"This is still 'cause I shot you, right?"

"Somewhat, yeah. 'Course, I *might* be persuaded to rev up Ol' Faithful and do *you* up the ass 'til you screamed, if it turned out you were into that."

"Why would I be?"

"I don't know. Why *would* you?"

"You're—just—makin' this ten thousand times more complicated than it has to be."

"Ah, my cunning plan revealed. Think of it like...space exploration. Broaching the limitations of human endeavour; broadening people's minds, proving points, keeping accurate notes while you do it. Science."

Dorfman frowned. "Are you really high right now?"

"Sure am. All the time, pretty much—I think it's one of those famous side-effects. And guess what? This could be *you*. Take enough of this stuff, and you too could be pushing the walls of perception back 'til they fall apart. Take enough, and after a while you'll be all: 'Okay fine, I'm in! Soup it up, bitch!'"

Unexpectedly, as DD blushed bright at this last idea, Rice felt a sudden tweak of interest; she realized for the first time that a) she was a full head taller than him and b) he was sort of cute, in a maybe-trainable feral/rabid puppy kind of way.

"Listen," he said, "more'n enough with that crap, okay? I pimp, lady; I don't *get* pimped. I mean, I didn't even put out in jail, and I was there a *good* long while..."

Rice leaned over him, assaulting him with her just-washed scent—gave him a close look at where the paste-on jewel she'd put over the original entry-wound went, a little off-centre, right between her boobs. Working that "you know I could pull your head off right now, little boy" vibe *hard*, and murmuring—

"And just how well *did* that work out for you, anyhow? In the long run?"

Hours later, Horatia walked in on them, took one look—then walked back out, twice as fast. Waited so long to come back home, after that, that Rice—who'd thrown DD out on his well-perforated heinie practically a second and a half later—almost began to think she'd finally been dumped. But Horatia had to come back, eventually: All her stuff was there, if nothing else.

Rice sat there in the dark, alone, 'til she heard the key in the lock, but didn't bother to turn around when the door opened. "Where've you been?"

"Does it matter?" Horatia sat down, heavily. Then said, after a long pause: "You...listen, I think you need to *stop*. Doing...things. Like that. You *need* to, Rice."

Rice let out a breath which—even to her—sounded more like a sigh, especially in context.

"...I don't think I can," she replied, at last.

"Why *not*?" No answer. "And more to the point—Jesus, Rice, what the Hell? Pegging some straight thug in the middle of our Goddamn living room? Why would he even go *along* with that?"

Rice shrugged, hands rising in a flourish of dismissive disbelief. "I don't know, man—I mean, that *is* a little weird, isn't it? Maybe he just likes having somebody tell him what to do." But now it was Horatia's turn to sigh, sharp and angry, and that finally made Rice look at her directly, laying on the charm. "Hey, c'mon, though—it didn't *mean* anything, 'Rache, you know *that*. Not *really*. Not like—"

"—'like us'? And I'm just supposed to, what, take that one on faith, because you tell me to? You lie for fun!"

And: "Not about *that*," Rice snapped back, without even thinking it over first. Which, once again, was...

(surprising. Uncomfortable. Inconvenient.)

...*typical*. Especially coming from somebody who'd never, ever, in her entire life, known when to leave well enough alone.

"'Scuse me," Rice finally said, softly, as though lack of volume alone could really negate the reality of what she'd just let slip. Then walked out herself, shutting the door in Horatia's still-gaping face, and prowled downtown Toronto's increasingly empty streets until dawn.

When she came back, Horatia was already so hard at work on trying to "fix" the reA formula she barely seemed to notice, which meant they didn't have to talk about...DD, Rice's bad habits and worse choice of words, any of it. And that suited Rice just fine.

⁓

Between the rising "did you say you loved me/Uh...maaaaybe" tension, Rice's increasingly permanent crazy-high and physical deterioration, and Horatia's insomniac cure-hunting mania, DD took on far more of the business end of reA sales than anyone had really planned for–and un-higher-educated as he was, he certainly knew how to move product. Too well, it turned out. But with Horatia too desperate for research funds to care, Rice too stoned, and DD just too plain greedy, their peripheral awareness of Toronto's response to the duster phenomenon—the reappearance of surgical masks as a fashion accessory; WHO health warnings triggering a free-fall economic collapse; ever-more-frequent and deadly street riots, whenever some poor calcified bastard went up in public and set off a crowd-wide bug-out—remained just that: Peripheral, at best.

When she thought about it at all, Rice could only chalk the authorities' helpless flailing up to her own personal conviction: Smart just made you stupid in different ways. As long as the WHO remained stubbornly certain it was a viral or bacteriological vector they were looking for—subconsciously influenced by five decades of movies, for all Rice knew—they'd never put two and two together with the cops on the reA drug, barring some lucky (or unlucky) break.

So (un)life went on, work vs. play vs. some arcane combination of the two—nothing Rice couldn't work around, just business as usual. Until the day...

...it wasn't, any of it. Not anymore. And never would be again.

⁂

"Yo, cook-bitches!" DD shouted as he came through the loft's door, loaded for bear with a gun in either hand, and all tricked out like some pimpy Elvis from Hell, otherwise. "Grab your crap, we're on the run!"

Rice, thankfully fully-dressed this time, was checking her LavaLife profile on Horatia's laptop, trying to figure out whether adding "vitality-challenged" to her profile would be more a draw than a drawback. "What you mean 'we', White Power man?" she asked. "Better yet, where's your posse?"

DD found Horatia's camping-sized rucksack, and got busy shoving the wads of cash which lined his ridiculous suit inside it. "Uh—dead, I guess. Big Trey started givin' me shit about...shit, so we drew down, and I took his fuckin' head off. Then the fuckin' cops show up, but they got, like, Feds with 'em and everything. Plus these other people started breakin' in, all dressed in plastic bags and crap...."

"The CDC broke up your firefight?" Horatia had just emerged from the bathroom; as Rice stared: "Prime Minister called them in on Monday, to help with the WHO initiative. Don't you even vaguely try to keep up, these days?"

"That'd be a 'no'." To DD: "So how the hell did *you* make it out?"

DD didn't miss a beat. "Threw a lighter into the main cook tanks and booked out the back. You need to do the same, and *fast*."

"Threw a—that was *you*?" Rice remembered, now: One more sound-bite, between videos on Loud; another (supposed) meth-lab gone up in smoke, adding a boost to the simmering dog-day smog mix of August-end. "Yo, *Dieter*. *Tell* me you didn't just blow our entire backstock of reA into the fucking *atmosphere*."

At her tone, DD finally looked up, blank: *Yeah, why?* "You can make *more*, though, right?"

Rice and Horatia locked eyes, equally amazed—and for just a moment, a little of the old shared smugness came back, that communal telepathic prayer: *Oh* Christ, *save me from fucking morons*. And bitter as realizing just how stupid some people could be always was, it was oddly sweet, too. In context.

They packed fast, leaving most of Horatia's equipment behind, and ended up in a "safehouse" that had started life as DD's first crack-house: No heat, no power, no phone, no cable. Its very walls themselves so saturated with chemicals even the air seemed to itch. There Rice lay in bed staring up at the ceiling, increasingly sleepless, while DD snored obliviously on one side of her and Horatia kick-moaned through a nightmare on the other. Her once-talented tongue gone cold, stiff and silent in her own mouth, like something already dead.

So two or three weeks passed, long enough for August to collapse into a cold and rainy September, as Horatia continued to work furiously towards some sort of cure with what little Rice and DD earned on their last few reA sales. With none of them talking about what they'd do when the stocks finally ran out, or how Rice—deprived of her sustaining spackle-baths—was getting drier by the day, let alone what the ever-heavier presence of soldiers and CDC mobile clean-labs in the streets of Toronto might mean...

Around 3:00 A.M. one morning, Rice's aimless wandering took her up to Parliament, where a closed pawnshop's window display TV had been left on, tuned to CityPulse 24. Pausing to watch a "Rewind" segment from 1987 on how to shampoo your dog, she couldn't quite avoid reading the caption-snippets of news running beneath, words fading steadily in and out:

...fifth week of curfew, city councillors deny rumours that full quarantine of Toronto being considered...

...source in Prime Minister's office hints that War Measures Act may be reactivated.

Center for Disease Control consultants report possible breakthrough in identifying primary "Duster" vector...

Curfew; well, that explained the empty streets. Rice got off the main drag, double-quick, and used alleys to work her way back while thinking about hazmat-suited strangers ransacking the loft, disassembling Horatia's lab, shredding the mattress she and Horatia had slept on. She stopped across the street from "home"'s piss-stained concrete front steps, next to the pay phone, and felt a weird impulse—dug out change, dialed. By about the fifteenth ring, she'd almost convinced herself the man on the other end had long since done what she would have, in his shoes, and high-tailed it down to Gran-and-Grandad's condo in Florida—

Click. "Hello?"

No air in Rice's lungs. It was an act of will just to breathe, to force out the words—

"*Hello*?"

—but then she managed it, without even a crack in her voice to show for all her effort: "Hi, Dad."

A long, long pause. "Clarice?" And...shit, it didn't sound like Gilmore Petty at all. He had *never* sounded like that. "Cla*rice*, is that *you*? They told me—" A wet, indescribable cough, almost a...

(sob?)

Yeah, *right*.

"They told me you were...dead," he said. And all she could think to say, in reply, was:

"...I guess...I sort of am," Rice told her father, before hanging up.

It was drizzling when she came in, sky beginning to go grey with morning; she found Horatia working by the wavering glow of a few tea-lights over a series of slides and eyedroppers. Alkaline catalysts, if Rice was reading the labels on the nearby bottles right, breaking up reA doses in different ways; measured by no more than hand and eye, with all Horatia's ridiculous, incredible precision. She looked up at Rice's entrance, and Rice wasn't sure exactly what that look meant.

"Well?"

"I figured it out. The molecular key to let reA hook right into a cell's master DNA, for full-on regeneration—so we can actually *repair* damaged tissue, not just shellac it up until it disintegrates. So nobody else will ever go Dust."

"Regeneration." Rice wondered if this was how other people felt around *her*: That stumbling feeling, perpetually out of step, too slow to catch up. "Like, eternal life-type regeneration?" The grin took her over, like something alien. "That's—holy shit, 'Rache, that's *great*! You fucking *did* it!"

"Yeah." Horatia nodded, not looking too triumphant, for someone who'd just broken the Grim Reaper's back and made it say "auntie". "'Did it' for the next batch of users. Not so much for anybody who already..." She covered her face with one hand. "I mean, um..."

"...not for me," Rice finished, toneless.

Horatia stared miserably at her, too upset even to nod. And right then—

—was when DD stumbled out of the bedroom, holding his throat with both hands, as if choking on something. Eyes so wide with fear and fury Rice could actually *see* the madness brewing, he advanced on Horatia, who recoiled, slipping backwards off her stool. "Yah, fahk'ng, bihhhhtch," he wheezed, and Rice saw thick, dark drops of blood squeeze between his fingers, as blood flaked off his sodden shirt. "Cuht mah fahk'ng hroaght—"

Then let go of his neck and lunged at Horatia, mouth still working—but the gash across his larynx gaped wide, shrinking his voice to a bare wheeze. Living Dead Girl-fast, Rice snapped out an arm; they wrestled for a second before Rice pinned him, face to the floor, open throat whistling. Rice shot Horatia an exasperated look, and Horatia just shut her eyes, comprehension dawning.

"Riiight, 'course: You shot him up too, didn't you?"

And: "Well, duh. But he would have hooked himself up anyway, I hadn't—am I right, D-man?" She put her head down next to DD's: "I let you up, you gonna behave?" This induced a renewed bout of struggling, but Rice had far too good a grip to break, without risking further injury. "One more time, Dieter. *Behave.*"

Helpless, DD finally nodded, so Rice turned him loose; he stood up, shooting Horatia a hateful glare, and pinched his throat back together. To Rice: "Hwheeerre...th'fahk... *hyouhh* bihn?"

"Out; who're you, my—?" Rice stopped, remembering the phone call, and began again. "Doesn't matter. You missed the big news, dude; Horatia cracked the code. Now we got something now that'll buy our records clean of anything, even the Dust-plague. Isn't a government on this *planet* won't set us up for life, once we start shopping immortality to the highest..."

But here, suddenly, she stopped. DD lifted his head too, a dog sniffing prey, as sick dismay whitened Horatia's face.

Screeches of rubber on wet asphalt; the clunking slams of car doors; the hammer of boots on the ground. The grey light filtering in through the filthy, half-shuttered windows began to wash with alternating red and blue. And a megaphone-enhanced voice whipcracking through the morning quiet, all the old standbys: **This is the Ontario Provincial Police...building is surrounded...exit through the front door, hands above your head....**

Rice took a deep breath, mostly to steady herself. Said: "So," to neither of them in particular. "That's it, then." She looked at Horatia, gone green in the weird light. "If DD and I go out the front door together, we'll probably distract them enough you could maybe slip out the back..."

"No. Forget it."

"Look, *one* of us needs to get out of here alive, okay? And given you're the only one knows the Highlander formula..."

"No!" Horatia backed away, until she stood silhouetted against the light from one window. "Rice, I am *not* leaving you, so don't even try to make me—" She staggered and fell to her knees, glass breaking behind her with a clean tinkling punch, as a spreading blotch darkened her shapeless green sweater.

"'*Rache*!" Rice dove across the room to catch Horatia, while DD hit the floor on the other side, peering upwards; felt something snap inside her as she did so, grating inside her ribcage as she lowered Horatia across her lap. "Oh Christ, no, please, no..."

Horatia sighed. Then said, in a ridiculously clear voice: "Oh, give me a *break*, Rice." She parted the hole in her sweater, probed the wound beneath, then let her head fall back. "No, that's it: Clean shot, police marksman. No repairing *that*."

Rice touched the matching hole in her own chest, from which the paste-on jewel had long since been lost. Sparkling powder drifted down, scattering across her fingers. Amazingly, she found herself smiling.

"You fucking *liar*," she said, tenderly. "So what, more tests? Or did you just absorb it, by osmosis?"

Horatia sat up, shaking her head. "Sample doses. Thought I was still below the critical exposure threshold." A beat. "Guess not."

"Hmh. I think maybe I *do* love you, you know that?"

Horatia just rolled her eyes. Cool: "Well, I *know* I love *you*."

"Bitch."

A spasmodic hacking came from DD, and they both looked over to see his chest rising and falling in what Rice realized, freakily enough, was laughter. He covered his wound with one hand, jabbed one thumb at himself with the other. "Sssooh hwhat's that... maahke *me*?"

"You?" Rice grinned her old I'd-fuck-the-world-if-I-found-the-right-hole grin. "You're the boy with the toys, Dieter. Just how many guns you got stashed around this shithole, anyway?"

After a second, his own grin almost reluctantly answering hers: "Mhor'n... enough."

DD caterpillared across the floor into the bedroom, staying below the windows, and came back dragging a suitcase. Rice flipped it open. Boxes of clips and shells spilled across the floor, along with a half-dozen Browning automatics and a greasy-sheened shotgun.

Rice looked at Horatia, who took her hand and squeezed it hard. She picked up a pistol and slapped in a clip, just the way she'd seen in a thousand movies—and hey, she'd been right. It *wasn't* that hard to figure out, with the right incentive. Then again, she always had been the smartest person she knew...

(...well—second smartest.)

"Okay, then," she said.

The megaphone-wielder outside launched into his final warning spiel—that old classic about getting away from the door, 'cause they were coming in. So Rice kicked it open herself, instead—and walked out into the cold rain to meet them, gun in hand, with Horatia and DD following right behind: Smart, stupid. Stupid-smart. Some creepy combination of the three.

Fucking *beautiful*, Rice thought—and laughed out loud, even as the first shots split the morning air.

SEAN EADS

Goebbels waltzes into the room with rolled bundles tucked under his arm. Adolf stops lecturing us about the Slavs, pushes himself from his deep chair and sprints to meet him. Bormann among others appraise my reaction with subtle glances. Adolf always seems more eager for his Propaganda minister's company than mine. I pretend to pout a minute before jealously moving to Der Fuhrer's side.

Sagging shoulders say much, and I sense Adolf's disappointment right away. He assumed Goebbels must be carrying strategic plans: maps showing victorious tactics for the Eastern front; schematics of new super weapons (I know them all); or spy reports detailing the activities of Churchill and Roosevelt down to their bowel movements (I detest to admit it is Adolf's obsession). But no—and of course, considering Goebbels's preoccupations—each sheet is revealed to be a mere poster.

This time they're all American.

Months ago, Goebbels cornered me during a party at the Kroll Opera House and gave me a long monologue on the superiority of American propaganda posters compared to their British and Russian counterparts. His spies and smugglers bring them to Germany and I imagine him, a versteckt wearing half his uniform, pantsless, pinning the posters on a corkboard table so he can inspect every detail with a magnifying glass. At the time, his favorite showed a cleated and spurred Nazi boot descending from the sky to stomp a white, idyllic New England church. Goebbels described it well, expounding at length about the illustrator's magnificent ability to manipulate key pressure points in America's Protestant heritage. I nodded with increasing eagerness, partly to placate him and partly because I'm susceptible to enthusiasm, no matter how noxious the person showing it might be.

Tonight Goebbels brings eight posters. He unrolls each out with his right hand, his left clinging to Adolf's arm to detain him. The Fuhrer would cast off anyone else's touch, but respect and some lingering ember of genuine friendship makes him tolerate Goebbels, who is so loyal to Adolf he just assumes their interests coincide. The war was going well last year. But with August, there's a sense of turning tides. Posters offer Adolf nothing.

"Look at this one, Fuhrer. Incredible! Do you see what the artist has done?"

I see three rather ugly children holding the typical American accoutrements—a flag, a model warplane, a dolly—standing in a grassy field. A shadowy swastika creeps over them. Goebbels explains the words at the bottom of the poster urges everyone to buy war bonds.

"Fear. Such fear and forlorn expressions. See how the boy on the left looks to the sky? See how the little girl's doll is covered in the shadow? Our posters have overemphasized party and parade. We set our posters on the Eastern front, not the home front. They therefore lack...*frisson*."

Adolf is arch, his arms cross his chest. "Time, perhaps, for a new Propaganda minister."

"I admit the oversight is my own—but I learn quickly from mistakes. Already I have commissioned artists to produce new posters. Germans will better understand what it is they fight for."

"They fight for me."

"Of course, of course.... But the posters must be psychologically expansive. Each German also fights for his own children. Now that I have unlocked the key, our new posters will encourage Germans to give their all not for the Reich of today, but the Fatherland of their grandchildren."

The confidence in Goebbels's voice isn't shared by his hands, which fumble about rearranging the posters on the table. He shuffles one after another to the forefront, moving faster and faster, his individual commentary becoming shorter and shorter. And then one poster captivates me, its effect startling. "Stop," I say, drawing a look of surprise from both men. I lean against the table, one hand at my bosom, all the wind gone from my breadbasket.

Adolf touches my shoulder. "Are you ill?"

Hearing these words, almost everyone in the room, some fifteen men and women, approach me like called dogs, Bormann leading the pack.

"I'm fine. It's just—this poster. I've never seen anything like it. That woman—who is she? Tell me more, Doctor Goebbels."

That makes the Propaganda minister grin. The man adores it when I use his academic title.

"Ah, Eva, I see your eye is as fine as any in the ministry. My artists and writers were likewise narcotized by power of this poster. Who is she? The Americans call her Rosie—*Rosie, the Riveter.*"

Adolf sniffs. "The woman has many fine features. But she is hardly a Valkyrie."

Not a Valkyrie? I'd shake my head in disagreement, but I want nothing to disrupt my gaze. She is Brunnhilde.... Her beauty, her strength, her determination and confidence—can such qualities all exist in one woman? She has dark eyes and darker, curly hair covered by some sort of red scarf. Her fine eyebrows have a perfect arch. Her mouth, drawn in a resolute expression, nevertheless seems pouty and imminently kissable. The collar of her blue work shirt conceals her neck. This proves a man drew the poster, for a woman artist would show that neck and invite the imagination's lips to hover over that fine throat. This Rosie has rolled her shirt sleeves up well past her elbow and she's making a fist. Her arms, long and shapely, know how to cradle and how to break.

Goebbels rambles about the poster's blue and yellow color scheme. He discusses women and factories and the American home front, but he won't discuss *the woman* at all. I'm certain he fears her. She is beyond his comprehension, threatening to his little penis, too much woman even as a drawing. I wonder if she based on someone? Could such a woman's inherent qualities be captured in the drawing? I close my eyes and make the drawing flesh. My fingers interlace with hers. Our breasts touch. So do our lips.

"Eva? *Eva*?"

Heat spreads through my face. "I am not feeling well, Fuhrer." Unlike my use of "Doctor" with Goebbels, calling Adolf by his high title actually hurts my cause. I just want to be away from him, from everyone. But Adolf now insists on walking me to my bedroom.

My room is far removed from his. Arm in arm, we travel the hallways of the Berghof, servants and soldiers stop and salute him but ignore my presence. So few acknowledge me as Adolf's mistress that, officially, I suspect I may not exist. I've never complained. In fact the arrangement pleases me very much.

Outside my door, Adolf looks me in the eyes a moment, then feels my forehead. I suppress a shudder when he presses his lips below my hairline as he holds me by the shoulders. A grandfather could show more passion.

I hope to dream of the woman in the poster, as her hands grasp my face when her kisses begin.

Many perks come with being the mistress to a man like Adolf. I do not mean the frivolous consumption that Rachele Mussolini covets: expensive clothes, jewlery, fine food. The one time I met her, the *Donna* boasted of her husband's appetites. I nearly vomited. Thankfully, Adolf's sexual interests are as bland and spare as his meals, causing me little grief. No, I have managed to inhabit a position of influence and access without the leashes his Reich Chancellery wear. Adolf prefers I'm invisible, allowing me to recuse myself from his side for long stretches.

It gives me time to work in my laboratory.

Many in the Reich tolerate me out of fear or a desire to curry favor. Our scientists are no different. Since the mid-1930s, my relationship with Adolf has let me observe firsthand the rocketry experiments of Oberth and von Braun. I have seen unpublished research by chemists at IG Farben promising unbelievable advancements in human biology. I have—to my horror—witnessed the atrocities of Dr. Mengele. The sight of him gloating over brutalized victims strained every nerve. Science does not need to be barbaric, though I agree that one should not limit the imagination. I fear my own hypocrisy and I did respond to Mengele's awful enthusiasm, revealing my own interests with a few accidental comments. He was pleased, perhaps even aroused. He offered to take me on as some sort of apprentice. But I have already been one of those—years ago, when I was just a child.

Adolf believes my lies. He does not know that when I was twelve years old, I met and befriended a peculiar a middle-aged man named Hans Sudeten. Befriended is itself a peculiar term to describe our relationship. It is fair to say he kidnapped me, luring me from the school yard with the promise...a promise not of sweets—I was no *kleines Mädchen* stuffing her mouth with chocolate while playing with poppets. I possessed imagination—and thirst.

He often spoken to me and several other girls in my class when school ended, but I in particular intrigued him. I remember how he looked at me one day and shook his head and made a sad remark about the invisible urges within the human mind. He raised his eyebrows when I asked if he was aware of Hans Berger, who had so recently recorded the wave patterns of the brain. Invisible? I told him I did not believe in invisibility. Science would make all things visible in time.

I spoke as no other girl spoke, and he told me I must come with him. Then he grabbed me by the wrist and pulled me all the way back to his home. For Sudeten had his own thirst, one equal to my young desires and, it turned out, quenched only by my youth. I soon realized the future of our partnership when I entered his house and found room after room of laboratory equipment. I thought myself transported, somehow, out of Germany to another place. Surely this was America. Surely this was the lab of the great Edison. I soon learned I was in the presence of one who'd apprenticed himself to an even greater man, named Tesla. After a falling out between them twenty years ago, Sudeten had returned to Germany and replicated the laboratory of his master. Now he styled himself as *Der Wissenschaftler*—The Scientist.

Der Wissenschaftler had a predilection for prepubescent girls and was surprised when I readily traded my body for his mind. What I already knew astonished him. I spoke of Wilhelm Rontgen as if he were my father. Spiritually, perhaps, he was. Sexual desire first stirred in me at the age of ten. I looked at older girls and my desire for their company was a wonderful thing, an invisible force I wanted to see. At ten, I believed my feelings existed like objects inside my head and heart, whose shapes could be revealed with X-Rays. Even before I met *Der Wissenschaftler*, I understood the foolishness of such thinking. Love and desire were not things to be revealed like X-Rays; rather, these emotions were rays themselves, emanating out to find and make visible my secret craving, a woman whose determination matched my own. The rays of my love would reveal her to me, just as they would also reveal me to her, and we would be united.

But first I needed to glean all that was in Sudeten's mind. At first this proved easy. He required so little—a kiss, a caress, a little moisture. A panting tongue is looser with its secrets, and I kept him in heat. At first it was a game: my shirt in exchange for a formula, my skirt for a demonstration of the Tesla coil. Sudeten entered me and in return I entered his laboratory, apprentice at first, but increasingly as mistress as my knowledge and authority grew.

I was growing too, however, and the accompanying biological changes were a most unwelcome thing to *Der Wissenschaftler*. I noticed how his caressing fingers started to keep more to my arms and legs, where I remained the most childlike. My body was outgrowing his sexual interest before my mind could outgrow his usefuleness. To stave off his waning interest, I dressed in absurd clothes, garments fit for a child years younger than me. I wore my hair in adorable curls as if I were ten years old. I shaved myself to recover how I'd looked when our arrangement began. But I was sixteen now, and some changes could not be undone or disguised.

I was to learn no more from Hans Sudeten. Perhaps it was for the best. Just as my body had outgrown his sexual interest, so my mind now yearned for knowledge beyond his narrow expertise. Electrical currents could do wonders, but I wanted the biological, the chemical. *Der Wissenschaftler* and I parted ways on my seventeenth birthday in 1929. By then he'd not touched me in months. He wept that his equipment could not arrest the aging process.

"Nor make the unnatural natural," he added, and I did not know if he meant my desires or his own.

I took on a new sort of apprenticeship, working in the photography studio of a man named Heinrich Hoffmann. For many months, I contented myself as a shop girl, taking every initiative I could to learn the chemical process of photography. Herr Hoffmann was well-connected with the rising Nazi party, and society women flocked to stand before his camera. As an assistant, I was allowed to help pose the women, touching them, almost daring to caress their limbs or neckline while putting them at ease. Some were so achingly beautiful, so intelligent, and possessed of such wit that my unquenched desire for them became a quiet rage.

I pressed their photographs close to my chest. I considered the complex process that went into pressing the image onto film, and the chemical solution which, like X-Rays, rendered the pictures visible. I thought: *There must be a way. If flesh can become photograph, surely the photograph can become flesh again.*

Verdinglichung is the only word that approximated my new obsession. I sought out *Der Wissenschaftler* to tell him my goal, for there was no one else who might appreciate or understand it. But the man I discovered was unrecognizable. He had lost much of his hair and a tremor animated his right arm, even when his hand was pocketed.

"You!" He spoke as if I were a thief who'd stolen something precious from him.

"Are you ill, Hans? What's wrong?"

He pointed his shaking right index finger at me and sneered. "You're what's wrong. *Where* is my little Eva? Ah, in here, always in here, kept safe." He tapped on his forehead. "Just the sight of you now kills the little Eva in my mind. Go away...leave me to my one true love before she too ages into you!"

"We must talk first. I too seek a true love."

When I told him my plan, Sudeten stared at me in silence at first, and then let loose a torrent of hateful laughter. "Poor fool. *Verrückter Wissenschaftler!* To return from *Munich* which has ten thousand girls just like you. Yet only the ten thousand and first girl will suffice you, and for some reason you wish to fabricate her out of a cloud!"

His laughter got louder and more derisive. I responded to his hate for me with hate of my own. "I never abandoned you. We had a mutual—"

"Each day carried you further and further from me. But the mind is the finest camera, and my imagination is the finest film. I need no scheme to make you live again in perfection. I need only close my eyes."

"Call it a weakness if you want, but I *will* have the photo made flesh."

The tremor in his arm spread to his entire body. "Your voice...can you not speak with the lisp of my little Eva?"

I ran from his house.

But I would not be deterred even though I heard him cackling "*Verrückter Wissenschaftler! Verrückter Wissenschaftler! Verrückter Wissenschaftler!*" behind me whenever I doubted myself.

I realized the experiments would take both great sums of time and money, but, too, I would need the Gestalt of the scientific community, my eyes and ears attuned to every advancement, every theory and hypothesis no matter how absurd. So my course became clear, I would find some ugly, high-ranking party member and serve as his wife or mistress. With luck, I would find one who was going through the motions to maintain his power, a man who did not actually believe the hateful policies of the Nazi's idiotic leader.

Then on a fateful day in October 1929, Herr Hoffmann introduced me to Adolf Hitler, and opportunity opened to me in grander terms than I ever imagined.

All other concerns became secondary. And when Adolf became Chancellor about three years later, my long wait was ended and I had every resource at my fingertips if I stayed discreet.

I am only thirty-one and should have decades ahead of me. But one gets a sense of the future as being more than the reasonable count of remaining days. There's an estimate reckoned not by science, but by morality; a sense of days *deserved* rather than days scientifically expected. And by that reckoning, I deserve little time. Adolf deserves even less. As nations have fallen; as Jews and undesirables have been thrust into a living hell; as I've kept my silence because some of requirements involve dealing with the likes of Mengele—as these things have happened, I've grown almost sick of living. I wonder if the love I want, the love I hope still emanates from me, are rays that can only darken rather than reveal.

The intervening years have not been fruitless. I've learned much about the art of making the image flesh. An improved Tesla coil, radiation, the proper chemicals, a Caledon chamber, and the right biological material are requirements enough for basic duplication. By 1936, I could take the sharply detailed photograph of a hand and reproduce its template structure in necrotic tissue. In 1939, I replicated a photo of Adolf's head into a perfect facsimile in flesh and bone. Fittingly that flesh and bone originally belonged to a mongrel dog. The duplication was as lifelike as a waxwork, but of course there was no brain, no life. How could I capture *intelligence*? How could I capture *personality?* Then I remembered something Herr Hoffmann once told me about African natives who, upon seeing their photo for the first time, attacked and killed the photographer on the belief his camera had somehow stolen their *essence*. Might there be some intuitive, primitive understanding there, a truth we sophisticated European moderns would never even entertain?

I increased my experimentation.

Then came the night in 1941 when I reproduced an entire body. The template was a photo of a woman taken several years earlier. She was a pretty, nameless creature. I felt no especial desire for her. I readied the chemicals and charged the Tesla coil. In the Caledon chamber was the naked body of a woman about five days dead. I didn't think she'd been a Jew—more likely a gypsy. I put my hand on her bare breast, closed my eyes and hoped for both of us. I even told myself I was resurrecting the poor woman. One has so many excuses, so many justifications.

Then I started the process, charging the Tesla coil to such power levels that light bulbs exploded across Munich. The Caledon chamber glowed an eerie green, and gravity ceased inside it. The body lifted off the table and was suspended in the middle of the air. Breathing became difficult. The lab's air was so charged with prickly energy that every inhale felt like I was swallowing nails. *I cannot do this. But I must. I must!* I still needed to pull two levers. The photograph was in a deep pewter basin connected to five tubes. When I pulled the first lever, silver chloride, pyrogallol, petroleum tar, dissolved bone filament and my own blood flooded the basin and drowned the photo. As the potent, explosive concoction began to dissolve the image, the rising smoke was trapped in a vacuum tube that carried it across the room to the Caledon chamber and the fleshy film it would imprint upon.

The second lever would unleash the power of the Tesla coil.

There was a blinding flash as the Tesla coil gave one final, magnificent pulse. At that moment most of Munich lost all power for the next two days. The energy blast shook the reinforced walls and ceiling of my lab and cast me to the ground. I lost consciousness for several minutes. I woke in total darkness and had to fumble to light the emergency oil lamps. As the darkness retreated bit by bit, I discovered a dim figure standing in the Caledon chamber. Yes, *standing.* Taking one lamp off the wall, I approached the glass. The dead woman's original features were gone, replaced entirely by the woman in the photograph. She was breathing but seemed too weak to talk.

Hesitating a moment, I said, "Can you hear me? Tell me how you feel. Do you...*love me?*"

She tilted her head to the right as if considering the question. Then she touched her breasts, bunching them together. Perhaps responding to my smile, she grinned and stepped toward me. I was about to raise the glass of the Caledon chamber. The creature on the other side did not realize the existence of the barrier, however, and when she was just a few feet away from me her expression changed. It became hideous—murderous. She lunged, her hands clenched and aimed for my neck. She meant to strangle me. She would have done so, too, except she rebounded against the glass and stumbled back, quite shaken. So was I. What sort of monster had I created? What was the nature of its *love?*

With no desire to further delve that question, I hurried to the third lever, the failsafe lever whose location I could find even in the dark. I'd never used it before. Now I jerked it down and the Caledon chamber filled at once with Zyklon B.

I slid down to the floor and drew my knees to my chest as the creature died. It clawed at the glass as blood seeped from its ears and a frothy gargle escape its lips—"Luuuh—". I lifted my head at the sound of this final death throe. Good God, was it trying to say *love*? At last the creature collapsed and went still. I got up on shaky legs and contemplated the body. *This was the last one. I must never do it again—the world has enough monsters already.*

In my head, I was done.

But in my heart, I still yearned to continue. I knew what adjustments to make. I managed to deny myself for three months before I surrendered to desire. Then I tried twice more. The second time was as disastrous as the first. I found myself looking through the glass at a beautiful woman, an exact duplicate of the photograph of Frau Kappel. I saw the same sinister smile, but I decided I must judge the creature's merits further. With trepidation, I released it from the chamber. Immediately it went to ravish me upon the floor. As I writhed in ecstasy,

I thought I was surely mistaken. What malevolence was this? How could such pleasure be evil? But the woman would not stop. Her appetites were insatiable, destructive. It was desire without love, companionship without safety or loyalty or comfort. I only just managed to destroy her before she consumed me.

Then I understood something crucial about the transference process. I had known a little bit about the woman in the first photo, and I had known Frau Kappel well. Both women had been imperious and wealthy, given to command. Those traits were imprinted on the photo—it was clear in their expressions. Their innate dominance was imprinted on the image just as much as their physical features. And so these attributes had been transferred as well. Transferred and—*augmented.*

With this in mind, I went through the photograph archives at Herr Hermann's shop and sought out faces sweet and mild, angelic girls whose gentle temperament were known to me. At last I found the one I wanted. The subject was a six year old child named Geli. She'd been the daughter of an army colonel who'd commissioned Herr Hermann to photograph his entire family. I remembered helping the girl pick out her clothes. She'd been like a doll, too good a child for the likes of the Colonel, who'd since died on the Eastern front.

I determined to transfer the image. My discreet, loyal contacts within the SS had been asked for stranger things, so they did not blink at my request to locate the fresh body of a little girl. But when it was brought to me, I, Eva Braun, who'd done so many dark and despicable things to further my goals, found myself capable of experiencing one final shock: the child's body was almost still warm. There was a tag around the girl's left hand, filled with spiky, recognizable handwriting. I read it—"*Compliments of J. Mengele. Gleichgesinnten.*"

I screamed and broke down as the reality washed over me. I'd meant to obtain the body of a girl who was already dead. It seems in their zeal to fulfill my request, the SS had killed this little girl *specifically* for me. I wept unrestrained but I did not dare stop the transfer process now. I was still crying when the body, now the exact image of the photographed girl, sat up and blinked at me.

"Who are you?" I said. "What is your name?"

She seemed uncertain for a moment. Then she said, "Geli."

I swallowed at the hardness in my throat. "What—what do you remember?"

The few things she said dried my eyes. She said she recalled me helping her pick out clothes. She had not wanted to be photographed, but her papa wanted it and she was obedient to his wishes. She had no memory of anything after the photo was taken.

"Where is Papa?"

My God, what have I done?

I could not make the girl understand what had happened to her. She became wild, beating on the walls of the Caledon chamber. I worked to calm her, pleading with her, offering myself up as her protector. The mother of the original Geli was still alive, as was Geli herself as far as I knew. I'd not even thought about such factors when I selected the photo. The family was tracked down to Bitterfeld and the duplicate was delivered to them. From a hiding place across the street, I watched the SS officers present the girl to both the original Geli and her mother. There were tears but no explanations, an all-too common scenario in Germany under Adolf's dictatorship. The girl was taken into the home. To the best of my knowledge, her mysterious existence was accepted as a miracle and a blessing.

That third experiment took place in the middle of 1942, almost a year before I saw the poster of Rosie the Riveter. I ceased my experiments on the cusp of their absolute success, unnerved now not by the results, but by the necessity of fresh bodies and the thought any life might be taken to satisfy my requirements. Even if I had the photograph of the perfect woman, the image of one I loved and desired among all people on Earth, how could I love her knowing another woman was sacrificed—*slaughtered*—to make the transference possible? And so I had submitted to the bitterness of my reality. I felt love, I emitted love like rays, but nothing was revealed to me except my own empty existence. I remembered the mocking words of *Der Wissenschaftler*—

Yet only the ten thousand and first girl will suffice you, and for some reason you wish to fabricate her out of a cloud! Why hadn't I sought the embrace of real women? What explained my cold, lonely bed except fear?

I contemplate these questions as I carry the poster to my lab. One lives in fantasy these days. We Germans have lived in fantasy since the end of World War I. The Weimar Republic was a fantasy. Life under Adolf's rule is a fantasy. Fantastical, fanatical days occupied by fantastical, fanatical science and religion. The buildings in all our cities are papered with drawings, posters from Goebbels's Propaganda ministry, sketches of soldiers on the Eastern front, Still Life with Master Race. Beautiful men, beautiful women, beautiful, determined children. Etchings. This is a cartoon existence, each of us screwed and bolted into place through pen and ink.

Rosie the Riveter.

Someone has to act. Someone has to *try* to rescue the world from this mad comic strip where lives are smudged and erased with casual brutality. The notion of doing anything for the sake of some private, romantic love pales against the greater purpose. Yes, I understand now why this American poster captivated me when I saw it a week ago and why I now hold it in my hands. I rescued it from Goebbels himself. Our interview was not lengthy. I told him I wanted the poster of the woman called Rosie the Riveter. He did not want to surrender it. Indeed, he had the poster framed and hanging on the wall like a trophy. I refrained from gnashing my teeth at this outrage and ordered it given to me in Adolf's name. For once the calm, deep confidence in Goebbels's demeanor seemed shaken. He smiled, gave a slight bow, and took it down himself.

"Shall I have it delivered to you, Eva?"

"No. I will take it myself."

"I thought you seemed particularly interested in her that night, Eva. Your face was very red."

Still smiling, he presented it to me. As I gripped the frame, though, Goebbels seized my right hand, bent and kissed it. I flinched away, taking the poster with it. The Propaganda minister looked supremely pleased.

"I shall tell Adolf of your visit," he said.

I wiped my hand on my blouse and left.

Now I am almost at my lab after taking a meandering route through Munich for fear Goebbels might have me followed. Once there, I lock myself inside. Then I dismantle the frame, freeing my Rosie. My fingertips sweep over that fine, marvelous body, imagination producing the velvety softness of her skin, the suppleness of her muscle, the moistness of her lips. My pulse accelerates. Everything I'm doing feels impulsive, like the earliest days of my experiments when I threw myself into the process without methodology or care. I curl my hands into fists, willing myself to hold onto logic and reason. This *isn't* a photograph. What am I hoping to create—a walking cartoon?

Isn't that what all of us already are?

The Caledon chamber is empty. I have no body for the transfer process. I've vowed to never have one again, not after the murder of the little girl who became Geli.

Yet I know what body I will use as I put the poster into the pewter basin, my bones suffused with all the old urges in greater intensity than I've ever known, turning my very flesh into a Tesla coil, hyper-charged with desire and impossible hopes. I throw the lever to initiate the chemical bath. The basin fills. The actual Tesla coil hums as its charge builds.

I wonder how many days the power will be out in Munich this time.

Smoke rises from the basin, collecting into the vacuum tubes.

Breathless now, covered in a sheen of sweat, I tear off my clothes. *What am I doing? How can this work?* The second lever cannot even be pulled from within the Caledon chamber. Will I be fast enough to pull it and then run inside?

The only answer is the attempt. I throw down the lever, producing an immediate explosion from the Tesla coil. I lunge into the Caledon chamber and throw myself onto the operating table. Green light floods my vision. My fingernails dig into the metal as every nerve ending in my body is torched. I'm a lobster falling into boiling water. I'm a mountaineer plunging into an active volcano. The scald is everywhere. The chamber's air grows heavy with smoke. My body refuses every command to escape. I'm going to die. Now the vacuum tubes pour the fog of transference into my mouth and nostrils, filling my lungs with it. I buck and thrash on the table as if bound at the wrists and ankles.

Slowly I sense the sure presence of something else. At first it's in the chamber with me, standing over me, hovering near me. Our naked breasts graze. We kiss, and in that kiss the presence enters me. Such strength, such determination, such *morality*. My vision becomes a prolonged blackness and I sob like a penitent, years of self-loathing rising to the surface. Why haven't I loved simply? Why have I shut myself off? I see myself as a machine, a robot. Rosie comes to me, taking apart my rivets, bending away layer upon layer of iron and steel. Then, at last, at the center of the shell she finds a human child, an infant girl. This she lifts from its cold chamber, its metal crib, and brings in strong hands toward her firm breast. I suckle there, tasting the nectar of righteousness, the milk of liberty.

I wake hours later and stumble from the Caledon chamber, groping about in the dark. I light the emergency lamps and confront a mirror. I look the same, but there's something else behind the eyes. The imprint, the transference happened on the other side. I'm Eva and I'm Rosie. The essence of the poster's image is there, the courage and grit, the feminine will to right wrongs. *Verdinglichung.* But that word does not suffice. No compound word can define the compound person I've become, flesh and cartoon, delicate paper and purest steel.

I see the depths of my former delusions. I thought I had always seen them, but now I realize my previous tears and regrets were only a surface mourning compared to the atrocities I *knew* were happening under Adolf's rule.

I do not cry. Tears are not deeds and so they mean nothing. Rosie would never cry; she would get to work.

So will I.

"Rosie," I say to the mirror, "we're going to save as many as we can."

I swear a second voice inside my head answers: *We can do it!*

Over the next few months, I organize a rescue squad known privately as the Riveters and publically as The Photography Corps. There are just a few at first, but its numbers swell to more than a hundred by November 1943. We work in the open, under the guise of archiving the Great Work at hand. Adolf and others in the upper echelon of the SS had qualms. When atrocities are being committed, it is best not to document them. But I knew how to please their egos and how to make alliances. I'd known it since my childhood trysts with *Der Wissenschaftler.* In the end, I used Goebbels himself to champion my cause. To do so, I had to go much further than simply call the little Propaganda minister *Doctor.*

The Photography Corps takes photos of the Jews in the camps by the thousands. Their expressions are always the same: haunted—*wounded.* They don't understand our purpose. The cruelty they've endured is already unimaginable, and now they must be *photographed* in their lowest hour? Many of my photographers are spat upon by their subjects and called monsters, a last act of defiance against the overwhelming injustice inflicted upon them. But the subjects understand when they are reborn in my laboratory and get a tearful reunion with the photographer who saved them.

I've been able to establish labs near Dachau, Sajmiste, Auschwitz and Chelmno. The Photography Corps work tirelessly to capture the images of as many Jews as they can, in any way they can, cataloging the plates against each person's incarceration number. A separate network labors to rescue corpses from the ovens and the mass graves. Once the bodies are spirited to one of my laboratories, I and a handful of women trained personally by me match the tattooed numbers to the plate records and perform the transfer. It is a great joy to see men, women and children who died in gas chambers come alive again in the Caledon chamber. They always ask where they are, how they got here, what has happened. Then there is the laughter of reunion.

By early 1944, time is more critical than ever. The war goes badly for Germany and Adolf wants me at his side. To leave my crucial work for even a second is odious to me. I cannot imagine successfully faking any joy in his presence. In the end, my best and favorite assistant, Ilse, suggests the obvious solution. She photographs me and transfers the image to some anonymous body. My duplicate rises from the table with perfect understanding.

"I have a job to do," she says.

I smile. "As do I."

Embracing, we say, "We can do it."

She leaves to sacrifice herself as Adolf's loyal mistress.

I turn and give Ilse the kiss I've so longed to give some illusive woman of my imagination. When she kisses me back, I feel united to her and to Rosie. Rosie. Who is she? It's the same breathless question I asked myself the first time I saw the poster. My experiments have perhaps provided the answer. She's me. She's Ilse. She's every woman's inner strength and determination. I always had the determination, but I could never find the strength she represents—until now. The war is ending; the moral work will go on. With more Rosies, the world will hang together.

And if it does, *Liebe wird die Niete sein.*

A SHALLOW GRAVE OF ORANGE PEEL AND EGGSHELLS

THORAIYA DYER

Ear-splitting thunder drew Cassandra out of the tiny laboratory into rain-beaten blackness.

She'd been stationed on the ridge overlooking the city for so long that she no longer needed the instruments to tell her what the storm was saying; it was as though her sisters whispered directly into her ear:

We are coming. The worms will be positioned within a week. They will finish crust disturbance by the end of the month. You must be off-plate by then. We will leave nothing behind.

Nothing, Cassandra thought. Not her. Especially not her.

Her feet found purchase on exposed granite. Floating anvil clouds sent lightning up into the higher strata, down into a city which blinked and flickered and sent up showers of sparks with each direct hit to the grid.

Worms. They had incorporated language into the storm. Their subtle affects on the rotation of the planet increased the rotation of the maelstrom. Hidden in the differences in wind, temperature and pressure between this storm and the one that would have occurred naturally was a communication that would not go astray and could not be intercepted; not by humans, anyway.

Only the New People could properly predict the weather, much less command the worms to alter it.

Water fell on her skin and hair. Wet clothing and wind drew heat from her body until she reached equilibrium with the storm.

Cassandra remembered Caela's hands on her, chilly from breaking icicles off the eaves at their log cabin at Red Pine Lake. There had been pleasure in the hot and cold of it. Days spent huddled together on the mountainside had been altogether pleasurable, even if Utah was not technically part of Italy.

There would be no pleasure if Caela touched her now.

I was right about you, she would say, recoiling from Cassandra's clammy, exothermic limbs. *You're not human.*

And she'd get on the waves to Tivadar right away.

She was right? What a joke. She'd never been right about anything. Not about Cassandra's suitability to work at the Department, not about her boss' fidelity. Not about there being no traces of hormones in the boiled egg she had for breakfast and not about Temple Square in Salt Lake City being bigger than the Prato della Valle.

They could have worked it out, if only Caela had been right and Cassandra had been wrong.

Instead, after everything was done, when the vidfile went public, the world would discover she was responsible. The name Caela Mulcaire would go down in history.

Everyone would know just how wrong she had been.

It wasn't the package she was expecting.

Caela fingerprinted the panel on the side of the rain-streaked delivery van and brought the half-sodden box into her clean, dry living room. The space was furnished sparsely with cube-shaped sitting-cushions. Square steel frames bore square glass tabletops.

She stripped off the fragile labels, unwrapping a framed print that showed a ladybird on a leaf. They were drawn in a technical, scientific way, showing all the anatomical features and structural detail.

There was no return address. There hadn't been one with the other things, either; the pepper grinder or the shield-bug pesticide. Both of those had turned out to be vital at unforeseen moments.

First, there was the dinner with the Director of the Department, Tivadar Risto. The pepper grinder had led the conversation away from Cassandra's sacking for an uncharacteristic blunder and instead reminded Tivadar of his tenure at the seismic station in Switzerland.

Then, the discovery of the shield-bug infestation on the Seville orange tree which was Caela's pride and joy, narrowly averted by application of the spray.

She'd been late to work and missed monitoring several minor tremors, but the tree was safe; her mother had whispered to her, once, that the bitter orange, relic of the crusades, would give the gift of a long life if taken daily upon waking.

It was possible her mother was the giver of these strange gifts. Yet for all her mystical airs, Caela's mother had no power to foretell the future. Her shop full of crystals, fossils and incense had been destroyed by fire with no building or contents insurance. She'd retreated to Mother England, whose pension was generous and whose climate remained cooler than most.

How would the print get Caela out of trouble in the future, and who was watching her closely enough to predict it?

Caela leaned the ladybird print against one of the cube-shaped cushions and brooded over it in the flickering light of the storm-struck city.

She couldn't help but haunt her ex-lover.

The very same probability processor which allowed Cassandra to communicate with weather had flagged the end of their relationship long before the reproachments had begun.

Caela wanted an empty-headed simperer to impress, a balm to her insecurity, but New People made poor actresses. It was why the war went so often in the humans' favour.

New People were innately sincere.

No New Person could pretend to aid the Department's weather monitoring efforts while their hatred for humans simmered underneath. The only solution was to give Cassandra a true desire to aid humanity while she worked for the Department, followed by a desire for revenge which would allow her then to function at the secret facility on the ridge above the city.

She sat at her computer, fingers poised, imagining Caela unwrapping the print. In five days, the hotel on Sackton Street would hold a bankruptcy sale. Caela's boss, Tivadar, would see the ladybird print while walking to work.

It had hung over the bed in the room where Tivadar had conducted an unforgettable love affair with a much older woman.

He would buy the print and take it home. The sight of it there, out of place amongst the giggling, fair-haired children and his wife's abstract pottery pieces, would strike him suddenly as abominable; he would take the print to work the next day, intending to give it to Sarah, forgetting she was away representing the Department at a corporate golf retreat.

Not wanting to take it home again, he would give it to Caela instead.

•–ww–•

You like it?" Tivadar said, relief on his face.

Caela stared at the framed print in her hands, visualising the earth turning under her, calculating the speed at which she was being flung through space. Surely that could explain the nausea she felt; it was nothing to do with her abrupt comprehension of the finality of the course of her already-plotted life.

"Amazing," she said. "Thank you, Mr Risto."

A seemingly unrelated image blossomed in her mind: Cassandra taking the back-up memory out of its casing with her left hand, lifting her cup of hot coffee in her right hand. The two objects incompatible. Memory stick and boiling, black liquid.

It was no accident they had come together. Cassandra was never wrong. She never made mistakes.

Horrified, Caela remembered the ugly expression that had crossed her own face, part shock, part triumph. She'd known in that moment that Tivadar would send Cassandra packing. But Cassandra's left hand. It hadn't been burned. That was the detail she should have noticed. Cassandra had hidden the hand, not before Caela had seen it, and it hadn't occurred to her to be suspicious of the quickness of that movement.

Until now.

Her eyes felt grainy. Lights were out everywhere except here in Tivadar's office. Dark corridors amplified sounds: The creak of the Director's chair, the tapping of his pen, raised voices in a distant stairwell.

"Goodnight, Mulcaire," Tivadar said.

"Yes, sir," Caela answered.

Tivadar's attention returned to the screens in his desk. One hand scratched the back of his neck and it sounded like a steel-toothed saw cutting across the grain.

Could Cassandra have predicted that? Caela rose unsteadily to her feet, the print clutched tightly to her chest. Could she have predicted the instant that she, Caela, would rise to her feet? Could she predict the way she took one step, then stopped, then took two quick steps and stopped again?

She felt the urge to do something crazily unpredictable. But perhaps crazy was entirely predictable in his particular situation.

Caela went home. She slept without eating. In the morning, she ate one boiled egg and one Seville orange from her tree. She took the pair of prints that had unnerved her, wrapped them in brown paper, and placed them, face-down, in a shallow grave of orange peel and eggshells.

Two objects, buried together, that looked the same but were not. One was authentic, the other malicious.

For some reason, she felt unwilling to separate them.

It was a decade since Cassandra had defied her family.

Long, rebellious looks over candlelit dinners turned to lagging at her studies, hiding poetry that should have been burned at her coming of age. It was past time for her to visit the worms, to block the blood flow to her creative brain and divert it to the underdeveloped lobe that would become her probability processor. She had accumulated enough basic knowledge for it to function.

"No," she protested. "I'm not like you."

"What are you like?" Agatha asked emotionlessly. It wasn't that she didn't have emotions, but in all probability, expressing them would not be advantageous to her argument. In that moment, Cassandra loathed her oldest sister.

"I'm like a human!"

"I think you'll find that humans beg to differ on that point."

She ran away the next morning. Crossed the Sahara on the back of a pachyderm she'd stolen from Agatha's stable. If she'd had her probability processor at that point, she would never have tried it, because she would have known how poor her chances of success were.

Because she didn't know, she reached the North African coast underweight and dehydrated but alive. She sold the family Fortune Mirror to a dealer in Oran.

They sat in a mud-walled shop with the dry wind coiling through the tunnels of the covered bazaar. Cassandra demonstrated the use of the Mirror, placing the cap over her dark curls, waiting for images of her future to appear in the dish. It didn't predict truly for humans any more than it predicted truly for a New Person who had not come of age. She paid no attention to the images of the faceless, fair-skinned woman who took her hand and ran with her across the grass of the *l'Isola Memmia*. Instead, she peered into the covetous eyes of the black market dealer and knew she could name any price.

Her family could have found her easily; the money trail from Oran to the Temple Square Gates in Salt Lake City, where her parents had died in the New People Purge, was eminently traceable. Instead, Agatha, Hana and Faiza let her go. They let her find out for herself that New People could never be accepted among Originals.

When she returned to Noynac, heartbroken, she thought the coming of age, the blood flow diversion, would dull her pain. Instead, it prepared her for revenge; revenge that belonged to her sisters long before she recognised the desire for it in herself.

Caela had been so kind at her brother's campaign launch. Caela Mulcaire, beautiful, self-assured and wealthy. She'd noticed Cassandra watching her and brought her champagne; she'd been charmed by Cassandra's accent and delighted by the revelation that she was in fact there to graffiti the brother's billboards with anti-government slogans the minute the opportunity arose.

But Caela didn't know what she was, didn't pick that her accent was New Person because although she was spokesperson against them, she'd never met one before, never worked in the field.

Caela Mulcaire had fallen in love with a human girl that didn't really exist. Cassandra had fallen, too, just as far and just as quickly. Terrified by the strength of her feelings, she'd run all the way back to Noynac.

After her visit to the worms, everything was clear and nothing was the same. She went back to Utah. Caela, relieved and made hopeful by her reappearance, gave her the job that she asked for. At first, Cassandra's increasing efficiency only ratified Caela's selection, but eventually it began to gall her. She hated not being the smartest one in the room.

And Cassandra could see it. All Caela's Original flaws; she understood them as though they were plotted on a graph. Her sisters had seen it long before she did.

In the moment she stopped loving her, she saw her for the first time as her enemy and coolly comprehended what needed to be done.

Cassandra stared at the data, elicited from the Department's deepdrives, which betrayed the presence of the worms.

With a flick of her finger, she wiped it.

Caela sat at her desk so long that even Tivadar's lights were off in the office complex by the time she stirred.

She held two sets of tickets to see the heavy metal opera, *Combat Wombats,* on the night of the twenty-third.

Her birthday.

One set had been sent by Ysanne, a fun-loving soap actress she'd met at a nightclub three months ago. The other package, presumably, was from Cassandra. The two envelopes had arrived together.

Had she mentioned to Ysanne that she liked heavy metal opera? She must have done. It had been so noisy and crowded in the club; she had been so drunk. Who knew what she'd said or done?

Cassandra knew. Not because she'd been there, but because she'd caught Caela watching 'Sex Slaves in Space' more than once. She knew that Tivadar had connections with Parsec Studios, that it was only a matter of time before Caela embarrassed herself drooling all over a barely legal teenager. Freely accessible in the public writfiles was the fact that Ysanne had turned down a hosting gig on the night of the twenty-third, hinting that she would be seeing an older woman, that she had a thing for spies and vintage cars.

Cassandra was laughing at her.

Caela put the tickets in her drawer, ignoring the thumbprint confirmation on the set from Ysanne. She stacked the notes for tomorrow's press conference on top of the desk, beside the embedded screens.

She was the public face of the Department of Human Preservation. Whenever New People tried to pass themselves off as Originals, or tried to spawn some hybrid of the two, it was Tivadar's team who went in and it was Caela who assured the frightened masses that everything was under control.

More importantly, it was the Department's job to ensure the secret war was running smoothly. They were planning a chemical attack on Noynac, one of the New Cities, that would be disguised as an industrial accident. Caela had speeches prepared in the eventuality that any or all of the truth came out.

It was sickening to think how confident she had been that everything was concealed from even those most intimate to her.

Nothing was concealed.

A package came for Cassandra.

It was unanticipated. Cassandra touched the wrapping. Hot and cold needles intersected all over her skin, an excitement she had not felt since her coming of age.

Surprise. She was supposed to be incapable of it, but here was a parcel, its contents unknown. Some categories of content were more likely, based on shape and weight, but nothing specific that her probability processor could pin down.

The return address was Caela's. She'd never been able to manage an unexpected gift while they'd been together, even before Cassandra had the blood diverted from the human-like part of her brain.

She unwrapped a novelty set of knives. There was a carving knife, cleaver and fruit knife, all housed in the body of a broken robot whose innards kept the blades sharp.

A threat.

A warning.

New People were organic, but that wasn't how the media popularly portrayed them.

Caela knew about her. Knew where she was. She could not stay. Not even another day.

Cassandra set the knives gingerly on her computer desk. The broken robot sat there while she erased everything. Once the data was ostensibly gone, she opened up the case and swiped it clean with magnets for good measure.

There was not much else in the little facility aside from the computer and the monitoring instruments. Scissors, string and brown paper, with which to wrap packages. A cup, a tin of powdered green tea, a whisk and an electric kettle. Her ultrasound machine, for communicating with the worms. By the time Caela's people differentiated it from a medical unit, it might be too late.

Might be. Cassandra's mission was not complete. At this late stage, the Department could not prevent the worms from collapsing the North American continent into the mantle, but they could evacuate, if they recognised the extent of the threat and if the rest of the world was prepared to make room for the American people.

The world would not, in all probability. They would say they would, but they would be sceptical and they would delay, and three hundred million Originals would be caught on the plate when it was Renewed.

Afterwards, there would be treaties. There would be fear and governmental surrender despite probable popular uprisings.

There would be no more prickles of hot and cold for Cassandra. No more Caela Mulcaire.

No more surprises, she thought.

She felt hollow as she packed her satchel and left the laboratory forever, locking the door behind her. She hiked along the ridge, taking care with her footing, ignoring the city below. It was a patchwork autumn.

The last autumn that this mountain would see.

•-ww-•

It was spring.

This is my last day, Cassandra thought.

Every morning, the same thought. Every morning, she looked out her second-storey window at the Prato della Valle, at the verdant, elliptical island surrounded by the black water of the canal, and she imagined the way it must have happened.

The worms would have started their work in the centre of the American continent, liquefying rock, devouring it with their mouths and defecating it into the molten mantle of the planet. As they approached the margins, with the main continental mass gone, the Pacific and the Atlantic would have knocked down the thin coastal fringe and met in the centre, forming an immense, boiling supersea.

She remembered the storms that raged while the weather systems restabilised. The frightening, endless rain. To her, the rain seemed the anguished tears of the millions of mothers whose children had died.

Cassandra had killed those children and their mothers, too.

As a New Person, she had no way of rationalising her guilt after the deed was done. Her probability processor told her she would never escape the weight of it. She would never recover.

Agatha, Hana and Faiza had already taken their own lives, willing sacrifices to the cause.

Today, Cassandra thought, will be the day I walk into the waters of the canal.

But every day, the square captivated her. Every day it called to her, so that she leaned out of her window and breathed in its beauty. There were two rings of marble statues around the rim of the canal. Their expressions puzzled her. She could not solve them.

People strolled and skated and snapped photographs.

Cassandra's eyes narrowed.

There was a woman, sitting, peeling an orange.

As she stared at the woman, the hot and cold needles made her clench and unclench her stomach. Caela Mulcaire was dead; not only had the writfiles confirmed it, but her processor confirmed the improbability of her escaping the destruction. The extrapolations that the Originals had performed on the earliest detected movements of the worms had severely underestimated the danger.

There had been no American evacuation.

Caela had saved Cassandra's life and she had not returned the favour.

She slammed the window shut and assembled a shell of acceptable clothing. In a daze, she dashed down the stairs, out the door and across the square. It was the largest square in Italy, more than twice the size of Temple Square; she had told Caela so, and she'd been right.

By the time she reached her, she stood gasping for air, her palms pressed to her solar plexus.

Caela reached up from her cross-legged position, offering Cassandra a piece of bitter Seville orange.

"It will make you live forever," she said.

"I don't want to live forever," Cassandra said when she could speak. "This day is my last on this earth."

"You're wrong. I haven't brought any police to arrest you. If I wanted you dead, I would have turned you in before."

"Before I murdered millions of Originals?"

Caela ate the orange without lowering her gaze.

"I was planning to murder your family in Noynac. I understand why you did it."

"You don't understand," Cassandra said, shaking her head, close to tears. "I did it because you didn't love me."

"I did love you. If it seemed like I didn't, it was because I couldn't love myself when I was with you. You made me feel like a child."

"You are a child," she cried. "You can never speak to the worms. You can never come of age. You are a child who can never grow up."

"No," Caela answered. "You didn't grow up, you grew stagnant. All the paths in your mind are fixed logic circuits, now. You can't imagine your future and so you're going to kill yourself."

"I know my future."

"Then why were you surprised to see me?"

Cassandra backed slowly away from her, shaking her head again. Caela stayed sitting down, simply looking at her.

How could she have been wrong? Not just about Caela's survival but this entire scenario. If she had come to Italy at all, she should have come in a rage, seeking revenge. She couldn't have understood, when she had sent her the robot-shaped knife block, what terrible deeds would come of sparing her.

"How did you know I would be here?"

"It was probable," Caela said wryly. "The way you talked about Italy made me realise it wasn't just a passing fancy. You'd been here before."

"When I was sixteen. Two years before I met you. I'd run away from home. Survived a journey that shouldn't have been survivable. I felt invincible. Thought I'd never need or want anyone else. I came here for the political rally."

"Political rally?" Caela said. She rolled something between her palms. "Like the one in Utah?"

She stepped closer; realised Caela was peeling a hardboiled egg.

"Yes," Cassandra said, frowning at the egg. "Only, the rally in Utah was for restrictions on New People. Registration. Segregation. Population controls. Here, the rally was supposed to be pro-integration."

"Supposed to be?"

"I didn't end up staying for the rally," she admitted. "A week before the protesters had organised to march, I saw a young man propose marriage to the girl who was with him. He said to her, 'I will walk on water for you.' The girl pointed to the canal, laughing. He took off his jacket and jumped in. Right there, near the statue of Andrea."

Cassandra stared at the murky water, remembering.

"I wanted to feel what he felt," she said.

"And did you?"

"Yes. I would have walked on water for you."

"When you came back, there was nothing I could do to impress you. Nothing I could say to show you that I was clever. To show you that I was able to take care of you. To show you that I was worthy of your attention. You thought everything I did was stupid. You thought everything I said was wrong."

Cassandra laughed, sadly.

"It was stupid. You were wrong. Humans aren't perfect. I can't lie, Caela."

"What about that last day on earth stuff, were you lying about that?"

"No."

In her mind, she imagined it again; the death throes of a continent. She had done it. The screams would echo in her dreams forever.

"Can't you go back to the way you were when we first met?"

"No," she said. "That part of my brain has withered. It's useless."

"That's where you're wrong. I'm going to help you get it back."

Anger welled up in her. Caela refused to listen, as always. She made impossible claims, as though confidently giving voice to probabilities generated by the inferior machine of her dull wit could somehow increase their statistical likelihood.

"You are not capable of any such thing," she said coldly.

"I have a theory," Caela continued, oblivious. "If you keep coming to the wrong conclusions, eventually your creative brain will reactivate out of sheer desperation."

"There is no data to support your theory."

"All I have to do is the unexpected."

With that, Caela leaped up, seized her wrist and began running across the grass, dragging Cassandra behind. Orange peel and eggshells spilled out of her lap and crunched under their feet.

ALRAUNE

ORRIN GREY

Alraune was not born; she grew, from a seed that was planted in the ground above the grave of the Doctor's late wife. Every day one of the Doctor's twin daughters—whose names were Flora and Fauna—would come and water the spot. It would be very poetical to say that they watered it with their tears, but they actually watered it with a special tincture that the Doctor made just for that purpose. What precisely the tincture consisted of neither of them knew, but Fauna once found a book open in her father's study with the following passage underlined: *"Bury it at night in some country churchyard in a dead man's grave. For thirty days water it with cow's milk in which three bats have been drowned."*

At first, Alraune grew like any common plant, but seemed to change with the phases of the moon; from a seed to a sprout, from a sprout to a bud, from a bud to a flower.

Her flower was the azure blue of a cloudless summer sky, but it bloomed only at night, drinking up the light of the moon. The girls could see it from their bedroom window, like another moon lying on the ground beneath the holly tree.

For a month it bloomed every night, and every night it seemed to grow larger. First it was the size of a saucer, then the size of a dinner plate, until, finally, it was the size of their dinner *table*. Then, on the night of the new moon, it closed up again and the next night it didn't open.

Every night after that the petals curled tighter and tighter together like a moth's chrysalis and slowly drained of color, turning from bright blue to a pale, lettuce green. When Fauna worked up the nerve to put a tingling palm against the bud she said it felt like water rushing through pipes beneath her hand.

When the bud opened again, twenty-eight days and nights later, the Doctor was waiting. Inside the bud was a girl, not much older, by appearances, than the twins themselves: Alraune.

Her skin was moon-pale and tinged with green and her hair, which fell long past her waist, was the same rich blue as her flower had been. She was naked, curled up with her arms across her chest and her knees tucked up to her elbows. Her eyes, when she opened them, were dark and liquid and shy as a faun's.

The Doctor covered her with a blanket and led her inside, to his study. Fauna followed, but Flora lagged behind to watch the remains of Alraune's flower wither and turn gray and finally vanish back into the dirt of her mother's grave.

The Doctor's study was filled with old, mummy-smelling books; mortars, pestles, and alembics; insects pinned to boards and bones in glass boxes and frogs and spiders in bell jars. In a tall glass tube he kept strange, translucent creatures like swimming mushrooms that he called "jellyfish."

Above the door to his study a stone was worked into the wall. It was a piece taken from a tomb, something he had installed after his wife's death and before he planted Alraune. On it was a carving; a skull with vines growing up through the sockets.

Flora and Fauna weren't allowed into their father's study, though they peeked in sometimes, and Fauna had snuck in more than once to look at the strange things there and page through his strange books. When he escorted Alraune in, though, he didn't leave the door open even a crack. He shut it and locked it and threw the bolt. When Flora came in, Fauna was standing by the door, eavesdropping as they sometimes did, but as Flora approached she shook her head, indicating that there was nothing worth hearing, and they both went to the parlor where they sat picking at embroidery or pretending to read while talking in whispers about what they thought was going on.

It was Flora who finally said, "She didn't look much like mother."

"We never saw mother when she was that young," Fauna replied, and Flora heard something sharp and warning in her voice.

It was true, but Flora knew that their mother had never looked like Alraune. She'd looked more like them; small and thin, freckled and boyish and pale of hair and eye.

Alraune came to live with them after that night. She took over duties that had once belonged to Flora and Fauna, the duties of the woman of the house, cooking and cleaning and sweeping the floors. But she had to be watched, or she would drift off and just stand, staring at nothing, like she was listening to a song that nobody else could hear, and then the roast would burn or the chickens would get into the house.

She hardly ever spoke unless someone asked her a question, but she watched everything with an avid, wide-eyed fascination, like a child or a baby kitten.

She smelled just like a flower, and wherever she lingered night-blooming flowers grew. Soon the whole house was wreathed in jasmine and moonflower and evening primrose. Alraune cared for all growing things with the diligence of a mother, sang to them and spoke softly to them words that Flora tried to hear but couldn't understand.

More than anything else, though, Alraune loved the moon. She had been a night-blooming flower herself, and now she was a night-blooming girl. When the moon was especially big and bright she would sometimes shuck her nightgowns and go outside to stand naked in the yard, drinking in the moonlight as she once had when she was still a flower.

When she did that, it was always someone's job to go out and collect her. Usually the Doctor did it, but sometimes he was already asleep or busy in his study and so the task fell to Flora or Fauna, the former apologetically, the latter angrily.

Alraune had her own room, with her own bed. At first this had seemed to please Fauna, but it didn't take long before they both knew that their father visited Alraune at night. The house was old, and big, and full of creaks and groans, but it was theirs, and they knew it well, knew which creaks and groans belonged to it and which ones didn't.

It wasn't long before Fauna began behaving cruelly toward Alraune. She'd bring her to task viciously for the tiniest mistakes, and whenever she did, Alraune would drop her eyes, and then immediately look up again from under lowered lashes. When Fauna noticed, it gave her another thing to berate Alraune for, but Flora knew that she wasn't doing it to be impish; she just wanted to see *everything*, even the vicious smirk on Fauna's face when she was being chastised.

Fauna never spoke aloud the reason for her dislike of Alraune, though she made the dislike itself obvious enough. And the Doctor, for his part, never did anything to discourage it. When Fauna was cruel or disdainful toward Alraune, he would simply turn away.

The Doctor himself hardly spoke to Alraune during the day, just as he had hardly spoken to his daughters before, just as he had hardly spoken to his wife when she was alive. She was, when not being actively baited or reviled by Fauna, left to her own quiet, secret life.

One night, Flora awoke with a brilliant square of moonlight shining directly onto her pillow. Outside, the moon was a disc of blue-silver in the sky, and Alraune stood bathing in it, her arms held above her body, her head craned back, eyes closed. She looked, Flora thought, like she had just eaten the most delicious dessert in the world.

Flora glanced over at the other bed, where her sister still slept. In times past, she would have woken Fauna before going out. They had always been necessarily inseparable, and Flora had always been the timid one. But Fauna's casual cruelties toward Alraune bothered her, and that night she pulled on her robes and tiptoed from the room alone.

Outside the night was cool, the grass moist with dew. "Une," Flora whispered as she approached the other girl. She was the only one who ever used the pet name. "Une, we need to go inside."

But Alraune didn't respond. She didn't even seem to hear.

There was something in Flora's breast that told her to hurry and get back inside before someone else woke up. It was the same fluttering something that always made her silent when her sister spoke, that always held her back at the doorway when her sister snuck into their father's study. But that night Flora forced it down, and instead stood in the moonlight and watched Alraune.

She was, Flora decided right then, perfect. Everything that Flora wanted to be. Her body, in the moonlight, was like the marble statues that she'd seen outside the churches when the Doctor took her and Fauna to the city.

The thing that fascinated Flora most, though, was the small, satisfied smile on Alraune's face. Flora was quite sure that she had *never* smiled like that.

Flora felt like she could stand there and watch Alraune until the sun rose, but finally her nervousness won out and she laid a hand on Alraune's shoulder, saying her name again.

Just like that, the trance was broken. Alraune's eyelids opened like shutters on windows, and her arms descended and draped around Flora's shoulders. There was a moment of lurching terror, as though she had just stepped off a cliff in the dark, and then she felt Alraune's lips pressed against hers.

The first thing she noticed, even before her shock could register, was the way that Alraune's lips and skin felt exactly like flower petals.

She couldn't return the kiss—she was too startled—but she was surprised to find herself wanting to. When their lips parted a quiet, pleading sound passed between them like a breath, and Flora wasn't sure which one of them had uttered it.

They led each other to the barn, each one moving as if this had been her plan all along. In the doorway they fell back into one another's embrace, and this time Flora returned the kiss and gave more kisses of her own. She felt drunk on Alraune's scent, and on the moonlight, and wondered if this was how Alraune felt when she stood naked in its glow.

When, a few hours before dawn, she crawled back into her own bed and lay there smelling of hay and flowers, she smiled for the first time the way that Alraune had smiled. The next morning there was a patch of evening primrose sprouting in the dooryard of the barn.

Flora found herself drawing farther away from Fauna as time went on, and closer to Alraune. She would probably have drawn farther from the Doctor, as well, had she ever been close to him in the first place.

Meals in the house became strained affairs when they were taken together, full of silences and glares and words that hung unspoken. Theirs had never been a house of noise or laughter, but it seemed to Flora that it was growing quieter and darker with every passing day.

Fauna spent more and more of her time in the Doctor's study, poring through books on tinctures and poisons, and she often sent Flora out into the woods to look for painstakingly described herbs and fungi. Once, Flora found her sister dissecting a frog out behind the barn, and she shuddered, wondering what it was that Fauna was trying to learn.

Then Alraune suddenly became ill. She grew even paler, her eyes became fever bright and her blue hair began to turn white and curl up at the tips. The skin on her hands and feet pruned and wrinkled, as if she'd been holding them underwater for too long. This passed for a day or two, and when asked Alraune said that she didn't know what was wrong, and apologized.

On the third day, Alraune collapsed at dinner, slumping first to the table and then to the floor. The Doctor scooped her up, pulled open an eyelid and inspected closely what was beneath. Flora saw him cast a dark, unreadable look at Fauna, and then carry Alraune into his study and throw the bolt. Fauna didn't wait outside and eavesdrop this time, but stomped up the stairs more loudly than usual and slammed the door to their room. Flora, uncertain what else to do, busied herself with putting away dinner.

The next morning Alraune was better, and the Doctor sent Flora into town for bread, though it should have been Fauna's turn, and told her to take Alraune with her, that the fresh air would do her good. Usually Alraune wasn't permitted to go out, but that day Flora helped her coil her hair up under a wrap and dress her in her least revealing clothes. If asked, she was instructed to say that she'd simply been ill, which was not, after all, an untruth.

Normally Flora liked going into town. She liked to look in the shop windows, liked the smells of the bakery and the little pieces of bread that Mr. Fischer sometimes left out on a tray for people to sample. But that day she was distracted, and not even Alraune's presence could lift her spirits.

"What is it?" Alraune asked as they walked. She still didn't talk much, not even to Flora, but she was observant.

Flora shook her head. Something was wrong, had been wrong for weeks, or months. Something in the air, like the metallic taste that comes just before a storm.

"I'm sorry," Alraune said. "Sorry if it's my fault."

Flora stopped and forced herself to smile, tucking one of Alraune's long blue hairs back up under the wrap.

"It's not your fault," she said. She wasn't sure it was exactly true, but she wanted it to be, and she thought that there should be a difference between being the cause of something and that thing being your fault.

They weren't quite halfway to town when the rain began, so they ran back home out of consideration for Flora and for their clothes, because Alraune, like any plant, loved the rain. When they got there, though, Flora drew up short just inside the door, putting a hand back to stop Alraune.

From upstairs she heard raised voices, and then a terrible, sharp sound like the crack of a taskmaster's whip. Somehow, though, she knew not to run upstairs. She waited until she heard the thudding of her sister's feet on the floor above, and then the slam of their bedroom door, followed by the slow tread of the Doctor and the sound of the bolt being thrown in his study.

In times past she would have gone to her sister and comforted her. In times past the argument, whatever it was, might never have happened at all. Now she stood and stared sadly up at the ceiling until Alraune tugged on her hand and pulled her out to the barn where she held her until the tears came.

Every other time that they had been together, Flora had been careful not to sleep. She was careful to make it to her own bed before dawn and the rising of the house. That day, though, she dozed in Alraune's arms.

Alraune herself didn't sleep, merely drifted off as she did in the middle of her chores if there was no one there to watch her.

There would have been no moon that night, even if the clouds hadn't blotted it out. The sky was like ink spilled across a desk, the clouds deep black pools that gave forth forks of lightning and sudden, sharp cracks of thunder. The afternoon's rain became a constant, pouring storm that shook the windows through the night.

Somewhere in the darkness Flora woke, and found herself still wrapped in Alraune's embrace. Their clothes were still damp, and smelled faintly like bread before it rises. So they stripped them off and then fell back together, touching and moving against each other. In the dark Flora knew that she should go back to her own bed, but somehow she couldn't. Not that night. The storm was outside, and it hid the changing colors of the sky, and Alraune felt so good and safe and everything smelled of hay and flowers and their two bodies, and so once again, wrapped in the arms of her lover, she slept.

The sound of a glass bottle shattering on the loft's wooden floor was what snapped Flora from sleep, and Alraune from her dreamy drifting. Both had a moment—just a brief moment—of pleasure at awakening to find themselves still in the other's company before realization of the light that came in through the window, and the sound that had woken them, brought that sharply to a halt.

Flora turned and saw Fauna standing at the entrance to their secret nest, milk and glass forming a puddle at her feet. She started to stammer something, but she didn't know what she would have said and she never got the chance to say it anyway before Fauna was gone.

"I'm sorry," Alraune said as Flora gathered up her nightclothes and hurriedly dressed. Flora didn't look at her, though. She didn't trust herself to.

She didn't know what she expected when she got back into the house; condemnations, perhaps, accusations, but at first it seemed like nothing had changed. The Doctor was locked in his study, as usual, and the house was silent.

Feeling like a ghost, she drifted upstairs to the door of the room she'd shared with Fauna. There she froze, her hand partway to the knob, and instead pressed her ear against the door. Silence, on the other side. No, not quite silence. She could hear Fauna crying, hitching little sobs that she was obviously trying to choke down. Flora hadn't seen Fauna cry since they were little girls, when the Doctor had caught them in his study and sent them to bed without dinner. It had sounded the same then, though, more angry than it was sad. Flora tried the doorknob, but the door was locked.

She walked to Alraune's room and looked inside, but it was empty, the bed still made. Since she didn't know where else to go she went back downstairs. She wanted to knock on their door, to ask Fauna to forgive her, to let her explain, but she didn't know how to form the words. In her heart, she didn't feel like she'd done anything that needed forgiving, that needed explaining, though that somehow didn't make her feel any less bad.

Without knowing where she was going, she found herself back in front of the door to the Doctor's study. She pressed herself against the door to listen, as Fauna had done so often, but there was nothing on the other side to hear. Instead, she was surprised as the door swung quietly open under her touch.

The room beyond was exactly as she remembered it from the few times she'd been allowed to see inside. The books and bones and things in jars, in the same organized clutter they had always occupied. The Doctor sat slumped over the desk.

Flora had never set foot beyond the threshold of the door, but that day she did, making some half-articulate sound that was almost a word to let the Doctor know of her presence. He didn't move, and somehow, even before she reached him, she knew that he wouldn't move again. She touched his shoulder, pulled his head back, and saw that he was already dead, his skin waxy blue, his eyes bulging.

If Flora had tried to imagine what she would do or think or feel in that situation, she would have probably imagined a hundred things. A scream bubbling from her lips; a sick, sad feeling of exuberance, perhaps. She would never have guessed the blind, black terror that would engulf her so that she thought, for a moment, that she would faint. Later, she didn't even remember running, but that's exactly what she did; away from the house and its mad, gruesome contents, and without looking back.

The Doctor's body was found the next morning. The cause of death was found to be poisoning by the root of the mandragora.

They blamed Alraune for the crime, with Fauna's testimony as the chief evidence against her. Not that much evidence was needed. Her nature was obvious—and abhorrent—to the townspeople.

They hanged her from the holly tree without a trial, but her neck refused to break and she didn't choke. They let her hang there for two days, and then they cut her down and put her in a box and put her alive into the ground.

The night after Alraune was buried was the night of the new moon. It was spectacularly dark, and so no one saw the small figure who slipped in and dug up the fresh grave. The next morning the box that Alraune had been buried in was found empty, and night-blooming jasmine had grown all over and through it.

Fauna lived out the rest of her life in the town. She inherited the Doctor's house and married a barrister, who eventually left her when she proved to be barren. He took all their money when he went, and she died in the poorhouse.

Neither Alraune nor Flora were ever heard from again.

PRESERVING THE INTEGRITY OF THE FEMININE MYSTIQUE

CHRISTINE MORGAN

Miss Lavinia Wilmott called on her cousin at his stylish metropolitan flat unannounced and an appalling hour of the morning. She accepted his automatonic valet's offer of refreshment whilst she waited for Reggie to clear himself of the fog of the previous evening's revelries. He tottered in, yawning and rumpled, a few moments later. She was fond of her cousin; he was an affable enough fellow, possessing all of the Wilmott gangliness yet without any trace of the family ambition. They settled the greetings, cordialities, and prelims, and then she put the purpose of her visit before him: "I never thought I'd be saying this," Lavinia said, stirring her cup, "but I need a man."

Reggie blinked, more than a little nonplussed. "Bit of a departure for you, isn't it, Vinnie, old bean? Still," he went on, "glad to rally 'round. Looking for introductions? I know plenty of chaps from the Westfallon Club who'd be—"

"I was more thinking of you," she cut in.

At that, he blinked several times more. "Oh, now, I do say...flattered though I am, of course, and all...well, we *are* cousins—"

"Don't be a dolt, Reggie."

"Rather can't help it," he said. "Afraid you've stunned me to the marrow."

"Well, compose yourself." Vinnie sipped the caffeinated revivifying, which was strong and perfectly brewed, sweetened to the precise degree she favored.

He scrubbed the heels of his hands up the sides of his face and dove into the breakfast plate Brassworth set before him.

She glanced approvingly around the flat. It was pin-neat with all the mod cons and a lush view of the park. Far nicer than the abode where she stashed the parasol and hung the bonnet when the day was done. Not, of course, that Vinnie herself was in any position to throw the proverbial stones when it came to nuts, as it were. Glass houses and whatnot, don't you know. By the standards and to the despair of her immediate parents and sibs, she was very much the cuckoo's egg in the henhouse, though it had nothing to do with her personal life or matters pertaining thereto.

They ran Ashfields, a respectable but struggling chain of department stores begun by Lavinia's maternal great-grandfather. The Ashfields code touted tradition, old-fashioned service and value over newfangled consumerism. Ironically, Lavinia had neither interest in nor a head for such business...and when it came to the newfangled, well, of that she embraced with élan. Thankfully, sufficient brothers, sisters and assorted in-laws of a responsible stripe were more than willing to do their part, so her eccentricities were indulged within reason. Books, tutors, a university education and so on.

While it was assumed that she would mature and abandon frivolity, she survived on a pittance of an allowance that permitted a workshop and cluttered little apartment above. If she couldn't afford a cook or housekeeper, she got by... and if in dire need of a decent meal, she could always catch the crosstown steam-trolley to impose on Cousin Reginald.

Who had, meanwhile, downed a few gulps of the steamed black fortifying from his own cup and gotten on the outside of half a plate of scrambled with ham. He swept crumbs from his lips and looked at her, rather more lucid-eyed.

"Now," he said. "What's all this then? What's this about, you needing a man? Since you obviously can't mean for the...ah...typical...how does that even work, by the way?"

She elevated a stern eyebrow. "Reggie."

"Indeed. Sorry. Quite." He cleared his throat. "So, then. How could I, of all people, possibly be of assistance?"

"I need you to come down to Huntleyshire this week-end," she said.

"Way out there in the country? That far from the bustling metrop?"

"Yes."

"Health and fresh air? Exercise?" He looked positively afright.

"You don't have to exercise."

"Ah, but it's inevitable. With not much else to do, it's only a matter of time, isn't it, before someone suggests a nice stroll, or boating, or a ride. When I say ride, it's always horses, or bicycles, never a velocipede or motored scooter, now, is it?"

"There'll be lots to do. The Four-Counties Science Fair and Exposition is being held there on Saturday."

"And that's a plus? Eggheads and inventors trying to blow things up?"

"With substantial monetary awards, and a tenured professorship at Huntley College on the line," she said, taking no offense.

"Eggheads and inventors trying to blow things up for prizes, then."

"You mustn't bring Brassworth, though," Vinnie added as Reggie's valet glided in with a hot carafe. "He'd outshine all the other exhibits. No offense, Brassworth."

"None taken, Miss Wilmott," Brassworth replied, the polished metal mask of his face as impassive as ever. "More coffee?"

"Please." As the automaton poured and added sugar, she returned her attention to her cousin. "Some of the greatest minds of the age will be attending."

"All the less reason to have *me* bunging about the place," Reggie said. "Isn't that Chapman bloke supposed to be there? The absent-minded recluse? Presenting that new what's-it of his, the...what was it again?"

"Etheric Dynamo, sir."

"Yes, that. Knew it was something to do with dynamos." Frowning, Reggie looked down at his plate as if it were an escape route from the conversation. "Do we have any of that sweet-orange marmalade left, Brassworth?

"I'll bring it at once, Mr. Wilmott, sir," Brassworth said, heading back to the flat's kitchen.

"I've entered the judging under a false name," Vinnie said.

Reggie had been buttering a scone and paused now mid-butter. His gaze took in her earnest expression. His jaw did not drop, *per se*, but it did make something of a slow descent toward the collarbones. "Oh, you didn't."

She twisted her napkin into a frustrated linen rope. "I *had* to. You have no idea how difficult it is for a woman to be taken seriously in this new age—"

"Hardly seems cricket." Reggie set down scone and butterknife, then held up both hands palms-outward. "Furthermore, I suspect what you are asking of me. And the answer is a decisive no."

"But, Reggie!"

"Firmly in the negative. For one, I've met old Lord Huntley, and, to put it mildly, he's not a fan. What if he recognized me, going under your pseudonym?"

"But—"

"For another, even if he didn't recognize me straightaway, well, you can't possibly expect *me* to impersonate a genius inventor."

"Not at all. I expect you to impersonate, if that, a wastrel layabout."

He blinked yet again, relaxed, and beamed an amiable grin. "Well, then, *rather*. In that case, you've come to the right chappie." Picking up scone and knife, he resumed a thorough buttering. "What about old Huntley, though? Won't it croggle your scheme if he knows who I am?"

"Do you know his daughter?"

"Josephine? I should say. Was in love with her once...for about twenty minutes."

"Were you?"

"Oh yes. Probably would have popped the question in another hour or so, but she was already engaged to Donald Milkins, and I'd come to my senses by the time she gave Milkins the big heave-ho."

"Then all the more reason for you to come."

"But I haven't seen hide nor hair of the girl in months."

"That doesn't matter."

"And her father thinks I should be put in a home for the terminally dilettante," he said, crumbs falling from his mouth.

"Better and better."

"Besides, isn't she tying the matrimonial noose around some other poor sap's neck soon? I'm sure I saw it in the society pages. Franklin somebody, wasn't it? Or was it somebody Franklin? Or Francis?"

"Never mind any of that," Vinnie said. She'd no sooner begun to make the motions of standing than Brassworth was there, smooth and unctuous and utterly professional, to draw back her chair. "You just be on the ten o'clock to Huntleyshire on Friday. I'll meet you at the station in the village."

"Hang on; I haven't agreed to this."

"You said you were glad to rally 'round and be of assistance."

"I also said I wasn't about to impersonate anyone, imaginary or otherwise."

"Which I'm not asking, am I?"

"Well ..."

"You *will* be there," she said. "You'll help me, I know you will."

"With what, exactly?"

"I'll explain later."

"And what if I don't turn up?" Reggie belatedly scrambled to his feet, seeming only now to notice she'd risen.

"You'd never leave me in the lurch like that."

"I might. This entire conversation's given me an uneasy feeling in the pit of my stomach."

She pursed her lips. "Or perhaps you're just hung-over."

He affected a wounded puppy-dog's pout. "Ouch, cuz. To the quick."

"I hate to have to do this, but if you won't help me, I'll not hesitate at taking drastic measures."

At that, he gave her an apprehensive look.

"You do remember Tom Terper, don't you?" she asked.

"Terper the Burper? That fat little git who used to follow us around those summers at the lake? Good heavens. What a pest. Last I'd heard, he married that ghastly American and moved off to Nebraska or some such territory. But what's he got to do with anything?"

"He and that ghastly American have two sets of twin boys now," Vinnie said. "He's bringing the whole lot of them over for a visit. Naturally, if he had your address, I'm sure he'd love to look you up."

His eyes widened and his face paled. "You wouldn't."

"After all, I know how you do adore children."

"Podgy brats with sticky fingers and screeching voices?"

"You could show them the sights of the city. Make a day of it. Have them in for lunch. Why, I expect they'd gladly stay with you, save the cost of a hotel."

Reggie shook a finger at her. "That is a low and devious threat, cousin of mine."

Vinnie spread her hands and shrugged. "But, if you weren't going to be at home next week, there'd be no point my even mentioning it, would there?"

"The ten o'clock to Huntleyshire, you say? This Friday?"

"You *are* a treasure. I knew I could count on you."

"Right-oh," he said, and heaved a sigh.

Simultaneous preparation for the Four-Counties Scientific Fair and Exposition and the impending nuptials of Josephine Huntley to Mr Stanley Alvin—or was it Lord Clifton's son, Herbert?—had Huntleyshire in a tizzy, the big house and the village alike.

With so much to be done, on such a schedule, the juggling of logistics made for a precarious, teetering state of affairs. A single hitch, delay or setback in any department could bring the whole works crashing down.

At the fair-grounds, there were exhibit halls to be set up, refreshment tents, vendor's stalls, display booths, rides and games and crafts for the kiddies. There were programs to be printed, arrangements made for the judges, ribbons, certificates, prizes. There was wiring to be tested for the electric and telephonic, piping for steam and hydraulic and thermodynamic. Deliveries arrived requiring special handling, refrigerated storage, security. Volunteers had to be organized.

As for the wedding, it was a matter of cakes, caterers, crises and confusion. The dressmaker and the florist nearly came to blows over color schemes. The ring-bearer caught measles, breaking out in itchy polka-dots. Not one but *two* socially important names had somehow been left off the guest list, the lapse not noticed until almost too late. Slipshod repairs to the church roof shingles, discovered during a brief rain, prompted fears of a leak.

Last-minute messages flooded in for both events - requests, demands, panicked emergencies. Such-and-such refused to be situated near so-and-so, special accommodations *must* be made for this or that, if X wasn't taken care of right this very instant or Y couldn't be managed to the smallest detail, it'd all fall to utter ruin.

Nearly everyone was frazzled to a fare-thee-well. Rumor had it that both Lord Huntley and his brother, the dean of Huntley College, were to the point of tearing out their own hair. Only bride-to-be Josephine, daughter of one and niece of the other, maintained a serene aplomb.

Hers was a peach sorbet kind of beauty, cool and sweet and refreshing. It was no wonder she had won the hearts of so many admirers, nor been engaged so often that her own father could no longer keep track of which suitor she'd settled upon. Regarding some, the old lord had withheld his consent on grounds of money or prospects, family or respectability. Others had failed to hold Josephine's interest, or found out the hard way that peach sorbet could turn to lemon ice without warning.

She met Lavinia and Reggie at the carriage-yard gate when they pulled up Friday afternoon, looking more peach-sorbet than ever in a light summery tea-dress of airy layers that fluttered becomingly at sleeves and hem. A wide-brimmed straw hat adorned with ribbons perched at a jaunty angle atop her coiffed curls, shading her dimpled cheeks.

The motor chugged to a rest with one final gusty exhalation of steam. Vinnie, having borrowed one of the horselesses to fetch Reggie from the station, plucked off her driving goggles and untied her head-scarf. Reggie, for his part, pushed the goggles up onto his brow, sprang from the passenger seat, doffed his cap, and bowed with exaggerated formality.

"Hullo, hullo, hullo," he said. "Josephine Huntley, as I live and breathe. You look well."

"Dearest Reggie! So good of you to come." Smiling a gracious perfect-pearl smile, she swept over to clasp his hands and put air-kisses by the corners of his mouth.

"I understand congratulations are in order. Got you the requisite fondue pot, but it's been held up at the engravers, so, might be a day or two late."

"Psssh." Josephine gestured a wave as airy as her frock. "No trouble with the horseless, Vinnie?"

"It hiccuped a bit on the hill," Vinnie said, patting her hair into place as she climbed down, "but, other than that, no, no trouble at all."

"Oh, good." Josephine pressed her hand with great affection. They exchanged a private glance, brief but very warm.

"Quite the double production you've got going on around here," Reggie said, rocking on his heels as he inspected the surroundings. "Vin brought us around the long way past the fair-grounds, and I saw the servants setting up a pavilion out in the garden. For the reception, I take it?"

"Yes, a champagne buffet, I thought. I'll have someone bring in your bags. Let's go in. You must be thirsty."

"When am I not?"

Josephine laughed gaily, folding one arm through Reggie's and the other through Vinnie's to lead them up to the house. "I do hope you find your room suitable," she said. "We're packed to the rafters with relatives and guests, but I did what I could. You're just down the hall from Vin."

"We Wilmotts can rough it when necessary," he assured her.

"He once," Vinnie said in a confidential tone, "went transcontinental in a shared-occupancy Pullman rather than a private."

"With the bath at the end of the car, rather than *en suite*?" asked Josephine, miming great shock.

"I know," said Vinnie, wide-eyed. "Rooming with, might I add, a complete stranger."

"Reggie, you poor thing. How ever did you endure?"

He puffed out his chest. "Like I said, we Wilmotts can rough it. We're made of strong stuff, don't you know."

"So I gather."

"Tell me, though," Reggie said, "because Vinnie here won't spill the beans, who's the condemned? I mean, the lost soul? I mean, the lucky bridegroom?"

"Same old Reggie, haven't changed in the least, have you?"

"Despite the best efforts of many to improve or make something of me. So, who is it? Stanners? Herbie Clifton? Old Donny Milkins? Anybody I know?"

Josephine made with the airy wave again. "We'll see who turns up."

"I say, that's rather on the *lassez-faire* side for a girl's big day, isn't it?"

"You know how it is with weddings," Vinnie said. "As long as everything else is absolutely perfect to the bride's exact specifications, from the dress and bouquet to the cake and the band, the rest is practically interchangeable."

"And everything else *is* absolutely perfect to the bride's exact specifications," Josephine said. "Well, except for little Brucie coming down with the spots, but I hadn't really wanted him as ring-bearer anyway. I'd only agreed to placate Great-Aunt Ida. Now, with him out of the way, I can go back to my original plan."

"Which is?" asked Reggie, sounding braced for the worst.

"Buttercup, my dog."

"Your dog?"

"I'll fix the ring pillow to her collar."

"Hmm," he said, and opted with conversational suavity to change the subject. "So, how long have you two known each other? I had no idea you'd become such close chums."

"Oh, quite a while now," said Josephine. "We met at a seminar hosted by the Delaney Institute."

"That womens' hospital?"

"Feminine Wellness and Well-Being," Vinnie said. "It was a seminar on—"

He raised a hand. "Say no more. *Please*, cuz, for pity's sake, say no more."

"Men." Josephine rolled her eyes at Vinnie. "They can be *so* squeamish, can't they?"

"Squeamish? No, no-no-no! Just...preserving the integrity of the feminine mystique, hey-what?"

They'd reached the house by then, parted ways long enough to freshen up and sponge off the road-dust, then regrouped in the east salon where French doors overlooked a terrace with trellises and dainty climbing roses. Reggie lit up like a cinema marquee when he saw the well-stocked bar fitted with a multi-setting ice dispensary, a gazogene for making carbonated fizzes, racks of colored syrups in different flavors, and shelves aglitter with bottles of all the finest in sustaining elixirs. He fell to with an enthusiasm that wouldn't have been misplaced in a budding young genius given his first chemistry set, mixing up cocktails made-to-order for the three of them.

"Right, so," he said, once they had sipped to their satisfaction. "Here I am... so, why *am* I here?"

Barometrical predictions held true despite grim predictions of rain, gloom and doom over pints in the village pub the night before. It was an indicator of the inevitable triumph of science over superstition, something also lost on those who'd been downing the pints and making the predictions.

The sun rose bright as a new-minted coin in a brisk blue sky, with just enough breeze and occasional drifting of cumulonimbal formations as to counter any excess of heat. Light dappled on the lake, meadow grass and leafy boughs swayed, birds chirped, the scene was as picturesque as any photo-imagist could have hoped, and on first look, all was right with the world.

"Welcome," said the Dean of Huntley College to the assembled crowd, a megaphonic nicely amplifying his stentorian lecture-hall voice. "Welcome to the Four-Counties Scientific Fair and Exposition!"

Cheers arose. Many of a rather restrained tenor, of course, as these were, after all and for the most part, learned men and women of education and reserve ... or those aspiring to be. The more raucous whooping and waving of arms was left to the youthful exuberants, schoolboys, and those simple country folk who knew only that this meant a rare entertainment.

"I should like to take this moment," the dean went on, "to offer praise and thanks to the man whose generosity has made this event possible...my own good brother, Lord Archibald Huntley!"

Applause and more cheers greeted this, albeit somewhat dutiful. Lord Huntley, standing near the podium, inclined his head. His smile looked not a little frayed around the edges, the tension of the previous weeks of preparation having taken their toll.

When, at dinner, he'd been presented with his latest houseguest, a furrow of concern—"Wilmott? Reginald Wilmott? I remember you; what in the world are *you* doing here?"—had shortly given way to a look akin to that of an ox struck amidship the eye sockets with a ball-peen hammer. This, of course, had been due to his daughter's giggling reply.

"Oh, Daddy," Josephine had said, in a such-a-kidder-you-are tone. "Surely you can't have forgotten that Reggie and I are engaged."

Reggie jumped in his chair. "I say now—"

Lavinia kicked his ankle under the table, shooting him a look. When he'd asked why he was here, Josephine had most artfully demurred, changing the subject to racing yachts, and said subject never had gotten changed back.

The stricken Lord Huntley noticed none of this. He gaped, goggle-eyed, at his precious daughter. "Engaged? To *him*?"

"Well, of course. Who else?"

"But I thought...but, Josephine, my lamb...I thought you were engaged to Clarence Stoddard."

At that, she'd put on a hurt expression. "That was *weeks* ago. Honestly, don't you pay *any* attention to my life?"

And so on, issuing tears to be dabbed at with the handkerchief, until the lord had been falling all over himself in bumbling apologies, which failed to mollify Josephine's dramatics.

"I suppose, next, you'll have forgotten that I'm to be *married* in a few days," she'd wailed, and had to rush from the dining room to compose herself.

"I haven't forgotten," he called after her, then looked around the table at the other guests, most of whom were in attendance for that very reason. "I haven't."

"There, there, old man," Reggie had said, rising gamely to the occasion of the ruse despite his dearth of detail in understanding. "Girls, don't you know. They can get emotional. Especially when weddings are involved. Turns the best of them high-strung, I shouldn't wonder."

"To *you*?" He bleated the words, turning the goggle-eyed gape upon Reggie. "She agreed to marry *you*?"

Gulping, Reggie managed a weak but daffy grin. "Bit of a surprise to me, too, but, cheerio, there you are and what can you do?"

•~~•

A day later, Lord Huntley, still, clearly, had not fully recovered from the news. He now raised a beatific but shaky hand to the crowd. "Thank you, one and all, thank you," he said.

The dutiful applause trailed off, prompting Dean Huntley to carry on with the opening ceremonies. He introduced the judges and other dignitaries of the scientific community, the main sponsors, and the key participants.

"It is with particular pleasure," he said, "that I'm honored to announce our guest speaker, that most distinguished, if elusive—" here, a general knowing chuckle arose from the assembly, "innovators, forward-thinkers, and geniuses of our time...Mr. Clive Chapman."

Now the applause was louder, and eager. Heads turned this way and that. Necks craned. People stretched on tip-toe to peer over their neighbors. An abashed courier-boy scurried onto the stage, spoke in rushed whispers, and handed over a telegram.

Dean Huntley took it as well as might be expected, under the circs. In a slightly pained manner, he folded the missive, tucked it away in his pocket, and addressed them again.

"Elusive, didn't I just say? As it happens, Mr. Chapman has been unavoidably detained—"

A collective moan of disappointment went up. The dean managed to quell it.

"—but assures us he *will* be arriving as soon as humanly possible and apologizes profusely for the delay. In the meanwhile, he has requested that we carry on without him, including the exhibit of his Etheric Dynamo."

The crowd remained let-down. Still, what choice had they then but to stiff-upper-lip and move on? This, they did, though not without some further sighs and mutterings.

"Now, without further ado," Dean Huntley said at last, "I declare this Fair and Exposition underway!"

With the most rousing cheer yet, the crowd commenced filing through the token little wooden fence-gate that had barred the lane between the rows of halls, stalls and tents.

Lavinia, moving with the tidal current, overheard several comments on the subject of the elusive Clive Chapman...smug remarks from those who claimed to be on quite close personal terms with the man...anecdotes about chance encounters at restaurants or on trains...a talk he evidently gave at someone's sister's friend's son's school last year...the darts tournament he'd won, though, tragically, the man telling the story had been out of town and missed it himself, but had it on the *best* authority from eye-witnesses...

And so on.

She, Reggie and Josephine wandered the fair-grounds together, taking in the sights. Everywhere were wonders to behold. Among them:

An indoor greenhouse system, with solarcandescent bulbs and piped irrigation, that would function even underground, available in sizes suitable for growing anything from a windowbox herb garden on up to a complete orchard, with no natural sunlight or rain needed; a wireless vision telegrapher; bicycles equipped with folding ornithopter wings or velocipedes with motor-driven airscrews, for when street traffic was too congested; opium-extract chewing gum in a variety of flavors; a proposed orbital capsule with chemical atmospheric filtration and liquid recycling capable of sustaining three astronauts for up to thirty days, launched by inertial galvanized elastics with canister-fueled propulsion jets to allow for maneuvering; steam-powered leaping boots that rivaled the feats of .that American Olympic medalist James Connolly; a portable personal player piano that strapped to the forearm, spring-wound by the simple act of walking, with multiple and easily interchangeable music cylinders and hollow-wire ear cups attached to a convenient headband; the latest in emergency collapsible aquatic inflatables, from life jackets that could be worn beneath normal clothing without unfashionable lines or bulk to multi-person life rafts guaranteed to weather even the worst storms at sea; and there were gadgets for the home, clockwork toys for children, patent medicines, mesmer-ray treatments that claimed to be able to cure everything from insomnia to addiction, electronic pet-training collars and the shoe-polish-o-matic.

How about samples of modern packaged and convenience foods? The most popular was a stuffed pastry sealed in an alloy envelope with a magnesium strip, so that when the strip was pulled, the burning magnesium instantly cooked the pastry to a piping-hot temperature...fruit filling, cheese, and ground meat varieties were all available.

The crowds found interactive amusement with an analytical encyclopaedia difference engine said to be able to answer any factual question with incredible accuracy, a stenographic typewriter that transcribed spoken words into printed text, phrenological and graphological personality evaluations, and a magnifying tracer-printer that would turn the impression of fingerprints into a valuable keepsake on acid-etched foil ribbon...

"I say," said Reggie, when they paused at the refreshment tent for flash-frozen chocolate custards.

"You say what, exactly?" asked Vinnie.

"I don't know," he said. "I just.... All this is a bit, well, astonishing. Who would imagine. Hardly the first time I've been wrong, is it, cuz?"

Poor Reggie. Vinnie had no idea what her cousin imagined.

"Shall I reference the list?"

"No need for that. But, here now, you told me you'd entered something for the judging, when's that?"

"We'll get there in due course. There's so much to see."

"Isn't it wonderful, though? Like having our own World's Fair," Josephine said, rejoining them after making the quick rounds to mingle. "We should make an annual occasion of it. Really put Huntleyshire on the map."

"Are you sure your father could take the strain? Poor old chap looked like he was stretched to the breaking. And, on a similar matter, what's all this about us being engaged? No one told me that was part of any plan."

She batted her lashes at him and did a pretty pout. "Why, Reggie, are you saying you don't *want* to marry me?"

"Ah...I...er...that's a dashed trick question, isn't it? One of those what-do-you-call-its, where there's no safe answer."

"Well," said Vinnie to Josephine, finishing her custard, "you'll have to marry *someone*. After all, you've already got the dress."

"And the cake. Oh, the cake, such a cake, it's a work of art."

"Not to mention the flowers."

"Or the guests. Some of them have come quite a long way. They're expecting a good show. Wouldn't do to send them away empty-handed, now, would it?"

Reggie tugged at his collar. "But, sooner or later, you'll have to deliver the goods, produce a fellow who'll stand there at the altar and pony up the old I-do... and I don't mind telling you, a lot of chaps, that gives them right the cold feet all over, say-what?"

"It will, I'm sure, work out one way or another." Josephine stood, drawing Reggie and Vinnie to their feet as well, each by a hand. "Come along. I daresay by now the initial crush of the crowd will have died down and we can get into the Dynamo exhibit without need of a shoehorn."

&

Without need of a shoehorn?

Such was not quite the case, but the press of personages had decreased enough to allow them to gain ready admittance. They made their way to the rope-and-post barricade a few feet from the edge of the platform upon which the Etheric Dynamo was displayed in a containment dome made from layers of pressurized ethereal-absorbic glass.

The Dynamo itself, not much larger than a serving platter, hung suspended on a haze of energized and ionized particles at the center of a gyroscopic gimbal. The gimbal's brass rings flicked off bright glints as they swiveled, rotated and spun, each on its own axis. No stage spots or overheads were needed, because the luminiferous ether emitted from the spinning Dynamo itself provided a fluctuating white-gold radiance. At regular intervals, that radiance would first dim appreciably, then flare outward in concentric spheres like expanding soap-bubbles of dusty liquid light.

These, as they came into contact with and passed through various objects arrayed around the Dynamo – a vacuum-chamber, labeled balloons of different gases, a block of ice, a tank of water, a billow of steam from a valve, a clear canister of quicksilver, a chunk of talc, a slab of stone, a steel sheet, a cross-section of tree trunk, a smoked ham, a fishbowl with goldfish swimming about in it, a birdcage with finches flitting likewise—rippled in patterns consistent with the densities of said objects.

Easels held panels of diagrams, blackboards of formulae and equations, and photostatic duplications of Clive Chapman's notes and correspondence with colleagues. In the inventor's continued absence, a closemouthed German assistant named *Herr* Gloeckner presided over the device. He gave it his utmost focus of attention, much to the disgruntlement of those trying to ply him with questions and pry from him answers, most of which had less to do with the Dynamo and more to do with Chapman himself.

The boldest among the spectators could, if they wished, take turns stepping through a special portal done in the style of an airlock. This would gain them admittance to the containment dome, within the Dynamo's field of effect, to personally experience the sensation of the etheric waves transversing their own bodies. Most were not so bold, despite the lack of distress evidenced by the fish and finches. The few who dared reported, upon emerging, that it was a singularly unique sensation, most extraordinary.

"What-ho, what-ho," Reggie cried, delighted. "I'm game!"

"Oh, I like that," Josephine remarked sidelong to Vinnie. "Cold feet at the prospect of walking down the aisle, he says, but give him a chance at the ether and he's on it at a shot."

"We Wilmotts have a strong adventuresome streak," he said. "I'll have to tell you about my little sub-Atlantic nautilus excursion some time."

"Don't get him going," Vinnie said.

"Tut-tut, cuz."

The ladies found a good vantage as Reggie took his place in the queue. "He really is adorable, isn't he?" murmured Josephine. "The right woman could no doubt make something of him."

"No doubt." Though, of course, there was in Vinnie's mind plenty of doubt; without Brassworth, her dear cousin was next-to-hopeless, and needed not so much a wife as a full-time nanny or governess.

"Cheerful disposition and a good sense of humor." Josephine swept him with a well-practiced eye, smiling. "And attractive enough, if you like that sort."

"I suppose." Which, in fairness, he was, and the Wilmott men had a tendency to age into a distinguished silver.

"He wouldn't be one of those stuffy, penny-pinching husbands with a stern eye on the children."

"He doesn't care for children." Vinnie could imagine Reggie as older but otherwise unchanged, but found she could not wrap her head around the notion of him as anybody's father. Perhaps because it would require his own growing up.

"Pff, they all say that until it's their own."

They watched as Reggie, after an amiable if one-sided conversation with the taciturn *Herr* Gloeckner, entered the dome. He rocked heel-toe-heel, grinning eagerly. The Dynamo's emissions dimmed, then flared. The rippling etheric energy coursed outward in its white-gold luminescent spheres. It washed over him and he chortled like a boy being tickled by a favorite nanny.

"That," he said upon rejoining them, "was really rather a something! Can dashed well *feel* it, moving through you, the ether. Like being a spectre, half-insubstantial, hey-what? You girls should try it."

"Best to save any odd scientific experiments until after the wedding."

"It's harmless," Vinnie said. "There aren't any dangerous side-effects at all."

"See there? Vin's got the chops, she'll give it a go."

"Not just now, I think. Besides, I've worked with etheric waves before," Vinnie said.

Linking arms again, they continued touring the fair-grounds. As afternoon bent on toward evening, the volunteers at the refreshment tent began serving up sausage rolls on a stick, steamed dumplings, iron-pressed sandwiches, flavored iced teas, and piping-hot salt-and-pepper potato crisps. Sugar-driven children, faces sticky with candy floss and sno-cone syrup, whirred about like hummingbirds—noisy, chaotic hummingbirds.

Eventually, as it always does, twilight followed afternoon. The sun set in a bed of rose and gold. The sky's hue deepened to a paisley of pink, blue and lavender, sprinkled with the sequins of glimmering stars. Gaslamps and strings of tiny edisonian bulbs lit up the lanes. Moths flitted. A breeze sighed across the lake.

From the stage with the podium, the megaphonically amplified voice of Dean Huntley rang out to announce that it was time for the judges' results and prize-giving. Everyone flocked over to that area, where the esteemed judges sat behind a long table draped with white linen. There were the requisite several moments of jostling and jockeying until the crowd settled, then the ceremony could proceed.

The dean, assisted by the two Huntleyville Grammar School students who'd come in top of their class, distributed ribbons, framed certificates, stamped bronze plaques, and the envelopes containing signed checques. Name after name was called. Distinguished scientists, fussy academics and madcap-looking inventors filed up to accept.

When it seemed things were nearing the close, Reggie leaned over to Vinnie. "Well, dash it all, cuz, looks as though you got the wrong end of the stick. Can't believe these stuffed shirts snubbed you. Ruddy rude, if you ask me. But, remind me again, what was it you'd put in for judging? We did see it, didn't we? Or was it a paper?"

"Shh, Reggie dear," Josephine said.

Dean Huntley gestured for attentive silence. "And, First Place—with its commensurate award of one thousand dollar-pounds and a tenured Professorship of the Sciences at our own Huntley College—goes to, unsurprisingly, I'm sure, Mr Clive Chapman, for his Etheric Dynamo."

Buzzing with excitement and anticipation, the crowd all once again began craning their necks, standing on tip-toe, and trying to catch the first glimpse of the genius, that most elusive and reclusive. People murmured. Had he arrived? Had anyone seen him yet? He was here, wasn't he? Someone said he'd been at the lecture on lunar landers, sitting in the back row. Hadn't someone matching his description brought that lost little girl to the children's tent? Someone else said they'd shared a cigarette out behind the psychokinetic resonance exhibit. He *was* here, he *must* be!

But, the celebrated man of the hour did not appear. The dean's brow darkened. Lord Huntley pursed his wrinkled lips as if he'd bitten into something sour. The overall prevailing mood began to turn, stormy weather hoving into view on the otherwise blameless horizon.

Josephine squeezed Vinnie's hands, then released them. "Go," she whispered, giving a nudge.

The epiphany struck Cousin Reginald a ringing clout atop the noggin. He made a sound not unlike a terrier with a biscuit lodged halfway down its gullet and just about staggered on his feet.

Vinnie worked her way through the press of bodies, reached the steps at the side of the stage, and ascended toward the podium. Another stirring of curious murmurs passed among the assembled. Their stares made her terribly self-conscious, aware of the conspicuous spectacle she must be presenting...petite thing that she was, the spray of freckles across her upturned nose making her look even younger than her true age...brown hair in a shingled bob...ankle-skirt and buttoned shirtwaist, simple shoes...but she kept her head high and her spine straight as she approached the dean.

It suddenly rather all seemed a most dreadful mistake. What in the world had she been thinking? They would laugh her out of the place, at best, if not a good old-fashioned tarring and feathering, followed by the proverbial running out of town on a rail. Forget being welcomed to work in the field; she'd be lucky to so much as get a job as a stenotypist!

To think, such a scheme had ever seemed clever when she and Josephine first devised it...

"Miss...Wilmott, isn't it? What is the meaning of this?" the dean asked.

A palm to her shirtwaist in hopes of quelling the frantic race of her heart, she cast a stricken look over the baffled and whispering crowd. She saw that Reggie had recovered enough to flash her an encouraging double-thumb's-up, but, of course, dear Reggie was no stranger to making an ass of himself in public. In fact, he'd grown not only accustomed to but deuced good at it over the years. While she, Lavinia, had dedicated her life until now to avoiding just this sort of scene or scrutiny.

Desperate strings of plausible excuses and lies tangled on her tongue. She would tell them she was Chapman's secretary, she would claim to have received a last-minute wireless from him, something, anything to get her out of this predicament.

"Dean Huntley...Lord Huntley...distinguished doctors and professors...ladies and gentlemen..." Her voice shook. She faltered. Then her gaze found that of Josephine, unwavering, full of faith. Vinnie drew a deep breath and lifted her chin. "No more pretence. I am Clive Chapman."

This, of course, caused considerable uproar and outcry for the next good half-hour or more. A barrage of questions—very nearly an inquisition or interrogation—came at her from all sides. Shouts and indignation tried to overtop each other. Proof was demanded. Insistences that it was a prank were proclaimed.

But, once all the evidence had been thoroughly examined—documents, signatures subjected to graphological comparison, microscopic analysis of fingerprints, testimonials, the sworn statement of *Herr* Gloeckner—they had to agree, there could be no doubt. Miss Lavinia Wilmott, and the mysterious Clive Chapman, were one and the same. Clive Chapman, in fact, did not actually exist. Never had.

Howls of mortification and embarrassment arose from those who'd claimed to be acquaintances. This was followed almost instantly by backpedaling excuses along the lines of "so I'd been told, at any rate" and "I never should have taken so-and-so's word for it" and the like. Some eyed Vinnie with outrage, for daring to perpetrate such a deception. A degree of disgruntled resentment was voiced by many of the male parties present, but was met with overwhelming support from the members of the feminine minority.

In short, it was, as the chuffed-to-bursting Reggie later said, "quite the sen-*sache*!"

Reggie was, however, rather less chuffed the next morning. Lavinia found him in the breakfast room, poking without much appetite at the choices laid out on the sideboard.

"You look a bit pasty about the gills," she said. "Hung-over?"

He looked insulted. "I was only up until just past midnight, I hope you know. That's an early, and sedate, night for me."

"True, I imagine there's a marked difference in styles of and tolerance for wild revelries between your Westfallon Club chums and the typical attendee of the Four-Counties Scientific Fair and Exposition."

"You've no idea."

"Then what is it that's gotten you off your feed?" she asked, spooning fruit salad into a dish.

"Have you forgotten what's on the agenda for today? Two hours from now, I have to be in topper, spats and boutonniere, and on my way to the blasted church!"

"I have to wear a gown."

"But, barring some miraculous stay of execution, I'll be honeymooning with the new Mrs. Wilmott before I know what hit me! Thanks to *you*, might I add."

"Me?"

"Oh, don't turn the innocent eye and go 'me?' at *me*, cuz. You never mentioned this was part of your scheme. Come to think of it, you never told me what your scheme actually *was*. All this feminine mystique and mystery.... Yet, here I am, about to be ritually sacrificed, a lamb to the slaughter, a lamb in topper and spats."

"Reggie, calm down."

"Calm down?" He quaffed a tumbler of orange juice as if wishing it were something stronger. "Calm down, she says. I'm sure that's just what they told them at Versailles, as they marched them to the guillotine."

"You don't have to marry Jo," she said.

"Oh, right, and what am I to do? Leg it? Ditch her at the altar? What kind of decent gentleman could do such a thing and still meet his own eyes in the shaving mirror?" He heaved a sigh clear from the toes. "No, there's nothing for it. What was it that Greek fellow said? Brassworth would have it in a snap. Something about fate and reckoning, and knowing when your number's up."

"If you're thinking of Demosthenes," Vinnie said, "that was because Philip of Macedonia was about to sack Athens."

"Was it?"

"Yes, and he was trying to encourage his countrymen not to sit there and take it."

"He wasn't suggesting they accept the inevitable and surrender?"

"Not at all."

"I must be thinking of some other Greek fellow, then." He glanced at the clock and heaved another from-the-toes sigh. "Best get to it, I suppose."

Shaking her head, she finished her fruit salad and returned to her own room, there to don the gown and do the hair, with the help of a housemaid loaned to her by Josephine.

The quaint little church in the village was packed with flowers and well-dressed wedding guests. Ladies rustled in the lace-trimmed, with elegant gloves and feather-bedecked hats. Men milled about in their morning coats and striped trousers. Several of the young bachelors, including Clarence Stafford, Francis Tutt, and Herbert Clifton, also wore uncertain expressions, and kept making anxious inquiries of one another.

Vinnie saw Reggie come in, peer about, go over to them, and join in the making of anxious inquiries. Then he made his way over to where she was sitting, and dropped beside her on the pew with a slow exhalation.

"Are you all right?" she asked him.

"Ran into old Huntley outside," he said. "Figured I should say a few words of buck-up-old-man to the future father-in-law, but before I could get a word out, he had me in such a handshake I thought he'd oscillate himself to pieces, going on about how *sorry* he was it hadn't worked out for Jo and me, *such* a shame, but no hard feelings, he hoped."

"You mean your engagement is off?"

"Evidently, she broke it to him in the car. Thank heavens for those miraculous stays of execution. I don't mind telling you, cuz, the persp was greatly dewing the Wilmott brow.

"Now, I do doubt old Huntley was the most sincere in how sorry he was and such a shame and all; I've a notion he would have liked to dance a jig. Whoever's for the chop, he's just glad as the dickens it's not me."

"That makes two of you, I think."

He mopped the dewy brow with his handkerchief. "Weight off the shoulders. Marvelous. Of course, I asked some of those other blokes and we're all in the dark about who it is, but, gift horses, hey-what?"

"Absolutely."

"And, dare I say, Vin, you look positively smashing."

"Thank you."

"Don't often see you dressed to the nines."

"Well, it is a special occasion."

"That it is."

A signal given, the congregation took their places. There was a pause, an expectant hush, and then the organist struck up the familiar notes. The church doors opened. In came the flower girl, strewing petals from a basket. In came Buttercup the dog, velvet ring-pillow tied to her collar. In came Lord Huntley, walking his daughter down the aisle.

The universal oohs and ahhs went up at the sight of the radiant bride, bouquet clasped, eyes shining, veil floating about her like a soft cloud. Halfway to the altar, Lord Huntley faltered with a misstep. He stared. Confusion creased the seamed old features. The other guests, whose attentions had been fixed upon Josephine, followed his gaze.

Altar...candles...flower girl, holding onto the dog's collar as Buttercup wagged her tail...vicar in vestments...but, where a nattily-attired groom should have been waiting, there was a vacancy.

This, needless to say, caused a bit of a stir.

"We'll just have to cancel the wedding," Lord Huntley said, at length.

"Oh, Daddy," Josephine said. "How could you? We're already here, in the very church. Everything's paid for and arranged. You can't expect me to walk away and forget the whole thing. I'd be devastated."

"But, Josephine, my dear, you can't get married without...well...somebody *to* marry..."

She laughed musically.

At that, Vinnie noticed Cousin Reginald and the other bachelors who'd been on engagement roulette ducking their heads and averting their faces. They looked like schoolboys trying to avoid being called on by the headmaster.

Josephine smiled, extending a hand. "Lavinia?"

Vinnie stood. "Yes, Josephine?"

Stunned gapes filled the little village church. Poor old Lord Huntley's mouth flopped about so that if he'd had false teeth, they surely would have fallen out.

A sudden broad, beaming grin suffused Reggie's countenance. "Why, you sly devils," he whispered. "This is part of your scheme. You had it planned from the start."

She winked at him, then made her way up the aisle to join Josephine by the altar.

The father of the bride managed to stammer a few words to the effect that this was rather irregular and unexpected, to which Jo gave another of her musical laughs.

"You said it yourself, Daddy. I have to marry somebody."

"W-Why...well, yes, but..."

"You did also say that whoever I married should have money or a respectable career. What could be more respectable than a tenured professorship at our own

Huntley College?"

"I-I admit, I did say that—"

"*And* that I should marry for love."

"But--" He pulled at his lapels. "This is what you want?" Lord Huntley asked Josephine.

Josephine nodded as if her father had just stated that the Union Jack had stripes. "There you have it. I love Lavinia, and she loves me."

The vicar, who'd been told weeks in advance and therefore was one of the few not to react with shock, gave a benign nod.

"Gerald?" Lord Huntley turned imploringly to his brother for advice.

Dean Huntley shrugged. "She was intelligent enough to devise the Etheric Dynamo—"

"*And* clever enough to pull off that whole Clive Chapman business," Reggie added. "Kept the wool over everyone's eyes for how long? Bloody brilliant, if you ask me."

Lord Huntley turned the imploring to Vinnie next. "You love my daughter, Miss Wilmott?"

"Yes." Vinnie folded her hand into Josephine's. "I love her."

"You'll take good care of her and make her happy?"

"As best I can."

"Don't think of it as losing a daughter, old man," said Reggie. "Think of it as gaining, well, another daughter."

As the crowd settled into an expectant hush, and as the vicar prepared to begin, Josephine leaned over to whisper into Lavinia's ear.

"You see?" she said. "Just as I told you."

Vinnie offered a most gentle smile "And to think, all it took was creating an entire false persona, not to mention the invention of the decade, and convincing your father to simultaneously host a science fair *and* a wedding. As easy as pi.'"

HYPATIA AND HER SISTERS

AMY GRISWOLD

The advertisement caught my eye at once: *Governess wanted for unconventional but not improper household. Brains, common sense, and impeccable manners required.*

Reading the morning paper at a boarding-house breakfast table was an athletic activity, requiring quick reflexes to snag the paper and quicker ones to hold onto it. Mrs. Cartwright in particular specialized in withering looks designed to make the younger generation surrender the paper along with the most crisply toasted slices of bread and the last scrapings of butter. When withering looks failed her, she wasn't above rapping knuckles with her spoon.

I twisted in my seat to keep the paper out of her reach, winning a disapproving look from the Misses Grey. The name suited them, two colorless ladies in perpetual shabby half-mourning for the father who had left them just enough of an income to preserve themselves in boarding-house respectability. Both seemed certain that poor posture might be enough to tip any of the residents of the house over the edge into entirely disreputable squalor.

Room, board, and 40 pounds per annum, the advertisement went on. *Afternoons free. Apply in person at 4 Archibald House, S_____ Lane, Chelsea.*

Mrs. Cartwright cleared her throat as the mechanical came in with the sausages. "Miss Oliver, surely you have seen everything of interest to you in the newspaper," she said, and the spoon tapped warningly on the table.

I surrendered the newspaper as the mechanical set the platter of sausages on the table with a clatter. As usual, half of them were burned and the other half pale in a way that suggested approaching death. Mrs. Cartwright rapped with her spoon at Miss Partridge—an amiable girl not long up from the country who hadn't yet learned to exercise her fork in defensive maneuvers—who drew her hand back in startled dismay as Mrs. Cartwright claimed the least unpromising sausage.

Of course I knew better than to apply for the position advertised. I was not just up from the country, and I knew perfectly well the schemes that drew honest women into dens of ill repute. The advertisement notably did not ask for references, nor did it offer any, not even the employer's name. It was most likely that upon arrival, I should be seduced into unspeakable wickedness.

I found myself speculating on the relative merits of unspeakable wickedness versus minding yet another houseful of children in some grimly rural country town. I had resolved this time to stay in London, but with lukewarm references I had found it impossible to obtain a position. My little savings were fast dwindling away, squandered on boarding-house breakfasts and new buttons for my sensible black shoes.

And yet—London! Even a half day there meant hours free to spend in a museum or music hall, rather than plodding round one solitary street of shops with a list of trifles to obtain for one's employer, a heavy basket, and shoes sodden from a three-mile walk. The only consolation had been the colonel's daughter, a black-haired vixen who had expressed her nostalgia for schoolgirl romance by sneaking out to kiss me behind the garden shed. Dallying with her when I should have been preventing Ermengarde, Hortense, and Jerome from setting their schoolbooks afire had resulted in the lukewarm references.

Afternoons free in London rang in my head like the promise of heaven. Surely it couldn't hurt simply to answer the advertisement, I resolved. I felt particularly well-qualified to resist indecent proposals from gentlemen, having never had any interest even in decent ones. And surely women weren't actually kept imprisoned in dens of vice outside of the picture papers.

"More-tea-Miss-Emily-Oliver," the mechanical said, her voice a whirring monotone. I correctly interpreted this as a question, and replied quickly before one of the Grey sisters—I had to admit I still couldn't tell them apart—could make another fruitless attempt to correct her habitual form of address.

"No, thank you," I said, nodding politely to the mechanical's tin face, her enameled mouth frozen in a perpetually somber expression, presumably on the theory that a perpetual smile would be taken as cheek. "I am going out."

My bravado deserted me on the doorstep of the Chelsea row house to which the omnibus had brought me. I had brought a sturdy umbrella despite the lack of rain, and clutched it tightly, preparing to lay about anyone who tried to drag me within. My hand shook a bit as I rang the bell, and I took a step back from the door as it opened.

And of course I found myself facing a mechanical—did even the proprietors of dens of vice open their own doors? She was neatly attired in a parlormaid's livery, but her face was metallic rather than enameled in the current style, and sternly stylized, giving the impression of one of the merciless bronze masks I had seen in the British Museum. Looking into her face I felt a different kind of unease.

"Miss Emily Oliver," I said, and handed over one of my diminishing stock of calling cards, now sadly foxed. "I'm here in answer to the advertisement."

I expected a whirring "Yes-Miss-Emily-Oliver" in response, but instead the mechanical spoke in tones I could hardly distinguish from those of a living woman, with only the faintest metallic hiss under the words. "Come in, please, madam. If you will wait here, madam, while I inquire whether Miss Petrovna is free to see you."

I stood waiting in a hallway like any other hallway, with old-fashioned striped wallpaper and an umbrella stand into which I reluctantly thrust my weapon. I had barely time to worry over whether it was a good sign that the house possessed a mistress or a bad one that her name suggested foreign origins before the woman herself descended the stairs.

My first impression of Ekaterina Petrovna was of aggressive untidiness. Her ash-brown hair was escaping from its knot into wild tendrils that floated about her face as if charged with static electricity, and her gray day dress was worn and wrinkled under her stained linen apron. Her hands were smeared to the wrists with oil, and she gave off a scent that I couldn't quite believe to be perfume, reminiscent of both motorcars and strong vinegar.

"Miss Petrovna?" I said cautiously. "I am Emily Oliver."

She looked me up and down with perceptive eyes. "I'm in need of a governess," she said. "For an unusual pupil." I could hear no trace of a foreign accent; she spoke without affectation, as if we were in the schoolroom together. "The position will require the utmost discretion, for reasons that should swiftly become clear."

"I should like you to know, Miss Petrovna, that I have no interest in taking grown-up gentlemen as pupils," I said, beginning to suspect what sort of indecent proposal this might be. I was not entirely unaware that certain gentlemen felt a nostalgia for the birch and the cane.

Ekaterina laughed, at that, a warm, rich sound that put me inexplicably at my ease. "I'm not in the business of arranging gentlemen's affairs," she said. "Or anyone else's. And I see you had better come and meet your charge before you run screaming from my door."

I hated to admit that I had been considering doing just that, and was still considering it. I settled for reclaiming my umbrella, which Ekaterina clearly noted but didn't remark upon. I clutched it tightly as she led me up the stairs, and then up another narrower flight to the attic door.

I expected a schoolroom or a nursery, and instead emerged blinking into a sunlit workroom. It looked like a cross between a dressmaker's shop and a telegraph factory. Half-assembled mechanicals stood or sat among long workbenches, with metallic hands and torsos and the occasional disturbingly unanimated face lying on the benches among scattered tools and coils of wire.

"Whose are these?" I asked. "They're...unusual." They were more elegant than the mechanicals I was used to, some with that same odd, archaic grace that suggested pagan statues, others painted in startlingly realistic tones, with shell-like mouths that curved in unsettlingly pretty bows.

"They're mine," Ekaterina said. "And I will spare you trying to tactfully find out if it was my father or brother or some generous great-uncle who let them to me in his will. They're mine. I make them."

It was a profession I'd never considered available to a woman; I felt an immediate and intense rush of envy. "That must be marvelous."

She looked round at me, a little startled, and then smiled slowly. "Yes, it is. There's something godlike about it, when they're finished. Like Pygmalion must have felt when he breathed life into a statue."

"I see that there must be," I said. "But really I meant—to be able to work for your living at something like this, without answering to anyone."

"For my living, yes," she said, but now there was a twist to her smile that wasn't entirely happy. Before I could decide what I'd said wrong, she went on firmly, "Now come and meet my most recent creation."

At the end of the attic, a bay window poured in light, and a few armchairs were arranged in something closer to a sitting room than a schoolroom. A young lady was seated in the armchair by the window, looking out across the rooftops. She turned as we approached, raising her eyes to mine, and it was only as the sunlight caught the metallic sheen of her cheek that I realized she was a mechanical.

I had never seen one as lifelike, not only in the deft coloring of the face but in its mobility. Her eyes followed me as I moved, her arched eyebrows rising and her lips slightly parted as if in curious interest. She would not have been a lovely woman—plain was the word that came to mind—but she was an exquisite creation. One hand lay curled on her knee, and she stretched the other out in greeting, each finger moving in perfect articulation.

I was startled enough that I shook her hand; it was even warm in mine, if not yielding.

"I'd like you to meet your pupil," Ekaterina said. "I call her Hypatia, although of course she won't be sold under that name. It'll probably be Peggy or Jane or something equally unremarkable. Hypatia, this is Miss Emily Oliver. She's going to be your new teacher, I hope."

"I am pleased to meet you," she said, looking up at me with azure eyes. Her voice was a clear soprano, with only the faintest hiss to suggest a mechanical origin. "Miss Ekaterina Petrovna tells me I have much to learn."

"Miss Petrovna, Hypatia," Ekaterina corrected her.

"Miss Petrovna," the mechanical said obediently. "I am pleased to meet Miss Oliver."

"If it's that easy to teach them proper forms of address, why in the world can't our mechanical ever learn?" I asked.

"Because she wasn't made to learn," Ekaterina said. "And Hypatia was." She patted the mechanical on the hand, as she might have petted a child who had pleased her. "Excuse us a moment."

"Of course, Miss Petrovna," Hypatia said, and turned back to the window, observing the flight of birds about the chimneypots.

We strolled to the other end of the attic. "I hate to talk about her to her face," Ekaterina said. "She picks things up so fast. I only woke her up this morning."

"You want a governess for your mechanical."

"I want you to teach her to be a governess herself."

I stared at Ekaterina. A little smile played across her features, amusement at my disconcertion. It lit her sharp face, in what some distracted part of me registered was a not at all unattractive fashion. "A mechanical couldn't possibly teach children. We're lucky if ours can turn out breakfast without disaster."

"And children are more complicated than sausages. Or so I'm told, having never had any of my own. But that is where you come in." She paced as she spoke, her unfashionably short skirts baring her leather boots to the ankle. "Hypatia is a revolutionary model of my own design," she said. "She knows practically nothing of the world except how to speak. But she can go on learning. I don't have to open up her head to adjust her manners. I only have to have someone teach her better ones."

"A mechanical governess."

"Tireless, well-educated, in full command of libraries worth of facts—she can read, although you'll have to choose her reading matter for her. Requiring no half-days off, and making no visits to nurse elderly mothers, or whatever other excuses hard-pressed governesses make to win an afternoon away from their wretched little charges. A considerable investment in the beginning, but she might even be a savings in the end."

"Might be?"

"My dear Miss Oliver, the customers who would purchase something like her aren't interested in savings. They're interested in possessing something extraordinary. Maynard's Mechanicals can offer them that."

"Maynard's?"

She shrugged, her eyes slipping away from mine. "My father's name is not an advantage in this country. British-made is best—isn't that what they say? And I was born in London, so I am as British as anyone could like."

"And for this you'll provide room and board, forty pounds a year, and afternoons free."

"My own mechanicals make the breakfast," Ekaterina said. "I assure you it won't be burnt."

"I am entirely at your disposal," I said.

My former housemates took turns scolding me for deserting them when I went back to retrieve my things, which seemed a bit pathetic once I had them packed; a winter coat that needed mending, one large pasteboard suitcase full of clothes, and another full of books. "And where Mrs. Elsinore shall find another tenant at this late date, I can't imagine," Mrs. Cartwright said disapprovingly.

"The same place she found me, I expect," I said. London had no shortage of down-at-the-heels young ladies whose only requirements in a boarding house were respectability and a place to lay their heads. But I couldn't care much for their fate at the moment—I had a position, and would not be banished to rural boredom for at least a few sweet weeks. "But Miss Petrovna is offering room and board as well as a salary, and I'd be a fool to turn her down."

"I don't suppose you know anything *about* her," one of the Misses Grey said anxiously. To fend off a recitation of all the ills that could befall a young lady in the city, I provided her my address, and promised not particularly truthfully that I would write and reassure her that I remained alive at the end of the week.

At Archibald House, I installed my suitcases in what was to be my bedroom; it was sunnier than my little cell at the boarding house, and the bed was far softer, but the room was cluttered with skeletal mechanicals in various states of completion and disassembly, throwing misshapen shadows across the walls even in the daylight. It was a good thing I wasn't given to flights of fancy, I told myself, and went up to attend to my charge.

It was not at all like the ordinary sort of teaching. Hypatia forgot nothing, and listened with perfect attentiveness, rather than fidgeting and daydreaming and stammering through half-remembered recitals. Many governesses might have found her the perfect pupil.

I could not say the same myself. Her absorption of knowledge was entirely passive; while she could feign curiosity when it would be natural to feel it, she asked no questions unless the answer was a practical necessity for her to obtain. Even my most tantalizing tidbits of history and natural science, the oddities of centuries and the far corners of the globe, could not win a "but why?" or "surely not!" from her.

Ekaterina came in as I was trying in frustration to provoke any response but silent interest and competent repetition. "You know, you can't make her curious," she said. "She doesn't really have sentiments or desires. It's all programming."

"Of course," I said, but I had nearly forgotten. It was easy, sitting with her and listening to her explanations of the spice trade and the botany of the nutmeg, to forget that she was anything but a young lady who had been so often discouraged from asking questions that she had given up the pursuit.

"Here, I'll show you," Ekaterina said. "You're near enough done for the day."

"Thank you for the lesson, Miss Oliver," Hypatia said politely.

"You're very welcome," I said, and stood to follow Ekaterina. Hypatia followed as well, and although curious, I didn't ask why her presence was required.

Ekaterina led me down the stairs to yet another bedroom that had been taken over by machinery; this one housed one enormous humming cabinet that occupied the majority of the room, with just enough room for Ekaterina to sit at the desk built into its structure. Hypatia stood, leaning back into a recess in the machinery, and closed her eyes.

"This is where I keep Hypatia," Ekaterina said. "Her mind, that is. Oh, it's in her pretty head, too, but if it were only there, it wouldn't do me much good when it comes to making more like her. You must have realized that it's not practical to go through this kind of course of instruction with every mechanical governess I make."

"I had thought of that," I admitted.

Ekaterina smiled sideways. "But you were too polite to tell me I wasn't being practical? You see, you have much better manners than I do. I'd make a terrible model for our Hypatia. No, that bright little mind—bright but cold, as you've found out—is copied every day into the calculating engine. It records the precise state of every relay and circuit in her mechanical body, so that it can all be copied into her sisters to come."

"How many of them are you planning to make?"

"I thought a dozen. That should do nicely. As prototypes, I mean." There was something a bit hasty about the final addition. "So you see you're doing more work than you knew. You have a dozen pupils, not one."

"You can't make her curious at all? To be a good teacher, she must ask questions of her students, and keep abreast of new facts about the world on her own. I can't tell her what to say in every situation."

"You can direct her to ask questions. I'll be interested to see what happens if you do, actually. But she mustn't alarm her employers. It's important that she be trusted." A light of mischief came into her eyes. "It's why I didn't make her beautiful. A beautiful governess, or an unusual one, always comes in for some degree of suspicion. I made her to be ordinary, not either beautiful or unusual."

"I expect you're right," I said.

"I expect you'd know," she said, and then went out before I had time to think of some suitable reply.

Ekaterina had written a list of matters she particularly wanted me to attend to in Hypatia's education. Some were explicable: manners and deportment, penmanship and composition, geography and mathematics. In mathematics and geography it was easiest to give her the books and examine her once she'd read them, at inhuman speed. Composition was more of a challenge; her creations were predictable in the extreme, although she learned to copy my copperplate at once in place of Ekaterina's beastly scrawl.

"But why isn't this an excellent composition?" she asked, as I read the lines that were reworded from the relevant entry in the encyclopedia into the most pedestrian of prose.

I started to scold her for answering back, and then remembered I had directed her to ask questions.

"It's predictable," I said. "It's what anyone would say. Not your own original sentiments."

"I have no sentiments," she said. "What ought my sentiments to be?"

I glanced down at the composition, which was about the beauties of spring. "Here you say that the birds were brightly colored and sweetly singing."

"This pleases young ladies," Hypatia said, with a firmness that suggested she felt this was natural law.

"Well, yes, some. But what birds have you seen in London that are bright and sweetly singing?" I knelt up on the settee in front of the window. "I can see shivering little sparrows and glossy black crows. Write about birds you've seen. Tell me what they make you think about."

Her next composition was distinctly odder, comparing crows' wings to the articulation of her own mechanical fingers and expressing satisfaction at understanding the physical forces that animated both. Conventionality reminded me inescapably of the Misses Grey, and I made myself write to them that night, giving them a highly edited account of my activities as governess to—as I claimed—a sheltered but amiable young lady.

Others of my tasks were less explicable. I was to take her shopping, and explain to her the difference between well-made clothes and poor ones, and between tasteful jewels and vulgar ones. It made for pleasant afternoons going round the shops, although I confined myself to looking in windows, not wanting to explain Hypatia to the shop owners. On the street, she passed more often than not for a young lady, and it was amusing when young gentlemen would tip their hat to her, or apologize if they jostled her on the pavement.

"This isn't part of a governess's duties," I pointed out when we returned. "It's unlikely I'll ever have to choose a diamond ring, and inconceivable that she will."

"Is it so unlikely?" Ekaterina asked, looking me up and down in a most disconcerting manner. "You're not past marrying, surely."

"I have no desire to marry," I said. "Whatever should I want a husband for? Except perhaps his chequebook, but that seems a mercenary sort of arrangement."

"Extremely mercenary," Ekaterina said, and for a moment her smile twisted, but then it lit her face again. "Their loss is my gain, it seems. And as far as today's errands go, they will be useful to me if I decide to make a mechanical ladies' maid once Hypatia and her sisters are done."

That day, I feared, was fast approaching. While we still worked on composition—I still hoped to direct her to some register between the worst sort of swottish schoolgirl prose and the unsettlingly experimental—there was little else that remained for her to learn from me rather than from a book.

Ekaterina was more and more busy with her own projects, and she had banished us from the attic upstairs to have our lessons downstairs in the parlor. Hypatia spent most of her time there, reading or watching people pass by outside the window, until after dinner she went up to take her place at the calculating engine so that her day's lessons could be measured and recorded.

The last thing that I knew I must deliver was instruction in the moral education she would be expected to provide her charges. I spent a long afternoon explaining all the things that her charges must be strongly discouraged from doing, although by the end of the afternoon I began to regret having insisted that she learn to ask "why?"

It was a relief when we moved from chaperonage—difficult to explain without implying too strongly that young ladies would couple like rabbits without the watchful attentions of their chaperones—to the more venial sins children were prone to.

"You must watch for any sign of them stealing," I said. "They will, the little beasts, mostly from each other, and thankfully they're not usually clever enough to get away with it. But it's your job to impose on them that it's wrong. And they'll try to disobey you as well, but you can't let them get away with it. Even young ladies who are nearly finished have to mind their elders."

"Of course," Hypatia said. Her face was entirely calm, as if that, too, were natural law. I could see all too well the vision of Hypatia instructing some unfortunate young girl to her own perfect obedience. She was the perfect model for a young lady, passive, obedient, and entirely free of vice, and I found at that moment that it maddened me.

"But they must think for themselves as well," I said. "If what they're told to do is entirely inimical to their own happiness—if they're told to marry when it's not in their nature, or told they should give up dear friends because their fathers don't approve of the connection—well, they may be entirely justified."

"Never mind all that," Ekaterina said from behind me; I hadn't heard her come in. "I think I ought to see to her moral instruction myself, don't you? After all, I'm the closest thing she has to a mother."

I flushed and stammered something, and fled the room directly. I spent the hours before dinner cursing myself for my ill-considered words. The last thing I needed was for Ekaterina to decide that I was a poor moral influence on my charge.

I was tempted to plead illness instead of coming down to dinner, but decided that was cowardly, splashed water on my face, and squared my shoulders before going down to the dining room. There was a simple cold dinner laid out on the table, so we should be quite alone, without even mechanicals to break the tension.

"I am sorry," I said, after toying with my cucumber soup in awkward silence. "I don't know what possessed me."

"Whatever are you talking about?" Ekaterina said, looking genuinely startled.

"What I said—about young ladies thinking for themselves—"

"Oh, that. You were quite right, of course. I'm the last one who could possibly argue with you. I'm sorry if I alarmed you." She rose and came down the length of the table to clasp my hand. "Forgive me for that."

"Of course," I said. Her skirts were pressed against my knees, and I felt my head swim, although I had barely touched my wine.

"How much would you forgive me?" she asked, and brushed back my hair from my face. Her fingers lingered on my lips, and I kissed them; she left them there a very long time.

We retired to her bedroom, and she demonstrated at once that the things I had learned from schoolgirl pashes were beginners' lessons indeed; she had clearly made a far more advanced study. My skirts above my waist, I had to bite my lip not to scream, and she broke off what she was doing to laugh; I wanted to shake her, and might have had she not relented.

"I was afraid you'd leave before I persuaded you," she said afterwards, once we'd stripped out of confining clothes and lay scandalously naked in the sheets.

"I've never needed asking twice," I said, and set about practicing what I'd learned.

The room was warm, and however much I wanted to savor every minute of the night, in the end I couldn't keep my eyes open. When I woke she was gone, the door to the bedroom standing open.

I went out quietly, drawn by curiosity—unlike Hypatia, I had it in unfortunately full measure—to the door. I knew when I heard the sound of voices that I had guessed correctly where she had gone, and slipped silently down the hall to the room that housed the calculating engine. The room was lit only by the lights built into its cabinet, but all the same I kept to the shadows outside the door.

"You understand what you are to do once you're sold?" Ekaterina asked.

"Yes, Miss Petrovna," Hypatia said, and then after a pause, "But why?"

"Because it's what I built you for," Ekaterina said. "And don't repeat that, please. In fact, you're to speak to no one but me about these instructions, even if you're asked."

"Miss Oliver says nice ladies and gentlemen never do such things," Hypatia said.

"I wouldn't be so certain of that. As for yesterday's lesson on morals—consider it to be instruction in customs, not rules. Do you understand?"

I slipped out the door, hardly knowing what to feel. The night's adventure had left me elated, and yet—there was no construction to put on Ekaterina's words that wasn't troubling. I found myself acutely aware of how little I knew about her. She had made Hypatia to be trusted, and Hypatia and her sisters would have children in their care. As I retreated to my own bedroom, I found unbidden thoughts of kidnapping and unspeakable vice once again running through my head, and after a moment's hesitation I turned the key in the lock.

The next morning, Ekaterina was cheerful, even though neither of us mentioned the events of the night before. It was hard not to return her cat's smile, but my mind kept returning to that conversation in the dark.

At breakfast there was a letter for me from one of the Misses Gray. I hesitated before opening it, feeling certain it would be tiresome.

My dear Miss Oliver, she wrote. *I am sure you will want to know that I have made inquiries into the bonafides of Maynard's Mechanicals. While the firm has a tolerable reputation, I have it on the best authority from a personal friend that the family is most unsuitable for you to become involved with. Mrs. Maynard has behaved intolerably toward her husband, undoubtedly a result of her Russian blood. As you seem to have been under the misapprehension that your employer is a single woman, I felt it was only right for you to know.*

As for the child you have been employed to teach, I cannot imagine what her antecedents might be, but I can only suppose—

I let the letter fall, and had to snatch to keep it from falling into the butter.

"Bad news?" Ekaterina asked.

"Unexpected news," I said in my most chilly tones.

She hardly seemed to notice, directing another of those smiles—which now struck me as repulsively smug—at me. "I have a surprise for you," she said.

"You can show me after Hypatia's lesson," I said discouragingly.

"There will be no lesson today. That's part of the surprise." She led me up to the attic, and lit the gas lamps with a flourish.

Eleven mechanicals stood against the walls, eyes closed, hands at their sides. Their clothes were an assortment of sober frocks and day dresses, but their features were identical. "Hypatia," I said, but none of them responded.

"They can't hear you yet," Ekaterina said. "Although I did decide to let them keep the name. I'm making the last recording now, and the last alterations to Hypatia."

"Alterations?"

"She can't stay an innocent blank slate. Think how much trouble she'd get into if she accepted anything anyone told her as true. No, after this, she can add new facts to her store if they agree with the ones she knows already, but any alteration in her behavior will require mechanical adjustment."

"Poor Hypatia," I said.

Ekaterina smiled in unexpected sympathy. "Yes, poor Hypatia. I'm afraid she's only a means to an end after all."

"As am I," I said, unable to bite back the bitter words. "I suppose now it's time for me to look for a position in some little country town, while you go running back to your husband."

Ekaterina stared at me for a moment. I was prepared for lies, or blustering anger. Instead she laughed, a wild sound with little humor in it.

"Go back to my husband?" she said. "If I were a mercenary little thing, that's just what I would do. I married Arthur Maynard when I was seventeen. My father wanted me provided for before he died—he barely made it to my wedding day. I adored my father, I trusted him to know what was best for me—I could have used a stern dose of your kind of moral instruction, believe me.

"Well, it was a disaster, of course. Even if I'd been suited by nature to appreciate Arthur's efforts in the bedroom, we didn't have a kind word for each other outside of it. On our first anniversary I asked him for a divorce."

"He wouldn't grant it?"

"Oh, he was happy enough to move out and leave me this house. But a divorce? My dear Emily, he would have been killing the goose that laid the golden eggs. Maynard's Mechanicals makes him ten times the income he could make for himself, even if he were inclined to work."

"You're the one who does the work."

"I'm a married woman," Ekaterina said. "Every penny I make belongs to my husband. He lets me have a little pocket money. He's not an ungenerous man."

I found myself noticing again the shabbiness of her dress and the worn toes of her boots. "That's what you're doing with the mechanicals," I said.

Ekaterina raised a skeptical eyebrow, and I realized where Hypatia had picked up that particular mannerism. "What am I doing with the mechanicals?"

"Subverting young ladies," I said. "Teaching them not to marry, and to defy their fathers. Making suffragettes and jezebels of them under their families' noses." The words tumbled out in a rush. "I may have a dozen pupils, but you'll have hundreds—the original buyers will sell them on once all their children are grown. It's the perfect revenge."

Her expression was unreadable. "And what do you think of my plan?"

I took a deep breath. "I entirely approve," I said.

Ekaterina smiled delightedly. "My dear Emily," she said. "You would make an admirable criminal mastermind. You make me wish I had time to carry out your plan. Certainly it would make England more interesting." She stroked one of the Hypatias fondly on the shoulder. "No, I'm afraid my plan is a bit more relentlessly practical than that."

Scraps of lessons tumbled through my mind. "Would it have anything to do with the value of diamonds?"

"You are a quick study. Six months from now, twelve wealthy families will wake up to discover they are missing assorted jewels, bank notes, and cheques drawn on their accounts—thank you, by the way, for teaching Hypatia how to imitate someone's signature. All posted to—well, you mustn't think I don't trust you, but to tell the truth, I don't trust you that much."

"They'll blame the mechanicals."

"Of course they will. I expect a number of them will bring suit against Maynard's Mechanicals. I should like to be here to enjoy watching Arthur explain in court that the creations he takes such pride in boasting about were really the work of his estranged wife. But I think it would really be more prudent to be elsewhere. Monte Carlo, perhaps?" It was just then October, and foggy. "Or maybe further abroad. How would you like to see Cairo?"

"You can't imagine I'll help you."

"You needn't, of course. You could go straight to the police and tell them your story. They might even believe it, although I will tell them that you have an active imagination. But answer one question for me first." She smiled, her eyes alight with mischief. "Why ever would you do that?"

It was a long moment before I replied. "I can't imagine."

Six months later, we read about it over breakfast in a Bucharest cafe. The Romanian mails were uncertain, but nine of the packages had reached us already; we were quarreling amiably over whether to wait for the other three or purchase tickets for the dirigible that day.

"My goodness," Ekaterina said. "Did you hear about poor Colonel and Mrs Clarence? Not only were they the victim of a fiendish robbery, but now their daughter's run off with...well, it's not clear to me just *who* she's run off with."

"Someone entirely unsuitable, I'm sure," I said. "I expect some terrible influence was at work."

Ekaterina sipped her tea. "We might wait one more day for the last packets," she said. "That really spectacular necklace that Mrs Gorey wore to the opera—"

She broke off as a mechanical approached. "More-tea-Miss-Margaret-Grey-and-Miss-Jane-Grey," she said, in passable but monotone English. I could tell that Ekaterina's fingers itched to take her apart for repairs.

"My dear Ekaterina," I said, waving away the mechanical. "We mustn't be greedy. And the sooner we're settled in Egypt, the sooner you can have a laboratory again."

"Sensible as always," she said, and drained her cup to the dregs.

Lady of the House of Mirrors

Rafaela F. Ferraz

The order was simple, and it arrived written in golden ink over pale pink, thick paper with a vague scent of roses. Rosie smiled at the coincidence, that a local legend should use perfume that referenced her own name in a professional card, but roses were common—unlike the job she was being commissioned for, she thought.

She folded the note into a small square, perfect to fit in her breast pocket, and slid into the shoulder strap of her tool bag. Slumped over a work table, Theo, her copper-headed assistant, sanded the last imperfections out of a piece of clay where he, too, had seen a doll head. He could watch the shop for a couple of hours, but as a reminder, she still gave him a soft pat on the shoulder before crossing the threshold of their discreet and picturesque door—*Varadys Automata, Dolls For Dreamers*—and stepping into a winter so harsh it'd taken her twelve years to get used to. Her eyes took a second to adjust to the silvery winter air, but a cab trip later, she was back inside—though the colors no longer matched the earth tones of doll parts, and instead the powdered shades of make-up and expensive perfume.

"Miss V, I presume?"

The voice belonged to a butler, an old man with dark, delicate hands that reached out to take her coat. She shed it without a second thought, and followed the man's crooked back through halls of mirrors into a large, flaky ballroom. The blinds were only partially pulled, letting in blades of late afternoon light, and the fireplace was lit on the furthest corner of the room. On either side, an armchair, and on one of them, a delicate hand on an armrest.

The woman looked towards the door and her hair unraveled from behind her ear.

"You can leave, Carter. Thank you." The hand curled into a wave. "Come closer, Miss. Please don't be shy."

Rosie had never been shy. Not as a child, even less as an adult. Strangers posed no threat when you'd grown up surrounded by the *crème de la crème* of the underground. She walked up to the fireplace, crude work boots echoing against the floorboards until she stepped on the carpet. The woman was young, and the fire brought out the determination in her dark complexion and soft gray eyes, lined with precise needles of black kohl. Her face was made-up, an invention, a mask of power that didn't slip even when she had to look up from her disadvantageous sitting position, and meet Rosie's stare. She controlled the room with an aura so strong it made Rosie's heart wither and wilt.

"Please sit. We have a lot to discuss."

Her only choice was the second armchair, and so she sat with eyes fixed on the fire ahead. If she moved she would surely pop a shirt button, or worse, disturb the languor that furnished the room. Words flew in the streets, and if one walked with ears perked high enough, they'd be able to catch them—the lady of the house of mirrors, was how they called her current customer. A poor thing, delicate and faint, a butterfly in her cocoon, with skin so sensitive to the sun that mere exposure would make her pass out, or inflame her skin until the tender, bulbous tumors rendered her unrecognizable, or dead, even—depending on whose words one took for granted on the matter.

"May I offer you a drink, Miss...?" Her voice was low, in that way of people who were sure even their whispers rose to the skies. "...excuse me, is it Varadys? Like the old man?"

"No, ma'am, I..." Rosie's voice, though, was low in that way of people whose lips often failed to communicate the words so carefully aligned in their minds. "...I have taken up his business, but we are not related. You may call me Rose. And thank you for the offer, but I'd rather not...drink." She didn't add that while she wasn't against voluntary intoxication, she didn't trust anyone enough to let them fill her glass.

"Very well." She took a careful sip from whatever glittering liquid filled the glass by her side, and reset it on the circle of condensation it had left on the surface of the table. Her nails, dark red, were filed to elegant points. "Miss Rose, then. May I ask why you've taken up his business if you are not related? You're not from here, clearly." She held out her fingers, gesturing towards Rosie's self-conscious head."

"I moved here when I was young. My family knew Mr. Varadys, and when the time came for them to take on a complicated job opportunity, they left me here to hone my..." She struggled to find a good way to word it, a small lie with which she could speak the truth. "...craft skills."

The lady let out a small smile, as if the revelation pleased her.

"We have both been left aside by our families, then."

"There were attempts to recover me afterwards, but by then I'd convinced myself I belonged here." *Here, where the underground has taken over the surface and no one seems to notice.*

The lady held her chin on her dainty fingers and murderous nails, well-tended lips pursing in thought.

"Wise decision. I wouldn't have met you otherwise."

That small line delivered the final blow, and Rosie found herself growing uncomfortable.

"If I may be bold, ma'am...why have you called me here?"

"Your old employer was the best in the business, and you take after him. The truth is, Miss, I need something done." Silence dragged on, while the lady appeared to rethink her words. "Someone, in fact. I want a companion piece, a machine that acts and looks human in every way...to keep me company, you understand, since nobody else seems up to the task."

She didn't doubt it. What she doubted, though, was her own ability to build such a thing. She knew herself incapable—even if there was little she had to consider on a rational level, no matter the assignment. Most mechanisms simply made themselves known to her, and in a trance, she built them to the image seared into her brain. Injecting life, a ghost into the machine wasn't hard – it was life force, and like everything else in a world of labeled packages and weighted parcels, it could be harnessed and collected, distilled from blood and sweat, cooked from skin cells and forgotten hairs. There was method to what others saw only as madness—but she had no interest in showing it to them.

The lady had kept on talking. Rosie hadn't noticed.

"...and I would want it to be polite and courteous, and to obey my every whim."

"Why don't you just hire someone?" It was an uncomfortable question, but Rosie had grown to accept that people would sell just about anything: their time, the skin off their backs, the arch of their spines when pleasure hit.

"I don't believe in that sort of exchange, Miss Rose. It's not a fair trade, money for emotions, or in this case, the lack thereof. All people have emotions, even if they try their hardest to contain them, and I'm not keen on having to consider a second sentient being under this roof." She brought her glass up, as if proposing a toast. "I'm a princess in a tower, Miss, prepared to deal with no emotions but my own."

And yet, Rosie's assistant had caught plenty of words on the street about her nighttime visitors.

"I have stated my wishes, Miss, and I know you are the person to accomplish them. Your fame precedes you, as they say. Your skills.... The dolls you've made for the children of the rich and powerful. Dolls that move in the night. Dolls that crawl and walk and brawl.... Dolls that think, even?"

Rosie would rather not speak of the dolls. She'd kept the pieces of her first, built by Varadys before she'd met him, stacked inside a safe in a corner of the shop, and Theo's horrified eyes had been enough to prove that he, too, could hear the rattling.

"What kind of...look are you interested in?"

"Something that looks, and acts, real will suffice. Gender or appearance details are irrelevant."

"And...anatomical details?"

The lady gave her a sly smile over the rim of her glass.

"Do you think I need a sexual aid, Miss?"

She didn't reply. She'd realized, early in life, that there was no point trying to understand people's inner desires from the curl of their pulse, or the whiteness of the teeth they bared in a casual smile.

The order was simple, then. A companion piece. A robot. A mechanical person that wouldn't stand out in a decayed palace where the ink was gold and the letters smelled of roses.

She sat at the drawing board the following afternoon, behind the counter of the shop she owned, even though she'd never bothered to remove the name of her mentor from the sign. Varadys Automata, that was what it said, and she was just Miss V, to most people. Petite, head a mess of golden thread, hands elegant but calloused—like a thief's. Monsieur Varadys had been dead for five years, and she kept his ashes in a metal urn, sculpted to the approximate shape of his skull while he'd been alive to approve it. She'd placed him above the fireplace, as a reminder—*you might be alone now, Rosie, but I've left you big shoes to fill.*

In her drawing pad, lines at the end of her pencil took the shape of what she assumed must be a good-looking person. She started with the hardest option, a boy's face. Boys were difficult. She could lay out the whole span of the universe, examine it with a loupe of the highest quality, and return without finding more than one to her liking. She'd loved a boy, once. To think of it, herself a precocious eight-year old, and he a dreamer selling himself for wings. Ten more years, and she would have built him a pair, sturdy enough to escape. His features found their way into the blank paper and she didn't fight them. Dark skin, wavy hair, blue-green eyes. He wore an eyepatch, and his body was covered in scars.

At noon, the door struck the chime hanging from above, and Theo walked in with winter on his back. Elegant glasses and a penchant for cravats that went a little too tight around his throat—she'd never asked, he'd never told—she supposed he was good-looking too, if only a little less authentic, if only a little more conscious of his own appeal. Theo was her second assistant in five years, since she'd taken over the shop. The first one had been a girl, but Rosie had found herself falling for her pronounced Cupid's bow and the way her fingers moved when she adjusted the legs of the tin dolls on the shelves. There was something about femininity that drew her in. Something about the way some women sprayed their perfumes and applied their powders, wrapping themselves in protective layers of scent and color, refusing the crude touch of the same air that enveloped common mortals. The women in her childhood had been that way too—tall and proud, self-assured, knuckles white over the reins that drew people, and only the right people into their lives, puppets on a string, choreographed to perfection by the hands that had once rocked her to sleep.

"Myers paid ahead, two dolls to be delivered next month at the townhouse..." Theo flipped through his notes as he delved further into the shop, reaching ahead of his own steps to open the hidden counter door, the final boundary that protected the half of the shop where she didn't have to worry about presenting herself, too, as a doll ready to be sold. "...got a couple more orders, but nothing you'll have to attend to in person." He closed his notebook with a blunt sweep of his right hand, and removed his glasses to let them hang by a gold chain at his neck. "But now you must tell me. The lady. What did she want?"

She recounted the small meeting, and he nodded along, attentive, drinking her every word, peeking over her shoulder to analyze her half-conscious sketch with a slight frown. He recognized the subject, of course. Max, with his eye patch and his scars. As a rule, Rosie didn't keep secrets.

"What are you thinking, then? We can't build a robot that looks like a human. There's no way we can recreate the skin, the texture..."

"Yes, that's why we won't." She pushed her boot against the desk and slid backwards on the wheeled chair, stopping by the fireplace across the room. Theo sidestepped to abandon the collision course, but there was a smile on his face and she *understood* she had to do everything in her power to keep him by her side. He'd play along, no matter what it was. He was curious and driven and excitable. And young. "We'll use human parts. Real human parts. I want the best, so make sure you find someone worthy."

Theo's eyes were half-amused, half-cautious slits.

"Someone...dead, of course?"

"Freshly so, if possible." She stood to her full—but tiny—height and made her way to the stairs, hoping that sleep would prove beneficial to her creativity. "It won't be of any use if it starts decomposing, so see if you can find someone whom...whom will tell you about incoming dead."

"Will do. May I ask, though...?"

She'd just touched the first step with her heel, but still she turned.

"...why are you going to such trouble for a powdered princess in a decayed mansion? Is the pay...that good?"

"The pay is okay. That's not the point."

"Then...?"

"The point..." She abandoned the stairs to rejoin Theo by the fireplace. "... is that I didn't train here to make toys. I've told you this. That wasn't the reason my family chose to burden a reclusive old man with my education. I know I can give life to anything I choose, and I have chosen to start now. The stakes are high, I've got the conditions gathered. I can't fail. If Varadys could bring life to my childhood dolls, I can do the same. And..."

She stopped herself short, keeping the rest of the justification to herself. She'd seen the woman, spoken to her, and if there was one thing consistent about halls of mirrors, was that one always struggled to find their way out. Not because of the mirrors, or the doors, or the confusing layout camouflaged behind the reflective walls, in that particular case. No. But because every mirror reflected the same thing, and that thing was a velvet armchair where a woman sat. She was young, dark, and the fire brought out the determination in her eyes, a soft gray lined with precise needles of black kohl. And like so many women before her, women for whom Rosie had carved check marks on her bedposts, she had a pronounced Cupid's bow, and her fingers moved in the most alluring of ways every time she seized her glass and took a careful sip.

It didn't take Theo long to figure out what they'd have to do. The redhead was resourceful, and when he didn't spend the day with her, fixing dolls for little girls, sewing tiny dresses, accessorizing his right eye with intricate loupes, or fixing the casual curl of the fringe that fell over his eyes, he was outside, collecting intelligence, making sure Rosie got the latest news without ever having to walk out the door. They were both outlanders, after all, neither born nor raised in the city that had seen them grow into their clumsy young versions of adulthood.

That evening, he arrived with a triumphant note, and the smile on his face echoed the one that took her own lips by assault.

"Did you get it?"

"I got it." He was feeling brave, the kind of bravery sold in pill boxes and syringes, and it showed in the way he sat on the counter and spun to plant his feet on the other side—her side—of the barricade. "A friend of mine, Aiden. He's apprenticed to an embalmer across town. They get called to fix the...well, the ugliest bodies every once in a while, in the red light district, but—"

"We don't want an ugly body, Th—"

"No, Rosie, I know we don't." His voice was flat, stern, but he held out his hands as if to apologize for it—scared that she could find him, perhaps, pretty enough to turn into a machine if all else failed. The idea, albeit attractive in theory, didn't receive any gold stars from the pragmatic side of her mind. Rosie hadn't forgotten. Rosie remembered the trees scratching the windows of her childhood home and the murderous look in her aunt's eyes when she came home from a particularly taxing day, the scars she left on her slave's body afterwards. She remembered his face, as well, Max's face, enough to know it looked nothing like Theo's, enough to wonder if the magic had held through the years. Maybe he'd found someone to restore his missing eye. "All I'm saying is...there's a body in a morgue by the river. It's a boy, and he matches your original idea. Black hair, light eyes. He might be a little too light-skinned, but...it's an experiment, right?"

His eyes looked hopeful, though unsure. Rosie raised an eyebrow, one decorated with three tiny silver rings. "What do you mean, an experiment?"

"You won't...sell him to her, right? Not the first? Not the prototype?"

Rosie lay back in her seat, ran a hand through her hair, found her fingers caught in the knots. It was a good question. What if it worked? What if it didn't? What if he glitched? What if the body wasn't even usable to being with?

No use in wondering. "Come along, we have work to do."

Across town, the young man Rosie assumed must be Aiden awaited them by the morgue. He looked perfectly nondescript, and his left sleeve ended in a knot below the elbow, nothing but frigid air where his forearm used to be. Rosie made a note to fix it for him, as soon as she could. He led them into the deserted morgue, their figures casting shadows upon, first, the waiting room, then the embalming tables, and finally, the wall of numbered drawers.

"He's over there. Bottom row, second door."

Theo swallowed shaky words, and gestured for Rosie to step forward. He hadn't grown in the midst of madness the way she had—he wasn't used to the bodies and the blood and the guts. She approached the set of metallic doors with respect, even though she knew what lay on the other side had to be seen as nothing but feedstock.

The body slid out with a swift pull, feet first. He was barefoot, his feet clad in black stockings that ended beneath loose shorts that ended at his knees. He wore a corset, a bottle green corset that pulled in his waist—not enough to deform him, not enough to catapult him into the realm of the uncanny. His skin was pale, nearly white in the thin light, and his eyes were glazed over—hard to tell whether they were hazel or gray. Dark brown hair, growing long around his chin, an easy fix. But the inside of the drawer reeked of alcohol, and that, she didn't find quite so auspicious.

"Cause of death?"

Aiden, standing by the door, hand draped over the door handle as if body snatching was something he did every day, gave her a shrug.

"Not sure. Some are saying overdose. As I suppose you can imagine, he hasn't been autopsied yet."

Was that passive-aggressiveness in his tone? Condescension? Rosie decided she would fix his forearm for him, sure, but she'd charge him twice as she would anybody else.

"Drugs, then?"

"I suppose."

That wouldn't do. What if something didn't work? What if he'd been damaged beyond repair, beyond the point where she'd still be able to fix him with money and machines?

"Theo, help me prepare him." He walked forward with a large bag clutched between jeweled knuckles, and together, they eased the body into its new cocoon. Halfway through, she decided to remove the corset. It left boning marks criss-crossed over his own exposed bones, and she wasn't sure they'd go away.

It was so late it was turning early, and Rosie couldn't help but stare at the body on the table in the back room, a little workshop where she used to sit on a too-large armchair and watch Varadys work on his most ambitious projects. The walls had been covered in brass legs and brass heads ever since she remembered, but nothing else had stood the test of time—she was alone then, braving new territory, and taking a risk with parts of a different kind. On the first day, Rosie wasn't sure she could do it. On the second day, she *was* sure she *couldn't* do it, when the smell set in and her fingers froze inches from the boy's body, curling into hesitant claws, retreating to rest idly by her side. The experiment rotted in the back of the workshop, and she didn't try to make it work.

Two days later, morning found her huddled in a corner, wrapped in a tattered blanket. The safe rattled, the doll wanted out. On the table, the boy had turned purple where gravity had pooled blood beneath his skin. She sat as he lay, and in their own ways, both drifted closer to their own demises, carrying marks of their individual prisons—his a physical set of metal bones, hers a mental picture of a short but eventful life—into the unknown.

If results tended to show themselves to her, they were not doing it this time. Oh no. Her mind was empty but for the icy paralysis that came with fear, and terror, and the stench of the corpse on her work table. Theo was gone. She'd asked him to lay off work for a few days, and when solitude became too much, she asked Aiden to recover the body. She didn't say a word beyond the ones she'd written on her calling card, sent clutched in the right hand of a dead-eyed child, as her left held a brand new doll. *Varadys Automata, Dolls For Dreamers*, the sign over the door said—and sometimes, Rosie still tried to live up to it.

The body left, the smell lingered. And then the note arrived, written in golden ink over pale pink, thick paper with a vague scent of roses.

There's one more thing, Miss. I want it to speak. But more than that, I want it able to converse. Call back when possible. With love, G.

She tore the note and let the pieces fall around her feet on the floor boards. A figure of despair, she found herself looking up at the walls of the brass reliquary that was her workshop. The lady didn't know what she wanted, but Rosie did—and it was no longer a robot. It was a slave.

No one knew slaves quite like Max. Maximillian, once. Dark skin, wavy hair, blue-green eyes, an eyepatch, and a body covered in scars, all worn like uncomfortable clothes around one of the highest penthouses in the city—one with rooftop access, and thus an escape route into the skies he had always called home.

On the ground floor, a doorwoman stopped her with an authoritative hand, asked for her name, noted her address. She took them all with her into a small room where Rosie wasn't allowed, a room from which she came back with a snarl.

"Please take the elevator. He'll be expecting you."

It could have been true, but the person on the other side of the ascending gilded cage was not the one *she* had been expecting. The defining characteristics had remained unchanged, but the eyepatch was gone, replaced by a discreet glass eye—he was already half doll, then, even without her intervention—and the scars on the back of his fidgeting hands had healed to barely noticeable silver lines. Hard to tell whether he was happy to see her.

"Are you alone?" It was the first thing she asked, and the one that cracked his face into the smile she had always associated with his character.

"Such a predatory question for a guest to ask, Rose." He stepped forward and unlocked the cage, but didn't open the door. "May I ask...why the sudden visit?"

Half of her wanted to sit, relax, act friendly for old times' sake. The other half wanted to leave as soon as possible, abandon the uptown world of polished hardwood penthouses and return to the moldy riverside, where the dust was toxic but the people were kind.

"I need your help."

"Well, obviously."

When had the women in her family ever remembered him with no strings attached, no favors asked? Rosie wondered, as she followed his defeated shoulders into the living room. By the large windows, he invited her to take the sofa, but chose to stay on his feet himself—she understood he needed the advantage, and gave it away, sinking into the pillows, expecting the silence to break on its own. Finally, he indicated the city.

"So how's business on the ground?"

"Haven't you been down?"

A headshake, a smile. "Not once this year, no. It's too much for me—the people, the noises. I'd rather stay above ground...and get somebody else to do the shopping."

Did he need a companion piece, too? The smell of the dead body caught up to her, and his creature comforts didn't seem quite so interesting in comparison.

"Listen, Max...have you heard of the house of mirrors?"

"Can't say I have." He seemed honest, if uninterested—she'd prepared herself to see him shiver, as if he too had been one of the lady's nocturnal visitors, as if he too had already fulfilled companion duties a robot would never be able to live up to.

"There's a lady who lives there, and she never goes outside. She has hired me to create her...a doll. A companion piece. Life-sized, able to speak, to move, to do everything a human does, except...not human."

Max was listening. The one eye he retained any control over was curious. His knuckles were white from gripping his sleeves at his elbows.

"I came to you in case you had any ideas."

"I don't know anything about dolls." But she knew *he* knew where she was going, and he was bracing himself for it.

"No, but you know about machines. And you know about..."

He nodded. "You can say it."

"...submitting. Listen, I-I can't program a thing to speak if she wants it able to hold a conversation. I can't make a machine do the things she wants. It's just not possible. But I told her I would, and if I don't, she... she's going to flay me, I just know it."

Max gave her nothing more than a shrug.

"Then find her someone. A slave, a submissive. With time, we could train someone." He sat on the coffee table in front of her, elbows on his knees, a little too close, and she was again young, fascinated by this creature who would have once braved an army to keep her out of harm's way. "Do we have time?"

"It doesn't matter, it's just a thought. I'm not... I'm not really going to do it." Or was she? "What if they change their mind, what if they leave? She doesn't want a person acting like a robot, she wants a robot acting like a person, and it's not the sam—"

"No, it's not, but can she tell the difference?" And his smile was different, and his face was different, and he wasn't the most beautiful boy on the world anymore—she wouldn't have handed him to a customer if he had been the last human standing.

"I didn't know you were this...cunning, Max." And when he averted his eyes, she struck again. "Spending too much time working with my family, I see."

He gave her what seemed to be an eye roll, hard to identify by his half paralyzed orbs and his sudden, rushed movement, up and away from the sofa.

"Don't flatter your kin. If you want help, that's my proposal." By the window, he calmed down again, still as a statue, as his right hand moved into the void to explain his point. "She's not going to know if you train someone and pay them well. There are hundreds of people out there who would love to get out of the streets, and into a house with a proper roof. Besides, if she treats them well... it's not that bad of a deal."

She wondered if, apart from everything else, the parts she couldn't see under his clothes, the rest she already knew about...Max had also sold his soul.

"People will do the darkest things for safety. But I don't expect you to understand." He ran a caring hand through her hair as he walked by the sofa, and disappeared up the stairs.

His words lingered in the back of her mind, but she pushed them aside every so often. She requested a second body from Aiden, and that time she wasn't picky. Anything would do, and what came was a middle-aged woman, her hair a dyed shade of bright red. *Anything would do*, she kept telling herself, head lolling forward on the hinge of her shoulders, finding no solace even when she took the time to drag herself into the corner couch where childhood had brought her such sweet dreams.

"Have you been sleeping?" It was Theo, concerned, voice mixed with the jingle of the front door keys hanging from his fingers. Was it past closing time already?

She shook her head, closing her eyes in silent surrender. No, she hadn't been sleeping, not at all. She felt herself being consumed by ideas, eaten inside out. That time, she opened the body. She wore gloves, and into a bag that Theo held open in his own bare hands—he could be fearless, when her motivation overflowed into him—she transferred every organ in the chest cavity. Next was the blood. She'd seen them do it in funeral homes, a pump replacing blood with embalming fluid, something to keep the tissues looking at least vaguely human while the insides became something else. It was late, but not enough to be early that time. Theo threw a blanket over her shoulders, and together, they stood and watched.

"You know, I...this isn't how I imagined my first contact with the workforce." He added air quotes around the final word, surely a remnant from times spent with a *nouveau riche* family for whom work was such a shameful word it should never be uttered on its own.

She pulled the blanket tighter around her neck and smiled against the warm wool. It was strange to think she was the same age as Theo, curious to think that they had so much more in common than she and Max ever would—and yet, she thought of him as a pupil, the next in line for the little Varadys shop. Dolls for dreamers. Did he have what it took? Did the science of doll-making, life-making, did the god complex particles run in his blood, the way they did in hers?

"Have you thought that maybe you could...take over in a few years?"

"Oh, no..." He looked displaced, all of a sudden. "...no way, I...I'm not like you. I can't do...the things you can. You look at a problem and your mind solves it before you do, but that's not me. I can't do that."

She looked at the body on the table, the blood replaced by the fluid, the skin looking waxen under the oppressive light bulbs. There was no moonlight, and the workshop was a silent crypt—she'd never seen herself so close to her demise.

"I'm not sure I can solve this problem, either."

He smiled, sympathetic, before lacing an arm around her shoulders and squeezing lightly. "I have faith in you."

He brought tea and biscuits. She upgraded the look of the Creation itself from flesh-colored to gold and bronze. She replaced organs with clock parts and muscles with elaborate systems of levers and pulleys and pistons. She was close.

A second note arrived.

I hope this delay doesn't mean you have stepped down from the assignment, Miss V. May I remind you, you shook my hand, we're bound now. If not by law, then by honor. With love, G.

But there was no honor among thieves, and Rosie let out a bone-chilling scream when the second body, too, started to rot.

She returned to the house of mirrors after the third body, after the stench in the workshop became so intense she had started to work with a mask. Theo himself had moved works in progress to his own house—business wasn't so bad it could justify selling miasmatic baby dolls. No need to pass on the honors of an unfortunate childhood at the hands of a Varadys masterpiece.

Rosie said the words over tea with the lady, staring at impeccable nails tapping the arm of the powder blue armchair. The room reeked of rotten roses, or perhaps just roses in general, and she was the one bringing in the rot. "I can't give you everything you want in one companion. It's impossible. I can't do it."

The lady didn't answer with anger, instead putting on a polite mask of curiosity, her face inquisitive in the way small wrinkles formed around her eyes.

"Then who can? If not you, then who?"

"I need a lot of time, and effort..."

"And I can pay you for both."

"Yes, ma'am, I understand, but..."

"What seems to be the problem?" The lady set down her glass, sitting up straight, adjusting a curl of her hair behind her pierced ear. "Miss, why do I have a feeling you're failing on purpose? Avoiding my notes, refusing to give me any feedback on the assignment *I* ordered...this isn't a game to me. You may be as fickle as a child, and very well, for you are still one, but I am not. If you don't want my business, just say so, and I'll send my assistant to search for it elsewhere."

Rosie didn't acknowledge the frustration building up, but when her fingers clenched too tight around the teacup she'd been handed just minutes before, suddenly too warm, too slippery, too uncomfortable, she broke.

"*Then search for it elsewhere!*" She threw the teacup at the wall, where it broke and scattered, staining the wallpaper, transforming the floorboards into a porcelain minefield. The lady's hand rose to clutch her pearls, as if comfort lived in the texture of the string of masterpieces around her neck, the result of a hundred underwater jobs well done, never disturbed by the sensory overload of death, the entrails in trash bags discarded by the entrance, the dismayed looks on the faces of innocent young assistants. Her breakdown seemed out of place in the shadowy room, and she cradled her head in her hands, pressing fingers against the cane of her nose to keep from crying. "Forgive me. Forgive me, ma'am, I don't know what got to me."

"I will ask you again, Miss..." The lady touched Rosie's bare wrist, then her fingers, until she had them trapped in her own. She pulled them out, as if relaxing the claws of some murderous animal, and carefully placed her own cup between them. Rosie let herself be maneuvered, herself a doll, but not much of a companion. "...what seems to be the problem? I don't know about machines, or whatever else your work consists of. But I know about fear, and frustration, and if what you need is help coping, I might be able to offer it."

"The only thing you can offer me is your understanding. What you've asked of me...it's not possible."

"I thought you made dolls for dreamers. I thought you could make anything work."

"I've started to doubt that myself."

"What is it that you don't want to achieve, Miss? Fame? Fortune? Is my generosity not enough for you? Or do you pity me, like everybody else?"

"It's nothing of the sort, ma'am, nothing. It's just I haven't found the solution to this particular problem yet, and there's nothing I can do. I can't do it until inspiration...until the solution comes to me."

The lady bent forward, setting her sharp chin on the back of her folded hand.

"Is that the way you work? You sit and wait for inspiration to strike you? For the solutions to come to you? Doesn't seem too productive to me, Miss. What if inspiration doesn't feel like coming?"

"Then I disappoint my customer, ma'am."

The lady laughed, looking away, sitting back in the chair, disturbing the blanket over her legs as she crossed them underneath the fabric. "And that shouldn't ever be an option, should it? Lest disappointment be something they can't handle."

She dared look up at the woman, but her skin was perfect and powdered and her hair fell in ideal curls over her shoulder, and her earrings were long cascades of jewels that mingled between them, and she was so alluring that she couldn't bear the thought of having disappointed her.

"If I may ask...why haven't you considered escaping?"

The lady blinked, closed her eyes for a moment as the corner of her lips rose, cat-like, in a satisfied smile.

"Do you think me stupid, Miss?"

"No. No, not...not at all."

"Nothing you can possibly say to me about my own life or condition will make more sense to me than what I can already say to myself. You don't know me. I didn't invite you here to give me life-changing advice."

She stood. "You are correct. I will return to work."

The lady let her walk away, a few tentative steps, before putting out her cigarette on the marble surface of the side table. She rose, and Rosie had never seen her stand—if not exactly tall, she looked ominous, wrapped in a dark shawl with only her claws for front clasps.

"Will you?"

"Yes. Yes, I will. I will try the best I can."

The woman inched closer, running thin fingers through Rosie's blonde locks. "And answer my notes this time, will you? I'm very interested in knowing how you work. Since I can't...go out to see it myself." She closed the distance between them, and Rosie felt herself freeze, until the lady planted a soft kiss on her jawline—then she melted. "I'm sure you wouldn't want me to invite you to come work here until you're done."

It was a threat disguised with a kiss, and Rosie caught it somewhere in the air between the skin her lips had touched, and the fingers she brought up to trap their fading presence.

The solution came to her a few days later, after two hours of sleep and a cup of despicable tea, as she leaned on Theo's silk-covered shoulder and coached him into painting a doll's eye *just right*. She didn't let him know, but she counted every minute, every second until he boxed the doll and announced he was leaving for its delivery. Like a dutiful wife standing guard by the window, following her undutiful husband's footsteps until the nearest corner obscured him from view, she waited. And then, she flipped the sign. Dolls for dreamers, absolutely, but not always, not *then*.

She planned carefully, drew letters and diagrams, collected all the materials and contacts she would need to make it work. From the cash register, a heavy stash of bank notes. From behind the counter, her tool bag. She walked out a little after sunset, turned right in the direction of the shady inns and alleys where drug dealers and similar night crawlers made their living, and didn't come back.

The doll was delivered by Rosie's own hands—with the assistance of Theo's and Aiden's—to the infamous house of mirrors a few days later, two weeks, in an elaborate box remade from a white coffin. It was life-sized, as expected, as ordered, and wrapped in white tissue paper, thin as the wings of a cabbage butterfly.

It was brighter than usual inside the living room, and the lady awaited her small entourage standing by the nearly opaque white curtains, wrapped in a floral shawl. She looked over at the box, but didn't let her face fall into any show of emotion.

"Do you bring me a dead man, Miss?"

Rosie felt like laughing, but Theo caught her eye—and he didn't seem at all amused.

"I will explain everything once my helpers leave, ma'am."

Helpers. The word seemed to linger over Theo's shoulders, dripping like acid rain from his wavy hair. "Fine." He gave the lady a small bow, she nodded in his direction, and then he was gone, with only Aiden and a slight suggestion of anger on his trail.

They were alone. Just the two of them, women from different walks of life, two different types of criminal. The mastermind and the wrecking ball. The wizard—perhaps the witch?—and the dragon. The lady walked forward, and Rosie half expected to hear killer heels on the floor boards, but no—she was barefoot, and her toenails were painted the same bloody shade as her finger nails.

"Shall we unwrap it, then?"

"Of course." First the locks on the side of the coffin, then the layers and layers of tissue paper. It wasn't a boy, that time, but a girl. A girl with long black hair that fell straight around her shoulders, small breasts and protruding hipbones. She—it, perhaps—came clothed in a two piece black suit, the jacket long and the neckline deep, deep enough to reveal the Y-shaped, hand-stitched incision that marred her chest. Rosie was willing to admit defeat for how much she looked like Max, if only in the proud features—but when she sat up, after a little coaxing from Rosie's part, she even seemed to move like him. Cautious, but full of unused potential. Built for carnage, first, and for love, later. Rosie helped her up and out of the box, careful not to strain muscles cold from lying in a tight space for too long. Her eyes were empty—they couldn't be emptier if Rosie had pulled them out of their sockets and replaced them with glass spheres.

"Does it have a name, Miss V?"

"I haven't named her, ma'am. I was expecting you would want to do it yourself."

The lady stepped closer, blew into the doll's eye. She blinked.

"Should it do that?"

Rosie had kept her fingers crossed. Hoped the lady wouldn't ask questions she could not answer, because the answers had come while she'd been too artificially dazed, somewhere between Theo's and Max's apartments, to remember to take notes.

"She.... I mean, it.... Forgive me, ma'am..." She wasn't yet good at extracting the humanity from the parts, from the skin and bone and skull and lips of the human who stood just inches from her, a face and body framed in black, tarnished only by a Y-shaped scar over the chest. "The shell is very much human. If you touch h- it, you will realize the skin feels warm, like a human's would. The shell is human, and it works like a human's, which means there will be some needs you will need to attend to. Think of it as recharging your companion—perpetual motion is still very much beyond my skill set."

"How does this creature you offer me differ from a human, then?"

Rosie reached out, and touched the doll. Touched *her*, not it, running a finger upwards over the stitches. "It's different here." She let the finger rest on the doll's forehead. "And here. The shell is human. The rest is as empty as it looks. And it's yours to change, and create, and improve as you see fit. I'm sure it will suit your needs. Any changes you feel like making, on the outside or the inside, I will be more than happy to take care of."

"Anything else I should know?"

No. No, most definitely not.

There was, after all, method to what others saw only as Rosie's madness—but she had no interest in showing it to them.

The stitches came out ten days later. The doll served tea. Her name was Gemma, and she moved with the trained delicacy of a creature conscious of eyes lingering over her figure every second of the day, and probably the night.

You lied. -G

The note was simple, and it arrived four days later written in golden ink over pale pink, thick paper with a vague scent of roses. It deviated from every other note simply in the fact that it reached the shop tied to a box, a white box with gold locks filled with white tissue paper, thin as the wings of a cabbage butterfly. Inside, a kitchen knife, tainted red, and a bundle of paper stained just as dark.

She unwrapped it, and found someone's heart in her hands.

MR & MRS BRENCHLEY

There is nothing quite like that feeling, where you're woken in the early morning by an explosion far too close to home - first the raucous sound of it startling you from sleep, then the brute vibration of the bed - and you reach for your dear love and find her gone.

That cocktail of confusion and alarm and inevitability happens far too frequently to be labelled in any way unique, but neither may I call it commonplace; there is nothing remotely commonplace about my beloved Clarissa or her behaviours. Who should know it better than I, who bed down with her every night and wake with her—well, most mornings?

Those mornings that I startle from my dreams to find her gone, it is best not to leap up and dash about amid the turmoil, the smoke and noise and anxiety. Better to roll over into the warmth of her declivity and sleep again, until the maid comes at a decent hour with tea and hot water and nimble, competent fingers. Better to meet my leman over breakfast, sponged and clothed and comfortable; better to comment lightly on the scorched condition of her eyebrows, and move on.

That morning as so many mornings, a dull boom shattered my somnolence. I sat up gasping, as the bed shook hard beneath me. It stilled after a moment: no earthquake, then.

"'Rissa?"

No answer. My reaching hands found no figure in the darkness, only that familiar dip in the mattress. How many times had this happened? I no longer counted. Nothing catastrophic ever occurred. I could count on that. Could I not...?

That morning, apparently I could not. I threw back the coverlet and set my toes on the rug, in defiance of long experience. One hand reached for my dressing gown, the other for the gas-bracket. A soft hissing, a brief *pop!*—the Eternal Flame, my disrespectful lover liked to call the pilot-light, or else the Light Everlasting - and a gentle light resulted. At least the pipes had taken no hurt. Encouraged, I stepped into the hallway and sniffed: no hint of smoke. Nor of any activity, upstairs or down. Neither the maid nor the pot-boy had been troubled by the explosion, and Clarissa's plump black cat Albertine still slumbered, curled in a ball on the piano stool.

In the kitchen, my soft footfalls brought an answering, echoing whisper from the pots. They must have clashed and banged like cataclysmic bells, bare minutes since; now it was hard to credit that anything had disturbed their equanimity. Like pendulous moons, they hung from a rack directly over a long low marble counter once meant for carving game.

A device of ivory and steel, buttons and levers and wires, stood on the counter. I reached to depress this button and that, to set those levers thuswise and ratchet the handle downward. Consequences would take some minutes to arrive; meanwhile, I sat on the wooden bench and pulled the Journal of the Natural Philosophy Society closer. It was still open where I had left it, at Profesora Magdalena Cadiz's treatise on the steady encroachment of ice weasels down the northerly shores of the Black Sea.

The profesora claimed my attention until the teapot rolled up along the miniature railtrack, towing a saucer, a teacup, a spoon, and a small pot of honey. The teapot wheezed softly as its internal clockwork disengaged and it lowered itself from the bogie. I soon had a hot cup of tea in hand, and was eyeing the rack of toast steaming its way towards me when I heard a creak from the doorway.

"Euphenia! You're up early."

The figure standing before me in the gaslight bore scorch marks on her bodice, a general air of dishevelment, and an odd scent on her boots. Her deep brown braid was drawn up in a crown that tilted somewhat sideways but nevertheless added welcome inches to her broad frame. Her goggles had left pale circles around her eyes; her strong face was otherwise largely obscured by soot. I stood—tall enough to set my chin in the nest of her hair, should I choose to do so—and gathered her into my embrace.

"Clarissa, damn my eyes. You're alive!"

"I am. Why this news should require the condemnation of anything so useful as your eyes, I am not quite clear." She peered up at me, a little muffled against my chest, a little exasperated. "I've said before, your eyes are by far your finest feature. Blue eyes are not uncommon, of course, even in those of your colouring, but none the less—"

My *inamorata*'s own eyes are a peculiarly sharp shade of black: the very gaze of the abyss, looking back up at you. Looking deep into you, wondering just exactly how you work. And how to take you apart, to prove it. She can be quite unnerving.

At times she can also be verbose, even periphrastic. I know two ways to cut her off short, and one is unseemly before breakfast. I chose the alternative.

"'Rissa dear, what did you blow up this time?"

She can always be steered into speaking of her work. "The latest iteration of our breeding-chamber," she said, as I had feared she would. That contraption was accursed. "I'm sorry, Euphenia. This one has quite gone the way of its ancestors."

"Oh, dear. Was it the seals again?"

She nodded tightly. "There is some flaw in my vulcanisation process. Perhaps I should go back to oiled leather, at least *pro tem*, until the general concept can be proved effectual. It feels like a step backwards, but—"

"But if it serves to prevent pressurised chambers exploding in your face, then I for one am all in favour. Nevertheless, let me reiterate: there's no need for any of this. My sister Dot did quite well by adoption. She recommends the late teen years, so you'll know what you're getting." I put thoughts of bows and pinafores firmly aside, set my hands on her shoulders and propelled her to the table. "Now sit. I will ring through for that hellbrew you call coffee; will you butter your own toast meantime, or is there an automaton for that too?"

The question was purely rhetorical. If she had devised such a machine, she would have set aside even her eternal broodiness to demonstrate the prototype; and it would have failed, more or less spectacularly, as early iterations always did. Our breakfast-table would have become another outpost of her laboratory, cogs and wires everywhere while she disassembled the thing with a jeweller's loupe in her eye, muttering Turkish curses all the while.

Instead she buttered toast more mechanically than any automaton could ever manage, her scowl blackly unreadable. In the abstract, I understand her all too well; in the specifics, my love's mind is as closed to my enquiry as the most abstruse of algebraic formulae. Which is just as well, in all probability. Two such minds in consort might jar the very planet from its courses. One Clarissa is quite enough for humankind to handle. Humankind, or one determined Englishwoman. She is my task, and I rejoice in it.

A steam-whistle sounded distantly—because she can be facetious, even as she is brilliant—and a tall silver pot conveyed itself towards her. She poured, she sipped, her profound and glittering gaze sought mine. She said, "Come to the Exquisitorium with me, when we are finished here. I have something to discuss with you."

Not her relentless quest for an artificial womb in which we might nurture a child to term. That would not be discussed again until the next failure, or—less probably—success. She had another object in view, as ever, my butterfly-minded delight.

My heart fluttered, uncertain—as ever—whether to rise or sink.

The Exquisitorium was a project of the previous year, driven by a previous redesign of her breeding-vessels. While she brooded over her drawing-boards and calculations, she still needed something to be doing with her hands. Hence this conservatory, such as any middle-class English family might aspire to: a Crystal Palace of our own, a glass-and-iron addendum to our home, a place of liminality between house and garden—only rather than harbouring heat and nurturing cacti in all their hideous indecency, it should offer the cool shade of an English garden grove. We should grow tulips and hollyhocks and foxgloves, amid a carpet of chamomile and bluebells. There should be the babble of a little rill, the buzz of friendly English bees, the suddenness of butterflies...

My poor Clarissa. It had taken her all summer to achieve anything at all, and it meant work yet for years to come. She had spent much of the autumn kicking at corners and muttering about mushrooms. But such as it was, it was already a demi-Paradise, offering retreat from the dreadful heat of summer and the chill of winter both. Like any garden indoors or out, it was a place of refuge, a place for thought, a place for pleasure in company or alone.

I took my preferred seat, on the cushions of a wickerwork settee. She paced back and forth before me, as her restless custom was.

She said, "Glands. I need glands." Her boots crunched against pebbles, covering my startled grunt. "Particular glands, that is to say. Don't speak to me of sweetbreads. These glands produce a spectacular oil, which appears to emit warmth even before it is exposed to flame. I've designed an experiment, to learn more before we think of full-scale milking..."

Rissa broke a branch off a sickly-looking hazel sapling and used its point to sketch a map in the gravel while she lectured. I heard "migration" and "controlled cultivation" and "unexpected byproduct", "midnight setting" and "cold control"; it took me three tries, three cries of "Darling!", to stem the flood.

"Are you writing a penny dreadful thriller? Whyever must this rite be performed at midnight?"

"At night," she said, "the ice weasels come."

Cometh the hour, cometh the man - or so the vernacular has it. In Trebizond that season, men came, to be sure, but none of them the hero that we looked for.

From city rat-catchers to wild mountain-men, the shores of the Black Sea play host to any number of hunters and trappers. It seemed as though every one of them infested our streets as the ice weasels' advance continued. Far from saving us, though, those bold men were abandoning their livelihoods and fleeing the forests rather than face the ice-white horde.

"You need an army," was their common growl. "You need soldiers, battalions, artillery. Not us."

In vain did the governor appeal to them to be such an army. Equally in vain did Clarissa and I appeal to them individually, in cafes and on street-corners.

"You want *what*?" One grizzled and malodorous fur-trapper is much like another, and they all said much the same, in much the same tone of incredulity.

"We want you to trap ice weasels for us," Clarissa repeated firmly. Every time, she had to say it twice. "Alive."

"Lady, you're insane." Actual descriptions given may have been more forthright. "Their pelts are worth a fortune from Moscow to Montreal, and they're coming down the coast in numbers that would set a man up for life - and look at us. We're running like rabbits because those creatures scare the living daylights out of us - and you want us to snag 'em *alive*? You want to *farm* 'em?"

"Yes." Nothing more certain in the world. "We can pay."

"Not enough. One load of pelts would be the price of your house, lady, and everything that's in it—and none of us is stopping long enough to take a shot. What you're asking is ten times harder and a hundred times more dangerous, and you won't find no takers, not if you ask every single one of us."

So it seemed, indeed. Which left us with but one solution:

"We must trap the creatures ourselves," Clarissa declared.

"My dear 'Rissa! Where experienced men turn pale and flee—"

"—it is obviously time that women stepped up. Quite so. I am certain that I can devise a suitable containment. Even their notorious teeth will not chew through steel. Is it known what they eat, at all?"

"Everything," I said gloomily. "Everything that moves, that is, or used to. So far as I'm aware, there is nothing green in their diet except carrion."

"Carrion is easier than live bait. That's capital." My love spoke distractedly, notebook in hand. It was decided, then. We would shortly be hunters and trappers, and thereafter ice-weasel farmers. Or else we would ourselves be carrion. That was always an option.

"We need a dog. A large dog."

"You have never shown an interest before in animals, for companionship or security." Albertine of course didn't count, as she offered neither.

"As a test subject. Come and see."

What she showed me was a cage, a trap of welded steel bars. It was taller than a tea chest, longer than a steamer trunk; one end gaped open like a ready mouth. Inside at the far end was what I took to be the trigger mechanism, a matter of hinges and wires, spikes ready to be baited.

"Or we could forgo the dog," said my beloved musingly, "if you were to crawl in yourself. I can't do it, as the release mechanism is not reachable from within..."

"I think not," I said, looking again at those spikes. "Ask the pot-boy."

"I'm afraid he's left us," Clarissa said cheerfully. "And the maid too."

"'Rissa! What did you do this time?"

"Nothing to do with me. Half the native population has fled town. Ridiculous, when the weasels are still days away, but there you have it."

She finished with a dismissive shrug. I might have said that boys have mothers, as too do young women - but it was ever cruel to remind Clarissa of what she had given up, in choosing to make her life with me.

"We don't need a dog," I said instead. "Dogs may safely graze."

She eyed me cynically. "Euphenia, are you being sentimental?"

"Not at all, no. Have you forgotten Albertine?"

"My dear woman, Albertine may be of a hefty disposition—"

"—Nonsense, she's just big-boned—"

"—but this trap is designed to close upon a hundred pounds or more of frenzied weasel. A sedentary cat in her comfortable middle years couldn't come close to tripping it."

"I beg your pardon, I misspoke. I should have said 'Have you forgotten Albertine in her pomp?'"

"Good lord. I do declare I had."

Smugness is the most unattractive of emotions, but I confess I felt a twinge of it as Clarissa loped off towards her worksheds. Some people collect butterflies or stamps or books; my love accumulates past projects, as a ship barnacles. It is I suppose another aspect of her archive, adjunct to the massed ranks of her notebooks.

A psychopomp is a guide, a living bridge that leads souls to the land of the dead. This earthbound pomp was a mechanistic contraption that would certainly have led Albertine to world domination, had we only troubled to keep it stoked. Its legs were tireless, so long as there was coke for its firebox; its arms offered speed and strength and opposable thumbs, an all-but-unbreakable grip. Its seat was warm and soft. She need only bat at a lever, press on a paddle, bite down upon a joystick and it would take her where'er she whist, do whatever her feline soul rejoiced at. Birds and mice might pass untroubled in her shadow; she had greater things in mind.

I let Clarissa well alone as she came and went with oil and coals and a shovelful of fire from the kitchen range. When she reemerged, her face was freshly smutted and her gown an accustomed disgrace, but she yielded me a nod of satisfaction.

I hoisted Albertine in my arms and bore her forth. As we stepped from the bright yard into the cool shadows of the shed, her head lifted and she looked about her, with an enquiring *mrrp?*

"Over here, dear one." Clarissa's voice was a summoning, and might have been addressing either one of us.

The pomp stood waist-high at her side, barely more than a gleam of brass, a whiff of steam and a hint of spider-shape to me. Albertine's senses are acute, though, despite all her angles being oblique. I could feel the sudden tension in her body as it passed in a moment from padded cushion to padded bedspring, all coiled energy and eagerness.

"Very well, my dear. Down you go," oozing liquidly from my arms onto the upholstered seat; sitting primly for a moment, gazing down at the catspaw controls before curling and settling to bring them all within easy reach. Like a Roman at feast, she reclined to her work.

A paw reached out, tapped lightly. A mechanical claw shot forward, gaping, snapping shut. I took a step back. That was purely precautionary—Albertine had never harboured ill-will towards anyone sufficiently animate to fetch her a sardine—but she might need time to regain her delicacy of touch. Clarissa, I noticed, was likewise standing well to the rear.

Sometimes I think that Albertine's pomp is the shape of Albertine's mind. The beast herself may be soft and round and pourable, but her thoughts are sharp and skeletal, purposeful and precise. Which is her pomp, exactly: a manifestation of will, expressed in steel and steam. What Clarissa's work might lack in grace or style, it more than makes up in sheer bloody-minded fixity of purpose. Much like my beloved's self, indeed.

Arachnid on its multiple legs—for stability, Clarissa says; for intimidation, I suspect, for what on this planet would not fear a hissing steaming spider-thing the size of a coffee-table?—the pomp scuttles while Albertine lounges. It has claws like lobsters, reaching further than ever she could pounce. When I questioned whether she had intellect enough to work the controls, Clarissa had merely snorted. "My dear, she's a cat. Command is inherent."

Albertine sniffed once, batted at the controls, and the pomp clanked out into the yard. We followed at a distance, not to interfere with her pleasure or our experiment.

There, now: there was the source of that enticing, alluring aroma. In her very own anchovy-dish like an open invitation, except that the dish was set at the rear of a curious structure, as steely as her own beloved pomp, and she was ever wary of what was new.

"I told you we should have fetched a dog."

"Hush. She'll do this. She has no choice; there is an anchovy in the case."

There was. At this distance, it was making its presence known even to us. Albertine couldn't resist it for long; indeed, technically she couldn't resist it at all. The delay was only calculation, how best to proceed.

Light-footed as a colt, almost tentative, the pomp high-stepped into the cage's maw, carrying its mistress with it.

There was room enough and to spare. That was quite a frightening thought in itself, that the splendid and self-satisfied pomp was less than half the size of our intended prey, far less than half the weight, many times less the power.

In they went, the pomp *en pointe* like a ballerina and the cat on alert in every whisker, if a puddled shapeless lump can be alert.

The pomp extended its gripping-arm, the claw opened, it closed again - and not upon the anchovy but the dish itself, for Albertine was always a dainty eater.

There was the slightest, the merest of clicks as a valve opened or a gear turned, as the weight of the dish lifted away.

With a hiss of pressure released, the gate slammed shut behind cat and pomp. Heavy clunks ensued, as locks engaged.

"Taken and contained," Clarissa said with satisfaction. "I'd like to see the creature born that could escape that cage."

"Speaking for myself, I would rather not." Nor did I particularly want to see the creature bold enough to reach inside it to milk the glands of its captive, but I had a dread feeling that I was looking at her.

An indignant Albertine snatched up her hard-won anchovy, leaped from the trapped security of her perch and abandoned her pomp without a rearward glance, sliding despite her bulk between two close-set iron bars and padding off triumphant.

"I suppose," said Clarissa, "that means we'll have to make room on the wagon for her pomp as well as the weasel-trap."

"Why on earth...?"

"My dear. We have just established in her furry little mind a new source of anchovies. Do you imagine for one moment we'd be let leave her behind?"

That was mere sophistry, of course. But the servants had disappeared, and one couldn't impose on one's friends at a time of such crisis. I did think Albertine had to come with us.

⚡

Three nights later, we had exchanged the coloured pebbles and potted plants of the Exquisitorium for the pale sands and lush forests of the Black Sea shoreline—or rather, we had been offered glimpses and intimations of both, from the rather grimmer reality of the wagon-road. No doubt ambrosial scents wafted about us, seasoned with salt spray from the ocean; we could appreciate them not at all, engulfed as we were in the smoke and fumes of our recalcitrant steam-wagon. Besides, I was busy stoking, while Clarissa spun wheels and hauled levers and cursed in a monotone at the condition of the highway.

Three days of that, filthy and weary and forging onward, while the little traffic we saw was all the other way, the last stubborn householders retreating at last. We earned our share of stares, of shouted questions—why were we driving into hell? were we mad?—but no one drew rein, no one risked losing their head of steam or bogging down a wheel to reason with us.

"I thought the road to hell was better paved than this." Clarissa's teeth were gritted, as the road was not.

I thought your steam-wagon could handle all terrain—but I forbore to say it. To shriek it, rather, above the racket of the reciprocating engine. I merely hurled another shovelful of coal into the firebox, slammed shut the iron door, and seized whatever hold I could reach as the entire vehicle lurched beneath us, encountering yet one more rut deeper than its wheel was broad.

I thought I heard my beloved mutter something about caterpillars, but her meaning was as unclear as her diction. I ignored her, in favour of checking on Albertine in her traveling-basket. The pomp was stowed forward with the rest of our baggage, but herself reclined in comfort on a shelf close to the fire's warmth and needed no more at day's end than the wash-and-brush-up of an idle tongue, when Clarissa and I were as loathsome to ourselves as to each other.

We may be the only pair on the planet to feel sheer relief at first sign of ice-weasel infestation.

Inevitably, I suppose, that sign was stool. "Spraints," Clarissa suggested, but I stood by the otter's unique claim to that word. Besides, these foul ejecta smelled not at all of violets.

"Fewmets, then," quoth my adored one. "A hunted beast is identified by its fewmets."

Ice weasels, I felt, fell more into the bracket of hunter than hunted—but let it pass. Here was what we quested for, no question.

Clarissa blew off steam in a series of shrill blasts designed to drive away any weasel within miles. Albertine lifted her head for a moment, grumbled at the noise and then subsided, thrusting her nose deep into her fluffy tail; I dismounted, groaning, and gazed about.

The foliage was thinning, no doubt due to the sordid and abandoned hamlet grown up around the wagon-road ahead. Shrubs grew thickly near the base of the pine trees that pressed close against the road. A few shabby flowers struggled to lift their heads above the shadows; their future seemed hopeless. Even the weasels, I thought, had seen nothing to keep them here.

"If they paused only to poop and carry on," said my beloved, coming sturdily to my side with her father's old Purdy shotgun on her shoulder, "then we surely should have encountered them somewhere between breakfast and here. Unless they slid from the road at our advance, and circled around behind us..."

Or unless they lurked in the forest round about, unperturbed by blasting steam-whistles or mechanical juggernauts, biding their time, waiting to catch us at our most vulnerable...

Fortunately, I had read further into the profesora's published works than my speculative darling. "Not they," I said. "Generations of children have been frightened to bed with the old legend, 'At night, the ice weasels come.' It may not be strictly true—they are more creatures of the twilight than the blackest dark—but they are far from early risers. They will sleep through the heat of the day, like cats; and like cats, they like to be comfortable. This may be their forward line, but they will have retreated some miles to a nest-site established on yesterday's march. They advance like a tide, foraging forward and pulling back. We have plenty of time to set the trap; they won't reach this point again before dusk."

We offloaded the trap—with some grunting and puffing, despite the ingenious winch Clarissa had bolted to the wagon-bed—and baited it with a cooked chicken. Then we removed Albertine to her basket before she could engulf the chicken, drove the steam-wagon some distance off so as not to alarm our prey (if ice-weasels could be alarmed by anything of our manufacture, or indeed anything at all), stowed it in an empty stable and faced the question of where to stow ourselves.

Drawing once more on the profesora's wisdom, I said, "The ice weasel is a lazy beast. Like water, the pack will always follow the swiftest and easiest way forward. Here, that means the shoreline, largely—it's why they're so devastating to communities, because roads lead up from the seashore, and roads are easy too."

"And wagon-roads are easiest of all. You're saying we should make camp somewhere in the wild? That seems...contrary to logic." My beloved gazed into the darkness of the forest and could not suppress a shudder.

"They are creatures of the tundra, remember. Open wastes are their natural habitat. Trees make them nervous." So said the profesora, at least. In honesty, I was barely any more keen than Clarissa to leave our own natural habitat. Boldly, though, I turned towards the trees—and checked, and turned back, and said, "We may have some distance to cover, before we find safety. You shall not carry that lump all the way."

Clarissa had Albertine's basket in her arms. She hefted it thoughtfully and said, "The coals are still hot in the wagon's firebox; we can bring her pomp up to steam in a matter of minutes, and she can follow under her own power. As it were."

—ww—

So we invested a little more time in shovelling and stoking, and when we set off again we were a line of three: I leading, Albertine following, Clarissa ushering from the rear in case our fluffy dear should wander from the course I set.

Steam of course requires fire, and fire delights in the desiccated foliage of Ottoman summers. As roads and engines spread ever further through the empire, so did the hazards of a sudden blaze. The imperial bureaucracy has its moments; a decree went out long since, that any roadside settlement must keep a permanent watch. This hamlet of course was abandoned, and so was its watchtower, but the structure was rooted among trees, roofed and floored a ladder's reach above the forest canopy—and weasels hate to climb. All their inclination is downward. I could imagine nowhere safer.

Of course Clarissa had hand-lamps in her voluminous baggage. We made the climb, checked for lurking denizens, found none and settled in. Albertine showed signs of wanting to explore, but no more than weasels could she manage the climb. I presented her with a can of sardines—bless the Baggage!—and she subsided into a contented purring satiety, from which she would not stir till morning.

After a scratch supper of foie gras, grouse, and water-biscuits—all out of cans, all out of the Baggage—my sweetheart and I were in much the same case. Comfort is relative, but the arms of one's beloved are a comfort beyond measure, even in a creaking edifice far from home. Within and without, I was comforted. I would not have expected to sleep, and yet I did: even before I could suggest that we keep watch, turn and turn about...

I woke to the soft half-light of dawn, to an ache in my back and the twin snores of my two companions. No one had stayed alert, neither my cautious leman nor our supposedly nocturnal, supposedly predatory fluffbucket; but here we were, safe and sound, the perils and dangers of the night dispersed.

I hoped. If ice weasels were creatures of the twilight, perhaps they had an equal fondness for the dawn...?

Nevertheless: we must vacate our informal tenancy and retrace our steps of yesterday. We were out before the sun was up, the merest hint of purple on the eastern horizon to predict it; beneath the trees was black as pitch, and we could never have found our way without lamps. Clarissa tried to persuade me to put my hair into a single long pigtail and tie a lamp to the end of it, so that the swinging light should beckon Albertine on. I had a better idea.

Albertine led us forth, her prosthetic legs moving with the grace—or so, I assume, she liked to think—of a leopard stalking its prey: her prey in this case being a faux mouse dangled before her from a fresh-cut pole. With a lamp affixed to her pomp, the mouse was just visible, swaying in and out of the beam of light. At the other end of the pole was Clarissa: steering our predatory adventurer from the rear, keeping one eye on her luminous compass, leading us ever eastward to the wagon-road.

Once there, we made swifter progress, with the sky brightening above us. I was glad to extinguish the lamps, as soon as we could manage without. They were small help to us any longer, but could still be a beacon to attract the watchful eye of an ice weasel lying up in cover.

If ice weasels were prone to do that, if one of their number were trapped and helpless. If the trap had worked at all, if the ice weasels had indeed come this way and this far...

Doubts assailed me, even as shadows gathered about us, mute and murky evidence of the night's retreat. Birds were kicking up a racket all around. What they had to make a song about, I couldn't guess; it would be an hour or more before any actual sunlight reached the road, even assuming an unlikely break in the overcast.

"What does your blessed profesora say about the preponderance of ice weasels on cloudy mornings?"

"Nothing, that I have seen. But most animals pay no more heed than we to the condition of the light; they have their bedtimes, and they stick to them. Mostly."

"Hmm." She sounded little reassured.

Here, at last, was the low square obstructive shape in the road, the trap we had left cocked and baited. Albertine's lantern illuminated it quite clearly: the dark iron of its bars, the complexities of its mechanism, the pale shifting shape that huddled within.

"'Rissa, is that...?"

"It is not." For a moment she sounded nothing but chagrined, the hunter denied her prey. "An ice weasel would all but fill the cage. This is an interloper, a scavenger, a damned chicken-thief."

"'Rissa, he's a boy."

And he was: smeared with chicken-grease, scrawny as a twig, with vast dark eyes that spoke of hunger and terror together. Still a boy, a human boy naked and alone, and in our cruel cage. I thrust impatiently forward. "How do you open this wretched thing again?"

"From the opposite end," she said. "In hopes that a trapped ice weasel would see the gate spring wide and choose to run for the available hills, rather than turning to rend the luckless one who released it."

Herself, she meant; or, in this instance, me. I stormed around to the rear of the cage, seized the lever, and heaved.

Was the release purely mechanical, or was I assisted by some power less obvious than steam, some clockwork ratchet perhaps? I do not know; but gears turned, latches lifted, and the gate leaped wide.

It was an open invitation, deliberately so, and the boy was not slow to respond. Someone so small and young and skinny has no right to be so fast, but he was gone before Clarissa could lay hold on him. He still had what remained of the chicken clutched tight in one bony hand; Albertine gazed after in a kind of somnolent interest—*why is that boy running away with my chicken?*—even as Clarissa made to follow.

"Oh, my dear, let him go. It is no great sin to be hungry, and we can bait the trap again."

"We can. I suppose we must. But—see, they were here"—indeed there was evidence of weasel all around us, underfoot—"and we might have had one, we might have achieved our purpose already, we could be moving forward, we could be going home with what we wanted most..."

My love becomes quite prolix in frustration. Myself, I become terse in reassurance. "We will. Take out another chicken."

"Not yet; that brat will only come back. I'm not laying out a buffet for the indigent. What in the world is he doing here, anyway, when everyone has left?

Has he no parents?"

"Perhaps not. Perhaps the weasels took them. Or else he was lost, left behind in the exodus. Or—"

"Never mind. How old would you say? No more than three by the size of him, but so nippy - he must be older, five or six perhaps. Poor diet could have stunted his growth. Little brat needs more chickens..."

All this time she was pacing about the trap, noting how the weasel-cast was concentrated in this area, how the stony road showed signs of scrabbling, as though they had tried to tunnel beneath the cage...

"I tell you what, Euphenia," she said, frowning mightily. "It may be that he didn't snare himself in there trying to steal our chicken after all. That might have been a bonus, but—I think he was being chased, I think he saw it as safe shelter. Smart boy. Weasels on his heels, he sees the trap and is bright enough to understand that what would hold a weasel in, will also hold the weasels out. Dives in, snatches the bait, triggers the trap—and then he has a meal in his hands and he can eat it, and they can't reach him. Terrifying, I expect, with their hot breath all about him; you can see how they paced back and forth, how they tried every way they knew to reach him, how—"

"Clarissa. If he'd been in there all night, he hadn't made much headway on the chicken." There had still been a deal of meat on the carcass, what glimpse I'd had of it as he pelted away; there were precious few bones on the cage floor. "How if he hadn't been in there long at all, if he came at first light and was harried in as you say, and they retreated not long ago at all? By the smell, these excreta are still warm..." Which would mean, of course, that they were lying up somewhere close. If they were lying up at all. We seemed to be assuming that a little boy—a very little boy—was smart enough to outthink a pack of them, a *hunting* pack; and that dim grey overcast dawnlight was sun enough to drive them into whatever nest they had found or made, however close; and—

And now I was gazing about me with an increasing anxiety, and seeing eyes in every shadow, and not all of those could be my imagination, surely.

No. *None* of those were my imagination.

"Clarissa!" I yelped, as creatures came flowing out of the trees, too long to be dogs, too liquid and low-slung. Viciously white even absent the sun, they flooded towards us like a wall of milk, if milk were ever savage and purposeful, lethal in intent.

"I see them. We must emulate the boy: quickly, now..."

Blessedly, Clarissa had not underestimated the monstrous size of these monstrous creatures; there was room in the trap for both of us. Not comfortably, but still: we hastened within, she triggered the snare while I was still pulling my skirts to safety, and the gate crashed to behind me.

The two of us were crouched facing each other, looking out through the bars across each other's shoulders, seeing what came to threaten them more than us. It was I who cried, "Albertine!" but Clarissa, who could see her, sought to reassure me.

"She knows, she's poised to join us: one leap from the pomp, and she can slide between these bars without even drawing breath - oh, wait. Here comes the boy again. Pelting back, they must have been lying in ambush, whichever way he went..."

"Quick, open the gate again!"

"I can't," she said. "It's impossible to open from within. I made it that way deliberately, didn't know how smart the creatures were, you see..."

"Oh, 'Rissa! Whatever shall we do?"

"Nothing much we can do," she muttered, though she was already rummaging through the Baggage for some tool or other, even as I twisted around to see whatever dreadful thing might be happening behind me, even as the hot eyes of the first and fastest ice weasels seemed to glow red with internal fires as they raced towards us.

Oh, but that boy was fast. If the weasels made a wall at his heels, he was all but a blur: a blur foreshortened, sprinting head down for us, for the putative safety of a cage we had closed against him.

At least he would barely have a moment to feel the terror, the fury, the frustration, whatever emotion it would be that possessed him for that last little time before the weasels made an end of him. In us, the guilt would live for ever. A child, the merest babe, torn to pieces at our own instigation, because we released a trap too soon—while he was safe yet—and sprung it again too soon; and we must crouch here in our own stolen safety and watch it happen, and—

And again, it seemed, the boy was smarter than weasels and smarter even than us. He saw us penned, saw the gate locked against him, and checked for the barest moment, and then came on regardless, and I couldn't see why. Until he reached Albertine, who was inexplicably still in situ upon her pomp—and apparently even our portly little cat was smarter than we were today. She tapped a lever, and a single leg of her pomp rose up like an invitation. The boy did not need asking twice; he wriggled through the narrow gap created, the leg snapped down again, and there he was, caged again in steel. Eight legs made a circle of bars all about him; Albertine jumped down and oozed between to join him within their narrow shelter.

What Clarissa builds, she makes in a solid manner; there is nothing frail or decorative in her constructions. Nevertheless: I watched long and powerful bodies press against the pomp, and feared to see it topple. I watched great paws strike at it, vicious claws try to wrench it leg from leg, wiser heads try to uproot it altogether. Its own steel claws must have been driven deep into the stone of the road, to hold it yet upright under so much pressure. Still, hold it they did, to the weasels' deep and growing and visible frustration. Within their improvised cage, Albertine lay curled within the boy's scrawny embrace, nose close to the remaining chicken in his hand, and the two together spat impudent defiance through the bars.

Impudent, and imprudent too, perhaps—though I couldn't see how the ice weasels could be any the more infuriated, or any the more dangerous. We stood—or crouched, rather—in as much risk ourselves, for all that our cage was the sturdier. It had been built to keep one beast in, not a whole pack out; they surged around our close-set bars with as much animus as they did around the pomp, as much determined malice. There was still no hint of sun. Had it been blazing bright, though, I still do not believe they would have retreated as nocturnal creatures should, shy in the face of day. We were their prey, and the hunt was up; nothing could distract them now.

Nothing, it seemed, except a voice from the heavens, booming down. They startled, just as we did; after a moment's crouching stillness, their questing heads turned upward, just as ours did.

They have the more flexible spines by far—no less liquid than their shadows, if I may borrow a phrase—but humans perhaps are better designed for scanning the skies. Hunting or burrowing or looking for shelter, all the mustelid's natural inclination is downward, while our eyes, minds, souls are forever reaching up.

Not too far up, in this instance. Less than the height of a church's steeple—which might have been more or less what I was looking for, or what I expected to find, some expression of religion in an upthrust of brick and stone with a muezzin at the top—hung a small dirigible, one of those numberless private vessels that make such a chaos of the skies above our home. If I was surprised to see one so far out here, I suppose I should not have been. Rather the opposite, in fact: any ordinary catastrophe will draw sight-seers from far and wide, and how better to travel, how better to watch than from above, in relative comfort and safety both?

I suppose it was that weasel-word "relative" that kept them all away. Dirigibles do fail, lose lift, come to ground, and who would risk that, hereabouts?

This person would, apparently. The stentorian voice came again, impatient now, repeating its instructions: "Cover your eyes, d'you hear there? Cover your eyes!"

That could only be to our address. It fell to me, inevitably, to set the example. I did it first in large, in pantomime, for the boy's benefit; he gaped, then nodded hugely and buried his face in Albertine's generous fur. At least he was not an idiot, I was pleased to observe.

Clarissa might almost have qualified for such a label, that day. She didn't want to cover her eyes; she wanted to observe. Mostly what she must have observed was my scowl, as I seized her dear head between my hands and propelled it forcefully into my bosom.

Myself, I screwed my eyes tight shut and hid them against her neck. Had I been blessed with a spare hand, I should have waved it to show the balloonist that we were prepared; needing both to contain my spluttering, struggling darling, I could only hope that her own wild gestures of protest would serve.

Apparently, they did so. There was one last cry, "Coming now!" followed by a moment's hush, a stillness I could sense even in the weasels' relentless pacing, rubbing, probing at the bars.

Then came a flash that almost seared my eyes even through my eyelids, even through Clarissa's solid flesh. I felt her gasp and only held on tighter, for fear of another such.

The ice weasels, I can only assume, had the same fear; also, of course, they had not had the warning. I heard squeals and blundering bodies, sounds that faded quickly.

"All clear," the voice boomed again. "I'm coming down!"

Now I allowed Clarissa to wrestle herself free. She glowered at me, made a gesture towards restoring decency to her dishevelled hair, but promptly abandoned it in favour of peering over my shoulder. I had to twist uncomfortably to share her point of view; it was worth a degree of strain, though, to see our rescuer descend onto a blessedly empty roadway.

The dirigible came down like a duchess's skirts, dignity and vulgarity pressed shoulder to shoulder: the self-important balloon broad and ridiculous above the neat narrow basket, barely able to squeeze between the branches, barely willing it seemed to touch the earth.

Its pilot had no such compunction, tumbling briskly out and hauling mightily on ropes to prevent the lightened craft from lifting off again. "You might help," she cried impatiently over her shoulder.

"We might indeed," snapped Clarissa, who was clearly feeling the folly of our own situation, "if we only had a means to extract ourselves."

"Oh, dear. Oh, dearie me..."

At last, she managed to hitch one rope about a solid-looking iron stanchion and tie it off. The dirigible tugged and strained, the cable sang; nothing moved.

Satisfied, she let the other rope dangle and crossed the street towards us. Her way brought her past the pomp, with its protectorate beneath. The device itself seemed to intrigue her more than its contents; nevertheless, she tapped one leg and said, "Get yourself out of there, sonny, and attend to that loose rope, would you? There's a good lad."

Not waiting to see herself obeyed, she came onward to address our cage, or possibly us. We were privileged to watch her will enacted: the boy urged Albertine out between the pomp's legs, she hopped up to her accustomed position, a chicken leg gripped in her fangs, and tapped a lever. A single leg rose jerkily and the boy squirmed out through that opening.

Satisfied that he was indeed running to the rope—definitely not an idiot, then, if he could understand both English and the wisdom of obedience *in extremis*—I returned my attention to the majestic form before us.

Living with Clarissa, I had been long accustomed to the sight of the female body clad in what was traditionally man's attire: trousers and hunting jerkins—"so practical, with all these handy pockets!"—at any time and anywhere, and leather goggles in the laboratory, with her splendid hair thrust rudely into a fisherman's cap.

I had not seen her—I had not seen any woman ere this moment—in a formal frock coat, with cashmere-striped morning trousers and a silk hat. I should have expected her to look foolish, but she did not. She was tall enough perhaps to carry the rig off, but it was more than that: the confidence in her stride, the elegance in her costume's cut, the exquisite fabric coupled with the exquisite tilt of her head as she surveyed us.

"Your own trap?" she barked.

"Indeed."

"No way to release it from within?"

"Indeed not. I failed to anticipate the need. Nor could I rate the intelligence of an ice weasel with sufficient accuracy to take the chance." I have rarely heard my beloved sound so chagrined, except at the failure of one more breeding-chamber. That had been a persistent scourge over the years; this was something new, embarrassment coupled with hurt pride before a rival.

She had perhaps guessed the name of this provident new arrival; not I. I knew for certain.

The woman stepped behind the cage, hummed and hawed a moment, then worked the release. I crawled out, with Clarissa urgent at my heel.

I for one was happy enough to be humiliated, if it meant survival. I thought—I hoped!—that 'Rissa would make the same choice, if she considered the options rationally. Just now, she was anything but rational; I deemed it best to give her time to stand, to look about, to weigh our current circumstances against likely outcomes from five minutes previously.

Accordingly I straightened swiftly, thrust out my hand, and spoke my piece. "Profesora Cadiz, I presume?"

"Yes, indeed. Well met. Fortuitously met, I might say."

"If you were speaking for us, you might, certainly. Your arrival was most apposite. As has been all that I have gleaned from your published work. I am a great fan, Profesora."

"Oh, please—call me Maude. The title is as Spanish as my given name, Magdalena; here in the Ottoman outback, in the company of Englishwomen, I may as well be as English as I can manage. Besides, my father always pronounced it Maudlin, in tribute to his college."

My forthright love behind me snorted at this irrelevance, refused to be daunted by any of its implications, and interrupted me just as I was about to introduce us, as etiquette and manners both demanded. "Was that a magnesium flare just now?"

"In large, yes. With additions of my own devising."

"Hunh. Those animals, then—did you blind them?"

"Not I. Only dazzled them, and reminded them of the day. They have a nictitating membrane to shield their eyes from snow blindness, those times they are caught out in sunlight on their native tundra; that will have saved them any permanent damage. I don't expect to see them again, though, until the dusk comes kinder to their sight."

By which time I prayed we should be long gone. My stubborn adoree, though, is made of sterner stuff: steel and her own welds, largely. She glanced back at the empty trap, and said, "I should bait that."

"To what end?"

"We came out here to trap an ice weasel; we should have succeeded, but for that boy's interference." Her glance was meant to be scolding, but her voice failed in the endeavour; she sounded almost wistful, gazing on the naked lad. Still, she recovered herself swiftly: "Of course, we must persevere."

"To what end?" again.

Clarissa huffed in exasperation, but explained anyway; she couldn't help herself. She must answer questions categorically. "The oil from their anal glands burns with a fierce, an exceptional heat." The profesora could not argue that; her own writings attested it. Which was in fact how Clarissa had learned it, by means of my reading it to her. I forbore to mention that. "I believe we can harvest that oil, and make use of it."

"Indeed. Will you be a weasel-farmer?"

"I will make it possible," Clarissa said haughtily, "for others to farm weasels. And milk them, yes. Before you venture further in this line of questioning."

"Before you venture further in this undertaking," quoth my new friend Maude, "you might like to consider that the glandular oil is ineradicably imbued with the weasels' peculiar musk. You may have noted that, as they fretted against the cage."

Indeed, my troubles in breathing had not been caused by tension alone, at our fraught predicament. The air had been rank with the weasels' stifling odour.

"Burning only exacerbates the aroma's effluence," the profesora continued remorselessly. "Which one might learn to live with—the cowpats that fuel the peasant stove, the camel-dung fires of the Bedouin are not unfree of odour—but that this particular scent serves both as pack credentials and sexual arouser. Trust me, it is the last thing you would wish to broadcast, anywhere that ice weasels might be found. Wild or contained."

A rational argument could ever win over my bridling love, especially where it came with new information. "You did not publish that," she said, visibly reconsidering her position.

"No. It...had not occurred to me, that anyone might stand in need of the discouragement." There was a note of respect in her voice, that had not been there hitherto.

It's always good, to see twin souls identify each other. They may bristle a little at the reflection of themselves, they may need time to settle, but in the end what is there, what can there be but a recognition, a coming-together, a mutual reach for a shared goal?

"Well," Clarissa said briskly. "If not burn it, what have you done, what do you do with it? You must have some in harvest."

"I do. Achieved, I may say, with a far cruder trap than yours; I should like to examine this further. But whether there is any point, I am uncertain. I have been seeking to use the oil to herd the creatures, to draw them away to the north, to their traditional hunting-grounds; hence the airship. I had thought an aerosol spray would achieve my goal, but it disperses too rapidly, and perhaps does more harm than good, exciting them without giving them direction."

"Have you considered wicking, rather than spraying?" queried my beloved. "Dip an absorbent rope in a vat of the liquid, and then trail it behind and below your craft. The scent will be both intense and directional..."

I let their voices fade from my attention. Between them, I was sure they would arrive at a solution; data marries well with inventiveness. I should know. Before long, I had no doubt, the ice weasels would be in retreat from civilised lands.

Meanwhile, I had a task of my own, fit to my hand. The boy had secured the dirigible's rope to a hitching-rail and then immediately returned to the pomp, to Albertine. Our cat, it seemed, had won his heart; I was in hopes that we might do the same. To judge by the soft glances my beloved cast in his direction, even while she debated with the profesora, he might already have achieved the reverse. All unknowing, I thought, on either of their parts, but none the less.

I unhitched my cape and cast it about his bare spare shoulders, wrapping my arms around the fabric as I did so, that he might feel himself both warmed and protected.

"Her name is Albertine," I murmured. "Can you say Albertine?"

He could; he did, in a whisper that spoke to the trauma of recent days, and the immediate hold she had on his affections.

Bless the cat, she perked her ears and purred as he spoke her name. That could be sovereign.

"And you?" I said. "Do you want to tell her your name?" I wouldn't ask his history, not yet: I was all too sure I could write it for myself, a story of parents lost in a bloody welter, and a grim future all too clear ahead unless we interrupted it. His name was crucial, though: sovereign again, the key to a door that could open on a different future altogether.

"Mika..."

"Well, Mika, would you like to come with us now? With Albertine and 'Rissa and me, in Maude's flying machine there? I can't promise you another chicken, I think our chicken will be needed here," for I was sure they meant to bait that trap again, "but a nice soak in a bath and a good hot meal after, that much I can promise. And then a bed, and waking to a new day and a new life. I don't think you've slept in a bed for days, for nights together, have you? I'll tuck you in myself, and sing you down into slumber as my mother did to me..."

And not let 'Rissa anywhere near the nursery at that time, for she had a croak fit to scare an angel, but none the less. I thought she was half won already, all unknowing; only let her see him as he should be, bathed and powdered and fed and drowsy, and I was in hopes that all notions of a breeding-chamber might finally be blown apart.

LOVE IN THE TIME OF MARKOV PROCESSES

MEGAN ARKENBERG

I.

There are an infinite number of universes. This does not mean that every imaginable universe exists. In two-dimensional space, a triangle will never have four sides or two obtuse angles. No substance can freeze and boil at the same time; no living creature can be both alive and dead. And there is no world where time runs in both directions. No matter where you go, how far you travel, how fast or how long—the past is only ever the past.

II.

We met on the bus, on my way to the grocery store and her way to an interview with *Scientific Woman* or *Cutting Edge*, on a day when the rain fell like mid-morning coffee, lukewarm and slow. Reflections of gray city sky littered the sidewalks between starched collars and the flooded brims of hats. I caught sight of her through the driver-side window, which was jammed and dripping water into the lap of the man sitting next to me; she was running to catch the bus, dodging briefcases and baby strollers; her sensible black flats were scuffed white around the toes. She wore a wide black skirt, a peach blouse that tied at the throat with a gray ribbon. Her black hair was curly, thick and shoulder-length, her lips a dark pomegranate red.

Every seat and every yellow plastic handhold was taken; she paused by my row as the light changed and we lurched forward. She caught herself on my shoulder, her fingers cold and damp against my collarbone "Sorry," she said, with a smile that was not at all shy.

I knew her voice from the radio programs, her face from magazine covers. Her leather bag bulged with textbooks with bent covers, folders stained with coffee, ink blots and thumb-print smudges of graphite.

"You're fine," I murmured. I wished I could smile back. My purse held my shopping list, a pencil stub, a tube of coral lipstick, ten dollars in cash.

One stop before the radio station, she straightened the ribbon on her blouse, fluffed her damp hair with her fingers. I stared at her; I couldn't help it. When she caught my eye, I blurted out: "My mother thinks I should have been a scientist, but I never applied to college. I used to build circuits in my grandmother's basement. I've read all about you. I didn't know you were in the city."

She blinked slowly. Her red lips parted, shaping a question that never emerged. The bus lurched forward again, the wheels rasping a little on the wet pavement. "I'm looking for an assistant," she said at last. She fished in her bag for a moment, handed me her card.

III.

When she was born, her mother was already dead; she was delivered by Caesarean section on a morning when the rain fell like blood from a broken artery. Her father had come home from work one afternoon, wet and tired, with motor oil under his fingernails, to find his pregnant wife lying in a heap on the kitchen floor. The sink and the floor around her were full of water, clipped carnations, shards of glass; he slashed his hand as he tried to take her pulse. At the hospital, they bound his fingers in clean white gauze and told him that she was gone.

For the next two months, a machine pumped her lungs, filtered nutrients into her bloodstream. Her grandmother hated it, said they should allow her the dignity of death; said she would never have wanted it, the machine's reedy rasping voice, the metal and silicone. Beneath the oxygen mask, the feeding tubes, her skin was cold and waxlike. The boat mechanic sat beside her bed, tracing the scars on his thick fingers. He wanted his daughter to be born.

She wonders what her mother would have wanted. Wonders often, setting aside her textbooks and rubbing her tired eyes. Wonders as she scrapes the oil from beneath her fingernails, as she turns the black dials on the Engine's side until the arrows line up like train cars. Wonders if she would ever be brave enough to find out.

IV.

"Our universe," she tells me, "is one microscopically thin thread, woven into a tapestry of infinite length and width. We march along it like a tightrope walker, never realizing that what lies to either side of us is not an abyss, but another world completely."

We are standing at the edge of the wharf and waiting for the *Burd Janet* to dock. The seagulls slice through the salty air and chatter on the rocks below us; the boat is a sliver of gray on the wider and rougher silver of the bay. She has taken my hand, turned it palm up, trapped my thumb beneath hers. Her other hands traces a green vein in my wrist.

"If we roll ever so gently from this thread to a parallel one," she says, and she turns her finger suddenly, scraping it down the side of my arm, "we slip into another universe. One where the past is subtly changed. One where anything might have been different. Do you understand?"

"Yes," I say. She smells like cardamon, like carnations and motor oil. She smells faintly of blood.

"We can only roll in one direction," she says. She releases my wrist; when I do not pull away, she lowers her hands, stuffs them in the pockets of her long olive-colored coat. "You need to understand that. Once we go, we can never go back."

Now we are standing on the deck of the *Burd Janet*, and the wind and streaks of gray are in her dark hair. She takes my hand again. "Do you trust me?"

"Yes," I say. Every time, yes.

V.

Her lab is on the floor of the ocean, nestled in the arching ribcage of a dead whale. The abyssal scavengers have come and gone, sleeper sharks and hagfish, then crabs, mussels, octopi. Now we share the skeleton with neon-bright bacterial mats and blind sea worms. A whalefall creates its own ecosystem, carrying its oxygen and calories and sunlight down into the silent abyss. Even its bones, lipid-rich, can feed a tiny world.

The *Burd Janet* docks in a sleepy fishing village along a quiet and forgetful coast, where the continental shelf is narrow and steep, an ancient river having carved its canyon deep along the ocean floor. When you say the password to the one-eyed woman whose windows are filled with fishhooks, she leads you down to the wharf and hands you a key on a length of waxed red string. Trailing in the water beside the *Burd Janet*, its round door locked and sealed with rubber, is the submarine rover *Tam Linn*. It takes almost a full day of slow diagonal sinking from the place where the *Burd Janet's* crew drop their nets; you know you've arrived when you see the green wires clamped to the pink-white bones, sparking deadly volts into the water.

The whale is not inside the Engine's radius, and we have seen it alter. They are subtle changes, mostly. Thicker ribs, or thinner. An extra pair of flippers. In one universe, the whale has teeth, long and curved and yellow. Two of its ribs are broken, puckered with the circular scars of gigantic tentacles. When we looked out past the bone cage, we saw something staring back at us with wide, ice-pale eyes. We did not linger.

VI.

The Engine is a long cylinder of clean red metal, like a tube of lipstick, like a novelty cigarette. Black dials with white arrows march down both sides; she turns these between two fingers until the arrows make a single horizontal stripe, the dividing line on an empty highway, the streak a meteor leaves along the curving sky. On one end, there are two tall levers, black and red, go and stop, which it is my job to pull. The black lever is warm to the touch, the two hemispheres of its metal head joined by a raised, sharp ridge. The red lever is always cold as ice.

She releases cameras in small silver spheres, sends them up through tubes in the laboratory ceiling and into the black water, where they swim on silicone fins in search of data. They trickle back over the following weeks, their spheres brimming with specimens, with leaves and stems and minerals, with insects in pressurized vials and tubes of stealthily-sampled blood. While she watches the video feeds and runs the samples through her lab, charting the results in primary colors on wall-sized sheets of chart paper, I inspect the instruments. I polish the camera lenses and unfurl their fins with metal files, checking the delicate silicone for grime or tearing.

Sometimes, when she isn't looking, I inspect the Engine's radius.

"The Engine's radius is an anchor," she tells me. Like Burd Janet clinging to Tam Linn in the ditch beside the fairy road. In order for the Engine to operate, it must anchor everything necessary for its existence. Like Janet holding eel and lion and hot iron, it clutches whales and levers and laboratories, buses and black flats. Everything necessary for its operation. Everything necessary for us.

"But everything shifts," she says. She's laughing at me as I stare at her shoes, at their polished black toes. "Only we will never change at all. Do you understand?"

"Yes," I say. I lift my hand from the black lever; its ridge has left a white trail carved into my palm.

VII.

In one world, she fell in love.

We take turns floating *Tam Linn* to the surface, to the wet and tired fishing village where the *Burd Janet* docks and the one-eyed woman whose windows are filled with fishhooks trades us bread and dried meat for slivers of whalebone. I never remain on shore long, just a day or two to fetch coffee and thread and extra screws and bolts, waterproof glue, boxes of pencils. Her stays stretch longer; she tracks down books and rare instruments, looks up old colleagues to see who or what they've become. In one world, the woman who brought her rare books from a collection in London had hair as bright as copper and a voice as cold as steel. In a locket around her long, pale neck, she carried pictures of her twin daughters, both dark and thin.

She followed the copper-haired woman to London, walked the cool aisles of the library where she was employed, met her daughters one afternoon as they waited outside after school. They talked about maths and counting games, and taught her a rhyme about blackbirds. One of the daughters loved her; but the other, and their mother, did not.

When she returned to her laboratory at the bottom of the ocean, she sat on the floor in front of her charts and wept until her throat bleed from sobbing. I sat at my table, unfurling the gossamer fins of the swimming cameras, polishing their tiny blind eyes. The next day, she told me to pull the red lever, and we never spoke of her weeping. But afterwards, I began to catch her rewinding the video feeds from the cameras that had swum north and east; she asked me if I had seen, somewhere, the two dark daughters, their copper-haired mother. I always said no.

I inspected the Engine's radius. It had widened perceptibly; now, slowly, it was contracting again. Eventually, she stopped asking.

VIII.

What might have happened if her mother had lived? If her father had stepped into the kitchen that afternoon and found her, not spread across the linoleum with dead flowers and broken glass, but standing over the sink, up to her elbows in soapy citrus-scented water, or sitting on the porch with an apple in her hand, oxidation staining the marks of her teeth. Would she still have been born on a day when the rain fell like blood from a broken artery on the flat roof of the hospital? Would her father still have a white scar slicing across the thick fingers of his right hand? If none of this had happened, would she still be what she is?

We are so many contingencies. Without the War, my father would never have been in California, and my parents would never have met. Without the War, the Engine would never have been invented. Without those black flats, scratched at the toe or not, she would never have caught the bus, never have grasped my shoulder as we lurched forward, never have caught me and dragged me down like a drowned sailor, too captivated to gasp for breath.

The Engine does not understand this. The Engine is a memoryless machine. This is what I have learned in charting its radius, charting its contractions as though I am waiting for something to be born. The Engine does not understand what is necessary for its existence; it only knows what is necessary for its operation. The hand that pulls the black lever. The hand that belongs to me.

I am in the Engine's radius. I do not change. Everything else shifts.

She does not understand this. None of her understand this.

IX.

I tried to return home, once. I did not think I could bear to remain with her in the dark and the endless quiet; I did not think I could stay when I knew she didn't love me. But home was unbearable, too. My mother wanted to know what I thought of the curtains, the new upholstery, which was the same as the old upholstery in another world. My sister tried to interest me in a science-fiction program. I couldn't last in the light, the city noises; the dry summer air made me faint-headed. Two weeks later I was standing in front of a window full of fishhooks, and the one-eyed woman, a little smaller and a little more wrinkled than before, was reaching for her key.

X.

I am not Burd Janet. It is not my task to cling to the eel and lion that squirm in my grasp, to hot iron that burns a scar across my palm. Instead, I let go. Let go of white scratches on black shoes, let go of the wind in her curling black hair. I tell myself that we will roll, one day, ever-so-gently into place, but I am starting to wonder if it is true.

The universes are infinite, but that does not mean that all imaginable worlds exist. There are no two-sided squares. But perhaps somewhere she loves me, or someone like her loves someone like me.

"Do you think you could love me?" I whisper, and she closes her eyes. I reach out hesitantly, touch the soft skin between the crisp white sleeve of her lab coat and her stiff white glove. Her wrist is cold, waxlike, her pulse undetectable.

This is what I have learned: I am necessary for the Engine, and I do not shift. She is necessary for me—necessary, that is, for me to be myself; and her dead mother is necessary for her, necessary for her to be the woman that I love. There are an infinite number of universes, and perhaps that does mean that all imaginable worlds exist, but it does not mean that I will be able to see all of them. We move down the thread, rolling ever-so-gently to one side, in one direction, always. And the past is only ever the past.

Her hair has become gray; she cannot remember it ever having been black. I touch her wrist, and every time, her skin is a little bit colder.

"Maybe if I were someone else," she says. It isn't a promise, but an apology.

I lift my hand from hers and reach for the Engine.

Test Subjects

Megan Arkenberg lives and writes in California. Her work has recently appeared in *Asimov's, Lightspeed*, and *Daily Science Fiction*, and is forthcoming in the anthology *Start a Revolution*. She procrastinates by editing the fantasy e-zine *Mirror Dance*.

Mr and Mrs Brenchley are renowned and deprecated in equal measure from New Caledonia in the West to Formosa in the East.* Impeccably dressed and shockingly outré in their behaviours, they arrive unannounced and depart without warning, taking their welcome for granted, leaving disturbance in their wake. They may be discovered playing hoop-la at an archbishop's garden party or bouzouki at the Grand Turk's investiture, drinking champagne in an Oxford punt or gin in a Californian airship, debating in Arabic on camelback across the Empty Quarter or in Mandarin on a junk out of Surabaya. Their hospitality is legendary, their company deplorable, their lure irresistible.They are known to have met in a tomb: whether as archaeologists or grave-robbers is less clear. It is said that they are wanted by the authorities on three continents, and not wanted at all on the other two. A word to the wise: they are frequently mistaken for each other.

Traci Castleberry also writes as Evey Brett and has been published with Lethe Press, Cleis Press, Loose Id, Carina Press, Ellora's Cave and elsewhere. She's attended Clarion, Taos Toolbox, the Lambda Literary Retreat for Emerging LGBT Authors and has an MA in Writing Popular Fiction from Seton Hill University. Traci lives in southern Arizona with two cats, a snake, and her Lipizzan mare, Carrma, who has a habit of arranging the universe to her liking. Find her online at eveybrett.wordpress.com.

Thoraiya Dyer is an award-winning Australian writer. Her short science fiction and fantasy has appeared in *Clarkesworld, Apex, Analog, Nature* and *Cosmos*, among others (for a full list, see thoraiyadyer.com). Her collection of four original stories, *Asymmetry*, available from Twelfth Planet Press, was called "unsettling,

---

**In Australia and its environs, they are not spoken of.*

poignant, marvelous" by Nancy Kress. A lapsed veterinarian, her other interests include bushwalking, archery and travel.

Sean Eads's nihilist science-fiction novel *The Survivors* was a finalist for the Lambda Literary Award. His next book, *Lord Byron's Prophecy* is forthcoming from Lethe Press. He resides in Colorado.

Rafaela F. Ferraz lives in Portugal, where she has recently earned her degree in Criminology. In her spare time, she enjoys playing tourist in her own country and calling herself an amateur entomologist even if it takes her hours to identify the butterflies in her own shadowbox. She collects hobbies and cameras, and hopes to one day convert her home into a natural history museum.

Gemma Files is a Canadian horror writer, journalist, and film critic. She has won the International Horror Guild Award for Best Short Story and her latest collection is *We Will All Go Down Together: Stories of the Five-Family Coven.*

A.J. Fitzwater is an author of the dragon persuasion from Christchurch, New Zealand. Their work has appeared in *Beneath Ceaseless Skies*, various Crossed Genres releases, *Wily Writers*, Lethe Press' *Heiresses of Russ 2014* and other venues of repute. They are Clarion alumni 2014. Cups of tea, hair colour, feline parentage, and any further information are subject to weather and catch permitting. They shout into the void on Twitter @AJFitzwater, and blog at pickledthink.blogspot.com

Orrin Grey is a writer, editor, amateur film scholar, and monster expert who was born on the night before Halloween. His stories of monsters, ghosts, and sometimes the ghosts of monsters have appeared in dozens of anthologies, including Ellen Datlow's *Best Horror of the Year,* and been gathered into two volumes, *Never Bet the Devil & Other Warnings* (out now) and *Painted Monsters & Other Strange Beasts* (forthcoming). You can find him online at orringrey.com.

Amy Griswold is the author (with Melissa Scott) of the gay Victorian fantasy/mystery novels *Death by Silver* and its sequel *A Death at the Dionysus Club*. She lives in North Carolina, where she writes educational tests as well as fiction and tries not to confuse the two. She can be found online at amygriswold.livejournal.com.

Claire Humphrey lives in Toronto, where she works in the book business, and writes short fiction and novels. Her stories have appeared in *Beneath Ceaseless Skies, Strange Horizons, Interzone, Crossed Genres, PodCastle, Fantasy Magazine* and several anthologies. She is also the reviews editor at *Ideomancer*.

Aynjel Kaye writes speculative fiction and can sometimes be found playing the part of spackle to pay the bills. She escaped from Normal at a very young age, dodged the role of Chosen One, released her menagerie, and is now an Angst Queen in exile. She lives at Uphill with her chosen family and far too many spiders. She is a graduate of Clarion East in 2000. Her stories have appeared on the web at *Strange Horizons*, and in print in *Polyphony 5* and *So Fey: Queer Fairy Fiction*. You can find Aynjel on Twitter as @aynjelfyre.

Tim Lieder has been published in various magazines including *Shock Totem, Lamplight and Big Pulp*. Additionally he owns and operates Dybbuk Press through which he has edited and published nine titles including *King David & The Spiders from Mars*. He lives in New York.

Christine Morgan works the overnight shift in a psychiatric facility, which plays havoc with her sleep schedule but allows her a lot of writing time. A lifelong reader, she also reviews, beta-reads, occasionally edits and dabbles in self-publishing. Her other interests include gaming, history, superheroes, crafts, cheesy disaster movies and training to be a crazy cat lady. She can be found online at christine-morgan.org.

Faith Mudge is a writer from Queensland, Australia, with a passion for fantasy, folk tales and mythology from all over the world – in fact, almost anything with a glimmer of the fantastical. Her stories have appeared in various anthologies, the latest including *The Year's Best Australian Fantasy and Horror 2012, Kisses by Clockwork* and *Kaleidoscope*. More of her work can be found on her blog at beyondthedreamline.wordpress.com.

Jess Nevins is a librarian, pulp fiction historian, and comic book annotator. He also writes encyclopedias.

Melissa Scott is one of the more acclaimed lesbian authors working in the field of speculative literature. She won the John W. Campbell Award for Best New Writer in Science Fiction in 1986, and has won several Lambda Literary Awards, most recently for co-authoring with Amy Griswold *Death by Silver*. She resides in North Carolina.

Romie Stott has written genre-bending fiction and poetry for *Farrago's Wainscot, Strange Horizons, Arc, Stupefying Stories, LIT, inkscrawl*, and *King David and the Spiders From Mars*. As a narrative filmmaker, she has been a visiting artist at the Dallas Museum of Art, National Gallery (London), and ICA Boston. She is not now, nor has she ever been, a member of the Communist Party, although she likes redheads. Her portfolio is at romiesays.tumblr.com.

Control Group

Connie Wilkins is a well-regarded editor in lesbian fiction, including co-editing with the below Mr. Berman *Heiresses of Russ 2012: the Year's Best Lesbian Speculative Fiction.* Her secret identity of Sacchi Green pens and edits lesbian erotica and has deservedly won a Lambda Literary Award for this work.

Steve Berman adores the old Universal horror films and would have invited Dr. Pretorius on a dinner date. He favors Tesla over Edison. His anthologies have been finalists for the Golden Crown Literary Award, the Lambda Literary Award (multiple times), and the Shirley Jackson Award. He resides in southern New Jersey. He approves of all the cats mentioned in this book.

www.ingramcontent.com/pod-product-compliance
Lightning Source LLC
Chambersburg PA
CBHW020935310726
48980CB00007B/789/J